S0-BSF-768

GOLD DUST
The Seventh Red River Mystery

"[An] unlikely game of polecat-and-mouse...unfolds in a series of developments as preposterous as they are richly enjoyable. The result reads like a stranger-than-strange collaboration between Lee Child, handling the assault on the CIA with baleful directness, and Steven F. Havill, genially reporting on the regulars back home."

—Kirkus Reviews

"Readers nostalgic for this period—songs by the Monkees and Tommy James and the Shondells blast from transistor radios—will find plenty to like."

—Publishers Weekly

UNRAVELED
The Sixth Red River Mystery

"Not only does Wortham write exceptionally well, but he somehow manages to infuse *Unraveled* with a Southern gothic feel that would make even William Faulkner proud...A hidden gem of a book that reads like Craig Johnson's Longmire mysteries on steroids."

—The Providence Journal

"This superbly drawn sixth entry in the series features captivating characters and an authentic Texas twang."

—Library Journal

"Readers who hang on for 200-plus pages...will be treated to a stunning finale, first in an evil fun house, then on a long stretch of oil-slick highway."

—Don Crinklaw, *Booklist*

"The book's strength lies in Wortham's ability to construct a world; it doesn't take long for readers to feel like kinfolk."

—Cevin Bryerman, *Publishers Weekly*

"The more I read of Reavis Wortham's books, the more impressed I am by his abilities as a writer...His understanding of family feuds, how they start and how they hang on long past their expiration date, is vital to the story line. Wortham's skill as a plotter is demonstrated as well. He's very good at what he does, and his books are well worth reading."

—Reviewing the Evidence

DARK PLACES
The Fifth Red River Mystery

Named one of the Top 10 Modern Westerns for 2016
by *True West Magazine*

Named one of the 12 Top Books for 2015 by *Strand Magazine*

Named one of the Best Small Fictions of 2015
by *The Dallas Morning News*

"Reavis Z. Wortham is the real thing: a literary voice that's gut-bucket Americana delivered with a warm and knowing Texas twang."

—CJ Box, #1 *New York Times* bestselling author of
the Joe Pickett series and Edgar Allan Poe Award-winner

"Replete with period details and a strong sense of place, this winning fifth series entry is as much a coming-of-age story as crime fiction. This series is comparable to Rick Riordan's Tres Navarre or Joe Lansdale's Hap Collins and Leonard Pine books."

—*Library Journal*

"Readers will cheer for and ache with the good folks, and secondary characters hold their own....The novel's short chapters fit both the fast pace and the deftly spare actions and details...the rhythm of Wortham's writing, transporting us back in time, soon takes hold and is well worth the reader's efforts."

—*Historical Novel Society*

"Once again, Wortham supplies something for everyone—especially fans of summer movies who love chase sequences so much that they don't care who's chasing whom."

—*Kirkus Reviews*

"A terrific suspense thriller that transports grateful fans to 1967 small-town Texas and Route 66. The Parker brood has their hands filled between corralling the runaways, and capturing a vehicular homicide killer and the businessmen murderers. Aptly named *Dark Places*, this is a superb period piece."

—*Midwest Book Review*

VENGEANCE IS MINE
The Fourth Red River Mystery

Named one of the Top 5 Modern Westerns by *True West Magazine*

"Reavis Wortham doubles down in *Vengeance is Mine*, the fourth in his Red River Series, and for mystery readers it's a Full House when Las Vegas intrigue invades Center Springs, Texas. Aces High, Constables Ned, Cody Parker and company are terrific riding and reading partners."

> —Craig Johnson, *New York Times* bestselling author of the Walt Longmire series that inspired the hit TV series *Longmire*

"Reavis Z. Wortham's *Vengeance Is Mine* is a winning and unusual book. Equal parts small-town tale and thriller, the combination is both entertaining and emotionally engaging. Wortham is at his best in the small Texas town of Center Springs, where this and his three other Red River Mysteries are set. The small-town characters carry the day but Wortham hits his thriller marks too, and the result is a solid and humane story."

> —T. Jefferson Parker, *New York Times* bestselling author and winner of three Edgar Allan Poe Awards

"Loaded with healthy doses of humor, adventure, and intrigue, populated by a remarkable cast of characters both good and bad and featuring one heck of an electrifying climax is a throwback to the pulp era in the best possible sense. A great read."

> —Owen Laukkanen, bestselling author

"This very entertaining novel, set in 1967, is reminiscent of Donald E. Westlake's Mob comedies *The Fugitive Pigeon* (1965) and *The Busy Body* (1966), which, like this book, feature offbeat characters getting themselves into offbeat situations—although this book also has a more serious side, too...."

> —David Pitt, *Booklist* Starred Review

"Wortham is a masterful and entertaining storyteller. Set in East Texas in 1967, *Vengeance is Mine* is equal parts Joe R. Lansdale and Harper Lee, with a touch of Elmore Leonard."

> —*Ellery Queen's Mystery Magazine*

THE RIGHT SIDE OF WRONG
The Third Red River Mystery

"A sleeper that deserves wider attention."

—*The New York Times*

"A gritty, dark, and suspenseful Western with a final explosive showdown that kept me turning the pages late into the night to see who would survive."

—Jamie Freveletti, internationally bestselling author

"Wortham's third entry in his addictive Texas procedurals set in the 1960s is a deceptively meandering tale of family and country life bookended by a dramatic opening and conclusion. C.J. Box fans would like this title."

—*Library Journal* Starred Review

"Top is an endearing narrator, full of childlike wonder, which is gradually being diluted by the realities of the adult world. In that sense, the novel may remind readers of Joe Lansdale's superb *The Bottoms* (2000). A very good mystery that will also transport readers to a different era."

—Wes Lukowski, *Booklist*

BURROWS
The Second Red River Mystery

"The cinematic characters have substance and style. They walk off the page and talk Texas."

—The Dallas Morning News

"Wortham's outstanding sequel to *The Rock Hole*...combines the gonzo sensibility of Joe R. Lansdale and the elegiac mood of *To Kill a Mockingbird* to strike just the right balance between childhood innocence and adult horror."

—Publishers Weekly Starred Review

"As in Ned's debut (*The Rock Hole*), his grandchildren, Top and Pepper, are on hand to provide welcome humor and lend perspective to the acutely and unobtrusively observed small-town landscape. The result is that rare bird, a mystery with something for everyone."

—Kirkus Reviews Starred Review

THE ROCK HOLE
The First Red River Mystery

Named one of the Top 12 Mysteries of 2011 by *Kirkus Reviews*

Finalist in the Benjamin Franklin Awards (Mystery)

"An unpretentious gem written to the hilt and harrowing in its unpredictability."

—*Kirkus Reviews*

"Throughout, scenes of hunting, farming, and family life sizzle with detail and immediacy. The dialog is spicy with country humor and color, and Wortham knows how to keep his story moving. *The Rock Hole* is an unnerving but fascinating read."

—*Historical Novel Society*

Gold Dust

Books by Reavis Z. Wortham

The Red River Mysteries

The Rock Hole
Burrows
The Right Side of Wrong
Vengeance is Mine
Dark Places
Unraveled
Gold Dust

The Sonny Hawke Thrillers

Hawke's Prey
Hawke's War

Gold Dust

A Red River Mystery

Reavis Z. Wortham

Poisoned Pen Press

North Central Kansas Libraries

Copyright © 2018 by Reavis Z. Wortham

First Edition 2018

10 9 8 7 6 5 4 3 2 1

Library of Congress Control Number: 2018935803

ISBN: 9781464209611   Hardcover
ISBN: 9781464209635   Trade Paperback
ISBN: 9781464209642   Ebook

All rights reserved. No part of this publication may be reproduced, stored in, or introduced into a retrieval system, or transmitted in any form, or by any means (electronic, mechanical, photocopying, recording, or otherwise) without the prior written permission of both the copyright owner and the publisher of this book.

Poisoned Pen Press
4014 N. Goldwater Blvd., #201
Scottsdale, AZ 85251
www.poisonedpenpress.com
info@poisonedpenpress.com

Printed in the United States of America

*This one is for Robert Reynolds, my father-in-law,
who once told me that he always looks forward
to the next Red River novel so he can catch up with
the Parkers who are like family.
You can't ask for a better endorsement than that.
Thanks for everything, Grandpa.*

Acknowledgments

I wouldn't be here if it weren't for the love of my life, my bride Shana. She puts up with more than any woman should out of this guy who's still a kid inside.

Others helped in the creation of these books. The idea of lost gold in Palmer Lake came from a friend I've never met, Dan Dancer. He's a fan of my work, and was raised in Chicota, Texas, which was once Center Springs. Dan sent an email that sparked one of the plots in this novel.

My old friend and former editor, Steve Brigman, suggested the Missouri setting for the climax and changed the direction of the novel in midstream. It worked well, Steve, and I look forward to casting a fly for McCloud trout with you sometime in the near future.

Much is always owed to John Gilstrap, who continues to be a mentor and brother from another mother. He is always there for me, and I look forward to many more real life adventures with this outstanding author. We've already had quite a few.

Thanks also to the authors who lend their names to my books. I'm afraid I'd forget someone if I try to list everyone, but their generosity, support, and friendship is overwhelming.

My editor at Poisoned Pen, Annette Rogers, was the first person to see the potential in my work. Instead of making *The Rock Hole* a standalone novel, she offered me a series. It was completely unexpected and welcome. Barbara Peters and Robert Rosenwald, the owners and publishers of Poisoned Pen Press, have championed my work from the beginning, and that support has led to the success of the Red River series. Thanks to all y'all at the Big PPP, for working so hard on my behalf.

My exemplary agent, Anne Hawkins of John Hawkins and Associates, has shown guidance and friendship since I was blowing in the wind, and she continues to believe in my work. I think I'd be back at square one without her.

And to all my readers, from my newspaper columns, to the magazine articles I pen, to all my novels, much obliged.

Chapter One

The Devil was beating his wife when the rusty green cattle trailer backed through an assortment of oak, pecan, elm, and hackberry trees surrounding a warped and sun-splintered catch pen. The rough gray corral full of bawling cattle almost disappeared in the shadows despite the rain cloud moving quickly to the east. The loading chute was rickety at best. The odor of wet dust, crushed milkweeds, and cowshit filled the air.

Nervous cattle bawled as two hard-looking men ignored the brief shower falling in the sunshine and herded them with whoops and hollers up the wooden ramp and into the trailer hitched to a two-toned blue and white Ford truck. The mama cows wore brands, but the red white-face calves and more than a few heifers were unmarked.

The current hit "Harper Valley PTA" came through the pick-up's open windows.

The men were halfway finished loading them when a green 1955 International pickup turned off the highway and crunched to a stop on the red gravel turnout at the gate. A slender, slow-moving farmer in a sweat-stained straw cowboy hat shoved the cranky door open with his shoulder and stepped out to wrestle aside the limp wire gate. He grunted at a sharp pain in his back that was iffy, even on good days.

The long shadows of the surrounding hardwoods almost prevented the landowner from seeing the trailer a hundred yards away. The glittering shower focused most of his attention on the streaked windshield made worse by wiper blades baked hard as a rock by the northeast Texas sun.

The front chrome bumper of the unfamiliar two-toned truck caught his eye through the open window. The farmer frowned at the sight, turned the wheel, and cut through the bitterweeds, throwing debris and tiny grasshoppers into the air and across his unpolished hood.

He killed the International's engine twenty yards from the catch pen and popped the door open, sitting half-in and half-out to study the scene. The men working the cattle stopped, as if expecting what came next.

Coming to a decision, the farmer de-trucked and stuck both hands into the pockets of his overalls. "Hey, fellers. What are y'all doing?" His voice rose above the bawling cattle and wavered, either in fear or anger.

A man, dark-complected under a cracked and battered straw hat, climbed over the corral. His shaggy, greasy brown hair hung limp over large ears that looked like the open doors of a Buick.

A redhead in a faded, thin plaid cowboy shirt stretched tight across a bulging belly lit a cigarette and rested his forearms over the top sun-dried board to watch. He unconsciously rubbed the edges of untrimmed fingernails crusted with dirt against each other.

Greasy Hair left the trailer's back gate and met the agitated rancher in the open pasture. The shape of his face and abnormally close-set eyes along with the flapping ears suggested mental issues, something he often played in his favor when people misjudged him. "Howdy."

"I said what are you doin'? Don't y'all know you're on private property?"

The restless cows on the ramp stomped into the green trailer and the others paused, bawling. The crew of sweating men who'd been loading the cattle were silent.

Greasy Hair ran long, slender fingers along the side of his head. "We're loading cattle." Balancing on one leg, he used a boot to rub at a smear of brown cowshit on the opposite leg of his jeans. "It's hot and nasty work, ain't it?"

"Them cows are mine. Nobody said you could load 'em up in anything."

"Guy Harris did."

The farmer shook his head. "I don't know no Guy Harris."

Greasy Hair frowned as if deep in thought and couldn't believe a mistake had been made. "He sold us these cattle. I got a bill of sale in the truck there."

"If he did, y'all got took. These are mine, and they ain't for sale. Y'all let 'em out and get gone."

Greasy Hair hooked both thumbs into the front pockets of his khakis. His shoulders were wet from the rain shower. A smell like sour milk rose from his sweaty skin.

He turned to gaze across the pasture at the milkweed and bitterweeds scorching in the sun. Cicadas cried in an undulating chorus from the surrounding hardwoods, their song rising and swelling in rhythmic unison. He slipped a hand under his untucked shirt and scratched his stomach. "Well, I don't know. See, Guy said this was his place and he gave us directions directly to this pen. Said we could round up all we wanted, 'cause he was selling out."

The farmer's face reddened in anger. "Mister, this is my land and them are my cows. Now you get shed of this place or I'm calling the laws."

"Aw, I wish you wouldn't do that. Look, it's too hot to stand here in the sun like we got good sense. Come on in the shade and let's work this out. I got some ice water over there."

"Nope. I'm staying right here."

Greasy Hair swiveled around to eye the cattle. A horsefly buzzed his head and he waved it away. "Well, I guess the mistake is ours. We watched this place for two weeks and never saw nobody."

"What are you talking about?"

"We never saw nobody come out here." Greasy Hair sighed and looked defeated. "Didn't see nobody feed, nor scatter so much as a bag of nuggets. And now you show up. Dale!" He called toward the truck. "C'mon over here and help us work this out."

"Nothing to work out." The farmer's attention flicked back and forth between Greasy Hair and the redhead coming their way.

Greasy Hair shrugged. "There's always something to work out."

"I been down in my back and ain't had time to come out…" the farmer trailed off, as if realizing he was volunteering information they didn't need.

The redhead named Dale was built like a fireplug. He took his hat off and joined them, wiping sweat with his left hand. A Newport cigarette bobbed between his lips. "What's the trouble?"

"Y'all're loadin' my cattle, that's the trouble." The farmer pointed at the trailer. "What do I have to say for y'all to get gone? How about I'm going to call the laws and they'll take care of this? Is that plain enough?"

Greasy Hair smiled. "Now, hang on a minute. See, I believe we made an honest mistake here."

Dale squinted from beneath thin eyebrows. Like most redheads, he couldn't tolerate the sun and his nose was burned. He drew on the cigarette and exhaled through both nostrils without taking it from his lips. "Owen, did we come to the wrong pasture?"

"Looks like it." Greasy Hair stuck out his hand. "Hey, I'm sorry. My name's Owen. What's yours?"

The farmer refused the offered hand and backed away to put more distance between himself and the strangers. "Name's Pat Walker and I'll be back with the constable and then we'll see what's what."

"I wish you wouldn't do that." Dale spoke to the retreating farmer's back.

Pat turned to address the redhead and Owen pulled a German Luger from under his shirt. "This is on you."

He shot Pat Walker in the back of his head.

The 9mm round punched through the hat's thin crown. Blood flew in a red mist. His hat went spinning away as the farmer collapsed with a heavy thump. Thick gushes of blood from his nose and the huge exit wound flowed into the barely damp ground.

Dale rubbed at his own blistered nose. "Possum, I told you we didn't need to do this in broad daylight."

Owen slipped the Luger back into his waistband and studied the still corpse at his feet as if looking for signs of life. He tilted his head along the line of Walker's body and raised his gaze. "I've told you I don't like that name. Don't ever call me that again."

People from his hometown called him by the nickname until one night outside of a bar when he beat a young man half to death with an axe handle for calling him that.

Fear flashed across Dale's face when he realized what he'd said. "I meant, it wasn't a good idea to shoot him right here in broad daylight."

Owen exaggerated a look around the pasture. "I don't see no grandstands full of people or nothin'. Like I told this fool, we watched the pasture for two weeks. The least he could have done was to send somebody around to check on his cows and we'd have knowed." He spun toward the trailer.

Dale paced him. "What now?"

Owen looked surprised at Dale's question. "Why, we finish loading these cattle and get gone. I got buyers waiting in Austin." Owen started back toward the catch pen. "When we're done, you drag him in the corral and pull his truck in, too. We'll have plenty of time before anyone misses him."

The rustlers turned toward the west at the throaty roar of an airplane. A crop duster suddenly burst into view over the tree-tops, dangerously low. A widening trail of mist spread over the pasture, covering the men standing in the open.

"What the hell!?" Despite his hat, Owen ducked his head as the cloud settled around them.

Dale used one hand to protect his eyes as a light mist blew under the bill of his cap. "What's he spraying *here* for?"

"Must be some kind of weed killer, maybe?"

"Naw, nobody sprays weed killer on a place while there's cattle on it."

"They don't spray *people*, neither." Owen wiped his sleeve and sniffed. "It don't have any smell." He absently rubbed at his dandruff-covered shoulders.

"Do you think he saw this dead sonofabitch?"

"Probably not. It's hard to see directly below you in one of those things, and he came over the trees so fast I doubt he even knew we were down here. That's why he hit us with that crap. It don't make no nevermind. Let's finish up here and go."

Dale took a deep drag down to the filter and dropped it on the ground. A deep, wet cough rattled his lungs and he shook another cigarette from the pack. "This next one'll help my cough."

A buzzard floated high above as they laughed and ignored Pat Walker's cooling body.

Chapter Two

A cow bawled in the pasture beside our little frame farmhouse, the sound hoarse and mournful. A mockingbird sang in the sycamore near the southwest corner, doing his best to brighten the already warm and sticky November day. A covey of quail caught my eye, working in single file down the bobwire fencerow separating what Miss Becky called the side yard from the woods beyond.

Fully dressed in jeans and a plaid button shirt, I was on my bed, reading in a soft breeze blowing through the rusty screen, when she called from the kitchen. "What's it gonna take to get you two up and out of this house?"

Mark Lightfoot was drawing on a sheet of lined paper. His jeans and button shirt were fairly new, because my grandmother, Miss Becky, threw out all of his old clothes when he came to live full time with us several months earlier.

He'd been drawing on what he called some house plans. He'd been at it for a couple of days, and when I peeked, it was our farmhouse with a wraparound porch and an extra room that we didn't have.

He's not blood kin and his last name is different from us Parkers'. Miss Becky and Grandpa Ned had Judge O.C. Rains draw up some papers last year so Mark could live with us full time since his people couldn't take care of him anymore. They were poor Choctaws from across the river in Oklahoma, and barely had enough money for coal oil.

"We will in a little bit." I had to raise my voice so she could hear me over the rattling pans. I think she made noise in the kitchen to run us out. "Then we'll gather the eggs and feed the cows."

"Five, four..." Mark pulled a strand of his long black hair out of his eyes spoke around the yellow pencil in his teeth, "...three..."

I marked my place in the book with a finger. "What are you doing?"

"...two, one."

Miss Becky appeared in the door, studying us with that same eye she used when she was trying to decide on making us go with her to Wednesday night services at the Holiness Church across the pasture. "I believe I'm fixin' to get a come-along out of the smokehouse to drag you two out on the floor."

"We're just feeling lazy."

"It's comin' on to nine o'clock already." She studied at us for a while. "Good Lord, deliver me from teenage boys. Y'all figuring on stayin' in bed all day? Your Grandpa Ned'll get y'all's goat when he comes home."

My Grandpa Ned had been the local constable for Center Springs since the beginning of World War II. "We'll get going in a minute."

"You'll get up right now. Y'all can't laze a whole Saturday away."

"We have plans. We're gonna camp out tonight."

Mark raised an eyebrow, knowing we hadn't discussed it. The idea'd popped into my head that second, because some kids in my book by Fred Gipson were coon-hunting and sitting around a campfire. I was burying myself more and more in books, on account of I was having trouble with one of the kids at school and it was the best way to escape to somewhere else.

It wasn't the first time. Cale Westlake gave me holy hell the year before, picking on me every day and beating me down with threats, pushing me around, and wartin' me to no end. It started the first week of school and didn't let up until him and my girl cousin Pepper ran off together to California.

He was the Baptist preacher's boy and learned a lesson while he was out there. After they got back he kind of faded into the background. But like Ms. Rosalie Russell always said in science class, nature despises a vacuum. When Cale straightened up, one of his former toadies, Harlan Ketchum, moved in and took over, and he was mean as a snake.

"I swanny." Miss Becky worked the dishtowel around her hands. She flipped it over one shoulder and absently wiped them on the sides of her blue and white house dress that reached mid-way to her knotty old calves. "Where do y'all figure to camp out?"

I propped my head on one hand and watched a white-face cow slap her tail at a swarm of pestering flies beyond the smoke-house. I knew how she felt. Me and Judge O.C. Rains hated flies with a passion.

"How about right down there by the old hog pen?"

She glanced out the window toward what was left of the empty pen by the bobwire fence. "Fine then, but y'all don't chop up nothing but them rotten planks off the pen to make your fire. Leave the good 'uns. Your granddaddy might want them for something."

Mark crossed his eyes to be funny. "It'll be hotter'n blue blazes out there today. Why're you wantin' to go camping?"

I didn't tell him about the book. "I'm bored. It'll give us something to do."

"That's all you Parkers have is adventure." He swung his legs over the side of the cotton mattress.

Half an hour later we finished putting up a smelly old canvas tent. "I don't know why we need this. It's too hot to breathe and there's no way we're gonna sleep in there tonight." Mark pulled his headband loose, pulled his hair back, and settled it back around his head.

My dog Hootie who'd been watching from the shade of a big bodark tree caught a scent and took off past the barn. The humid air was thick enough to cut with a knife and the only thing that broke up the blue bowl of sky was a couple of skinny little clouds off to the southwest.

"What are you two up to?"

I looked up to see Pepper standing back at the gate in her Sunday clothes. We hadn't heard the car come up the red gravel drive. Her mama, Aunt Ida Belle, was talking to Miss Becky beside the porch. Hootie ran ahead to greet Pepper, wagging his tail and barking to beat the band.

Mark and I left our camp and met her at the fence fifty yards away. I seldom saw her in a dress. "Ain't you purty standing there in the weeds. Where you going?"

My near-twin cousin rolled her eyes. "Kiss my lily white ass. We're going to town. Mama's aunt is visiting from California and I have to go sit and look at that old lady for a couple of hours."

Standing there in a bright jersey pullover shift, she didn't look like herself, softer and not as hard-edged.

"She won't let you stay here?" Mark patted her head like she was a puppy.

She grinned and slapped at his hand. If it'd been me, she'd-a got mad, but they'd been making goo-goo eyes at one another since Mark showed back up. "No, dummy. Don't you think I asked? I'm not interested in going to Aunt Earline's house to sit on her plastic-covered couch and try not to get her white carpet dirty. I swear, I can't *stand* that old woman."

Miss Becky and Aunt Ida Belle went inside at the same time Curtis Gaines popped up over the big red oak tree in the pasture. His Stearman crop duster was lower than I'd ever seen.

Afraid of the low-flying plane, Hootie made a bee-line for the house and slipped under the porch. Mr. Curtis was so low I could see him twisting around, busy with something behind him.

"Whoo wee!"

Mark whistled. "Man, he's low!"

"He's going down!"

The plane's engine roared and started to climb, like Mr. Curtis does when he gets to the end of a field. He was spraying something right then, but it wasn't the crop-dusting cloud I was used to seeing. Two thin streams of white vapor widened out overhead.

A white mist settled on us. Mark and I ducked and squinched our eyes shut.

Pepper covered her hair with both hands. "Well, shit!"

The mist fine as a cloud collected on my arms, but disappeared as quick as our breath in the winter. I rubbed my hair. "What was that?"

"Well, it wasn't cotton poison." Mark looked toward the bottoms where Mr. Curtis' plane disappeared. "I know what *that* smells like, and this ain't it."

I sniffed at my hand and arm. There was no odor at all. "I wonder what he's doing."

"Probably running water through his tanks to clean 'em out and wanted to aggravate some kids." Pepper ran her hands over her clothes and hair. "And he damn-sure did it."

The women came back outside before we could answer. Miss Becky looked up at the sky, probably to see the airplane, but it was long gone. There wasn't anything up there but a couple of turkey buzzards spiraling high overhead, looking for something dead or dying.

Aunt Ida Belle waved her arm. "Let's go, hon."

Pepper looked like she was going to the electric chair and I could tell Aunt Ida Belle was getting frustrated with her daughter's slow speed, walking like she had dead lice falling off of her. When she got in their old yellow Bel Air and slammed the door, Aunt Ida Belle started giving her the what-for as they backed up and drove away.

Chapter Three

"Come on, baby." Curtis Gaines pulled back on the stick and cleared the trees at the end of his dirt runway. Despite a long flying career, he could never get past that pucker moment when the wheels of his Stearman left the ground and the air finally took hold of the biplane.

The Stearman growled toward the sky and he banked right, toward the Red River Bottoms north of Center Springs. The workhorse crop duster was as familiar to Curtis as his Chevrolet pickup. His heart was pounding with excitement, not from the job, but from the thousands of dollars tucked in his shirt.

He'd been flying the biplane since coming home from the Japanese Theater in the second World War, but for the first time in his life he had the money to put down on a *new* plane. The last year of the decade, 1969, was less than two months away, looking to be a banner year at the Gaines' castle. He was even thinking of asking his girlfriend to marry him.

The two retrofitted canisters attached to the spray bar hung just beyond each wing's aileron were much smaller than the standard setup mounted below the wings. They didn't add any noticeable weight. The plane was light as a feather, an unusual feeling directly opposite of when he was spraying fields and loaded with liquid chemicals.

The wind was cooler on his face than at ground level and he breathed deeply. He flew to the western tip of Lake Lamar,

Texas' newest water impoundment. The blue, dragon-shaped lake quickly came into view. It was the starting point of the experiment funded by two men in dark suits from the Department of Agriculture waiting back at Curtis' dirt airstrip, along with the remainder of his money.

He pushed the stick forward as he'd done tens of thousands of times and dropped fifty feet above the tree-lined lake, as instructed. He opened the valve and glanced backward, expecting to see the usual wide spread of thick mist, but this time there were only two streams of vapor stretching out behind.

Mr. Brown did most of the talking when they hired him that morning, but both well-dressed men told him not to expect the usual cloud. "We're testing air currents and water movement. We need you to drop low and spray the lake, then up along the river. The wind is from the northwest and we need to see which distribution method reaches Chisum first."

"Won't that be dangerous?" Curtis had never been asked to do anything like that before. "I don't believe it's a good idea to put chemicals in the water."

Blank-faced, Mr. Brown and Mr. Green exchanged glances. Mr. Green spoke up for the first time since they shook hands, talking around the ever-present cigarette in the corner of his mouth. "These canisters don't contain dangerous chemicals. They're full of microscopic metallic particles our scientists call 'Gold Dust.' It will dissipate in the water without harming fish, animals, or humans. We have people at the pump station who will be testing for the particles to see how fast they reach Chisum. It's all very scientific and as safe as Pepsodent."

"Is it real gold?"

"No. That's just what the eggheads in the research labs call it."

So there he was, flying only forty feet above the lake. The dam quickly came into view and he shut off the flow. He pulled the stick back and the plane rose. The boomerang-shaped dam quickly disappeared under the wings. He banked over the Sanders Creek bottoms toward Arthur City, Texas, five miles away.

His next target was the muddy, serpentine Red River.

Two gas stations and a country store on Highway 271 were his markers. He thought of the stories he heard when he was a kid of a bustling Arthur City before the turn of the century, perched on the edge of the river thick with runoff in wet weather. Wide in places and narrow in others, the river twisted like a snake between sandbars and hardwood-lined banks.

He banked into a sharp U-turn on the Oklahoma side of the river, buzzing the cluster of rough cinder-block gun and knife honky-tonks nicknamed Juarez. They looked worse than the trio of structures in Arthur City, and were the source of trouble and worry for both states.

When Curtis passed over the iron railroad bridge spanning the Red, he checked his altitude once again as instructed. At one-thousand feet, he followed the river west for four miles. The contents streamed out until he saw Palmer Lake in the distance. He pushed the lever into the *Off* position and relaxed.

His job was finished and he settled back to enjoy the flight, thinking of the Ag Rep's explanation. It made sense that the light breeze would catch the particles and they could estimate the time it took to travel from the point of distribution to the county seat in Chisum twenty miles south.

Lots of potentially dangerous chemicals came out of Curtis' nozzles in the course of a year and he'd always said the cotton poison and defoliants were dangerous to bugs, plants, and people alike, despite what the vendors said. This one seemed as safe as… what did they say?…*toothpaste!*

You'll wonder where the yellow went when you brush your teeth with Pepsodent! Curtis checked his watch and grinned as he recalled the familiar commercial.

For the past two years it had become his habit to buzz Constable Ned Parker's house after he finished a job so Ned's grandson, Top, could wave. He felt sorry for the skinny, asthmatic youngster who reminded Curtis of himself when he was that age. He'd already decided to ask Ned if the boy could go up with him soon for a ride.

He winced when a sudden sharp pain lanced from his colon to knot his abdomen. Hissing, he tightened up, waiting for the familiar jolt to go away. They were getting fewer as the weeks passed, and he was thankful for that.

The polyps Dr. Heinz had removed were gone, but it was taking longer than he liked for his body to heal. Doc told him not to worry, that he'd been forced to be what he called "more invasive" than he'd planned, but the doctor had removed everything during the surgery that had posed a danger and said Curtis was well enough to fly.

The jolt passed and he relaxed. That one was much shorter than they'd been only a few days earlier. In the aftermath of that brief spasm, Curtis felt remarkably better.

He banked into another U-turn and bled off enough altitude to fly over Center Springs' two country stores and domino hall. He wig-wagged the Stearman's wings at the farmers, who stuck their heads from under the porch overhang at Neal Box's rural general store. The Wilson boys jogged down the unpainted steps and waved their arms, pointing behind the crop duster.

Curtis frowned and twisted around to look over his shoulder. Twin streams of vapor stretched as far as he could see. "Oh hell!" Something was wrong and he forgot he'd been hurting only moments before.

He hit the shutoff valve again and again, but the streams continued uninterrupted. The unfamiliar equipment worried him from the start and he'd argued that they should use his spray rig, but the Ag Reps wouldn't hear of it.

"Damned low-bid government crap!"

He reached under the dash, thinking it might be an electrical short. After jiggling the wires with his fingers, he twisted in the seat to peer over his shoulder at the flow that was much thicker than he expected. Curtis fought the malfunctioning equipment until he caught a flicker in his peripheral vision of drifting down to barely above the treetops. Ned Parker's house appeared dangerously close off the point of his starboard wingtip.

"*Jesus!*" Muscle memory took control and Curtis pulled back the yoke, accelerating at the same time. The wasp junior Pratt and Whitney engine roared and the plane quickly regained altitude. He banked left over Sanders Creek and the pastureland beyond. When he was clear and in a safe zone, he thumped the solenoid, hoping it might close the valves.

When he glanced back up, he was too close to the tall oak trees again. Putting both hands on the yoke, he flew straight for several minutes, deciding what to do. The bottoms appeared, green fields of varying colors and patterns bordered by roads and trees.

A straight dirt road running between two fallow fields was the perfect place to land. He adjusted his flaps, cut the biplane's speed, and landed, taxiing slowly in a cloud of dust before rolling to a stop near a large red oak tree. Sighing with relief, Curtis climbed out of the cockpit while the engine idled.

Alone, he wasn't worried about the contents still hissing from the nozzles. It didn't take but a moment to tap the canisters' valves closed with a wrench. The first tank was easy. He walked around the tail. Small bubbles formed and popped from the brass aperture opening. Curtis tapped that one also and it closed, but not before he realized the tank was empty.

Some of the contents were on his hands. Curtis sniffed his fingers to find no scent at all. "Gold Dust, my ass." He absently rubbed his palms dry on his worn khakis, stowed the wrench back in the toolbox, and returned to the cockpit.

The government Impala was still parked under the pecan tree beside his pole-barn hanger when Curtis landed and rolled to a stop beside their car twenty minutes later.

The government men in fresh crewcuts were sitting on the Impala's fender, smoking. They slid off and waited for the plane to completely stop before approaching. The tallest, who called himself Mr. Brown, took one last drag from his cigarette and thumped the butt away.

Curtis climbed down. "Well, that's that."

Mr. Brown pushed the dark shades up on his nose. "Did you make the complete route?"

"Sure did."

Mr. Green popped their trunk and joined them wearing a thick pair of rubber gloves reaching to his elbows. Slender and bent at the shoulders, the gloves over his suit coat made him look like a mad scientist. Without a word he knelt under the starboard wing and disconnected the tank and spraying equipment.

Curtis started forward to help, but Mr. Brown took his elbow. "You need to let him do this."

"Two are faster than one."

"I know, but he's practiced this hundreds of times, and besides, those tanks are so cold they'll strip the skin from your hands." He reached into his jacket, distracting Curtis from what was happening under his plane. "As we agreed. The remaining five thousand."

"You fellers sure are free with my tax money."

Mr. Brown chuckled as Mr. Green placed the first canister into a metal box in the back of their car. "Well, that's the good ol' US of A for you, ain't it? I bet you'd rather get it than have someone else get it, though, wouldn't you?"

"You're mighty right. Say, what's the real name of that Gold Dust stuff, anyway?"

Mr. Brown gave his arm a pat. "It's a long name that neither one of us could pronounce, let alone understand. I don't ask the scientists too much. My job is to deliver it to you and bring the tanks back."

"All right, then. Say, when does that next payment come in?"

The lid on the box slammed shut. Mr. Green stripped off the gloves and dropped them into a second container, which he latched shut. "These sure did feel light. I expected them to have more fluid left in them." His voice was gruff and abrupt.

Mr. Brown raised an eyebrow, noting his partner's face was white as a sheet. "The lab boys set the flow rate."

"Yeah, well." Mr. Green closed the trunk and wiped a sheen of sweat off his face.

Mr. Brown returned to their conversation. "As we agreed. You'll get it in six months—that is, if we haven't heard a word of discussion from you or this community on today's experiment. Then you'll get the next payment one year from today. If our secret is kept, you'll get another ten thousand for the next twenty years on this date."

Greedy for the first time in his life, Curtis licked his lips thinking about all that money. It was more than he'd ever imagine making as a crop duster, and it required just an hour's work. A tickle ran up his spine and he shivered. It was his only reaction to the nagging thought that he should have at least questioned them a little more. Still, he never questioned the folks who asked him to spray all that insecticide and defoliant all over the county. And, besides, money talked.

"And I don't have to report this on my income tax, since it's cash and all."

Mr. Brown lowered his shades and winked. "I wouldn't, if I were you. This is just a little secret between us."

Curtis winked back. "Say, do you need me to do anything else?" He wished he could see the government men's eyes. It always made him feel better if he could see into what his grandma called "the windows into people's souls." Their shades and blank faces made him think of them as ghosts more than real people. "You know, by this time next year I'll have a new plane and we can work out a deal…"

"Time to go." Mr. Green opened the passenger door with a shaking hand. The muscles in his jaws flexed over and over again, as if he were trying to choke down bile.

Mr. Brown patted Curtis' arm again. "I don't think we'll be back. But if we do make it up here again, I promise you'll be the man for the job."

"All right, then…" Curtis' comment floated unheard in the air. Mr. Brown had already headed for the car. He started the engine and shifted into drive almost before the engine smoothed out. They made a sharp turn onto the blacktop road leading south.

Curtis watched the car disappear and frowned. "That tank wasn't cold when I worked on it." He studied on it until they disappeared, then returned to his plane to replace his original spray equipment, but only after stuffing both envelopes into the bottom of his toolbox.

Chapter Four

We killed the rest of that hot Saturday puttering around the camp. It was late evening when Aunt Ida Belle finally brought Pepper over to stay. She'd changed out of her Sunday clothes into her cutoffs and what she called a peasant shirt. The shorts were an old pair of jeans, but they weren't as short as those I'd see them hippie girls wearing on TV. None of the old folks in our county would put up with a girl showing what she had.

Pepper drifted down to see what we were up to while Aunt Ida Belle and Miss Becky shelled peas on the porch. Her music arrived before she did from the transistor radio in her shirt pocket. She was filling out pretty fast, and it was a little crowded in that pocket. "Y'all still planning on camping out in this heat?"

"It'll cool off after dark." Mark used a rubber band to pull his hair back on his sweaty neck. Grandpa told us that every time we complained that it was hot. The thing was it always *did* cool off then, some, but it didn't help much. It was that time of the year, in the late fall, when the temperature bounced like a rubber ball. It was hotter'n a six-shooter and we were all waiting for the norther that was sure to come at any time and bring us some relief.

It aggravated me that Mark could have hair down to his shoulders since he was full-blood Choctaw, but I had to get a boy's regular about every six weeks.

"Far out." Pepper turned up the radio and The Rolling Stones new song "Get Off My Cloud" filled the air. "That's not the way you do it." She spun a finger and Mark turned around. She took the rubber band off and did it her way. It looked the same to me, but I knew she only wanted to touch him. "So you guys are going to spend the night out here?"

"Why not? It's gonna be hot in the house anyway, and besides, it's something to do."

A Monkees song came on and she turned it down. "I might join you."

I sighed. I liked the Monkees, and with her there, I'd be the third wheel again.

Despite the humidity, the night sky was coal-black and the stars glittered bright and distinct. A glow on the northern horizon came from Hugo, Oklahoma. A similar glow to the south was Chisum, on our side of the river. Neither was enough to dampen the Milky Way that looked like smog in outer space.

The fire wouldn't start and after we wasted half a box of strike-anywheres, I had an idea. Ten minutes later I was back at our camp with half a soup can of gasoline. I splashed it on the thick boards. "Try it now."

Mark struck a match, and pitched it toward the planks that were nothing more than a dark mound on the ground. The fire caught with a yellow *whoosh* before it landed. Yellow flame filled the air and the gush of heat burned the hair on my arms. I fell back and we went to stomping out the tent.

"Hotamighty!" Mark's stomping was frantic.

I laughed. "You look like a Comanche doing a war dance."

"My shoes are on fire!" He kicked off his tennis shoes and rubbed them in the grass to put 'em out.

Pepper laughed like a loon. "If that don't beat all. I don't know why y'all need a fire, anyway. It's already so hot I've about cooked down to clear grease."

A pair of headlights came up the drive. I recognized Uncle Cody's El Camino. That meant he was off for the night instead of out being sheriff of Lamar County. There'd been a lot of meanness in Chisum and our little community of Center Springs for the past few years, but we'd finally reached a dry spell and all the adults were feeling pretty good.

The porch light was off, and it was too late to see anything but shapes and shadows in the yard. Hootie'd been lying in a hole he dug under the bodark tree to keep cool, but he took off like a shot. Redheaded Aunt Norma Faye laughed at something Uncle Cody said, and her voice washed over me like a cool drink of water, as it had since they married four years earlier.

The wooden screen door closed behind them with a *slap, pop, pop,* and Pepper sighed deep and leaned against Mark's shoulder. She adjusted the volume and "Midnight Confessions" by the Grass Roots filled the night. She squealed. "Outta sight!" She started dancing around our small campfire.

Mark grinned and shook his head. "Ain't she something?"

"Something, or the other. She looks like you putting out your shoes a few minutes ago. You want to turn that down?"

She flailed around like she had ants in her pants. "Why? It's not bothering the old folks."

"It's bothering *me.* We wanted some peace and quiet, and all that jumping around's making me hot just watching you."

For once she didn't argue.

Pepper fiddled with her radio and sighed. "I wish I had a drink of water. I'm about to get the dry wobbles." She stared off into the dark for a second and I could tell she was thinking of something else. As usual, she switched subjects in midstream. "I know some history around here."

Mark barely looked up from the coals. "What?"

She ran her hand up and down Mark's arm, finally tangling her fingers in his. "There's a lost gold treasure in Palmer Lake."

A little over ten miles to the northwest as a crow flies, Palmer

Lake was a shallow spread of water not much more'n a deep slough. I'd been there several times with Uncle Cody in the last couple of years, hunting ducks. "No they ain't."

"Is too. I heard Daddy and the Wilson boys talk about it up at the store. About a million years ago a Mexican mule train on the way to Louisiana was attacked by Indians and the Mexicans buried a bunch of gold real fast. Most of 'em got killed, but a couple got away. People talked about it for years and then one day this Mexican General showed up with a map and poked around for a long while, but didn't find anything."

She paused, thinking. "Then they told about a farmer who plowed up some people bones and rusty old rifle barrels back before Daddy was born, right there where the General camped out. They thought that's where the gold was buried, but folks dug up most of that land and didn't find anything else."

Mark laughed. "That old boy probably made it up and got his land broke up by treasure-hunters before he plowed it. He was pretty smart, if you ask me."

"I don't know nothing about that." Pepper dug a gold coin from the pocket of her jeans. "But I know gold when I see it. Take a look at this."

We put our heads together to see the firelight reflecting off the coin. I felt something uncoil deep down inside. "Let me hold it."

The metal was heavy in my hand and I knew it was real. Someone a long time before had worked a ragged hole at the top of the coin to wear as a necklace. "What is it?"

"Dad says it's a gold *escudo*, whatever that means."

It was the first time I'd ever felt the need to own something. "How come you to have it?"

"I snitched it out of his sock drawer."

Mark took the coin from my hand and weighed it in his palm. "How'd Uncle James get it?"

She glanced up at the house to make sure no one was coming down to check on us. "That snooty sonofabitch Bill Preston came into the hardware store to get some building materials for that house he's having built not far from the river, about a mile from Palmer Lake. He traded Daddy what he owed for this. That feller said he's been collecting gold for years, but he wouldn't tell him nothin' else. Daddy says he thinks it came from that treasure at Palmer Lake."

I'd seen Bill Preston half a dozen times up at the store. He always wanted to pay with one of those Diner's Club credit cards, but Neal Box wouldn't take it. He insisted on cash. "I know him. Grandpa says he runs a Ford house out of Dallas."

A wolf howled and we scooted toward the fire. I was already sweating like a pig before the fire collapsed and got hotter. I rubbed my finger over the gold eagle. The thought of a mule-train load of coins buried close by sent a tingle up my spine.

"Yeah, and Uncle Cody's mad because he's tearing up the land with a bulldozer he bought." Mark fiddled with a strand of Pepper's hair. "He's pushed over fences that ain't his and started cuttin' roads through other people's land that he calls easements. I heard Uncle Cody say Judge Rains' already hauled him in for it, 'cause the way he's doing it ain't legal. He's even killing trees somehow with poison. Said they'll block his view to the river."

I saw a blue-white flash as my Poisoned Gift flared to life— dreams and visions that haunted me at night, and sometimes came true during the day, but they weren't clear enough that I could figure them out.

For a second we weren't in a pasture, but in a wide meadow full of grass lit by a full moon above. A glittering golden stream of mist drifted down on a house perched on a ridge lined with crying skeletons standing in the yard, holding bony fingers toward the sky.

The vision went away as quick as it appeared, leaving me tired and empty inside. Neither of them noticed what happened. My mouth was dry and I had to work up some spit before I could talk. "Well…" I stopped when my voice broke and I waited to get hold of myself.

"You're voice is cracking!" Pepper pointed and laughed. "That means your balls are gonna drop soon."

"Hey!" Mark shoved her shoulder, but lightly. "I don't want to hear that."

I sure didn't want to get into *that* discussion with my girl cousin. The psychedelic, space-age lead into "Reflections" by Diana Ross and the Supremes came on and sounded like robots, or that TV show *Lost in Space*, at the same time a wolf's howl filled the air, much closer than before.

Another wolf joined in and they took to fighting and snarling, just beyond the edge of the firelight. One of 'em choked on an ear, or maybe a mouthful of hair, and belted out a hyena laugh.

"I'm done." Pepper snatched the coin from my hand and took off toward the house.

"Good idea." I followed her and Mark wasn't much behind me as we sprinted toward the house.

Chapter Five

That same Saturday night, Mr. Green sat at the round table in the Howard Johnson's motel room he shared with Mr. Brown. The Austin traffic outside was muffled by *The Wild Wild West* on the color television. Moisture cloaked the Texas capital in a wet blanket of heat and humidity that poured like a river from the Gulf Coast, and the government agents were enjoying the motel room with refrigerated air.

Mr. Green plucked a pack of Camels from the pocket of his white shirt, shook one out, and fired it up. His tie was off and both sleeves were rolled up. He was on his third pack of the day, one up from his usual two. "We may have a problem."

Wearing nothing but a sleeveless undershirt and suit pants, Mr. Brown kicked off his shoes and leaned back against the wooden headboard screwed to the wall. The motel's neon lights illuminated the full parking lot and empty swimming pool in the center. "You looked like you were going to puke back there at that airstrip."

Mr. Green didn't take his eyes from the snowy picture on the screen. "Got too hot."

"It wasn't that hot."

"*I* was." Mr. Green wiped at the side of his crewcut and tapped the ash off the cigarette. "I can't stand this humidity. Remember, I'm from the Pacific coast, where it's cool. Look, you think that pilot's going to stay quiet?"

"He won't talk."

"How do you know that for sure?"

"I grew up around people like that." Mt. Brown switched over to an authentic Texas accent. "He gimme his word and he'll keep it, 'sides, them two stacks of cash'll keep 'im quiet."

"Wow! That's great. I always thought you were from the Midwest by the way you speak."

Mr. Brown realized he'd made a mistake and revealed a tiny bit of his past. It was bad business to do that, even though he knew more about Mr. Green's own history than he'd like. "I meant farm people."

"I always figured you for a city boy."

"It doesn't matter where I'm from. I lived close enough to the country to know those people. He'll also feel guilty for taking the money from the government, tax-free."

"If you follow that line of thinking, he might feel guilty for more than that. Both nozzles were dented. I saw it when I took them off. Not much, but a little. That brass is soft and it looks like something hit them."

Mr. Brown tucked his chin into his chest in thought. "You didn't say anything back there."

"I had to think about it."

"You looked like you'd seen a ghost."

"He'd monkeyed with the sprayer. That worries me."

"Maybe they were like that when you installed them."

"Nope. He did something after he left."

"That means he landed somewhere."

Mr. Green blew two streams of smoke through his nose that looked a lot like the vapor that flowed from the plane's nozzles. He dug under one fingernail with the other and examined the results. "Why do you think he'd do that?"

"I don't know." Mr. Brown plucked a bottle of Scotch off the nightstand. He poured two fingers into the water glass from the bathroom, added ice, and swallowed half. "Don't say anything about it."

"I don't intend to. I got some on my hands." His voice broke and he held them up as if to offer proof and maybe find some sympathy. "Look, I know the people we work for, and this scares me."

Mr. Brown lit a Lucky, and crossed his sock feet. He balanced an ashtray on his lap to keep both hands free to handle the Scotch and cigarette. "They said it's nothing but water with—what did they call it?—a benign bacteria. Marcus says we already have those bacteria in us. A little extra shouldn't be a problem."

"Sure. That's why they gave us those gloves and the lined boxes."

"You use them?"

"I did, but there was a tear in one finger that I didn't notice until it was too late." Mr. Green's chin quivered. "Do you think it's safe, like they said?"

Mr. Brown drew a lungful of smoke. "Relax. We have to believe those eggheads, but the truth is I believe *these* damn things'll kill us long before anything in those tanks will."

Mr. Green took a long drag and blew smoke at the swag lamp hanging over the table. "You're right. We'll all die of *something*, sooner or later." He attempted a sarcastic laugh that dissolved into a wet, phlemy cough.

"Yep, and if they find out we're building our own retirement plan, it'll be sooner." Mr. Brown pondered a valise sitting on the floor beside the television stand, thinking about the unused ten thousand dollars he'd split with his partner.

Chapter Six

On Monday, the cotton town of Chisum baked in the hot sun that was breaking all records for that time of year. The chuckling marble fountain in the town square pumped warm water that did nothing but hint at refreshment. Heat waves shimmered above the streets.

Texas weather could change in a matter of hours, and late fall was the worst. It was still nothing for the temperature to reach near triple digits and cause the whole town to look toward the north, waiting for the first blue norther of the year.

An old gentleman carrying a battered suitcase pulled the Woolworth's glass door open. His black Stetson, dark coat, and faded Wrangler jeans were unusual for northeast Texas. The brass bell jangled as he entered the cool five-and-dime that smelled of plastic, cosmetics, astringents, with a touch of Pine-Sol.

The ceiling above was the original stamped-tin panels. The wooden floor creaked underfoot. On the left-hand side, a lunch counter ran the length of the building, paralleled by rows of cosmetics, toys, household items, and over-the-counter drugs and ending at a perpendicular aisle. It gave customers free access to turn down aisles at both ends of the store. The building was filled with an electric hum as ceiling fans moved the refrigerated air.

Helen Humberstone glanced up from behind the red and white Coca-Cola fountain and watched him pass the row of red vinyl stools with surprising ease for his age. His back was ramrod straight, evidence that he'd not lived a life of stoop labor like so many of the farmers from outside of Chisum.

The Beach Boys' "California Girls" came through the tinny Bakelite radio on a shelf behind the counter as Helen constructed a Coke float. The old man took the last seat under the lighted plastic Dr Pepper sign at the far end of the counter. She recognized most of the old-timers in town, but the man in the dark sport coat was a complete stranger.

He tilted the cowboy hat back to reveal a lock of white hair. Smoothing a thick, well-trimmed gray mustache with one finger, he folded his hands on the Formica counter and began reading the menu board secured above two shelves full of plain off-white cafeteria plates. After a moment, he glanced down and studied a pasteboard menu with the daily specials.

The waitress slid the finished drink in front of a businessman at the end near the doors. He pulled the frosty glass close. "Thank you, Helen. This'll sure perk up a pretty sorry Monday."

"You're welcome." She winked and made her easy way toward the stranger, wiping her hands on a damp rag. She leaned her elbows on the counter, refolding the rag. "How-do. Looks like we have a new sheriff in this hot town. Can I get you a coke with lots of ice?"

His eyes were bright, promising mischief. They flicked to her beehive hairdo. "What kind do you have?"

"Co-Cola, on the fountain. We got Dr Pepper, RC, Sem'm-Up, Diet Rite, Big Red, and Fresca in the bottle."

"I sure would like a grape Nehi."

"Don't got. Them I said is all we have."

He nodded toward a two-foot-high glass dome covering round shelves full of sliced pie. "Well then, how about a piece of that coconut and a cup of coffee?"

"Hot coffee in this weather?"

"Down south they say it helps you feel cooler."

"Down south?"

"In the Valley."

"I don't know about that." Helen pulled an order pad close and plucked a pencil from behind her ear. Thinking, she drew a tiny tornado in one corner to start the flow of ink. Never been down there. "Pie and coffee. Comin' right up."

The white-haired man turned sideways on his stool, resting his right elbow on the counter. He watched a farmer in overalls leave a few coins on top of his check and walk into the bright sunshine. His eyes flicked through the large windows and rested on the Plaza marquee down the street, announcing the new Dean Martin western, *5 Card Stud.*

Farther down the counter, a gray-haired woman shared a banana split with her grandson. The businessman with the Coke float checked his Timex and drew long and hard on the straw.

Helen returned with the pie. She slid an empty cup and saucer across the Formica and filled it. "Sugar's right there. Here's some cream." Returning the pot to the burner, she leaned both elbows on the counter again and nudged the shot-size container toward his cup.

"Don't need any sweetener, but thanks."

She left it there and rested her chin on her hand. "So, you live here or just passing through?"

He cut a bite with the edge of his fork and chewed for a moment before swallowing. "I lived out in Center Springs here-while-back." He blew across the surface of his coffee, cooling it.

"You got kinfolk around here?"

He raised an eyebrow. "Yessum."

Two scruffy men in their twenties came in under the jangling bell. Dressed in bell-bottoms, tie-dyed shirts, and worn-out sneakers, they split up. One with hair to his shoulders and long sideburns to his jawline veered toward the back. The blond sporting a wispy Fu Manchu mustache slouched onto the stool closest to the door. Despite the heat, he wore a denim vest with the sleeves cut off.

"Be back in a sec." Helen pushed off from the counter to take the young man's order. "What'll it be?"

Fu Manchu barely glanced away from the door. "A coke."

"What kind?"

He shrugged. "A Dr Pepper?"

"We only have it in the bottle. You okay with that?"

"Fine."

"You want a straw?"

"Yes."

"Your buddy want anything?"

His frustration was apparent. "I doubt it. Ask him your own-self."

"Well, *excuuuse* me." Helen opened the cooler and cold bottles rattled.

The old cowboy put down his fork. Taking another noisy sip of hot coffee, he watched the young man from under thick gray eyebrows. Between them and oblivious to everything except her grandson, the woman at the counter laughed and wiped chocolate syrup from the child's face. She lit a cigarette, blew a cloud into the air, and rested it on a nearby glass ashtray.

As if it were a signal, Fu Manchu dug a crumpled pack of Camels from his jeans and lit one with a kitchen match scratched alight on his thumbnail. He cupped the flame between two hands, as if there was a breeze blowing in the building. His hands moved with the tiniest of shakes, and he waved the match out like it was soaked in kerosene.

The old man's right eyebrow raised ever so slightly.

Helen returned. "Something wrong with the pie?"

He slid the half-empty cup toward her. "Not a thing. That much sweet stuff hurts my teeth, so I have to sneak up on it and eat a little at a time."

"I don't believe that." Helen refilled his cup. "Them pearlies of yours look better than most that come in here. You either have great choppers, or they're dentures. I bet you weren't born in Lamar County. You don't have the look."

He tapped a tooth, the wrinkles in the corners of his smiling eyes grew deep. "They're mine. Your daddy a lawman?"

Helen frowned in surprise. "No, why?"

"Just asking. Brother, granddaddy in that line of business?"

"Nope. You still ain't said why you're asking."

"Because you're inquisitive. Most little gals your age start conversations with their customers to flirt, but I'm too old." The prominent crow's-feet in the corners of his eyes cut deep with smile. "So you're just gen'ly nosey."

Helen's couldn't decide whether to get mad or laugh. "I'm a waitress. I flirt with everybody."

"Gets you better tips, huh?"

Get mad, or laugh? "Sure does. Look, the reason I'm interested is that you're sittin' there in a hat, sport coat, jeans that ain't Levis, and boots. You're a whole 'nother animal for this part of the world."

He watched the businessman finish his float and leave. "I've been told that before."

She smiled, relaxed "So, you here on business, or visitin' somebody?"

He laughed softly. "Yep."

"My name's Helen."

"You can call me…Stranger."

"Well, if you don't beat all." Helen rolled her eyes in fun and drifted down the counter to slide a check toward the grandmother. At the far end, Fu Manchu watched out the window. The bubbles from the carbonation pushed the paper straw high in the neck.

Stranger's eyes took the measure of the counter as tense male voices rose two aisles over near the fabric section and ended abruptly. Ignoring his pie, the old cowboy slowly spun on the stool to face the door and Fu Manchu fiddling with his untouched Dr Pepper.

A soft yelp came from the manager's office, accompanied by the sharp sound of breaking glass. Stranger put down his coffee cup. Resting his left foot on the floor, he twisted to look over his shoulder. Other than the radio and the grandmother whispering to her little one, the five-and-dime had gone quiet.

Stranger's gray eyes flashed with lightning-bolt electricity. He tapped the edge of his pie plate with the fork to get the waitress' attention. "Helen."

Filling a glass at the fountain, she cut her eyes at him. "Yessir?"

His voice came low and steady. "Call the laws."

"What?" She glanced around the store. "Why? What's wrong?"

His voice whip-cracked with authority. "Call the laws right *now!*"

Helen's face went white as a sheet at the order. She wheeled toward the pay phone.

The slap of running feet on polished tile broke the silence. Sideburns rounded the far end of the perpendicular aisle behind Stranger, charging past the display of hair curlers, brushes, and combs. "*Go-go-go!*"

A quavering voice howled from the rear. "Help! Robbery!"

Sideburn's faded jean jacket flapped open, revealing the butt of a revolver stuck in his waistband. Either from fear or drugs, the man's pupils were wide, dark pits fixed on the glass door. He tucked a small brown paper sack under his arm like a running back and ducked his head, sprinting flat out and desperate.

Fu Manchu jumped to his feet and held the glass door open, spilling hot air into the store. "Nobody move or I'll shoot!"

Stranger stuck out his black boot as casual as a businessman checking the leather's shine, locking the fleeing man's ankle as he charged past.

Sideburns slammed face-first onto the hard tile like he'd been heeled by a professional roper, landing with the smack of a dropped steak. The bag shot from his hand across the floor and slid to a stop beside a clearance display of unsellable plastic items from Japan, fanning loose, wrinkled bills everywhere.

Stunned by the impact, Sideburns groaned and tried to rise,

blood pouring from a broken nose, crushed lips, and a missing tooth. Stranger kicked one arm out from under him and drew a Colt 1911 with the smooth, fluid ease of practice. He pointed the muzzle down the counter toward Fu Manchu. "Hold it!"

Moaning on the floor with blood spilling from his broken nose, Sideburns twisted, trying to draw the revolver from his belt. Stranger kicked him hard in the side with the toe of his pointed boot.

He dropped a bony knee on the young man's neck and glanced up to see Fu Manchu squirt out the door. "Looks like your friend's done run off." He checked over his shoulder. The waitress' eyes were wide and she held the receiver against her ear. "Helen, I believe somebody's talkin' to you on that thing."

She snapped back and spoke into the mouthpiece. "Uh, somebody just tried to rob the Woolworth's. Y'all better get somebody over here."

Satisfied, Stranger returned to the unsuccessful thief on the floor. "Criminal, you make one more move and this forty-five's liable to go off." He flipped the young man over and plucked the snub-nosed .38 revolver from his waistband.

The big-bellied Woolworth's manager appeared at his side, wiping sweat from his bald head with a wrinkled handkerchief. "My money."

"Gather it up. It's right there."

The manager's voice broke with relief. "I thought he was gonna shoot me."

"Might have." Stranger put the worn revolver on the counter and holstered his forty-five. "You're under arrest, son."

The manager raised an eyebrow. "You making a citizen's arrest?"

"Naw. It's a little more'n that." He pulled his jacket back to reveal a round badge. "Texas Ranger, retired."

"Sure lucky for you to be here."

"It was, that."

A siren wailed from the direction of the courthouse only a block away. The stranger smoothed his gray mustache. "Criminal, you roll over on your belly and lay right there and I won't have to shoot you. Put your hands behind you, hoss."

"I ain't going nowhere." The would-be robber's pronunciation was mushy from the blood and missing tooth.

"I know it." The Ranger plucked a pair of handcuffs from the small of his back and clicked them around the man's wrists. "Now be still and you might prove to me that you're smarter'n you look."

He spat. "I'm bleedin pretty bad."

"That's liable to be another charge, spittin' in public."

A minute later a black-and-white sheriff's car slid to a stop behind the vehicles parked in front of the Woolworth's. A female deputy in a straw Stetson and khaki uniform popped out and rushed inside with a revolver drawn. She slowed when she saw the bleeding would-be robber lying on his stomach at the feet of an elderly cowboy perched casually on a stool.

She advanced and stopped with a pistol in her hand. "Sir, would you stay right there, please? And don't touch that pistol there on the counter, either."

"You bet." Calm as a wooded stock tank, Stranger leaned his right elbow on the counter and laced his fingers. She kept an eye on him from under the brim of her straw hat as she glanced at the cuffs on Sideburn's wrists. "Don't move."

Sideburns turned his head and grunted. "I done been told that by him. He threatened to shoot me."

"You're lucky he didn't." The deputy met Stranger's eyes. "So you have a pistol?"

Using two fingers of his right hand, Stranger opened the sport coat to reveal the cold blue 1911 in a hand-tooled leather holster. "Yes, ma'am." With the gentle motions of a magician, he flicked his coat with the other hand to reveal a badge stamped from a Mexican peso.

The deputy recognized it at once and relaxed. "Well, leave it right where it is." She knelt to make sure the cuffs were tight and glanced up at the white-faced manager. "Pete, you all right?"

Pete stepped forward, wiping his mouth with a nervous hand, forgetting the handkerchief in the other. "This old feller stopped the robbery all by hisself." He held out the bag of money. "They didn't get a dollar. That man's a hero."

The deputy finally holstered her pistol and held out a hand to the old man. She met his gaze for the first time. "Deputy Anna Sloan. I believe you might be a Texas Ranger."

"Retired." He took her hand in a firm grip. His voice was as soft and calm as it had been when he ordered pie and coffee. "Name's Tom Bell."

Chapter Seven

We took our seats after recess on Monday. Things hadn't changed much in our little frame community school since Mama and Daddy went there. The windows of the WPA project from way back in 1932 were open to catch any breeze, and the wooden floors echoed with the footsteps of those barely making it to class before they were counted tardy.

Green squares with cursive letters were stapled above the blackboard, and around one side of the room. Miss Russell called that type of writing the Palmer Method, and it was one of my favorite lessons. She'd erased our English lessons while we were outside and put up the day's math problems. The board was filled with numbers and letters that were confusing to me as all get out.

She passed out our math tests and I left mine face-down on the desk. I knew I'd failed it on Friday the minute I looked at all the questions. I gave every problem a good try, despite all those letters that had no business being in there with numbers and minuses and such.

I raised my hand.

Miss Russell used her pen almost as a wand, granting me permission to speak. "Yes, Top?"

"May I use the restroom?"

"Is it an emergency?"

"Yes ma'am."

"You may."

I left the classroom, eyes stinging with the knowledge that I'd surely fail the next six weeks and would suffer the consequences. Grandpa, Miss Becky, Uncle Cody, and even Norma Faye would get on me, and I wasn't sure I could take it.

My nerves vibrated as tight as guitar strings while I walked down the empty hall to the boys' room. The windows were open and the fencerow full of oaks and hackberry trees out past the swing set was as tempting as a slice of coconut pie. The bathroom smelled like Lysol and was silent except for the drip of a leaking faucet.

Trying not to cry, I turned on the water to wash my face and that's when the door opened on the only stall and in the mirror I saw Harlan Ketchum step out. His hair looked like it was cut with a brush hog, sticking up and gapped in several places.

His face widened in a grin, showing the space between his front teeth and the missing incisor that had never grown in. "Well, howdy Mouse."

I ignored him and bent down to throw water on my face in order to hide the tears. It was exactly the wrong thing to do. As soon as I ducked my head, he grabbed me in a headlock.

"How does *that* feel? Huh! You like it?"

He was half again my size and I couldn't pull away. He ground down with his bicep and it felt like my ears were on fire. "Stop it!" My voice was high as a girl's and even in a headlock, the squeal was embarrassing.

Harlan spun, nearly taking me off my feet. "How about I flush your stupid head?"

"Quit!"

My tennis shoes squeaked on the gray penny tiles and I struggled to get free. He let go with his left and punched me in the head. "Squeak, Mouse."

"Stop it!"

"Squeak!"

We were halfway into the stall when I heard Principal Stevens' voice in the hall. He was talking to someone just outside the restroom. Harlan turned loose of me and went out the screenless window like a shot.

I stumbled out of the stall just as Mr. Stevens came in. "What's wrong with you, boy?"

My face and ears burned with shame and the exertion of fighting back. My nose was running and I wiped tears from my eyes. "I don't feel good."

He studied me for a minute, then pointed at the sink. "Well, wash your face and get back to class. And be sure to turn that water off when you're finished. You kids are wasteful."

My throat tickled and I swallowed down a cough. "Yessir."

Chapter Eight

Constable Ned Parker was sitting in Judge O.C. Rains' sweltering office Monday morning, arguing as usual. The two old men had been friends since before World War II and fussed at one another like an old married couple, flaring up and cooling off to laugh together minutes later.

"Goddamn it, O.C., I can't believe Wes Clay's back running the streets like nothing ever happened."

"Me neither." O.C. ran his fingers through a head of white hair. The barrister bookcases overflowed into every available space. His oak file cabinets were filled to capacity. Files and papers were stacked on the floor in constantly growing towers.

"But you're the one who let him go."

"I didn't have anything to do with it. The Grand Jury no-billed him. Said cuttin' up Olan Mayfield was self-defense."

"Well, I don't like it one damn bit."

O.C.'s chiseled face remained as somber as it looked when he was on the bench. "Neither do I, but there ain't nothin' I can do about it. Go arrest his sorry ass again. He'll do something sooner or later, and that'll add up with the next jury."

"I got better things to do than sit around and wait for Wes Clay to break the law."

"You won't have to wait long." O.C. shot a look out the open window at the blistering sun. "But I'd sit in the shade if I's you."

"That's a fact."

They paused, faces gleaming in the airless office. The city council refused to provide the funds for refrigerated air conditioning or even water coolers, so everyone in the Lamar County Courthouse suffered in the last heat wave of 1968. Dark patches under the arms of Ned's blue shirt widened.

O.C. picked up a wire flyswatter and slapped a fly walking on one of the many stacks of paper on his desk. The hot street below hummed with traffic noise. People on the sidewalks sweltered in the thick air that belonged three hundred miles south where the folks who lived in Houston suffered the heat, humidity, and mosquitoes by choice rather than whims of the weather.

He swept the corpse onto the floor to join a dozen others. "Well, it's too hot to fool with you anymore. Let's go down to Frenchie's and get us a cold drink."

Ned stood, hat in hand. "You only want to go watch her transmission shift every time she walks by."

"It's better than sitting here listening to you yak." O.C. plucked his black coat off the rack and slipped it on over a limp white shirt. "I was already tired of your temperament back in forty-eight."

"You're gonna die in that coat out there."

"I might. You be sure and have it cleaned before they bury me in it, though. I want to leave a good-looking corpse."

Ned grunted and followed him into the stifling hallway. "It'll be the only good-looking thing in that casket, that's for sure."

O.C. punched the elevator button and watched the half-moon dial creak up from the ground floor. It jerked to a stop, jolted up an inch, and they heard the accordion safety-gate rattle back. The metal doors opened to reveal the oldest man in Lamar County sitting on a tall stool beside the control panel.

"Mister Ned. Judge."

Ned stepped aboard. "Howdy, Jules. You doing all right today?"

The wrinkled old man well over a hundred years old was born into slavery. He'd worked the fields until he took a job as the Lamar County Courthouse elevator operator where he worked for over fifty years, well past the time when most folks retired. "Tolerable well, sir. First floor?"

"Yep."

Jules closed the outer doors, then the safety gate. "Y'all done been to breakfas'." He knew the routine of everyone who worked in the courthouse.

O.C. grinned. "That was an hour ago. Now I need a cool drink."

"Miss Frenchie'll be glad to see you, but I doubt it'll be cooler in there. That place ain't got no circulation in the front, or the back."

Though it was the dawning of the Age of Aquarius, white folks still ate in the front of the café while colored people took the rear.

"O.C. don't speak for me. I plan to eat a bite." Ned chuckled. "At least it'll be a change of scenery."

Jules wiped at the sheen of sweat on his forehead and steadied himself with one hand against the elevator wall. "Marse Ned. Mind we stop on the next flo' and open the do' fo' some air? I ain't feelin' too good."

Ned rested his hand on the old man's shoulder. He'd never heard Old Jules speak that way. Though his usual speech reflected his culture and the people he lived with, the strange pattern sounded old…very old.

"Sure we can, Jules."

The elevator jerked at the second floor and the old man reached a shaky hand to open the safety gate. Slightly cooler air flowed in. O.C. saw Jules' eyes go glassy and fanned him with his hat. "I believe you might need to get out this box for a while and catch some air."

"It sho' was hot when I's a kid in 'em fields down south. I reckon I can handle this little spell of weather."

"You may be having a spell yourself."

"Sho' nuff, Marse Watson."

Ned and O.C. exchanged concerned looks. Neither knew anyone named Watson. O.C. mouthed "stroke." While the judge continued to fan Jules, Ned hurried out of the elevator to the nearest phone.

Jules shrank on his stool. "My daddy and mammy was Charley and Liza Bunton and Marse Philip Watson brung dem from Loosiana to Lamar County 'fore freedom. Dey was ten chillen and I's borned when de Yankees come. My folks stayed with Marse Watson and he daughter Miss Em'ly till dey went to de reward where dey ain't no mo tears." Jules' eyes rolled back in his head.

His voice full of fear for the old man, O.C. cried through the open door. "Ned, help!"

Jules went limp as a dishrag and it was all O.C. could do to not let him fall. The old man's chin dropped to his chest as the judge lowered him to the floor.

Ned was back seconds later and knelt in the door. "They're calling an ambulance."

"He was talking out of his head. Sounded like them real old coloreds talked when I was a kid. Help me get him fixed right."

"Let's get 'im to the lobby." Ned pulled Jules' foot inside the elevator and punched the ground floor button. It was stifling by the time they reached the first floor. Though the lobby was far from cool, it felt like air conditioning. They took Jules under his skinny arms and pulled him out onto the black and white penny tiles.

"Watch his head, watch his head." Ned cradled Jules' neck as they stretched him out on the floor.

The lobby was empty, except for Albert Shames sitting on the stool in front of his shoeshine stand. He dropped his paper and rushed forward. "Lordy. What's the matter with Jules?"

"He fell out in the elevator." O.C. loosened the old man's collar.

Jules' eyes fluttered. He grabbed Ned's shirt with a hand covered with tissue-thin skin. "Mr. Cody?"

"It's still me, Jules. Ned." He held the skinny hand that felt like it was full of bird bones. "O.C.'s here with us, and Albert. You lay easy. Help's on the way."

"Marse Cody. Thankyee for the water."

"You need some water?"

"Dat water taste fine now."

Ned and O.C. exchanged bewildered glances until Albert explained. "He's talking about the drinkin' fount'ns. It always bothered him to see the colored and white signs there, but he never said nothin'. When Sheriff Cody ripped them signs down here-while-back, I saw Jules almost dance in 'at elevator 'fore he closed the do' that day."

Ned's throat closed up as his chin quivered. He squeezed Jules' hand and patted the old man's chest, barely feeling the life there. "Hold on old-timer. Help's a comin'."

"He here. Lily, I got to go."

Ned glanced over his shoulder. The old man was talking out of his head. "Not yet, you don't. Stay with us, Jules."

"'at Angel's right dere, I see her. She's beautiful, but I'm held back, sump'n cain't let go yet."

The hair rose on Ned's neck and a wave of dread washed over him. "Oh, no." A low hum filled his head and his ears burned as if he were embarrassed.

Jules quivered, fighting something deep inside. His heels hammered against the floor with frantic rhythm.

Mouth dry, Ned felt a once-familiar electric charge build deep in his core and rise to his head. He quit patting Jules' chest and backed away. "Not again."

"Help him." O.C.'s voice was sharp as it sounded in his courtroom.

The tone shocked Ned as much as a physical slap. He met O.C.'s eyes, this time with stomach-dropping fear. Dread weighted his shoulders and he shook his head. "I'm done with that. He'll go."

"No you ain't. You never was." O.C. shook his head, eyes glittering in anger. "He's having a hard time of it. He don't deserve this. Help him go on."

"You know what happened to us back then." His voice plaintive, Ned held up a hand, as if to ward off a blow. Images flickered like a Nickelodeon peep show as the humming in his head increased.

Wasted bodies.

Weeping relatives.

Miss Becky praying over her Bible.

Men, women, and children dying in Ned's arms.

Angry, unbelieving residents of a Chisum long ago.

The Lamar County courtroom, and a young O.C. arguing Ned's fate as the equally young farmer sat at the defense table, staring at his hands.

Ned weeping in anguish every time he was called upon to help others pass.

He shook his head, gritting his dentures. "The Lord'll take him directly."

"I can see it coming on you, just like before. This ain't the time to argue!"

Jules convulsed again. He reached for something unseen.

O.C. gripped Ned's bicep with a surprisingly strong hand. "*Help* this man, Ned."

"I want to be shed of this."

"That's between you and God, but right now you're needed."

With tears rolling down his sun-browned cheeks and shaking like a leaf in a gale, Ned gave in to the weight of the dread resting on his shoulders. A crowd gathered as the word spread and the onlookers whispered, wondering what they were arguing about.

Ned watched Jules struggle with Death for a moment more. He reluctantly dropped his hat on the floor and sat on the hard tiles with a grunt, crooking his leg. "Get ahold."

Albert paled under his black skin. "I heard 'bout this years ago...."

Still on one knee, O.C. braced himself. "Not now, Albert. Help me get his head in Ned's lap."

Jules struggled to breathe. Spittle ran down his cheek. His body trembled even harder, like a mule struggling against the plow.

They tugged the fragile old man around until he half-lay on Ned's cocked leg. Ned cradled Jules' gray head. Mouth dry as dust, his voice came out low and hoarse. "You ready? You sure, Jules Benton?"

For a second, the dull, rheumy eyes opened and fixed somewhere over Ned's shoulder. "Marse Wats'n. Sweet Jesus, hep me to Glory. They's a big ol' rusty chain holin' me back. I knows you can do it. Lily! Lordy, that angel over your shoulder's beautiful, but she won't take my hand. Mama! Tell her to take m'hand."

Seen by only Jules and Ned, sparking electricity fractured storm clouds hovering near the ceiling. The high-pitched humming filled Ned's head and the pressure in his skull built until he felt it would burst like a ripe melon. Ned closed his eyes and pulled Jules close enough to feel his feeble heart.

It was the long-forgotten but intensely personal act of putting his cheek against Jules' wrinkled face that completed the mysterious, unwanted circuitry that allowed Ned Parker to help others pass on. Ned's body went rigid. His body snapped as if hit by a jolt of electricity from the silent clouds against the ceiling.

Energy and a burst of pain, fear, and longing flowed from Jules and mixed with a warm glow in Ned's chest. For a moment, aches, pains, and a lifetime of sorrow filled Ned and just as it was about to run over and take him into a deep pit from which he knew he'd never return, Jules' life experiences fled.

A ray of light shot down on Jules' face, but no one in the courthouse saw it, except for the old elevator man. His eyes opened, then narrowed at the intensity of the beam, then closed. He took one last breath and let it out with a slow sigh.

Shuddering sobs filled Ned's chest as he did what he hadn't done in exactly forty years. He used his own Poisoned Gift to help a soul struggling with death to pass on.

Chapter Nine

The black oil road leading from school to Neal Box's store was mostly in the sun, except for a patch of shade here and there. A wide pasture with scattered trees and bushes was on our left, and a fencerow full of hardwoods on the right.

A trailer full of cattle roared past, not giving an inch to the three of us walking to the store. I didn't recognize the driver, but I threw a wave anyway, because that's what was expected.

"That ain't cool." Pepper threw her middle finger into the air. "That asshole ain't got no manners."

"I don't believe what you just did was very nice, neither." I kicked at a rock and watched it skip across the oil road. The air was thick enough to chew and my tee-shirt was already sticking to my back. I was looking forward to a cold drink from Neal's musty smelling cooler.

"Shut up, Zippy."

I hated when she called me that. She picked it up at the traveling carnival a while back and liked the sound of it. It was my fault she kept on wartin' me with that stupid nickname. I played the devil the first time when I told her not to call me that anymore. Now she knew it aggravated me and wouldn't turn it loose.

Pepper had changed some in the past few months, but the old Pepper imp was still in there, kicking to get loose again. I sure hoped she wouldn't call me that name at school. If Harlan heard it, he'd have two nicknames to hold over me.

I saw Miss Mable Truitt coming back from the post office. She was a little odd and always tickled me to death. Miss Becky said the midwife who helped deliver her in a house in the bottoms hurt her on the day she was born. She was one of the few people in Center Springs that I wasn't kin to, and that made her special to me and Pepper both.

She was in a blue-and-white housedress, the kind most Center Springs women wore only at home. I thought they were the ugliest dresses on the planet, and not even Twiggy could make one look right. She had her hair curled nice, though it was glued into place by so much Aqua Net hair spray that we could smell it before she reached us.

Pepper brightened. "Howdy, Miss Mable."

The old woman stopped and grinned. The skin on her legs below the hem of her dress looked like scarred leather. "Hi, hon. How're you today? You're supposed to call me Sissy this week."

"We're fine." Pepper rubbed the old gal's spotted arm. "Whatcha got in your bucket?"

Instead of a purse, Miss Mable always carried a different container everywhere she went. Most of the women in Center Springs toted big purses, but Miss Mable didn't. This time she had the skinny bail of a nursing bucket full of mail in the crook of her arm.

You never knew what she had in 'em, neither. I heard Grandpa say she'd carried around everything from puppies and kittens, to rocks, to a baby doll. At Sunday school one time, Miss Becky made Miss Mable give her something she real quick wrapped in a scarf before anyone could see it, and though I'd asked her a hundred times what it was, she'd turn red and refuse to answer.

Miss Mable glanced down at her galvanized bucket as if she was surprised to see it. I 'magine there was a nursing bucket in every barn in the county, but you usually didn't see 'em carried down the road in the crook of somebody's arm. The size of a regular milk pail, the bucket had a six-inch pink nipple that looked like a cow's teat sticking straight out to the side. Folks used them to feed baby calves.

She reached out and squeezed the nipple like she was milking a cow. "Why, ain't got no calf to nurse. I believe it's mail."

She kept squeezing and stroking the nipple while she talked and Pepper pressed her lips together to keep from laughing. Her ears turned red for the first time I could remember. "Is it *your* mail?"

"Why, I reckon." Her crooked old fingers fluttered around the envelopes. "See, here's some right here. And this is my lead rope." She pulled out the tail of a worn out rope.

I had trouble taking my eyes off of Pepper's red ears. "You have a baby calf at home?"

"Why, no. I ain't got no barn or corral neither. Why you think that?"

"I can't think of an answer, Miss Mable."

Mark peeked into the bucket and his eyes widened. He stepped back. "Something's *moving* in there."

I knew Miss Mable well enough to back up too. I was surprised to see Pepper get closer. "You got something else? Maybe a baby chick or two?"

"Why no, hon." Miss Mable reached into the bottom of the bucket and drew out a sluggish two-foot chicken snake that wrapped itself around her wrist.

Me and Mark were set to run, after my dealin' with a rattlesnake a few months earlier, but Pepper only laughed. "Miss Mable, how come you to be carrying around a snake?"

"Why Pepper, I forgot I put it in this mornin' when I went to gather th' eggs." She bent down and gently put the snake in the grass beside the highway. "It was in one of the nests and I couldn't leave it in there to eat m'eggs. Well, I got to get goin'." She took off without another word.

Pepper waited for a minute before she busted out laughing. Mark gave her one of those looks they'd been trading back and forth. "Did you see the way she was handling that…?"

His eyes sparkled and I thought he was gonna say something funny, but he just gave her a nudge and we headed for Uncle Neal's store. I couldn't figure out what they were talking about, but it sure had 'em both laughing.

We each had a quarter to spend, and I was trying to decide what kind of coke I wanted. A coke could be anything in the cooler including oranges, strawberries, Chocolate Soldiers, Dr Peppers or even a Grapette. I was kinda in the mood for an RC, though, and was thinking about putting some salted peanuts in it.

Our cotton shirts were wet by the time we circled around to the front of the white frame building that was the Center Springs Courthouse back in the 1800s.

The usual members of the Spit and Whittle Club were on the porch, talking and watching cars and trucks pass on the highway, but there was a difference I picked up right off. Every man there was straight and attentive, even the ones on the two-by-six rails, facing a young woman who was perched like a magazine model at the far end.

We slowed on the wooden steps to get a look at what was going on. Pepper reached out and snapped a knuckle sharp against the bottom of my chin. She leaned close. "Close your mouth, Zippy. Flies'll get in."

It was open for good reason. I'd never seen anything like that gal in a white mini-skirt held tight on her hips by a chain belt around her waist. Her sleeveless blue blouse was unbuttoned lower than I'd ever seen on a woman. And she wasn't wearing a brassiere. Every time she moved, and she did that about ever' ten seconds, there was a chance that something would get loose.

From the looks on the men's faces, I figured they were praying for that to happen.

Ty Cobb Wilson rested an elbow on his knee and leaned forward. "It's hotter'n a two-dollar pistol today."

Even though they weren't twins, his brother Jimmy Foxx did the exact same thing at the same time. You didn't see either one of the Wilson boys without the other. Those middle-aged men more than favored each other, with hooked noses, long, scraggly hair, and their ever-present hip waders folded down at the knee and looking like bell-bottoms.

The woman threw her head back and laughed, reaching out a bare foot and nudging Ty Cobb's leg with her bare toes. Her sandals were on the dusty boards. "You boys are so *funny!*" She batted her eyes, and I heard Pepper growl behind me.

It was all I could do to take my eyes off the woman, but when I did, I saw Pepper push Mark through the door. His head was down, but I knew good and well that he was sneaking his own look through the long hair hanging down in his eyes.

Pepper threw another glance toward the lady. "Something else's cheap around here, and it ain't no pistol."

"Watch your mouth, missy." Uncle Neal glanced up with a pencil in his hand. His shirt-sleeves were rolled to the elbows and the red-and-white plaid material was soaked under his arms.

She threw her hands up. "Who's that hussy out there?"

"Keep your voice down or I'll have to call your Daddy." He leaned on his bare-board counter crowded with everything from tubes of BBs to cigarette lighters, to coils of string. He pointed with his pencil stub that was barely visible in his thick fingers. "That there's Scottie Graham, or at least that's the name she gave me when she bought her an Orange Crush."

"I don't know no Grahams."

Uncle Neal sighed. "You ain't as old as my shoes, so I don't reckon you know everybody."

"Well, how come you to ask her name in the first place then? You don't care who spends their money in here."

"Pepper!" His voice was low and sharp, a tone I'd never heard from Uncle Neal.

"Well, those men out there need to get their eyeballs back in their heads and them tongues off the floor."

"She ain't hurtin' nobody. They're just out there talking."

Pepper stalked over to the coke cooler, the big bells on her jeans slapping with her anger. Mark raised his eyebrows Groucho-style and tagged along behind. I held back beside the rusty screen door to listen.

"Say he found a fifty-dollar bill?" Scottie's voice was light and full of life. There was something else in there, too, that made me feel funny in my stomach. "Mason what-his-name?"

"Two Crow, Mason Two Crow, and that's what he told me." That was Jimmy Foxx's voice. "Said it was old and might-near rotten."

I didn't like not seeing, so I went to the clear glass case by the door, pretending I was interested in the bags of Gold Nugget chewing gum on display under the open window.

She took a tiny sip from the orange drink and straightened up. The material of her shirt stretched tight. "Where was it?"

"Up on that far bend in the river north of Colbert Lake."

"Where's that?"

Emory Daniels snorted, interrupting. I never liked him much. He was the kind of man to leave his tools out in the yard to rust. "I don't see why they call it a lake. Hell, it ain't much more'n a mudhole."

"Well *I* didn't name it."

Scottie frowned, but the smooth skin between her eyes didn't wrinkle, like a baby's frown. You could tell she was irritated that Daniels had butted in. "What was he doing up there?"

"Went fishing." Jimmy Foxx Wilson scratched at the hair hanging over his collar. "Said he had some throwlines in the river and saw it when he was climbing up the bank. It could have washed out of the bank, or down the river."

"Hey!" Pepper's voice was loud and I jumped.

"*What?*"

"You want to get your eyes off that gal's titties and talk to me?'

Uncle Neal grunted. "Beatrice Parker. I'm about to get your goat."

Pepper sighed long and loud at the public use of her real name, but we knew whenever an adult resorted to a kid's full title, they were about out of patience. "You want a coke or something?" she asked me.

I picked up a wire flyswatter with the tag still on it and turned it in my hand, keeping up with my charade, even though all three of them knew what I was doing. Uncle Neal met my eyes and winked. Heat rose in my face. "Yeah, get me a Dr Pepper."

The bottles rattled as she guided them through the slots. The men outside laughed and it irritated me that I hadn't heard what was said. Uncle Neal chuckled real soft, tallying up the monthly bills. He carried half the community on credit, but might-near everyone paid up at the end of the month.

Skinny little Ike Reader always wanted to be the first with any information and talked fast, but he was twitching even more than usual, like he was hooked up to electricity. "Listen listen. It might be from that robbery back in the fifties."

"Which one was that?" Scottie didn't know nothing.

The jerky little farmer cleared his throat. "It was somewhere around fifty-five or fifty-six, after two men robbed the Hugo Trust and Loan."

Pepper and Mark went up to the counter to pay up. Uncle Neal tallied the total and we trooped back outside at the same time the conversation stalled. Pepper's expression shot daggers across the porch and I almost laughed out loud.

Scottie noticed her and her eyes went dark, and cold. "Hi, hon."

There was a long pause before Pepper took a long swallow of her Dr Pepper. "Hidy."

"I bet you *kids* have heard about this buried money these boys are talking about."

Pepper didn't like that kid part one little bit. "You talking about the *gold* that's buried out at Palmer Lake?"

A look passed across Scottie's face that I didn't like. Now I knew for sure and for certain that she was there for something else besides a cold drink. "I hadn't heard that one. The boys here are talking about bank robbers. You say there's gold?"

"Sure. Ever'body around here's heard that story. Where you from?"

"Dallas. Bill Preston hasn't said a word about it."

"You kin to him?"

Preston was a Dallas businessman who was busy buying up as much of Center Springs as he could. He was one of those city people who enjoyed the country, but then tried to change it into something else. "No, he's just a really good friend. I came up with him a few days ago to see the new house he was building. I heard a story about some found money and came up here to see if it was true."

"I bet." Pepper's eyes lit up, and I didn't like that one little bit. "Hey, you want to know a secret?"

"Sure."

The men leaned in and the corner of Pepper's mouth twitched. "Come around to the side of the store for a minute." She took off down the steps, twitching her bottom in a way I'd never seen before. Barefoot, Scottie slid off the porch like a water moccasin right behind her and, believe me, that woman went down the steps like warm oil.

Me and Mark started to follow and Pepper held up her hand without turning around. "I didn't invite you two."

We stopped, and my ears burned when the men laughed.

"I believe she told *you* how the cow ate the cabbage." Mr. Floyd slapped his knee as if was a good joke.

Pepper and Scottie weren't around there but for just a minute or two. They came back and Pepper was smiling like a possum eatin' green persimmons. Scottie's face was flushed and she was chewing her bottom lip. She gave Pepper's arm a little squeeze and slithered back to her shoes. Pepper sat on the top step.

Mr. Floyd noticed Scottie suddenly had something on her mind other than robbers. "You hear something you liked?"

"Sure did." She grinned wide. "Something a lot more interesting than some old rotting bills." She stopped when a horse came loping up to the bottle-cap parking lot. Scottie stood to see better and leaned on the rail with both hands. The skirt pulled high and tight across her bottom and the only people looking at the horse and rider was her and Pepper.

It wasn't unusual for folks to ride up to the store. A lot of the locals worked cattle on horseback, and came in for a lunch of sliced baloney, rat cheese, and crackers. Uncle James had horses at one time and we rode them up to the store just for somewhere to go.

The man under a sweat-stained Stetson was a real cowboy. Mack Vick worked Mr. Bill Preston's new ranch. He wasn't much older than Uncle James, but he'd cowboyed out in West Texas before he came to Center Springs about the time I lit at Grandpa and Miss Becky's house.

He reined the dun up in the parking lot and grinned at the men on the porch. Deep creases on his cheeks made me think of the movie actor Randolph Scott. "I was wondering where you'd got off to. Bill didn't know you were here."

Scottie frowned. "I got bored. I don't have to tell him everywhere I go."

"That's between you and him. I was just sent to find you." Mr. Mack's eyes locked on Scottie as he built a hand-rolled and stuck it into the corner of his mouth. "I guess you boys ain't heard."

"So you noticed I was gone?" She cocked a hip and squared her shoulders to keep him involved in their conversation.

It was the first time in my life I'd ever seen a woman's nipple hard against the material of her shirt and I almost dropped my Dr Pepper. Mark swallowed loud beside me and even Pepper was quiet for once.

Mr. Mack lit the cigarette with a wooden kitchen match and squinted around the smoke. "Only because more work's gettin' done today."

Scottie straightened and wrapped her arm around the corner post. It was enough to release the men so they could turn their attention to Mack Vick.

Floyd cleared his throat. "Heard what?"

Mr. Mack looped one leg over the saddle horn and didn't seem to be in a hurry to tell his news, and I kinda got the idea that he was enjoying the moment.

Ike Reader finally couldn't stand it anymore. He always liked to be the one with fresh news and it was killin' him not to know. "Listen listen, what's your news?"

Mack came back to the conversation, though he was still looking at Scottie. He dropped a bomb on us hard and fast like he was telling us the sun was up. "Tom Bell's alive and he's back."

Chapter Ten

Two matronly women in print dresses reaching to mid-calf stopped on the courthouse staircase overlooking the high-ceiling lobby, watching Ned and O.C. kneeling beside Jules' still body on the black and white penny tiles.

More people pushed in through the brass and glass doors as news of the crisis swept down the hot streets like wildfire. Curious individuals in suits and overalls flowed around the edges of the lobby like cold molasses.

Sheriff Cody Parker pushed through the clot of townspeople. At first he thought Ned was hurt and a knot of dread tightened his gut, then he saw him on the floor, cradling Jules' head in his lap. "What happened?"

Tears streamed down Ned's cheeks. He looked twenty years older than when Cody saw him the day before.

Still on one knee, O.C. rested a hand on Ned's shoulder. "I'god he was talking one minute and the next he just fell off his stool."

Cody knelt and lifted Jules' eyelid. The old man's face was completely slack. Cody placed two fingers against the artery in his neck. They waited in silence while Cody felt for a pulse. "He's gone."

Ned rubbed the old man's short gray hair. His voice was low and quavered like a man twenty years his senior. "You were a good man, Jules. A good man."

Cody removed his hat and waved at a circling fly. "Did someone call an ambulance?"

"Ned had somebody do it." O.C. glanced up to see a ring of quiet people standing around them. Women were wiping tears. Others openly wept. From the expressions on their faces, several men fought a tide of rising emotions.

Jules had operated the elevators as long as most could remember. He was hired not long after the courthouse was built to replace the one that burned in the Great Fire of 1916. He traveled up and down the short elevator shaft through the Roaring Twenties and the Great Depression when sad, tattered folks came in and begged to keep their farms and homes, through the Second World War as a steady stream of drunk, battered, and black-eyed soldiers traveled up to the top floor cells and back down again the next day, and through the good years of the 1950s. He was a constant everyone expected to see each morning when they came to work.

An era had ended.

Ned kept patting the old man's still chest. Great BBs of sweat mixed with the tears rolling down his cheeks. Concerned that Ned might be in danger from his own heart, Cody met O.C.'s eyes.

The judge leaned in. "He helped him pass."

Shocked at the revelation, Cody inhaled sharp and loud. "He said he'd never…"

"Of course he would, when the time came. It was a given. We always knew he'd do it again to help family, if they needed it. Jules is family."

The glass and brass front doors flew open and the trio looked up, expecting to see the ambulance drivers with a stretcher.

Instead, Deputy Anna Sloan pulled a ragged young man in cuffs into the rapidly filling lobby. It was a good thing they were already on the floor, because Ned and O.C. would have been there anyway when Tom Bell followed her inside.

Ned frowned at the apparition. "Tom Bell. Are you a ghost, or real?"

"I'm real as you, Ned. Howdy."

Emotionally exhausted, Ned bowed his head and cried like a baby.

Chapter Eleven

The smog-filled air in Austin was so thick it looked like the central Texas hill country was burning. The population of the state capital weighed in at over two-hundred-thirty-thousand, twenty times the size of Chisum. It provided plenty of anonymity for those who wished to operate without notice, moving like ghosts through the city.

The team of operatives assembled by senior agent Mr. Gray blended in with the populace in their dark suits, dark ties, and bare heads. The only hats in evidence on the streets were older men refusing to follow current fashion trends by keeping their three-inch brim LBJ's.

At the opposite end of the spectrum, the city was a magnet for the Flower Children who preferred the emerging laid-back music scene on Sixth Street, only blocks from the Capitol. The college kids at the University of Texas embraced the raw new music of The Flying Burrito Brothers, Jimi Hendrix, The Thirteenth Floor Elevators, Janis Joplin, and Crosby Stills & Nash.

Fresh in from northeast Texas, Mr. Brown hung his coat over the back of a wooden chair in their nondescript office above Leland's Western Wear, eight blocks down the street from the Capitol Building. Nothing more than a front for their mission, the rented space contained a metal desk and wooden swivel chair, two blond-stained chairs, a leaning coat rack, and a dented metal file cabinet painted green. He adjusted the revolver in the shoulder rig and pulled his sweat-soaked dress shirt away from his chest.

Mr. Gray closed the top drawer of the desk that contained a thirty-eight revolver and picked up his pipe. Clamping the stem in his teeth, he adjusted the metal desk fan and leaned back in his chair. "Mr. Brown. Any problems?"

He chose the simple names that were easy to remember. No one in their business went by their real names. Even their organization had no name in most places and was merely referred to as The Company by those who worked there.

Mr. Brown ignored the uncomfortable chairs and stepped to the open window. He studied the traffic on Congress Avenue two floors below. "Nothing to write home about. The folks in that one-horse-town drive a hard bargain."

He angled himself toward the UT campus, disappointed that he couldn't see the tower made famous by Charles Whitman, a former Marine sharpshooter, who took rifles to the observation deck and killed or injured forty-nine people only three years earlier.

The Company provided orders and the money, lots of it to test a new concept in biological warfare. A dozen metal canisters full of a substance code-named Gold Dust rested in a rented house in the small community of Round Rock, twenty miles north of town.

The canisters contained *bacillus globigii*, considered to be harmless to most people, and an added stimulant, *bacillus subtilis* commonly found in hay, dust, or water. The CIA had experimented nearly twenty years earlier with another bacteria, *serratia marcescens*, with disastrous results they buried and never spoke of again.

The new bacteria was guaranteed to be harmless this time. Mr. Gray's assignment was to test the germ's dispersal and viability by distributing it across the rural part of a small county via air and water. A team under a completely different supervisor tested those samples after they reached town either from the air or through the municipal water system, determining the rate of distribution, the area, and the saturation level.

Gray chose Chisum in Lamar County due to its remote location, similar atmospheric conditions to nearby Dallas, and the relatively small population which allowed them to monitor the results. He packed his pipe and lit it with a paper match from a book bearing the name Pittman Radio and TV Service.

Gray scratched at her bare rear with a thumbnail. "How'd it go?"

"Fine. Found a hayseed crop duster that thinks a lot more of his little plane and abilities than he should." Mr. Brown answered with his back to the room, surveying the stores below. He found it easier to lie with his back to Mr. Gray. "He sprayed two canisters up along to the Oklahoma border and wanted a buttload of money to do it."

"Get it done?"

"Yessir. I'd expect the other team to have the results in less than a week."

"Any problems?"

Mr. Brown hesitated a beat, then turned back into the sparse room. "Not a one."

"What did you do with the empty containers?"

"They're back at the house, sealed in the box."

"You guys didn't get exposed, did you?"

Brown's stomach dropped. "No. There shouldn't be a problem anyway, should there?" They'd assured him the bacteria was benign, but Gray's question was alarming in light of Green's accidental exposure. "You said the bacteria wasn't dangerous."

"I never trust anyone in this business." Mr. Gray fiddled with his pipe. "Those eggheads say we built up immunity thousands of years ago, but it pays to be careful. Hell, you shouldn't even trust *me*."

Brown grunted as Mr. Green came through the door and into the stifling room. He shucked his suit coat to reveal a snub-nosed .38 on his hip. His coat joined Mr. Gray's hat on the rack beside the door. He coughed, lit a cigarette, and snapped the Zippo closed. "What are you guys talking about?"

Mr. Gray nudged an ashtray in Green's direction. "Those things will kill you. Look at John Wayne." He spoke through a blue stream of smoke rising from his pipe stem. "They say he lost a whole lung from those coffin nails he smoked."

"Yeah, but look how good he's doing on just one." Green coughed again, deep and wet. "I've been hacking like this since I was seventeen years old."

"When'd you *start*?"

"Twelve." He rolled both sleeves to his elbows while they chuckled.

The harsh jangle of the phone interrupted their conversation. Mr. Gray waited, and the black rotary phone rang again, then a third time, the bell resonating in the office for a full second after the last ring.

They stared at the device resting on a phone book as if it was about to move.

It rang again exactly thirty seconds later. Gray picked up the receiver. "Yes?"

A tinny voice was clear in the quiet office. "Update?"

Mr. Gray told him what the other two men had reported and listened. "Fine then." He hung up the phone and rested the pipe in the ashtray. "We need to wrap this up as soon as possible. Come by here on the way out of town. If the door is open, I'm still here. If it's locked, do what the kids say, and split."

Mr. Green stood and rubbed out the butt. "And the remaining canisters?"

"They'll be gone tomorrow. I have people taking care of that. Get the results from those eggheads and let's go back home. We have another assignment waiting."

"Where?"

"That's for me to know and you to find out. See you in D.C."

Chapter Twelve

It was threatening rain Monday afternoon when Miss Becky lowered her sewing at the sound of Ned's car crackling up the gravel drive. Heavy clouds to the northeast seemed to rest on the treeline beyond the hay barn. Wind freshened, rattling a piece of loose tin on the chicken house.

The windows and doors were open and the familiar pop of a John Deere in the bottoms floated on the breeze. A scattered covey of quail in the pasture called each other back together with their familiar bob-white whistle. Field larks moving through the grass and weeds lifted their heads, raising their own lilt.

She'd already turned on the lamp beside her blue cushioned chair to better see her mending. Moments later, the house echoed with his footsteps on the porch, then through the kitchen.

"It's coming up a cloud." Ned stopped just inside the door and dropped his hat on the television. He'd been in town, so he was dressed in black slacks and his trademark blue shirt. He unbuckled his belt to slip the holster off and the look on his face spoke volumes. She knew he wasn't concerned with the breaking weather, though he dearly dreaded dark thunderstorms.

"What's wrong, hon?"

Ned's usually sharp blue eyes were dull and full of sorrow. He laid the holstered pistol on top of the television. "Old Jules died today."

Her breath caught. "Sweet Jesus! Bless his old heart, he finally got to Heaven." She stopped. "What are you not telling me?"

His hands shook. Ned focused his attention on unpinning his badge. "I had..." He choked on the words.

Miss Becky waited. She knew her husband, and something was terribly wrong. She seldom saw him so full of emotion.

Ned took a breath and started again. He ran a hand over his bald head.

"I had..." Tears welled and he wiped them with the back of his work-hardened hand. His watery eyes skipped through the room before finding the window screen and the pasture beyond. "He couldn't let go."

It was Miss Becky's turn to catch her breath. "Oh no."

"I had to help him."

The storm was moving fast, pushing cold air into the hot, humid mass that had been smothering them for over a week. Lightning cracked nearby and thunder rolled over the house, vibrating the dishes in the china cabinet. The lights flickered and went out.

She rose, dropping the mending to the floor. "Oh!" Her exclamation wasn't over the power outage. It was so routine during storms that they were often surprised when the power *didn't* go out during a cloudburst.

An old dread had finally reappeared. Two steps later she was in his arms, and felt Ned trembling. "Dear Lord. Not again."

The bottom fell out of the clouds. Heavy raindrops hammered the shingles.

"I didn't want to."

It came out, *I din't wont to.*

She pressed her cheek against his chest and held him close. "I know. You didn't want to ever do it again."

"He fell out and we laid him on the floor. He was a-strugglin' and strainin' for breath. It was pitiful. He was talkin' out of his head, sayin' he was seein' angels, but couldn't turn loose."

Ned's shirt soaked up Miss Becky's tears that welled for Jules, Ned, and the troubles they'd suffered so long ago from his own Poisoned Gift, one she'd prayed would vanish and never return. "I thought all that was behind us."

He wrapped his arms around her. "He was layin' there, his eyes rolling around. O.C. said I had to help him turn a-loose."

"He didn't have no right to say that."

"It wasn't right or wrong. It never crossed my mind to help Jules, but when I heard O.C., it dawned on me that I was there for a purpose. Like I've heard you say a hunnerd times, the good Lord puts us in places for a reason. I sat on the floor and pulled his head in my lap and I heard that same buzzin' in my head and felt the air suck out up above me."

The downpour arced off the eaves in a wide waterfall. They were silent for several minutes. Holding on in the midst of two different kinds of storms.

She pulled her head away from his tearstained shirt. "I'm remembering what happened."

"It was a long time ago. Most of those people are dead, or moved away. The rest probably won't know nothin' about it." He drew a long, shuddering breath.

"My stars, Ned. People around here hold onto stories until the day they die."

"I don't care."

His trembling lessened. Ned swallowed so loud she heard it. "It won't make no difference now. I'm too old for jail or prison. If it all starts up again. I'll just sit down and give it all up myself." Thunder punctuated the end of Ned's sentence.

She pushed back and met his blue eyes. "You'll do no such of a thing, Ned Parker. We'll fight them again like we did the first time."

"It'll be different these days." He absently patted her back. The memory from forty-five years earlier felt like a physical presence in the room. Their roles had reversed, making it his turn to comfort his wife. They both remembered how close he came to being convicted of assisted suicide, while others said what he'd done was nothing short of murder.

"Now we have television and reporters and folks'll stay on the phone until their ears fall off. We're just lucky you can't walk around town holding a telephone or these people wouldn't ever get out of one another's business." Miss Becky wiped her eyes with her apron. "I don't know why you Parker men have that burden to bear. But I'm glad you finally used it again to help Jules get Home."

Ned drew a long breath and straightened. She could tell he felt better now that he'd gotten it off his chest.

"Your shirt's damp, hon."

"I sweated through it."

"Go get you a bath and I'll fix us something to eat."

"It's not suppertime yet."

"Rain makes me hungry. Let's make a plate and sit on the porch and watch it rain. I'd dearly love to enjoy it before the kids get home."

She was taking leftovers out of the icebox when he came back around the corner still in his damp shirt. This time he was stepping lighter and she was stunned by the transformation that had taken place in only five minutes. The light in his eyes had returned, as if she'd taken some of the burden away with only a hug and her presence.

"What, hon? Are you all right?"

"I can't believe I almost forgot." His face smoothed and a smile awoke. "You better put that bowl back and set down."

The corner of her mouth twitched. "I swanny. One minute you're as blue as the ocean and the next you're bright as a star and tellin' me what to do. What did you remember?"

"All right then, if y'ain't gonna listen to me. There was *another* miracle today and I plumb forgot it for a minute."

She raised her eyebrows, feeling the dried tears on her cheeks. "Tell me."

"You sure you don't want to set?"

"I said tell me, Ned Parker, and quit this foolishness."

He reached out and took her arm. "All right then. Tom Bell's back. He ain't dead, and ain't no ghost, and I saw him and hugged his neck. He'll be here in a little bit."

The sound of a bowl full of cold mashed potatoes shattered on the floor to blend with Miss Becky's shriek.

Chapter Thirteen

I'd never seen such laughing and crying in my life. Mr. Tom Bell was back. I couldn't get enough of him.

The storm pushed through leaving the sky clear and blue. The grass dried in a hurry once the humidity was gone, and Grandpa sat him in one of the metal shell-back lawn chairs outside our house under the shade of the sycamore and mimosa trees Miss Becky planted when her and Grandpa got married.

The old two-bedroom farmhouse with its wraparound porch sat on a hill overlooking the Sanders Creek bottoms, only a couple of miles south of the Red River. The whole place was about nine hundred square feet, if you didn't count the porches. The kitchen and living room took up the west side. A short hall separated the two bedrooms with a bathroom between them.

The yard was busy as the county fair with folks coming and visiting. It looked like the biggest family reunion in Lamar County, except that even though I'd heard all my life that we couldn't talk about anyone in Center Springs because we were most likely kinfolk, there was still a lot of people who I only knew by sight.

Folks gathered around Mr. Tom and Grandpa that Monday evening, sitting on anything they could, including straight-back wooden chairs with their legs digging deep into the soft ground, the kitchen chairs brought out from the house, and even a milk bucket. The rest stood to see over them and hear the old Ranger that was a long ways from dead. Cars and trucks lined the side of the road when there was no more room on the gravel drive.

Pepper was like a gnat around Mr. Tom. One minute she'd squat on the grass beside him, then she'd stand up and put a hand on his shoulder or arm. Every time I looked over, she was touching him somewhere else. I could tell she wanted to sit on the arm of the chair and hold his hand, but she had sense enough to know she'd be smothering him and in the way.

"We ought to move this get-together up to the gym," Neal Box said, referring to our WPA school. He'd closed the store so he could come visit with the rest of the neighbors.

"No." Mr. Tom looked embarrassed. "Y'all don't need to make a fuss over me. Besides, it don't seem right to sit here like this with Mr. Jules laid out up at the funeral home."

Grandpa's face fell for a moment. His usually cold blue eyes were moist, and I'd never seen him like that. "He was a good man, but we'll tell him goodbye in a day or two." He stopped to clear his voice. "Right now we need to hear what happened to you down in Mexico." He paused. "Tom, we'd never a-left you down there if we knew you weren't…"

Mr. Tom grinned and his white mustache widened. "Dead? Hell, Ned, You don't have to account for yourself. You did what you had to do and so did I."

A couple or three years earlier Mr. Tom, Grandpa, and Mr. John Washington drove down south of the border to get Uncle Cody out of a Mexican jail. The guards almost killed him before they broke him out. Mr. Tom was shot up pretty bad and stayed back to cover for them as they escaped back across the river.

Mr. Tom trailed off at the sound of a siren coming over the creek bridge. A deputy sheriff's car blew around the curve half a minute later and squalled to a stop at the bottom of the hill. The driver pulled to the side of the road and Mr. John Washington rose from behind the wheel.

The biggest man in Lamar County pushed up the hill and

folks separated the same way they would if a bull was to get loose and come charging into the crowd. "Tom Bell!" He stopped and spread his arms wide. Tears rolled down his dark cheeks and a sob caught in his big chest. "Lordy mercy!"

Mr. Tom rose and Mr. John gathered him in a bear hug. "If ida knowed…" His deep voice broke.

Their hats fell off, and them that was closest jumped to catch them before they hit the grass. "Don't say nothing else, John. It was all meant to be."

"But…"

"But nothing. Now turn me a-loose so I can breathe or you'll kill me sure."

The crowd laughed as Mr. John let go and stepped back. "Lazarus."

"I wasn't dead, but dang near."

"Listen listen." Mr. Ike Reader couldn't stand it. "Tell us what happened."

Uncle Cody laughed and put his arm around Norma Faye. "Hang on, Ike. He'll get around to it."

Mr. Tom sat back down. Even though it was hotter'n blue blazes, he looked cool as a cucumber in that black coat of his. "Well sir, I was shot to pieces and thought I was a goner when y'all took off down that alley. Them Mexican guards saw you leave and a bunch of 'em started to take off after you, but I had enough rounds left that I poured it on 'em 'til the B.A.R's magazine ran dry.

"That got their attention, and the next thing I knew I's in a hailstorm of bullets. Before you know it, I was down and nothing worked. I figured I was dead, and so I laid there and closed my eyes and waited for Death to come get me."

"Praise the Lord." Miss Becky raised her hand.

"Ain't that the truth?" Mr. Tom grinned again and nodded. "Well sir, I passed out and when I came to, that old Mexican sun was in my eyes and wasn't anyone but dead people around me.

"They must have thought I was buzzard bait like the rest of 'em, and just left me laying there. Two guards were dragging bodies of those prisoners out of the front door of the jail and danged if they hadn't been piling 'em around me. Folks were coming from all over. They heard what happened and came to claim their kinfolk.

"There was women wailin' and crying' wandering through all that death and when they found their friends or kinfolk, they'd get even louder. After a while I heard a voice from a feller standing right beside me.

"He was speaking Spanish, so I didn't get all of what he said, but the gist of it was that he wanted to take the body laying next to me. One of the guards said it was all right, and before you know it, two people wrapped *me* in a blanket and carried me off."

"Who was it?"

"Well, Ned. It was a stranger, the daddy of that young boy and girl that helped us get in the jail. Remember? Those kids were about Top and Pepper's age. Well sir, him and another big fellow hauled me to a pickup and laid me in the back and the next thing I knew I passed out again. I woke up in a bed with a doctor standing over me. He said he'd taken six bullets out of me and part of my intestines."

The looks on the faces of those around me told me they were just as shocked by Mr. Tom's story as I was.

"It took me almost a year to heal up. Those good folks smuggled me out of that sorry town and to Progresso. They had family there and they treated me like one of their own until I got on my feet, and here I am."

Grandpa took off his hat and ran a hand over his bald head. "Well, hell! That don't answer all the questions I have."

"I can imagine."

"Why didn't you let us know you were all right?"

"'cause I wasn't sure I was. I expected to die and there was no reason to get y'all's hopes up and maybe try to come get me.

You three were hot down there and I didn't want you to wind up in that same jail we got Cody out of."

"But you had cancer!" Norma Faye's voice was full of excitement.

Mr. Tom nodded. "That's what that skinny old doctor said. He told me that one of those bullets hit me right where the Big C was growing, and they took it out with everything that was torn up in there. The doctors down in Houston told me they couldn't get it all even if they went in, and that I's so old I wouldn't survive the surgery. Shows what they know."

The crowd laughed, then laughed louder and longer, and I realized their laughing bled off all the sadness and tension they brought with 'em. Mr. Tom looked embarrassed by all the attention. "Look folks, I sure appreciate all y'all for coming by to say howdy, but you don't need to make a fuss over me."

There was a rattle of dishes behind me and I saw somebody'd put up some sawhorses and laid boards and one door on them. Miss Mable was pulling a tablecloth out of a bright Easter basket she carried that day and I almost busted out laughing. There were so many people, I hadn't seen her show up.

Mark was grinning from ear to ear. "Mr. Tom, are you staying?"

"Here? No, son, I believe Becky's only got two bedrooms."

"We can put the boys on the floor."

"No ma'am. I'll get a room in town."

Aunt Ida Belle shook her head. "No you won't. Me and James bought the Ordway Place. The whole second floor is empty. It's yours and I won't take no for an answer."

I couldn't think of anything worse than to live in the same house with Aunt Ida Belle and her sour mouth and loose eyes, but the idea of having Mr. Tom close by again sure gave my spirits a lift.

"Y'all don't need me around all the time. I only came back through to see everybody and then I'll be on my way."

"You may as well give up, Tom." Uncle James chimed in. "We owe you a debt for helping out here and in Mexico. It's settled. You can live upstairs with us for a week or forever if you want to."

Folks clapped and Mr. Tom gave in. "Fine, then. But only for a while."

"Praise the Lord." Miss Becky clapped her hands. "Ever'body, I have a refrigerator full of food, but why don't y'all go home and bring something back and we'll have a covered-dish supper out here tonight since the weather's turned cool."

Folks clapped again and the crowd broke up, leaving just our family under the big sycamores for the time being.

Miss Becky hugged Mr. Tom again and headed back to the house with Pepper in tow. "You come help me, Sister Sue."

"Aw…"

"Enough. Come on."

Mr. Tom lowered his voice and leaned in to Grandpa. "Ned, did you get that big envelope I had sent up from Mexico."

He brightened. "Sure did, and thanks for…"

Mr. Tom held up a hand and cut his eyes toward me and Mark. "Did you open all the envelopes inside?"

"No. You wrote when I was to open 'em, and I did what you said."

"Good. I'd like it back now, please, what's left."

"Sure 'nough."

Mr. Tom looked relieved, as if Grandpa was going to argue. "I'll give 'em to you again when the time comes, but I need 'em right now, since I know I'm gonna live a little bit longer."

Mr. Tom started to say something else, but was interrupted when a pickup came roaring up from the creek bridge. Mr. John watched him come. "Uh, oh."

The truck slid to a stop behind Mr. John's car and a man I recognized was Pat Walker's boy standing on the running board to call over the cab. "Ned, Cody! I just found Daddy dead out by his catch pen."

"Heart attack?" Ned knew Pat had been in the hospital for the past two weeks and was back on his feet.

"Not hardly." He broke down in tears. "He's been murdered."

Chapter Fourteen

Frenchie snagged the coffeepot off the burner and brought it around to the rear booth where Ned Parker, Judge O.C. Rains, Sheriff Cody Parker, and Tom Bell were finishing a late lunch. They'd been to Jules' funeral that Wednesday morning and their mood was still somber.

She set empty mugs on the table and filled them without asking. "Now that you boys are finished, how about dessert?"

Cody leaned back. "I'm full."

Tom and Ned shook their heads no. Frenchie topped the judge's mug. "O.C.? I got peach today."

He sighed as if she'd told him the café was closing for good. "That sounds mighty good, but I have an appointment coming in to see me in about half an hour."

The corners of her mouth fell for a moment, then her bright smile returned. "Fine then. Maybe next time."

She left to make her way past the booths lining the wall opposite the counter. Facing the door, O.C.'s eyebrow rose before he tested the coffee. Frenchie passed Deputy Anna Sloan who came through the door, jangling the bell. She made a beeline toward the back booth.

Her eyes twinkled as she placed her Stetson upside down on the countertop with the others. She rested one hip on the stool and raised an eyebrow. "You gonna have peach pie today, Judge?"

Ned sighed before he could answer. "I swear. Y'all talk about pie more'n anyone I know."

Judge Rains frowned. "I didn't bring it up nary time, and no, I'm not." He blew across the coffee's hot surface. "Tell me what y'all found out about Pat Walker's murder."

"It wasn't murder for killing sake." Cody leaned forward and laced his fingers. "It looks like he came up on some rustlers. They took his cows *and* his life."

"Yeah, and they got plumb away." Ned worked his dentures to make sure there wasn't anything under them. He hadn't been hungry since Jules passed away in his arms and he was surprised that the hot steak sandwich had sounded good at all.

Tom Bell smoothed his white mustache in thought. "Weren't y'all having this same conversation the last time I was here?"

"Yep." O.C. sighed. "It's been going on since I was knee-high to a grasshopper. It don't happen all the time, but we get a crook through here every now and then that don't mind taking stock that belongs to others."

"But they haven't killed anybody doing it." Cody sprinkled a few grains of salt into his coffee to cut the bitterness. "I had a meeting with George Nobles." He saw Anna's questioning look. "He's the stock detective who works this part of the state and up into Oklahoma. He thinks they might have taken them south, maybe to Fredricksburg or Kerrville, or Austin."

"There's a lot of stock down thataway." Ned ran a hand over his bald head to think. "But they check brands and bills of sale down there too."

"Yeah, but that only works if the rustlers try to sell 'em through the barn." O.C. sipped his coffee, watching Frenchie wipe her counter. "Cody, how about if somebody who had a big ranch and just slides some money across a table in some honky-tonk and unloads the trailer in a back pasture somewheres? I doubt stock inspectors drive them big ranches lookin' for brands. After that, you can sell every calf they drop for pure profit."

"I can see it happening."

The judge drew a long breath, thinking. "So what do you think? Tom?"

"I think these are some bad folks. They ain't your usual rustlers. They're the kind that need killin', in my opinion."

Cody pushed a plate out of the way. "I'm with Tom. This ain't like some river rat loading up a few head to sell under the table. These boys are mean as snakes, and they're different. I believe they took them cows south, and I'm gonna send Anna down to Austin to check around."

She was obviously surprised. "You are? How come you to settle on Austin?"

"I got a phone call up at the office from somebody who wouldn't leave their name, and it ties into what George thinks. They said something suspicious was going on down there and it traced back here to Chisum. My bet is the caller was some of the rustlers' kinfolk, or somebody they made mad. They wouldn't give me much more, but it might be enough to scare up some clues or information."

"What exactly did they say?"

"It was short, that's for sure. Said, 'I know for a fact that two men from northeast Texas is moving other folks' stock through Austin and on down south. Folks have done been hurt and more are sure to follow. You might find the right people in the Broken Spoke who can give you more than I can.' That's the best I can remember. I wasn't planning on hearing something like that and didn't write it down."

Ned nodded. "I'd bet that call came from family. I get 'em like that ever' now'n'en."

"Anna, go look around without your badge showing." Cody chewed his lip in thought. It seemed like a safe enough assignment. After she was shot in an ambush when she first came to Chisum, he'd worried over and over that she'd get hurt again. "You might want to start with the sale barns, and I bet if you drop by 'The Spoke' you might hear something."

She grinned. "A woman won't draw nearly the attention a male deputy will."

Ned chuckled. "Aw, you'll draw attention, all right."

"Be yourself and have a good time." Cody grinned and tried to hide it. "Pretend you're on vacation."

"I need a vacation after what happened yesterday outside of town."

Cody frowned. "What was that? I haven't heard anything about trouble."

"Oh, it was trouble all right, but not like what you think." Anna stuck the tip of her tongue out, like a little kid telling a story. "I pulled over this car full of men heading for the Mountain Fork River up in Oklahoma to catch some trout. They said they're fly-fishermen."

Ned frowned. "Is that them guys who tie their own little bugs?"

"That's it. Well sir, there were two guys in the backseat shaving a dead squirrel and a raccoon."

Cody put down his cup. "Hope the coon was dead, too."

Judge Rains almost spit out his coffee. Tom Bell grinned.

● ● ● ● ●

It wasn't full dark when Anna lit up the late model sedan and pulled them over. The driver hung one arm out the open window when she walked up. "Help you, Deputy?"

She glanced into the backseat where two men were awash in flying hair. Using scissors and a new battery-operated beard trimmer, they were cutting the hair off two animals. "Good lord, what are y'all doing?"

The man with the scissors paused. "We're collecting hair for fishing flies."

The driver twisted completely around and saw the look on the deputy's face. "They're both roadkill, and it's squirrel season. We didn't see any harm in getting the coon hair. It's the best of all, but the squirrel tail hairs would drive the trout crazy. Did I do something wrong to get pulled over?"

"Well, you're driving with the dome light on and using flashlights. It looked suspicious, so I wanted to find out what y'all are up to. What are you gonna do with the bodies?"

The driver shrugged. "I guess throw them back out on the highway?"

"That doesn't seem quite right to me, but I can't tell you why. You'll have to find somewhere else to dump the carcasses."

"We will—"

His response was cut short when the man with the scissors screamed and flailed as the nearly naked raccoon came alive in his lap. Apparently concussed naked coons don't like to wake up while getting shaved in the backseat of a car. Eyes wide in shock, it bared its teeth and clawed at the man's lap to gain traction.

Anna recoiled as the man with the electric shaver threw open the door and took cover behind her. The other man in the backseat slapped at the pink coon wearing only a moustache and low-cut socks and dove into the front seat at the same time the front seat passenger wriggled out the window like a worm from an apple. Shocked into immobility, the driver responded by doing nothing but make a high, keening sound.

The coon stumbled through the open door and onto the highway where it staggered and fell over dead, as it should have been in the first place.

Anna twisted around to find the man hiding behind her still holding the buzzing clippers. "You can probably turn that off now. Driver, get your coon here and y'all go bury them somewhere. You other two quit hiding in the ditch and get gone. Y'all don't come back through here doing nothing like this again."

They drove off, and she staggered to her car, laughing until she was almost sick.

●　●　●　●　●

O.C.'s face lit up. "That's what the story in *The Chisum News* was all about this morning! It was a long story about shaving animals for satanic rituals."

Anna nodded soberly. "They barely got around the first curve from where I stopped them to pitch the carcasses out. The paper called it 'Unholy Rituals,' sick people doing strange things to animals. I didn't have the heart to call them and explain."

They were laughing when Deputy John Washington came through the front door, drawing a half dozen looks from Frenchie's customers, and at least one glare. He ignored the attention and stopped at the booth full of law officers.

"Judge. Miss Anna. Mr. Tom. Hate to break up y'all's fun, Sheriff, but Mr. Ned, you got a call to run out to Center Springs. Some feller out there's moving a bulldozer on a trailer and the axle's broke. The dozer snapped a chain and slid off. The highway's blocked both ways and since the owner don't seem to be in any hurry to move it, somebody called the laws."

"Say who the owner is?" Ned answered the unvoiced question.

"Bill Preston. Big wheel out of Dallas."

Ned gathered his hat and slid out of the booth. "Yeah, and he thinks he's God's gift to Center Springs."

Chapter Fifteen

The same day they buried Old Jules, Aunt Ida Belle had us up on the dusty second floor of the Ordway Place after school, helping clean it up for Mr. Tom. I didn't feel worth a flyin' flip, but I wasn't going to miss being with *him*.

I woke up that morning with a tickle in the back of my throat and a dry cough. I figured it was the smoke and dust from the cotton gin. It usually locked me up something fierce and most of the time I wound up sick. I made it through the school day, feeling like I wanted to lay down and die, but I didn't want Mr. Tom to think I was trying to get out of helping.

Uncle James had painted the downstairs and it looked as good as it did the day Old Doc Ordway first built the place. But the upstairs smelled like a musty old building full of dirt dauber nests. Furniture and wooden boxes were stacked and piled everywhere. Piles of dust-covered lumber took up half of the west bedroom. It was separated from the east bedroom by an open area at the head of the stairs that I always thought was a living room.

Mark was whistling like moving old furniture was fun. "Man, I wasn't feeling too good when we woke up this morning, but I like this place. I'm glad we came. I kinda wish me and you could stay here after all."

"It'd be fun, all right, but this is where the ghosts came from that time I saw them walking down the stairs." It didn't matter if was daylight and people were with me, that old place made me as nervous as a cat in a doghouse. I propped a metal headboard of a bedstead against one wall and stopped, wheezing. "I think I'm coming down with something."

Mark gave a soft cough. "Something's in my chest, too. Hold that headboard steady and I'll put the rails in."

A thought crossed my mind. "You know, if we get sick enough, we might get to miss school together."

"You'd trade a bad ol' chest cold for school just so you won't have to deal with Harlan?"

Aunt Ida Belle was downstairs looking for more cleaning rags. I glanced over to make sure Pepper wasn't listening. She turned up the transistor radio she'd propped on the windowsill to get the best signal. "White Room" by Cream was blaring something about rooms, curtains, and horses. Her hair was tied up in a scarf, leaving her ponytail to bob free. She was wearing one of Uncle James' shirts and it was already dirty, but for once she wasn't complaining about having to work.

I didn't like to admit Mark was right. "You know Harlan's the second toughest kid in our grade." I didn't need to say the first was Mark. "He's wearing me out, and I can't fight him. I'd just as well take a runnin' start at the side of the gym and knock my own head in to save him the trouble."

"I'll take care of it for you."

"No. You can't take up for me all the time."

"What are you gonna do, then?"

I couldn't find an answer that suited me. Pepper saw me looking at that scary little attic door in the wall at the head of the stairs. She wiggled her fingers. "Wooo!"

Mark saved me again, changing the subject. "I'm not afraid of spirits."

"Wookie wookie!" Pepper snorted. "You would have been scared if you'd been around that day Top and I heard footsteps up here clear as day."

Mark's eyes sparkled in excitement. "It was probably some bum who was squattin' for a while." He pointed. "He probably lived in there."

The little door suddenly looked evil. "Let's just keep it closed."

"Keep what closed?" Aunt Ida Belle puffed up the steps with Mr. Tom right behind her, carrying a bucket of water and a mop.

I pointed. "That door."

"Y'all don't need to be in there anyway."

Pepper snapped her rag at me. "He's just being a titty baby."

I dodged out of the way and got to coughing so much that Mr. Tom came over and whacked me a few times on the back. "Your asthma acting up, hoss?"

"I guess." The tickle was down deep in my lungs. "It's never started like this before."

Aunt Ida Belle looked concerned. "Where's your puffer?"

"Left it at the house."

"Well, come get in the car and I'll take you to get it." She waved for me to follow. "We don't need to let an asthma attack get out of hand. Miss Becky'll get my goat if you get sick."

Mr. Tom nudged a little leather suitcase with his toe. He called it his grip, and it was the only thing he brought with him. "Ida Belle, y'all shouldn't be doing so much up here. I can clean this place up just fine by myself. Let them kids go out and get some fresh air and I'll settle in here in my own good time."

She gave him a hug. "It won't take much. They're not giving it much more than a lick and a promise."

I felt heat rise in my face and knew it wasn't all from feeling bad. Aunt Ida Belle might have seen my expression, because she tickled the back of my neck with her fingernails like Aunt Norma Faye did when she was loving on me. It didn't feel the same, though. Aunt Ida Belle didn't have long fingernails. "We'll get everything swept out and I'll wash down the walls and floorboards. James brought home some paint for these walls."

Mr. Tom's voice was firm. "I'll do the painting, then."

I coughed again and Pepper whacked me on the back hard enough to rock me on my toes. "Get it up."

Before I could answer, Mark gave a soft little chuff that he caught in his hand. Aunt Ida Belle frowned. "It must be this dust."

Mark shrugged. "I think it's something else."

"You gettin' sick too?"

He shrugged. "Might be."

She flapped her arms at us like we were chickens and shushed us down the black-painted wooden stairs. "Well, y'all get on down. I'm taking you two home. Pepper, bring up the mop bucket and some Pine-Sol. We need to get this dusty smell out of here. Mr. Tom, I'll be back directly."

He shrugged off his black coat and draped it over the stair rail, then slapped his black hat on the newel post. "Me and Pepper'll have this place swept and mopped by the time you get back."

Aunt Ida Belle followed us down. By late that night, I started to spiral down.

Chapter Sixteen

On Wednesday, four days after they paid Curtis Gaines to spray Gold Dust on Center Springs, Mr. Green took off his shades and met Mr. Brown in front of Nau's Enfield Drug on West Lynn in Austin. The sun was almost down and the busy street was solid with cars parked along the sidewalk.

The overhangs in front of the stores stretching down the block advertised Carlson's Hardware store, office supplies, Winn Furniture, Woolworth's, and the Majestic Theater. The neon lights on the hardware store's Holiday Inn-shaped sign already glowed with blue neon light. By full dark, the sidewalks would be lit with dozens of bright logos beckoning late evening shoppers.

Mr. Green looked like a walking corpse with dark circles under his eyes and pasty gray skin. He dragged deep on his cigarette and blew the smoke out his nose. "At least *you're* not sick. I've been coughing my lungs out since we got back here."

Mr. Brown felt the blood rush from his face. He stopped when a car passed with its windows down. "So Happy Together" by the Turtles washed over them. "Maybe you're just coming down with the flu or something."

"Could be. My throat's so sore I can barely swallow. I'm gonna get some Parke-Davis throat lozenges and see if they have anything else in there that'll help."

Mr. Brown watched his associate take another drag on his cigarette. "Why won't you go to the doctor?"

"I don't want to leave a trail to show we were here."

"Pay cash."

"Doctors ask all kinds of questions and I don't want to take the chance that I'll slip up, or he'll get suspicious."

"There's no reason to get suspicious. Besides, Mr. Gray said there was nothing to worry about." Mr. Brown ignored his own admonishment and glanced around by habit. They'd been walking on the thin side of the law so long it was second nature to check his surroundings from time to time. "You feel like eating? They have a malt shop inside. We can talk in there. I need to get something off my chest."

Mr. Green coughed again, bringing up thick mucus that he spat into the gutter. "Hell, no. I'm too old to eat in drugstores. Let's go to Frisco's and get a steak."

"That's six miles out of town."

"So?"

"You're not that sick, then."

Mr. Green started to laugh, but the moment was lost when it dissolved into a series of wracking coughs.

Mr. Brown dug into his pants pocket for a dime. "Let me call Mr. Gray and tell him you're sick. He might have a safe doctor here."

"I'll see a company doctor when we get back. I'm probably overreacting. All we need to do is wait for Mr. Gray to contact us and then we're out of this shit-kicking state and back to civilization. Until then I'll wear it out with Scotch and cough syrup."

"You don't like Texas much, do you?"

"Not a bit." Another cough, deep, wet, and tearing. "I don't care if the Gold Dust really is bad and kills every damn person in it."

Taken aback at the venom in his worsening voice, Mr. Brown inclined his head like a dog studying a stranger. "Are you sure you're up to eating?"

"I have to have something. We'll eat, get a few drinks, and I'll get a cab to take me back to the motel, and then," he mimicked Mr. Gray's penchant for quoting the hippie kid's slang, "as the kids say, we can blow this pop stand."

He folded over, wracking his lungs. Mr. Brown resisted the urge to move farther away.

"Fine, go in there and get some Velvo. That'll help with the cough."

● ● ● ● ●

The cough syrup worked and Mr. Green was able to finish his meal in Frisco's without calling attention to their table. Dark-stained wood-trimmed booths filled one side of the long and narrow steakhouse. A similarly trimmed counter stretched down the other with empty wineglasses waiting in front of each unoccupied stool. Polished cabinets behind the counter gave the establishment an elegant feel.

Mr. Brown snapped his Zippo to life and lit another cigarette for dessert. "I have a question for you."

"What is it?" Mr. Green finished his iced tea and caught a soft chuff in his hand.

"We've done a lot over the years, everything the Boss asked us to do, and his boss before him."

"So?"

"What we did here bothers me. This is *our* country."

"Thanks for letting me know. Who cares what happens? Even if a few get sick and die, it's for the betterment of millions."

"You know what I mean. I didn't have any problem with what we did overseas with Third Chance and Derby Hat. Those LSD experiments and mind control stuff on those Asian volunteers…"

He stopped when the waitress in a white apron came to their booth at the rear. "Coffee?"

Mr. Brown gave her a brilliant smile and she grinned back. Mr. Green had seen him do that in restaurants and bars across the country and it never failed to get him what he wanted. "Sure.

And would you do us another favor?" He continued when she lifted an eyebrow. "I really like that music. Would you mind turning it up just a little more?"

The middle-aged brunette with an up-doo curl was genuinely surprised. The hairstyle was much too young for her. "You really like this stuff?"

"Sure do. Who is that singing?"

"It's the Cowsills. I think the song is 'The Park' or 'I Love My Flower Girl' or something. My teenagers like it and that's all I hear at home. Now they're piping it in here."

"I know, but we travel a lot and most places don't play the current stuff."

She finished filling their cups and winked at him. "I'll see what I can do."

Minutes later the music rose in volume, covering their conversation. It was obvious the older patrons at the nearest table weren't pleased with "Born to Be Wild" that followed the bubble gum music. The white-haired gentleman snatched the check off the table and rose. His wife followed.

Mr. Brown noted the dark circles under Mr. Green's eyes and felt a fresh pang of worry. "Anyway, the things we're doing over *here* are bothering me. Releasing bacterium over Winnepeg was one thing, but to take that shit to New York and releasing it there isn't right."

"Our job isn't to question it."

"I think we should have questioned San Francisco and Georgia and Florida. Those experiments didn't go exactly as planned, either. How many people got sick? You'd have thought we'd learned our lessons in that one."

"So why do you think this thing in that little hick town bothered you so much?"

Mr. Brown dug another cigarette out of the pack and tapped it on the table. "I was raised in the country and those are the same kind of people. Good people who just want to live their lives and not be bothered."

A patriot to the core, Mr. Green dug a throat lozenge from the flat box and crunched it between his teeth. "They'd rather be bothered by the communists when they come marching over here and say, 'Thanks for building such a great country, but it's ours now,' those kind of people?"

They were silent as Mr. Green chased the Parke-Davis throat lozenge with another toonie. "Everything we're doing is for the safety of this country, and our families, your mother and daddy, and everyone."

"I see what you're saying. It's just that we're on American soil."

Mr. Green choked down another small chuff in answer. "I signed on the dotted line to protect our country. We're doing what needs to be done, so I don't have any regrets. You better get your mind right about it. You're either on the side of right or wrong. If you start questioning *that*, then you need to find something else to do."

Mr. Green's hand shook when he shot his cuff to check the time. "Think about that a little more before they send us home to Fairfax. I'm headed back to the motel."

"Go to the doctor if you're not feeling better tomorrow morning."

Mr. Green drained his water glass with a shaking hand. "Probably a good idea."

Chapter Seventeen

Thursday morning, Ned let the kitchen's screen door clap behind him. The sun was barely above the trees and the damp air was thick with the odors of cow flop and pasture weeds. "Mama, why's Tucker out there in the yard, sleeping in his car?"

One of many nephews, Tucker, head back and mouth wide open, was asleep behind the wheel of his rump-sprung Buick under the sycamore near the drive.

"He's been working the late shift somewhere up outside of Hugo and was so sleepy he couldn't make it all the way home this morning."

"I didn't smell no whiskey."

"My lands. He's not drunk. Not everybody who comes across the river at night's been drinkin'. The boy's tired and he probably didn't want to go home, because the kids'd wake him up if he did."

Ned reached through the door into the living room and dropped his hat on the television before circling the kitchen table to sit in his usual place. "Well, he shoulda' come in the house. That boy's past thirty-five and still bouncing around taking odd jobs like a teenager." Ned glanced through the screen. "He needs a haircut, too. At least he could have laid down on the couch. He's gonna get a mouth full of flies."

"Yeah, and you'd be shaking him awake to ask why he was here."

"Wouldn't have done no such of a thing."

Miss Becky rolled her eyes and slid two fried eggs on his plate. One of the boys coughed softly in the bedroom and her brow furrowed. "I believe that cough's getting worse."

"Which one was it?"

"Top. Mark's better this mornin'."

"Well, his lungs are weak. That's why he's having a worse time of it."

Halfway through his eggs, they heard Tucker's car whine to a start. Ned saw it pull onto the highway and head toward the store. "Top gonna be able to go to school today?"

"It's just a cough."

"He's been doing a lot of that these past few days."

Their conversation was interrupted by the jangling phone. Miss Becky let Ned keep after his breakfast and hurried to answer before the phone woke the boys. She wanted to give them at least another half hour.

"Hello?"

"Is this Constable Parker's house?"

"Yes it is."

"I need to talk to him. I know where there's a still out toward the Boneyard Slash. It's the biggest one I've ever seen."

For the first time in her life, Miss Becky questioned a caller. "Have you seen a lot of stills?"

"Yes, ma'am. Ran a few in my day."

"That's what I figgered, Doak Wheeler."

The caller on the other end was silent for a long moment.

"Doak. I know that's you."

The man on the other end cleared his throat. "Yessum."

"When'd you get out of the pen?"

His voice softened. "'bout six months ago, Miss Becky."

"And you're right back in it?"

Her scolding brought Ned into the living room. "Who is it, Mama?"

"Doak, you're out and free. Don't go messing up again." She handed Ned the receiver and returned to the kitchen, a world she knew and controlled.

Ned came through two minutes later wearing his hat, badge, and pistol. "I'll be back directly."

"You be careful, Daddy. He might be up to something."

"I 'magine he's trying to get rid of the competition so he can go back to cookin' 'shine." Ned pecked her wrinkled check and left, letting the screen slam behind him. "Get them boys up. They're sleeping the day away."

Chapter Eighteen

Owen the cattle rustler sat behind the wheel of his truck parked in the dirt lot in front of Dickey's Beer Stand that same morning. Dickey's wasn't a honky-tonk like the joints across the Red River from Powderly, more than ninety miles to the east. It was the roughest place to buy beer that Owen had ever seen, and he'd been raised in the mean oilfields outside of Odessa, Texas.

Nothing more than a square cinder-block building, it had only a metal front door and one rectangular window barely big enough to slide a case of beer through. Customers knocked on a steel flap, ordered, then slid the money through. Moments later, the beer appeared and the transaction was complete.

To Owen, it looked like a fort in the Oklahoma wilderness.

That appearance was reinforced by a thick stand of trees surrounding all three sides and broken only by the two-lane highway leading north to Yuba, and south across the river to Bonham, Texas, fifteen minutes away. Thick hardwoods grew right to the shoulder on the opposite side of the road.

Owen scratched the back of his neck through the greasy hair hanging over his collar and watched Dale take a case of Miller High Life from the slot window. Resting the cardboard box on the narrow sill, he cracked the pop-top and took a long drink.

The owner's voice came through the small window loud and clear. "Hey, feller. You can't drink that on the property!"

Ignoring the man, Dale kept the can to his lips and swallowed until it was empty. He belched and pitched the can against the cinder-block wall. "Okay."

"Hey Good Looking" filled the truck cab as Dale pushed the beer through the open passenger window and dropped it on the dusty seat. "This is the damnedest place I've ever seen."

"Rough country." Owen pulled the case to the middle of the bench seat.

"They don't know rough." Dale got in and slammed the door.

"You probably shouldn't be dickin' with these people. We need to keep our heads low."

"Hell, all he saw was the money."

"You don't know that. I bet he keeps an eye on this lot."

"What's he gonna do, yell at me some more?" Dale popped the top on a fresh can and took another drink. "Man, that's good."

Owen shrugged and plucked a beer from the box. He cracked the pop-top and took a long swallow, stopping only when a banged-up Ford pickup with Texas plates slid to a hard stop in the lot, only three feet from the building. Startled and thinking it might be the local constabulary, he lowered the can below the door sill.

He relaxed when a hard-looking red-faced man in overalls emerged from behind the wheel. From his dark tan, Owen took him for a farmer and watched him reach back inside the cab and withdraw a twelve-gauge pump shotgun. His jaw set, the man's manic look and unruly brown hair stuck up as if he'd just gotten out of bed.

Owen tilted the can as if he were watching a movie at the drive-in. "This oughta be good. Wait a minute. I'm curious to see what's about to happen."

The metal plate thumped down on the inside of the slot window, but the owner's voice came through loud and clear. "Lester! Get back in your truck and get on outta hea'!"

Lester shouldered the weapon and pointed it at the window. "You owe me that money!"

"You put your money on the wrong team, man. The Pirates lost and that's that!"

"You know damn good and well that I bet on the Astros."

"Nossir! You put your money down on the Pirates."

"No. I didn't! I don't never bet on anyone else, and you owe me a thousand dollars."

"You were drunk and you know it. I've never put them kinds of odds on a game no how. You just dreamed it."

Lester cut loose with the shotgun, punching a hole in the sky and startling Owen so bad his foot came off the clutch and the engine died. Lester moved with dream-like speed and slowly shucked another shell into the chamber. The window's metal slide dropped and he threw another load into the steel and surrounding cinder blocks.

He jacked another shell into the magazine. The empty hull made a hollow click on the packed gravel. His dull eyes flickered back and forth as he took the measure of the two men in the truck. "Y'all want some of this?"

Dale slipped the Luger from his waistband and held it out of sight, waiting.

Owen raised both hands from the wheel as casual as if he were waving. "That's between y'all. Not us."

Lester turned away with glacial speed and walked past the front of the truck and around the corner as if he didn't have a care in the world. The cattle rustlers waited, listening.

The shotgun crumped again, echoing off the trees around back. Two deeper reports coming a millisecond apart reached the two men waiting in the truck.

Moments later, Lester came around the corner, the front of his overalls covered in bright red blood, the material shredded. He stumbled and caught himself with one hand on Owen's hood. Their eyes met through the bug-splattered glass and Owen saw dozens of small holes from a shotgun blast weeping blood through the bib of his overalls and the shirt underneath.

Lester pushed off and staggered toward his truck. Throwing the shotgun through the open passenger window, he opened the door and followed it inside, falling sideways in the seat.

"Damn! You weren't a-kiddin' this is rough country." Dale drained the half-empty beer in his hand.

Owen twisted the key and the engine roared. "I believe we better get out of here." He shifted into reverse as the front door opened and the owner in wrinkled khakis and a stained plaid shirt emerged with a sawed-off double-barrel shotgun. His unruly gray hair stuck out in tufts and he hadn't shaved in days, but it was the ten-gauge in his hands that caught the rustlers' attention.

"Dayum!" Owen felt the back of his neck tingle at the sight of the twin bores that looked as big around as culverts.

The owner jerked his head back toward the cinder-block building. "Y'all don't leave. I need you for witnesses."

Dale shook his head. "We're gone."

The muzzle rose, but Dale was faster and the Luger centered on the owner's chest from a distance of only six feet. "Don't you raise that shotgun."

Owen shifted into drive and slowly pressed the foot-feed. They pulled out of the parking lot and Dale kept the muzzle on the man with the shotgun until they hit the highway. Owen glanced over his shoulder to see the owner walking toward Lester's truck, but it was the flashing lights on the Oklahoma Highway Patrol car appearing over the rise a mile away that worried him the most.

"Uh, oh." Dale laid the pistol on the seat and threw the empty can out as they crossed the Red River bridge into Texas.

"Don't worry." Owen's eyes flicked to the mirror. "He's so far back he won't be able to recognize the truck. For all he knows, we were just driving by."

Watching over his shoulder, Dale took a deep breath and let it out slowly. "He's pulling into the beer joint."

"See what I told you." Owen opened another beer with one finger and saluted the windshield with the can. "Man, that was *intense!*"

"If that's what you want to call it." Dale swiveled to face forward. "Where to now?"

"Where we were going in the first place. The sale barn in Childress. I want to see what they've got moving through there."

Chapter Nineteen

An hour east of Center Springs, Ned and John Washington pulled their cars off the highway onto a winding dirt road that led to a heavily wooded area in far northeast Lamar County. Sheriff Cody Parker and Deputy Anna Sloan turned in behind them in separate cars.

A career moonshiner, Doak Wheeler described the landmarks leading to the still on Boneyard Slash Road, and even the game trail cutting through the woods. Following his instructions, they cruised the twisting road until it finally stopped short of a cut bank not far from the creek. A rotting barn leaned against two walnut trees, as if they refused to let the weathered old structure give up.

The sun was straight overhead. Unseen blue jays screamed in the woods and a breeze shook the leaves. It was far from silent when they killed their engines on the shaded road. A nearby grove of oaks outlined the footprint of a house long gone. The grass was beaten down where vehicles had recently parked. They faced their cars outward, just in case there was trouble.

Armed with his Remington pump and a pocket full of shells, Deputy Washington led the way into the woods, speaking softly. "Mr. Ned, the last time me and you saw Doak, he was on his way to the pen after we arrested him for making whiskey. Mr. O.C. didn't think he'd ever get out."

"Well, he did." Ned trailed behind with a double-bit axe over his shoulder. He glanced back to keep an eye on Anna. He'd never had a woman deputy go along to bust a still and didn't know what to think of the idea.

Little light passed through the dense woods as a breeze rustled the leaves overhead. The earthy smell of thick humus filled the air. Game trails spider-webbed through the trees, but the one they followed was beaten wide by many feet. Birds sang and an unseen animal rustled just out of sight, breaking into a run at the approach of the officers.

Cody brought up the rear. "Y'all be careful. This could be some kind of ambush."

"Doak ain't like that. I've spent half my life taking that boy to jail, but he ain't no liar. There's a still up ahead. In fact, I just caught a whiff of woodsmoke."

"You know he's gonna be back in business pretty soon." Cody's voice was low. "If I was to guess, I'd say he's wanting us to take out the competition."

"Might be, but it'll be one less still, and if Doak goes back to work, I'll find him. He makes the best whiskey in the county, but that boy don't know a hill of beans about hiding his equipment."

John raised his head and sniffed. "Smoke, sure 'nough." His voice was so low. "And grass."

"Huh? I don't smell no grass."

John stifled a grin. "Marijuana, Ned. Somebody's smoking weed up ahead."

Cody didn't try to hide his amusement. "Give me a minute. Anna, be careful."

"You didn't tell anyone else to be careful. Cody, I'll be fine."

"Well, I don't want you to get hurt's all."

"I'm going to stay with you, Mr. Ned." Anna spoke over his shoulder and into his ear, barely mouthing the words.

Ned watched Cody disappear into the woods to come in beside the still itself. When he turned back, John was gone.

They'd done this so many times he knew the big deputy was headed for the opposite side.

Ned waited for a full two minutes before continuing. Anna was breathing hard behind him. "He worries about you."

Anna sighed. "I know it, but he doesn't have to. He doesn't worry about John."

"John wasn't shot with a shotgun. Cody's still guilty about that."

"Why now? I held up my part of that feud a while back."

"Cain't say. We've waited long enough. Let's go."

Pistol in hand, he crept forward until the odor of smoke grew stronger, avoiding thick grapevines dangling from branches sixty feet off the ground. Ned stopped beside a large sycamore and peeked around the trunk to find the biggest boiler he'd ever seen. It sat in the dappled sunlight under the tall hardwoods that broke up the column of smoke. Using his head, he indicated to Anna that he wanted her to move up to his left side. She slipped around a buckeye bush and stopped.

John's deep, powerful voice came to them from across the clearing. "Sheriff's Department. Y'all don't move. Get them hands up!"

Pistol ready, Ned stepped into full view to find two long-haired young men rising from quilt pallets almost at his feet. He lowered the muzzle to cover them. "You hippies be still!"

Cody was louder. He popped into sight from behind the still. "Don't!"

John cut loose with the twelve-gauge, the shot rattled through the leaves above. He shucked another round into the chamber. "The next one'll cut you in two. Hold up your hands like I said!"

A bearded man with a ponytail raised his hands as high as possible in a comic reach for the limbs high overhead. "Hey, don't shoot me!"

"He'll do it if y'all don't listen." Cody stepped into full view. "Everybody on your knees. Hands behind your heads and cross your ankles."

"That's a lot to listen to, Sheriff." Ponytail stood stock still, complaining. "And I don't like no woman deputy in on this."

"I don't care what you like." Cody's voice was sharp. "Do what I said. Everyone on your knees, now!"

One of the hippies on the pallets in front of Ned turned their attention to Anna. "Dude. Be cool. Which do you want us to do, man? Get on our knees or cross our ankles?"

Ned wondered if he'd directed the question to Anna because she was the only female. He didn't let her answer, though. "Do both, like the sheriff said." Ned's voice was filled with frustration. "It ain't that hard, boys. Knees first."

"It is if you're high."

"Hands behind your heads...*then* cross your ankles."

"Don't shoot." Still another moonshiner stepped into view from Ned's left, tugging his zipper up as casually as if he were alone. He was a river rat Ned recognized from the joints across the river. "I'll do it, but I didn't want anybody to see my tally-whacker."

It startled him so bad Ned almost pulled the trigger on his pistol aimed at the closest prisoner on the ground in front of him. Anna swung around and covered him. "Get those hands up or I'll shoot it off."

"She can do it, too." Ned had to take a deep breath.

"She ain't got nothin' but that little thirty-eight."

"She's a good shot."

Anna's voice finally came through loud and clear. "Not much of a target, though."

• • ● • •

With the moonshiners cuffed and transported to the Lamar County Courthouse by two highway patrol deputies, Ned returned to the still and stared at the gleaming copper boiler.

Anna joined him. "What?"

"That's the biggest and prettiest still I've ever seen. I believe somebody's been shinin' that copper."

She examined the huge boiler. The whole thing was as polished as a brass musical instrument. "I guess I'm ruined for the rest of my life since this is the first one I've ever seen."

Ned didn't get her joke, but Cody's laughed filled the air as he and John joined them. "That's why I'm gonna do something special with it."

"What's that?"

The look on the Cody's face showed that he wasn't completely comfortable with the whole idea. "Just came through on the radio. The mayor wants to show it off as the first still to be busted under his office. There's a truck coming. I'm gonna set this still up in the old wagon yard for the paper. They're gonna take a picture of it."

"O.C. might not like that idea, this being evidence and all."

"It'll only be for a little while, and besides, we're gonna have to make some room to store it."

Ned hefted the axe in his hand. It was his tradition to chop holes in a boiler so it could never be used again. He pointed at the crates of quart fruit jars filled with clear whiskey. "So what are you gonna do with all this?"

"A cameraman from *The Chisum News* is on the way. He's gonna take a picture of everything, then we'll pour it out."

Ned shook his head and turned away. "It ain't like it used to be. Now we're putting on shows."

"Changing times," John said. "Changing times."

Chapter Twenty

Three hundred and twenty miles to the southwest, Mr. Gray took one last look around the empty office they'd been using for the past six months to be sure he hadn't left anything. All the humidity was gone, and Austin breathed deep of the air scrubbed clean in Canada. The room was fresh and comfortable for the first time since he'd rented it.

The desk drawers were empty, and the only thing he found was a dust bunny on the floor. He was about to leave for Washington when the phone rang three times before it stopped. He rested an index finger on the receiver and plucked it off the cradle on the next ring.

"Yes."

"We might have a problem."

Gray recognized Mr. Brown's voice. "What's that?"

"Mr. Green woke up dead this morning."

Unmoved, Gray stared out the open window at the buildings across the street. "Heart attack?"

"I didn't ask him."

"Forgo the levity. What happened?"

"He didn't answer the phone when I called to say we were leaving. I had other accommodations and went by the motel, but he didn't come to the door. I had to badge the desk clerk before he would let me in. Mr. Green was in the bed. It looked like he died hard."

"I'll get a cleanup crew out there."

"Too late. While I was sanitizing the room, that nosey desk clerk went back and called an ambulance. I didn't think you wanted any more attention, so I backed off."

Mr. Gray's stomach clenched. He'd hoped to get both of his crews in and out of Austin without incident. Now things were *complicated*.

"I told him those damned unfiltered coffin nails were gonna kill him."

"I don't think it was the Camels."

"You think somebody killed him?" Mr. Gray went cold, thinking that Soviet agents might have become involved in the operation. If they stole information about Gold Dust or, God help them, one of the canisters of bacteria, every man, woman, and child in the free world was in trouble. His gut feeling was that the "benign" bacteria were, in fact, dangerous.

"I do. I think it was us."

"What are you talking about?"

"I think it was the Gold Dust. He came down sick not long after we finished."

"Watch out with the details. You aren't on a secure line."

"I know how to do my job. I'm in a phone booth."

"Are you sick?"

"No. What do you want to do?"

"Nothing." Mr. Gray's mind raced to create an explanation for his associate's death. "People die every day from a million causes. You said you sanitized the room?"

"I have his real papers and gun."

"Good. We're finished here. You go deep until further notice."

Mr. Brown was silent for a long moment. "We're just going to leave his body there?"

"What would you like for me to do?"

"Have him transported back to his home. He has a family."

"I assume you remember the contract you signed." Mr. Gray

picked up the phone by the finger well under the cradle and walked to the window, trailing the long cord.

"Yes, the one that said we were on our own if we got caught."

"Correct."

"But I thought that referred to foreign countries."

"It wasn't location-specific." Gray watched the activity on the street. All looked normal, but he never took anything for granted. A blue '63 Chevrolet sedan had been parked in the same place for three days in a row. The sun's glare prevented him from seeing inside.

A long sigh came through the receiver. "I just think he deserves better."

"His family will get a call in a day or two, how about that? They'll also get a nice check from Humbold Industries to satisfy his contract."

"All right. I'll wait to hear from you."

"Fine then." Mr. Gray hung up, wiped the phone down with a handkerchief, and finished by polishing the doorknob as he left.

Chapter Twenty-one

It was dusk when a car passed on the two-lane highway beyond the trees blocking the road from Cody and Norma Faye's house. The tires hissed on the pavement. A hawk sailed over the treeline and a squirrel scampered out of sight in a pecan tree.

Center Spring Branch chuckled over a two-foot waterfall not a hundred yards away from the house, the clear water continuing downstream over gravel and skinny sandbars. Late evening shadows stretched across the pasture, shading Cody's front yard.

"Supper sure was good." Tom Bell mimicked Cody and leaned his straight chair on its back legs against the wall on what used to be his own porch. The first cool front of the year had pushed out the humidity with the promise of changing leaves in the near future.

"Norma Faye learned from her mama. Don't tell Miss Becky, but Norma Faye's fried chicken is the best I ever tasted." Cody worked a toothpick between two teeth. "Listen, about Mexico…"

"You know, this house fits y'all better than it did me." Tom rebuilt most of the old house in the months he lived in Center Springs. "I believe the best thing I did was make this porch bigger."

"You can have it back, if you want. Me and Norma Faye can move to Chisum. A couple of folks on the city council want me to live there anyway. Said a sheriff ought to live in town."

Tom rested his hat on the porch rail and scratched his white hair. "Nossir. I deeded it over to you, legal. I don't need a whole house. It was good of James and Ida Belle to let me move into their second floor. You know, I doubt I have very many more years left on this old Earth anyway."

Cody didn't like the direction their conversation was headed. "Hey, I just remembered. There's still a trunk full of your stuff in Ned's barn."

Tom grinned. "I wondered what y'all did with it. I'll get and take it over to my new digs in a day or two."

"It was pretty heavy." Cody felt oddly embarrassed. It was almost like he'd been snooping in Tom's dresser or closet. "You know, we opened it up. There's still a lot of ammo for that BAR of yours. There's some letters and stuff, pictures, clothes."

"I sure wish I had that rifle back. I had to leave it and my pistol both down there in Mexico."

"Well, we didn't take nothing out of it."

Tom chuckled. "Wouldn't have missed it if you did. I was dead, remember? I've about forgot what all was in there. What went with those gold coins I had in there?"

Startled, Cody cropped his chair to all four legs. "Gold? You have money in there? Why, it's in the barn…"

Tom's wry grin was as close as he came to laughing out loud. "Settle down. I'm just kidding you."

A soft cough stalled their conversation. Cody watched the kids walk down the drive in the late evening shadows. Pepper joined them on the porch, sitting cross-legged beside Tom. Hootie followed and curled up on the greenest patch of grass in the yard to catch a breeze. The boys sat on the steps.

Cody knuckled her head. "What are you outlaws doing out this evening?"

Top leaned an elbow on the porch. "We wanted to come see Mr. Tom."

"It's a school night, and besides, I thought y'all were sick."

As if Cody's question reminded the boys they still weren't feeling up to snuff, Top coughed and Mark cleared his throat. Pepper pushed Mark's shoulder. "They say they don't feel good, but they manage to get up and come over *here*."

Mark pulled a strand of hair behind one ear. "I *don't* feel good, but it ain't bad enough to stay in bed."

Top shot Pepper a glare. "I'd be in bed if Miss Becky'd let me. This cough's wearing me out and I think it's getting worse."

"How'd you know Mr. Tom was here?" Norma Faye came out on the porch with a handful of warm teacakes and passed them around.

Pepper held a knee and leaned backwards. "I was listening in on the party line and old lady Whiteside was telling Thelma Prichard she saw you turning in here a little while ago."

Norma Faye felt the boys' foreheads to see if they had fever. "You're both warm."

Top coughed into his hand. "Throat tickles."

"Is it your asthma?"

"Partly."

Norma Faye grinned and nudged his shoulder. "I bet you didn't bring your puffer with you."

"Naw."

"Y'all probably got some kind of bug that's going around." Tom bit into a teacake and chewed. "I heard up at the store that there's a dozen folks around here, hacking and coughing." He grinned at the kids. "Y'all should have been here a minute ago. I had your Uncle Cody going pretty good. Told him I had gold hid in my old trunk."

The kids exchanged glances and Cody frowned. "All right. What are y'all up to?"

"Nothing."

"Pepper, your nose is growing." Norma Faye leaned on the porch rail.

"Tell 'em," Mark said.

Pepper almost rubbed *her* nose, but instead threw him a look that said shut up. For once the boys were working on her. Top's grin was white in the gathering gloom. "Go ahead and tell 'em what you told that nasty gal up at the store."

Norma Faye's eyebrow rose. "Nasty gal? Top, you should be ashamed of yourself."

"She was." Mark wiped the crumbs off his hands. "She showed up with a shirt that was near-bout painted on, asking questions about buried treasure."

"It wasn't buried treasure," Pepper interrupted. "She'd heard that somebody buried stolen money up at Palmer Lake."

"And you got her going on something else."

The look she shot Top was electric. "Fine then, but you two can't keep a secret to save your lives." She watched the adults for a reaction. "Daddy has a gold coin he got from Bill Preston for some building stuff up at his store. Said he didn't have his checkbook nor cash on him and offered it up instead. I took it to show these two loudmouths here and still had it in my pocket. That gal they're talking about was poking them big boobs of hers at everybody on the porch and it kinda made me mad, so I showed the coin to her and told her I found it out by Palmer Lake last year."

Top couldn't help himself. "And then she told her that old story of buried gold and that gal got all worked up. Just 'bout that time, Mack Vick rode up on his horse and told everybody you were back, Mr. Tom. We lit out right then, but I heard she talked Mack into taking her out to somewhere around Palmer Lake and they've been looking ever since."

Top quit talking and coughed long and deep. He leaned over and spat a thick wad of green mucus off the porch.

Cody watched Top rub his chest. "Gal, you need a whippin', but that's a good story. I know who you're talking about. She was there with a couple of other men. That's why I keep seeing strange cars up at the store. I think you might've started a gold rush."

"So you noticed her too?" Norma Faye raised her eyebrow again in fun.

"Sure did! She's staying at Bill Preston's house…"

"Isn't his wife in Dallas?"

"As far as I know." Cody grinned. "Anyway, she's been up at the store a couple of times since, and she's hard to miss."

Tom plucked a crumb off his white mustache. "You know, I bet there's gold buried all over this county."

"What makes you say that?"

"People didn't trust banks back during the Depression. If they're like everyone else, most of 'em buried their hard money in the ground. I'm sure more than a few died without telling anybody, and for sure it'll still be there."

Cody cut his eyes at the old Ranger. "I've heard stories like that, too. But we don't need strangers showing up out here and trespassing on private land. Me and Ned have enough trouble dealing with drunks and cattle rustlers."

"Gold rush." Top's face lit up. "Hey, how about we go out to Palmer Lake and do some looking ourselves?"

"That's not your land. You want to look for gold, dig around some of these old house places where Ned knows the owners."

Pepper rested her chin on one fist. "Mr. Tom, where do we dig, if we decide to go looking?"

"Well, I'd try around trees that were close to the house. Look for three that form a triangle and dig there. Maybe near a well, in a toolshed, or around something on the land that'll last for a while. I heard tell of an old man who kept his burn barrel on top of his gold stash. He'd roll it out of the way to get at it, then move the barrel right back where it was."

Norma Faye rose. "You two are worse than these kids. Y'all are just pouring gas on a fire. These three'll dig up half the county now. Folks won't be able to walk without twisting an ankle in a hole."

"Yep, and you two remember, I heard a story about a feller who was digging for gold in one spot and gave up." Tom winked at Norma Faye. "Along come another feller and saw the hole and thought, 'hey what if he didn't dig deep enough?' and then turned up a treasure chest with one push of a bilduky."

"You're mean. Don't listen to him." Norma Faye rapped Tom on the top of his head. She nudged Pepper with her shoe. "You three need to get on home. It's full dark and Miss Becky'll be expecting you."

Stars were shining overhead when the kids left after their goodbyes. Cody watched them disappear into the darkness. Hootie rose from the cool grass and followed. "I wonder why that patch there is so green when the rest of the yard's burning up."

"That's where I burned the scraps when I was working on this house." Tom finished his teacake. "The grass always grows back better because of the ashes."

Cody slapped a mosquito. "Well, I guess I'll tell Ned tomorrow about these gold hunters. I swear, I'm gonna jerk a knot in Pepper's tail one of these days."

Tom chuckled. "They're just kids. One of these days you'll look up and they'll be grown and you'll wonder how it happened so fast. Enjoy 'em while you can."

Chapter Twenty-two

Friday morning, Ned and Tom Bell parked behind the Chisum Courthouse, but instead of going inside, they strolled north on Main Street, enjoying the morning sunshine. The dry, cool air put a little spring in their step.

The pair seemed to have been created in a Hollywood wardrobe department. Ned's black slacks, blue shirt, tiny star on his pocket, and three-inch brimmed Stetson represented a world that was sliding away.

On the other hand, Tom Bell was a western icon that would never change in his wide-brimmed black Stetson, black sport coat, jeans, and Lucchese boots. "We going somewhere special?"

"We busted a still the other day. Biggest boiler I ever saw in my life. Our new mayor wants to make a name for hisself, so he had Cody bring it to town. I heard they're doing something with it on the square."

"Taking pictures and such?"

"Your guess is as good as mine."

They passed the side door of Duke & Ayers. Inside, a bald man in a limp white shirt was steaming a crease in a Bollman hat to suit a farmer wearing overalls.

Ned stopped at the intersection of North Main and North Plaza. "I'll be damned."

Tom Bell's slight grin was his only reaction.

"What'n hell are they thinking?"

"Well, Ned, it looks like somebody's set up a still here on the square."

It looked exactly as it did in the woods that previous day, all the way down to cases of jars waiting to be filled. Ned shook his head as they crossed the street.

Sheriff Cody Parker saw them coming and met them at the corner, clearly embarrassed. "Don't say nothing, Ned."

"Say something hell! This is the damndest thing I've ever seen. The only thing y'all haven't done is build a fire under that boiler and start cooking."

Cody refused to make eye contact. "Mayor Stratton suggested that."

"Neither Mayor Clay ner Mayor Haynes would've had that kind of stupid idea."

"Well, they aren't here anymore. It's Stratton."

"I never did think him or his daddy had sense enough to pour piss out of a boot."

"You might want to keep your voice down. He's over there talking to that reporter from *The Chisum News*."

"I don't care what he hears. This is evidence, you know."

"I tried to explain that, but he said something about budgets and I knew good and well what he meant."

"That if you didn't go along with this nonsense, then you might find your funds a little lighter than last year?" Tom Bell's voice was soft and even, but with a hint of danger.

"Yessir. Morning, Tom. Stratton's tightening the screws on us, and he wasn't too happy when I hired a female deputy. Then she nearly got killed right off the bat, and he says if anything like that happens again, he's gonna cut my budget, starting with the newest deputy, Anna."

Ned took off his hat to rub his bald head. "Does O.C. know anything about all this?"

"You talking about Anna, or this damned still?"

"Well, the still, right this minute. If I's you, I'd yank this down and put it away as soon as Stratton's through prissing around."

Cody looked as if he hoped the ground would swallow him up. "That won't happen for a day or two." He cleared his throat. "There's a news crew coming from Dallas, and another one all the way from New York. They want it to stay up there until they get their stories done."

"O.C.'s gonna have a rigor."

"I imagine so."

Tom Bell tilted his hat back as the *Chisum News* reporter finished with the mayor and saw them. "Uh, oh."

The young reporter hurried over as if he thought they might bolt. He stopped and flipped to a fresh page in his notebook. Another man joined him, holding a Speed-Graphic camera. "So was there trouble when you arrested the moonshiners? I hear y'all exchanged gunfire."

His attitude immediately irritated Ned. Tom Bell smoothed his mustache and took half a step to the side, trying to appear disinterested. Ned's forehead wrinkled. "You got a name, boy?"

Cody sighed loudly at the "boy" reference that could have been used in friendly conversation, but was a minor threat that the reporter missed.

"I'm Larry Michael Hagger."

"How long you been working for the paper? I don't recognize you."

"Uh, couple of weeks. Now, the mayor says you…"

"You from around here?"

"Huh? Nope. I worked at the *Commerce Journal* for a while, then for the *Hugo News* in Oklahoma, and now I'm…"

"What did the mayor tell you?"

Obviously irritated that he was being questioned when he should have been interviewing Ned, Hagger spoke a little sharper than he should have. "I got his side. Now I want yours."

Cody rolled his eyes and Tom Bell worked his mouth into

a frown to keep from grinning. Cody stepped closer to get the reporter's attention, and to be in a better position if Ned lost his temper. "How about you and I talk for a minute so Constable Parker can get an idea of how your questions are structured?"

Confused, Hagger gave his head a slight shake as if to clear the cobwebs. "Fine, then. I heard you were notified by an unnamed source."

"Yes."

Pen poised, Hagger waited for more. "And?"

Cody nodded. "You heard right. Our information came from an unnamed source."

"But you won't give me a name."

"Nope. Then it'd be a named source."

"Right. Where was this still located?"

"In the woods west of 271. That's all I can tell you right now."

"When can I see?"

Ned snorted. "There's woods everywhere. Go look at 'em."

Hagger paused and his photographer stepped in. "How about we get a picture of the three of you in front of the still?"

Tom Bell held up a hand and faded back. "I wasn't there."

"No." Ned's blue eyes flashed. "Make a picture with the mayor. He's the one who wanted this set up here."

Hagger looked at Cody for help. "I need a little more than that. Can you name those who you arrested?"

"That'll be released later."

"Do they have criminal records?"

"They do now."

Hagger reddened. "Look, I'm just trying to write a story."

Ned paused and Cody was afraid he was going to blow up. Instead, he relaxed. "I know you are."

Cody relaxed as well. "Here's what I can give you now. We arrested four men who surrendered once we identified ourselves. Their names will be released as soon as they are charged. Right now, the mayor thought folks here in town would like to see that we're doing our jobs. I can give you more in a day or two. How's that?"

Hagger didn't say anything for a long moment as he finished writing. "Good. Now, Constable, I hear you somehow *helped* an old man die the other day in the courthouse...."

Tom Bell moved with surprising speed for his age. He stuck his hand out and stepped between Ned and the reporter. "Name's Tom Bell. Texas Ranger, retired. I'm the one helped arrest them that tried to rob the Woolworth's the other day."

Frozen for a moment, Hagger couldn't decide what to do, but the tension on the sidewalk was so thick he made the right choice. "Yes, sir. Can you tell me what happened?"

The old Ranger took the reporter's arm and led him toward the fountain gurgling in the middle of the plaza. "Sure can. See, I've been gone for a while and came to town for a visit and walked right into a robbery...."

Hagger met his deadline, but the next morning he had an even better story. During the night, someone stole the still.

Chapter Twenty-three

The windows were open and our bedroom was almost chilly. The house smelled fresh and clean as another cold front pushed down to our little community on the river.

Mark and I both had the crud that Friday morning. I'd been fighting the sheets for a couple of hours and it seemed like I was going to cough my lungs out.

Mark was hacking up a storm when Grandpa came stomping into the kitchen. We heard them talking before Miss Becky brought the sugar bowl and set it on the dresser. She put the back of her hand on my forehead. "Hon, you're burning up."

She leaned over and did the same to Mark. "I swanny. Yours ain't near as high. Just that cough."

"I don't believe I feel as bad as Top. I'm not bringing anything up like him."

"It's probably his asthma making it worse." She took the lid off the sugar and unscrewed the mantle from the coal oil lamp on the opposite side of the drawer stack.

Mark rose up on an elbow. "What are you doing?"

"It sounds like y'all have the croup. This should stop it."

I knew what was coming. She dipped the corner of a dry rag into the coal oil and squeezed two drops into a spoonful of sugar in her other hand. "Open up." I got the first dose and the taste wasn't too bad, despite the coal oil.

The best part was we didn't have to go to school that day.

Chapter Twenty-four

Cool, dry air on Friday afternoon made a bull calf kick up his heels in the pasture beside Ned's house. A deep blue sky accented the dark green leaves of the massive red oak behind the hay barn and the other trees across the two-lane highway that wound around Ned's hill.

A V of geese passed overhead on their way to the rice fields west of Houston, their cries reached the farmhouse and announced the arrival of autumn. Clean Canadian air had reached as far south as the Gulf Coast.

Ned was working on his tractor parked by the big gas tank between the house and barn when the phone rang through the window screen. His wrench slipped off the nut at the same time Miss Becky stepped out onto the porch.

"Woooo! Ned!"

"You knuckle-busting son of a bitch!" He flicked his hand a couple of times to shake off the blood. "What is it?"

"Tomm'lee's on the phone, and you watch your language. The boys probably heard that."

"What does he want?"

"Well, my stars, you know I don't ask."

He pitched the wrench into the toolbox and stormed toward the house, talking all the way. "I swear, a man can't work on his own tractor without kinfolks wanting something."

Ned let the screen door slam shut, just to make a point. He sat with a thump on the telephone table's barely padded seat and picked up the receiver. "What?"

"Ned, I swear. Most folks at least say howdy."

"Most folks weren't under their tractor."

Tommy Lee laughed. "If I didn't love you, I'd pull your cranky old head off."

"Might let you do it to get some relief." Ned couldn't help but grin back at Tommy Lee's infectious laughter. "I haven't seen you in a month of Sundays. What's going on?"

"Somebody's been in the pasture I lease from Old Man Wilshire."

Ned's blood ran cold. He imagined rustlers parked in back of the pasture not far from Palmer Lake. "They cut the fence to get in?"

"Naw, went through the gate, big as you please."

"How many cattle'd you lose?"

"Why, I don't believe they was here to steal any cows. I saw the tracks when I went to feed this morning. All m'stock was there, but I saw where a truck cut across the pasture. I don't know what it's all about, but I bet they dug two dozen holes."

"Holes?"

"Yeah, some was shallow, but a couple not far from a stand of old sycamores were deep and more like trenches. It looks to me like they was looking for something."

Ned paused, thinking. "Pot hunters?"

"Huh?"

"Grave robbers. Folks who rob Indian graves."

"That's illegal."

"Laws don't matter to criminals. That's why they're the bad guys."

"Well, I can't say."

"I can. I'll be out there directly. Meet me at your gate."

Tommy Lee was waiting at the gate half an hour later. He was one of the last men in Lamar County to wear a fedora. "There wasn't a trailer or nothin'. Just one set of tire tracks."

Ned sighed and rubbed his bald scalp. He replaced his Stetson and stared down at the seven-foot-long trench and the dried dirt piled on the edge. "You're an expert on tires and trailers?"

"I've pulled enough in my life. So why do you suppose they dug all these other holes?"

A dozen piles of fresh dirt were scattered across the pasture. At first they looked random, but after a few minutes Ned recognized a pattern. "They ain't pot hunters or grave robbers, I don't believe."

"How can you tell that?"

"I can't for sure, but looky there. Some of 'em are dug by the biggest, oldest trees. That one right there, close to where that gully bends. They're looking for something else. I don't see where they took nothin' out, neither. These holes are as empty as their damned heads."

"I wish I knew what they were after, then."

"Gold. My granddaughter told a big fib to some city gal who's staying at Bill Preston's house. She's gone and spread that story that's gonna go like wildfire if somebody don't stop it."

"You don't say."

"I do say. Wrap a chain around your gateposts and lock it. That oughta keep 'em out."

"That No Trespassing sign shoulda done the same thing."

"Yeah, but a lock carries more weight."

"My daddy always said locks only keep out honest people."

Ned surveyed the pasture and nearby woods. "He was right about that. And if they come back, don't you come out here looking. Call me or Cody."

"Hole-digging ain't enough a crime to call the sheriff."

"It is now."

Chapter Twenty-five

A truck slowed on the highway and turned into Neal Box's lot, unusually crowded for a Friday. Cars and trucks parked haphazardly on the bottle-top pavement in front of the porch. Between the vehicles, farmers in light jackets and barn coats, khakis and overalls, visited with strangers who looked out of place in the country.

The cars glistened in the light beside local sedans and trucks covered in dust. A steady stream of customers clumped up and down Neal's wooden steps, their thin leather soles grinding sand and small pebbles into the rough planks. Neal's deep voice boomed through the open door.

"Howdy! Come on in! What can I do you for?"

Ned and Tom Bell sat on the porch, watching. A strange car pulled to a stop beside a dozen other unfamiliar vehicles in front of Oak Peterson's store, which was just as busy, if not more so.

"Tom, I believe we got a gold rush on our hands."

The old Ranger built his wry grin. "I believe this little burg's gonna get to be something you won't recognize before long."

"What do you mean?"

"You've never seen anything like this, but I have. I was still wet behind the ears when the Rangers sent me out to Rusk County after the Joiner strike came in."

"That was oil, and it was there. This is about gold, and there ain't none 'cause Pepper told a story."

"Don't matter. It was rough and got rougher when folks poured into East Texas looking to get rich. It brought all kinds."

"But there's nothing like that here."

"No? People talk. Pretty soon somebody's gonna say they found something, or knew somebody who knew somebody who found some gold somewhere, or they heard about buried cash and people'll pour in causing trouble. You'll be up to your eyeballs in trespass charges, and that's not the worst. With those joints across the river, it'll be a party every night with drunks and meanness coming back here in Lamar County at all hours."

They watched still another unfamiliar car pass. Two middle-aged men stopped at the edge of the porch and looked up. One had a nose that hooked sharp like a hawk's beak. "Sheriff!"

Ned frowned. "Constable."

"All right. Constable, do you know anybody who owns land out near Palmer Lake that would let us rent it for a day or two?"

"For what? A *day* or *two*?"

"Well, just to look around. We don't want to get into no trouble, but we heard about treasure buried out there and thought we'd check it out."

His friend lit a cigarette. "We'd be careful."

"Boys, there ain't no treasure. It's just a story that my granddaughter started. It'd be for nothing." Ned leaned an elbow on his knee. "Look, nobody around here's gonna let you on their place. They either don't want any trespassing, or they've already rented their land for grazing."

Hook Nose nudged his friend. "See, I told you. They're not going to let us look around. Thanks for nothing, *Constable*."

Ned rubbed the back of his neck as they walked past the domino hall and joined a group of strangers in front of Oak Peterson's store. "All because of that knothead Pepper and her mean streak."

Tom watched with his arms crossed. "I heard it was a joke when she got aggravated at some big-titted gal here at Neal's."

"Yeah well, Pepper's daddy got her goat when he found out she was carrying that gold piece around."

Tom chuckled. "That's kids for you. I got in trouble enough myself when I was about her age, and at least one time it wasn't my fault."

Ned grinned. "The jail's half full of men with that same excuse."

"Yeah, but I ain't lying. I was kinda sneaky when I was a kid, not in a bad way, I just didn't want anyone to know what I was up to. One day I was at a friend's house and found a gold Waltham railroad pocket watch laying in the yard. I had an idea who it might have belonged to but I wanted it. I figured lost and found, right?

"Well sir, later that evenin' after supper, I got to thinking I needed to hide it. I had an idea that I might try and sell it for cash, and believe me, hard money was hard to come by in the Valley. I stuck it between some newspapers in the rack beside my old daddy's chair, but I be danged if he didn't decide to read that night."

A truck pulling a boat trailer came from the Lamar Dam and parked on the shoulder, parallel to the highway. Two men tromped into Neal's store, but not before giving the two old men a long look.

Ned pursed his lips, unconsciously touched his little badge with his fingertips.

Tom didn't take his eyes off them until they were inside. "Dad pulled a paper from the rack and that watch fell on the floor. It was like somebody'd throwed a live rattler into the living room, it got so quiet. Both my brothers and a sister wouldn't take their eyes off of it. Daddy asked where it came from, and none of us fessed up. He quizzed us all night, but I didn't say a word, because I was scared. Of what? I don't have any idea, but everything froze up in my chest and I just sat there with the rest, shaking my head.

"The longer Dad asked, the less we had to say, and the madder he got. Mama finally cooled him down and we all went to bed. I didn't get a wink of sleep. He started in on us the next morning before chores and I was so groggy I finally gave in and said I'd found it."

Ned turned his ice blue eyes on the Ranger beside him who nodded like he'd been asked a question. "Wore my ass plumb *out*, once for lying and saying I didn't know anything about that gold watch, and again because he thought I'd stole it."

"And all it woulda took is you saying you picked it up."

"Ain't that the truth? That's how things start, bad little decisions. We walked down the road to the house where I found the watch and I had to knock on the door and ask who it belonged to. The old man inside said it was his and I had to apologize, saying I took it. Stole it."

They were silent for a long moment.

"We went back home and Dad put a hoe in my hands and worked me for two days straight without stopping until I fell out at the end of a row of cantaloupes." He smoothed his mustache. "I never lied again after that, and never stole so much as a piece of penny candy, either. I believe that's why I became a Ranger, to atone for something I never did."

"What'd your daddy say when you finally told him?"

They watched the two strangers emerge with packets of white paper, probably containing fresh sliced baloney and cheese.

"You know, that's always bothered me."

Ned raised an eyebrow. "What?"

"I never did, and he died thinking I stole that watch."

Chapter Twenty-six

Friday night, two miles north of Austin, Texas, smoke hung heavy below the Broken Spoke's low ceiling. Neon lights advertising Lone Star Beer and Pabst Blue Ribbon filled the walls, bathing the interior in the soft pastel glow of advertisement.

Dozens of tables covered with red checkered tablecloths covered with beer bottles and highball glasses were arranged in a semicircle around the golden oak dance floor. The floor was packed with couples two-stepping counterclockwise in a rhythmic whirlpool of bright plaid button-down shirts, cowboy hats, and women wearing tops that glittered in the stage lights. The long-haired Cosmic Cowboys were beginning to infiltrate the traditionally older western crowd.

The rest of the overflowing crowd gathered along the walls two and three deep, waiting on the night's top draw. Deputy Anna Sloan watched a man in oiled hair and a silver and white Nudie suit step onto the honky-tonk's low stage after the last notes of a new style of psychedelic rock ended with a polite response from the primarily country crowd.

"That was Roky Erickson and the 13th Floor Elevators. They'll be back tomorrow night to open for Earnest Tubb. Thanks guys, and I hope that Janis Joplin gal really does join up with y'all!"

The more progressive patrons at the back of the room yelled and whistled at the mention of Janis' name. A number of men wearing cowboy hats turned to glare at the long-haired young-sters.

"Evenin' folks! I'm James White and I hope you're all here to have a good time tonight. For those of you who'd like to hear more of that new sound, go on over to the Saracen or the Jade Room tomorrow night. You won't get much more of that in here."

The good-natured crowd whooped and clapped. Anna sat at a table by herself and had already turned down half a dozen dance requests before the headliner was supposed to start playing.

"Now I know you're here to dance, so I've got just the man for you. Ladies and gentlemen, Mr. Willie Nelson!"

The hatless country music star took the stage wearing a cream-colored suit. His short hair was oiled back and glistened in the light. Deep dimples bracketed his smile. "Hello. I'm Willie Nelson and I'm glad to be here again for…what James, the umpteenth time?"

"That's right!"

"Well, let's get to it." He hit a chord and the band joined in. "*Each night I make the rounds…*"

Couples poured onto the hardwoods at the same time a wait-ress in jeans and tight-fitting western shirt appeared at Anna's table. Dodging the flow of happy dancers, she sat a fresh Miller High Life down beside an empty bottle. The lights and smoke softened the hard edges of the waitress' face, showing Anna what she'd looked like fifteen years earlier, when she was young and fresh out of high school. "Here ya go, hon."

Anna handed her three dollars. "That should keep me paid up for a while."

The waitresses face fell. "It sure will. Some feller let you down?"

"Huh?"

"Well, we don't always get single women who stay that way for very long. You've been settin' there for two hours and haven't danced a dance."

Anna realized she was standing out in a crowd, the exact

North Central Kansas Libraries

opposite of what she wanted. "Well, I can't listen to the music and dance too. The guys are always trying to talk, or be funny, or running their hands around where they shouldn't be."

The waitress glanced around. "I know what you mean, hon." She popped her gum. "Some of these old boys in here sure are watching you though."

"Well, I could have gone to hear something else like Steppenwolf or Jimi Hendrix, they're playing across town, but I was raised on western swing and would rather hear country myself."

"Did you know Hank Williams and Elvis played here?"

"No!" Anna saw a square-jawed guy at the bar who looked like a true working cowboy. Most of the others were townfolk, or what her daddy called "drugstore cowboys," but the man who caught her attention was in worn-down boots and a sweat-stained straw hat that had seen better days. "Do you know who that is?"

The waitress looked over her shoulder. "Hon, I thought you said you were in here to listen to music."

"Well, Willie *does* make me want to dance."

The beer gal laughed big and loud. Her just-rolled-out-of-bed pageboy haircut reminded Anna of Goldie Hawn from the *Laugh-In* television show. "He does at that. You're looking at Stan Ewing. He works on a ranch out west of town. Comes in here pretty regular. He mostly just sits there and drinks beer, though. I don't remember seeing him dance more than two or three times."

Willie finished his song and held up a hand to see past the lights. "Any of y'all like the nightlife?" The crowd whooped. "I thought so. I wrote this one about the Esquire Ballroom in Houston." The crowd cheered and he started singing before the first chord. "*When the evenin' sun goes down...*"

Ewing saw her looking in his direction and nodded. Anna held up her beer and his eyebrow twitched. The waitress gave her a pat on the shoulder. "Good luck."

A minute later, Ewing appeared at her table with a cold, sweating beer in each hand. Anna took a sip of hers. "This one's fresh."

"These are for me." He grinned. "Did you want another one?"

Beer almost shot out of her nose and she immediately liked him. "Sit down, cowboy."

He hooked the chair leg with the toe of his scuffed boot and settled down beside her. "Name's Stan."

"Anna."

"What brings you here?"

"My daddy's looking to buy some cattle."

"You won't find any in *here*."

"Got in early. I'm heading for the sale barn tomorrow."

"Yep, Saturdays are always busy."

She took a long swallow. "That's what I'm hoping for. Some good stock moving through the ring, and I might even get some names there and go out to a ranch or two."

Ewing drained his first beer. "You want to dance?"

"Sure." Anna tilted her bottle and took a long swallow. "I'll even let you lead."

Chapter Twenty-seven

It was nearly dark on Friday when Ned stopped by the Chisum sale barn. Even though the stock inspector had already been there, he had to do *something* and he indulged his theory of poking around until he stirred up a hornets' nest.

The cold front had backed up, bringing a strong south wind that stretched the flags outside, meaning that in a day or two, another front was going to drop the temperatures once again.

There were only a handful of pickups in the parking lot so late in the day. By ten the next morning, the lot would again be packed with cars, trucks, and trailers. The owner, Sammy Alison, was still in the office, feet on his desk and Bailey hat tilted low over his eyes, chewing on a cigar. He put down *The Chisum News.* "Evenin', Ned. I reckon I know why you're here."

"Bet you do." Ned tilted his hat up to cool his forehead. The picture on a black and white television resting on a file cabinet was the clearest he'd ever seen. The only station Ned could get at home, Channel 12, was always snowy, no matter which way they turned the forty-foot antenna. The evening news highlighted race riots in Miami. "You on the cable?"

"Yep. They ran it out here last week."

"You have to pay for that, don't you?"

"Sure do."

"You ought not to have to pay for TV. That's like paying for radio."

"Changing times, Ned."

He cut his eyes toward the images of police and rioters. "This ain't right."

Alison grunted around his cigar. "It's a shame about Pat Walker. You find out anything new about his murder?"

"Naw. I was hoping you might have thought of something you didn't tell the stock inspector."

"I'd have called him if I did." Alison had started at the sale barn by working cows in the pens. His voice and attitude were gruff. "You know we're careful here."

"I know it. You hear tell of anyone y'all don't know hanging around?"

"There's always people coming in to watch the sales."

"Nobody trying to work deals in the parking lot?"

"Hell!" Alison removed the cigar and laughed. His belly jiggled under a blue western shirt straining at the snaps. "There's always folks tradin' in the parking lot, and every one of them are looking for a good deal, but none of it had to do with Pat Walker that I know of. I hear he'd been down in his back for a while before he was murdered."

"Yeah, he hadn't been up to snuff for a couple of weeks. Where would you take a load of stole cattle, if you was to try and sell 'em somewheres else?"

Sammy chewed on his cigar in thought. "Well, I wouldn't go to Oklahoma or anywhere around here. I might think about high-tailin' up 287 to Amarillo, but they watch pretty careful up there, too. I believe I'd either haul 'em into the Thicket, or down west of Austin."

The 3.3 million acres of heavily forested land in southeast Texas called the Big Thicket had refused to be tamed since white men first arrived. It was said some parts still weren't explored, and the families who lived there kept to themselves. Lawmen had been known to disappear forever.

"Hell, it could be happening right under our noses with

unbranded cattle. There's a little larceny in all of us and even though a feller might know them cows should be branded, they'll say 'well, it's only a heifer or steer,' the laws ain't gonna find out. Then it's only between them and God. Ned, you're looking for a needle in a haystack. I'd bet a dollar to a donut that Pat hadn't branded ninety percent of his cows."

"You're right. A lot of folks around here don't take the time for branding no more, but they should."

"Yep, and they wind up paying for it in the long run, too." Sammy swallowed tobacco juice and chewed his cigar back into place. "From what I've heard, those old boys that steal cows usually just take a few from first one place, then another. They don't steal every single cow a man has."

"Pat hadn't been out there for a while. It means they were watching and got greedy. They didn't need to take the man's life. Those people turned from thievery to murder, and that's why I'm a little more inclined to know if you'd seen anything suspicious."

"Can't help you. What I don't understand is *why* they killed ol' Pat."

"He saw 'em and they shot him for it." Ned set his hat. "All right, holler if you hear anything."

"You know I will."

Back in the empty parking lot, Ned settled into his car and started the engine. He plucked the microphone off the bracket. "Martha, this is Ned."

"I know who it is." Martha had been in dispatch so long she knew all of the officers and their families, even the inlaws and outlaws that moved in and out through the years. "You need to get on over to the hospital."

Ned's stomach sank. "What for?"

"It's not real bad. Miss Becky called and said your grandboy's there."

"Which one?"

"Top."

"How come?"

"Didn't say."

His tires spun on the gravel, sending a roostertail of dust into the air that quickly disappeared in the wind.

Chapter Twenty-eight

Ned hated the astringent smell in hospitals. He avoided eye contact with the nurses in nuns' habits who carried covered trays full of unidentifiable items. The bare walls echoed with his footsteps and it seemed like an eternity before he found the third-floor corner waiting room full of family members. Other folks visiting patients half glanced at him with a look that said, 'I'm sorry you're here, too.'

"Is it his asthma again?" His question was directed at anyone who would answer.

Miss Becky clutched her Bible in one hand. "No hon. Dr. Heinz says it might have started that way, but it's turned into something else that came on fast. He was coughing up blood when Cody drove us in."

Top was in X-ray. Cody and Norma Faye sat together in the uncomfortable chairs by the windows. Looking pale and weak, Mark waited beside James, Ida Belle, and Pepper, who were huddled together on one of the bench seats at the end. An expressionless Tom Bell in his black coat stood with his back against the wall, hat in hand.

Mark was still coughing, but not as much as before. Ned stopped beside his granddaughter and absently pulled her head against his side, addressing the Choctaw boy. "You feeling all right?"

"Yessir. I believe I shook it off."

"Good." He cupped the back of Mark's head and turned toward Cody. "What are they X-raying him for?"

Elbows on his knees, Cody worried at the brim of his hat. "The doctor's thinking it might be pneumonia."

"But it's not pneumonia, yet." Looking every bit like the elderly slope-shouldered doctor he was, Doc Heinz stepped into the waiting room with a clipboard in his hand. His white lab coat hung heavy with bulging pockets. "The boy's lungs are filling with fluid from a bacterial infection called *Serratia marcescens*. The thing is, I've never seen it before this week. Only read about it."

"Then how do you know what it is?" The tone of Ned's voice was stern, almost aggressive.

Dr. Heinz held up his hands. "Cool down, Ned. I know you don't trust us doctors, but I'm trying to help the boy, not hurt him."

James cleared his throat. "Mark here's coughing, too, but it ain't as bad. Is it contagious? We don't want Pepper to come down with it."

"I don't know yet."

"You don't know much."

Miss Becky rubbed Ned's arm. "Hush hon. Let him talk."

Dr. Heinz scratched at his thin white hair. "I'm gonna check Mark out and put these two kids on a round of antibiotics. That'll help with the infection. Their lungs are stronger than Top's, and I believe they've already fought it off.

"I believe Top's in bad shape because his lungs are weaker. That's how this kind of thing usually spins up. It gets ahold of whatever's wrong with the people carrying it and then goes to work on those weak spots and other organs. To tell you the truth, I've loaded him up with a stout IV antibiotic drip. I don't want it to get to his heart or brain."

"Oh, God." Miss Becky's hand went to her mouth. "What if it does?"

"It wouldn't be good, but I'm not gonna let that happen. Any of the rest of y'all showing any symptoms, coughing?"

The adults shook their heads. Cody patted his empty shirt pocket looking for the pack of cigarettes he used to carry. "You said you'd never seen it before, but you know exactly what it is. How?"

"The first case came in four days ago. You know Curtis Gaines?"

Ned straightened. "Sure. We all do. Curtis lives in Powderly. He's sprayed my crops for years. He got it too?"

"I believe so. He came in with a urinary tract infection. I ought not be telling y'all his business, but I guess it doesn't make any difference now. Curtis had some minor surgery down in his privates a while back. I'd released him to fly again, but then he got to feeling worse and worse with an infection in his kidneys. He was bad enough I put him in the hospital a couple of days ago and, despite everything we could do, the infection dug in down there and went to his heart and he passed away yesterday."

The news hit Ned hard. He pitched his hat onto an empty chair and rubbed his head. "Curtis was a young man!"

"He was too young to die, and that's a fact. I only for sure found out what it was after he'd passed, and that's why I've loaded Top up on antibiotics, so it won't do the same thing to him."

"He most likely caught it here, right?" Tom Bell looked surprised that he'd said anything. He cleared his throat. "I've had some experience with hospitals and secondary infections."

"No, Mr. Bell. We've never had a case of it before. The worse we've ever had is staph, and damn near every hospital I've ever been around has *that*. He picked it up somewhere, though. Have y'all heard of anybody else in Center Springs with these symptoms? Coughing, secondary infections from other illnesses? How about folks with lung problems, smokers?"

"Nobody that I know about." Ned worried at his bald scalp. "But folks don't usually come around when they're sick."

Miss Becky's cracked thumbs rubbed the leather cover on her Bible. "How long will it take for that medicine to start working?"

"That depends on Top. Besides his lungs and the asthma, he's healthy, so we should start seeing some improvement tomorrow at the earliest, the day after, for sure. Mark here'll be better tomorrow when the antibiotics kick in, and for her, it's preventative."

A young nun with smiling eyes appeared at Dr. Heinz's elbow. "Doctor, the Parker boy is back in his room."

"Fine. Y'all can go in there with him, but leave the kids out here."

Miss Becky followed the nun to Top's room while the rest of the Parkers and Tom Bell waited where they were.

Ned paused in the hallway. An enormous dread weighed on him. He walked to the window in the silent room and stared down at the dark parking lot, feeling he was falling down a deep well with no way out. His throat was tight and a swelling pain ballooned in his chest.

Overcome with emotion, the muscles in his arms and legs twitched. He slipped his hands in his pockets to keep them from shaking and blinked away a rising flood of tears.

I've done a lot of things in my life. If something happens and that boy was to need help from this damned Gift I have, I can't do it. I won't hold that boy in my arms as he dies, no matter if Becky believes he's going somewhere better or not.

Losing him's one thing. Helping's another.

There was a thickness in his throat and that balloon in his chest swelled even larger. Weak with fear, he stepped inside and dropped heavily onto a vinyl chair to gather himself.

Chapter Twenty-nine

I wasn't feelin' much punkin when they brought me back into the hospital room after the X-rays. Miss Becky, Aunt Ida Belle, and Aunt Norma Faye popped through the door not five minutes after the nuns got me off the gurney and into the bed.

They were wearing masks over their mouths and noses, and that scared the pee-waddlin' out of me. If they were afraid they'd catch what I had, then I was in trouble. The room was small and full of people, crowding in around my bed and the hospital table. Besides that, there was nothing in there but a thin cabinet that reminded me of a chifforobe, a built-in sink, and one uncomfortable-looking chair.

"Can you get me another pillow? I can breathe easier if I'm propped up."

A young nun with kind eyes who didn't look much older than me grinned over the mask and came back with two pillows. She and Miss Becky propped me up while Grandpa came in and sat on a chair in the corner and studied his hands. That's how he always thought when he was worried. Some folks might have got the idea he was just sitting there and doing nothing, but I knew he was working something over in his mind.

The nurses left and he looked up. "The doctor asked if any of the kids at school have this."

"Nossir." I chuffed deep in my chest, trying to keep from coughing.

"You been around Curtis Gaines lately?"

"Nossir. He said he'd take me up sometime, but I haven't seen him on the ground in a month or so." I coughed again and gagged on the lump that caught in my goozle.

Miss Becky pulled me forward by a shoulder and beat on my back. I'm not sure it helped any, but it made her feel better. "He must have took sick after he flew over the other day."

Grandpa looked up when I said that. "You saw him?"

"He went over the house last Saturday while we were camping out. He was flying low." My chest rattled deep inside, crackling like newspaper. "He usually comes over the house and wags his wings. He likes me, because he said he had asthma when he was a kid and knows how it feels when you can't breathe."

Miss Becky picked up her Bible and ran her hands over the leather. "I wish we'd-a known it was more'n just the croup. I'd-a got you in to see the doctor right quick, if I'd known that."

A tickle built in my chest and swelled. The back of my throat picked it up and almost itched. "Miss Becky, you don't think that stuff he was spraying made me sick, do you?"

Grandpa took his glasses off. "What stuff?"

I could tell Miss Becky didn't know what I was talking about. "We were standing by the gate when he went over and water was coming out of his sprayer."

"He didn't spray y'all with no cotton poison, did he?"

I knew what that stuff smelled like. I choked down a cough. "Nossir. It was just water, and there wasn't much of it."

Grandpa's face tightened. "It wasn't water. A man don't waste gas spraying water."

I started to answer, but that itch in my lungs and throat that'd been building broke loose and I got to coughing so hard I thought my insides were going to tear loose. The nurse came in and checked on me, then she went out when I settled down.

Grandpa left with a look in his eye, and I dozed for a while, but when I woke up, ever'body was gone except for Miss Becky.

I was still hacking up green stuff, but it was turning red. I tried to tell her, but the next thing I knew I couldn't draw any air.

Miss Becky hollered for help. Doctors and nurses filled the room as my head spun and I struggled to get a breath. It had been too long and I was suffocating. Panic took over and lights sparkled behind my eyes.

The Poisoned Gift exploded in my head.

Dark people in suits were surrounded by white marble, and buildings with columns like those Roman ruins we'd been studying, only it was all fresh and white. Other people walking around them were coughing out great clouds of red vapor and Grandpa and Mr. Tom were running in slow motion towards them. The dark people hid behind the columns and I tried to warn Grandpa, but he couldn't hear me.

A giant hand yanked me into a cold operating room. Everything was white, the floors, walls, and equipment. A big gray rat popped out of nowhere, running along the baseboards, following a dusting of fine gold powder that trailed toward a white door.

I sat up on the operating table. "You need to get out of here, Mister Gray Rat. It's too clean in here for you to be running around, dropping turds on all that pretty gold dust."

It turned its head toward the sound of my voice and grinned at me with them nasty rat teeth, then scurried along the edge of the room to the door that swung open to the outside. The rat ran through and stood on its hind legs and waded into a clear-water creek and ran up a hill.

Golden dust filled the air and my lungs and I couldn't breathe. I heard people hollering and praying before everything went dark.

Chapter Thirty

Deputy Anna Sloan, dressed in jeans and a western shirt, sat in one of the tiered wooden chairs surrounding the show ring at the Round Rock sale barn. Saturdays were always busy for cattle buyers and the auction was running on all eight cylinders. Her boots rested on the back of the empty chair in front and she leaned back in a comfortable slouch.

The odor of cowshit mixed with dirt and perspiration filled the noisy interior of the metal building that echoed with the bawling of cattle and hum of male customers. Twenty rows of creaky tiered seats, most of them filled, rose in a semicircle around a system of gates and steel corrals that funneled livestock into the center ring, and out again. The auctioneer on the raised podium at the opposite side of the ring rattled away with his machine-gun sales pitch.

"This one taken?"

She glanced up to see Stan Ewing standing behind the empty seat beside her. A small piece of toilet paper was stuck to his chin where he'd cut himself shaving. "It is now."

Stan stepped over and down, his long legs making the task look easy. Sand crunched under his boots as he folded himself the chair next to her. "I had fun last night."

"Me too."

"Didn't think you'd really be here."

She raised an eyebrow. "I told you I was looking to buy some cattle."

"Well, pretty gals in honky-tonks on Friday nights sometimes don't tell the whole truth."

"Like what I'm doing there?"

"Yep, and if you're really single."

She held up her left hand. "No ring. Not even a tan line."

He mimicked her action. "Me neither. So we're honest with one another."

Anna's chest sank dark and empty at the comment. "Looks that way."

Snapping short whips, the "ring men" opened the gate into the sale ring and pushed a herd of numbered and tagged heifers through the chute. The auctioneer called the price based on the animal's type, age, and weight in his rapid-fire cadence as they circled the ring.

Anna watched the cattlemen bid in ways others couldn't see. "You know the brand inspector back there?"

Stan tilted his head back and glanced toward the pens out back. "Known him for years, why?"

"I'm not from around here and want to be sure I'm not buying stole cattle."

He grinned. "He's a *state* inspector."

"I know it, but anyone can be bought."

"He's as honest as the day is long."

"And you know that for a fact."

"Sure do, as much of a fact as we had fun last night."

Anna fell silent, watching the stock move through the ring.

"Your daddy sure must trust you."

"How's that?"

"To send you down here with a wad of cash to buy cattle."

Her face reddened. She was playing a part, but it always got her goat when men looked down on a woman. "You don't think I know enough to do this by myself?"

Stan held up a hand. "Easy, gal, I was just staying that you don't see many women in a sale barn. Look around you. You're the only single girl in the place."

"I've done this before."

Stan crossed an ankle over the opposite knee. "You're not bidding."

"I don't see anything I want."

"So what is it you're after?"

"Cheaper stock than this. The prices are higher here than back home."

"Where's that?"

"Chisum." She wanted to kick herself for spouting out where she was really from.

"Never been there."

"You haven't missed much."

He laughed. "Why're you here, then?"

"Daddy sends me out for good stock to replace what he's sold. That's all."

"Cow-calf operation?"

"Yep. He never did like stockers."

"So the market value's higher than back home? What is it there?"

She was getting into dangerous waters. She'd read half a dozen stock magazines at the Chisum Library before leaving, but knew that his experience would quickly reveal that she was a fraud. "You know any local folks that might sell?"

"Naw. Most of 'em bring their cattle and horses here."

"How about someone who's getting out of the business, or in trouble?"

Stan cut his eyes at her. "So *that's* how you and your daddy do business?"

"What do you mean?"

"You take advantage of them who're in trouble. They sell cheap to cut out the middleman and take what they can get. Cash on the barrelhead."

Though her cover story was a complete lie, she didn't like the way she sounded in his estimation. "It's not like that at all."

"Yes it is. I know people who've had to sell out before. What y'all do ain't crooked, but it's not right either."

Anna watched the ring clear again. "That doesn't make us bad people."

Stan straightened. "I'm hungry. Didn't eat breakfast. Let's you and me go to the café. I'll buy you dinner."

"It's not a date."

"No, but I want to eat. There might be a fellow or two in there you can talk to."

Knowing that as much business was conducted around the tables of a sale barn restaurant as was in the ring, she stood. "Lead the way, cowboy."

Chapter Thirty-one

Seven days after Mr. Brown hired Curtis Gaines to spray Gold Dust on Center Springs, he paced his nicotine-permeated motel room in Austin. He'd done a lot of things in the past that he wasn't proud of, but this mission was weighing on his mind.

The depressing room in the St. Elmo Motel advertised "Color TV by RCA, for only $12 per night." Instead of watching, he sat at the small round table beside the window, peeking through a narrow crack in the thick gray curtains. One of the two double beds was still made. The other contained a valise. Inside, a snub-nosed .38 in a shoulder holster rested on packets of money. Half was his part of the split from the skimmed cash. The other was Mr. Green's.

Outside, a boy and girl played on a swing set without enthusiasm. Surrounded by the horseshoe-shaped motel, the grassy area was an oasis in the middle of pavement and parked cars.

His co-worker, Mr. Green was gone and there wouldn't be a funeral. It went against his small-town raising, where people took care of each other and paid their respects when a friend or relative passed on.

He'd lost a lot through the years with the Company. Sneaking around and lying had become second nature, making him a ghost to most people, but the wall of indifference he'd built over time crumbled a little more with every new falsehood.

Operating in Texas was just wrong, and he knew it from the outset. Some things you didn't do, and as his grandfather used to say, you don't shit in your own nest. The whole thing had a sour taste from the moment he was briefed, and he wished he'd done more to get out of the entire operation.

The jangling phone startled him. Heart racing, he answered. "Hello."

It was Mr. Gray. "We need to talk. Find a phone booth and call within the next ten minutes."

Mr. Brown hung up and slipped into the shoulder holster, covering the thirty-eight with his suit coat. Five minutes later, he dialed Mr. Gray from inside a glass phone booth outside of a Woolworth's. "I'm secure."

"The team that is collecting the Gold Dust data there in Texas notified me of more issues with the material."

"And they are?"

"Your pilot died. In addition, an elderly man is also dead, and a kid with a strange first name is in..." Papers rustled in the receiver. "...St. Joseph Hospital in Chisum. Top Parker."

Mr. Brown's stomach sank. "This doesn't look good. How did they get this information?"

Mr. Gray was silent on the other end and Mr. Brown could have kicked himself for the sophomoric question. He'd been in the business long enough to know Mr. Gray wouldn't release those details. "All right. Orders?"

"Come in. We need to determine where the failure occurred."

"It sounds to me like it was on the eggheads' end. We did everything right."

"My office. Tomorrow at the latest."

"Yes, sir." Mr. Brown hung up the phone and walked back to the silent motel room, smoking and thinking. Half a pack later, he came to a decision.

He was heading back to Chisum.

Chapter Thirty-two

The Parker family gathered in the hospital's stark waiting area to gather strength from one another until the attendants brought Top back to his room on Saturday morning. A bad copy of *Madonna and Child* hung on one wall above uncomfortable vinyl chairs and bench seats. Reproduction prints of the Seven Patron Saints for Healing and Comfort graced the remaining walls.

Dr. Heinz joined them, looking as if he hadn't slept in days. "It was a long night, but even though we got him back, he's in bad shape, Ned."

"Well, get back in there."

"We've done all we can do. Like I told you before, the infection was spreading and I think we caught it in time. If we hadn't, we might have lost Top already. It's touch and go from here on out. We just need to wait and let his body do the rest."

Miss Becky laid both hands on her Bible. "And pray."

Heinz nodded. "That'll help."

"I shouldn't oughta tell you," Heinz fiddled with the stethoscope around his neck, thinking, "but there's one more dead with this stuff."

The ring tightened and James slipped his arm around Pepper. "Somebody else from Center Springs?"

"No. An old man who's lived in Powderly all his life. His granddaughter brought him in about an hour ago, but it was too late. He showed the same symptoms and had been in for surgery."

"It's the hospital, then." Ned's eyes flashed.

"Nope, and remember, Top was already sick when he came in here. The man was a heavy smoker all his life. I'm seeing a pattern here that involves folks with weak or damaged lungs, and then a secondary ailment kicks in. In Top's case it's his asthma. In Curtis Gaines', it was that small surgery and probably the fact that he's sprayed chemicals all his life. I doubt that did him any good in the long run."

"One feeds off the other?"

"Both pull the body's defenses down." The rattling wheels of a gurney caused Heinz to turn and watch the attendants roll Top down the hallway. Ned and Miss Becky started toward the door, but Heinz held up a hand to stop them. "Give 'em a minute. We're putting him in an oxygen tent and keeping up with the antibiotics. From there, it's up to him. He's in crisis right now. The next twelve hours will tell the tale."

"The Lord'll bring him through."

Pepper coughed softly into her hand and the response was electric. She gave the adults a wide-eyed look. "What? I just inhaled some spit."

● ● ● ● ●

The weekend passed slowly. James and Ida Belle took the kids home, but the older folks stayed at the hospital. Miss Becky sat with Top while Ned and Tom Bell fidgeted in the waiting area with friends and relatives who came to offer their sympathies and support.

Frenchie dropped by with a box full of food after she closed the café. "I've got fresh coffee here and donuts. Y'all call the house if you need anything."

Ned gave her a pat on the arm. "Thank you, gal."

Judge O.C. Rains stepped off the elevator. "Any news?"

Ned turned from Frenchie, who gave the judge a hug. She patted O.C.'s arm. "Didn't bring any pie."

"Probably won't want any for a while."

She gave him a sad look and left.

Ned moved closer to his old friend. "Tonight'll tell the tale."

"Heinz is good. Top'll be all right."

"This is all wrong, O.C." Ned lowered his voice that quavered. "If he don't make it, and can't let loose, I don't think I can—"

The judge cut him off and scanned the room, nodding at the worried adults. "Let's not think about that right now."

The elevator arrived and Cody stepped out. He paused at the door of the full waiting room and motioned for Ned, Tom, and O.C. The somber men followed him to the end of the hall and into an unused room with two empty beds.

Cody took off his hat and placed it upside down on the over-bed hospital tray. "I did a little digging after I heard that Curtis Gaines died from the same thing."

"Figured you would." Ned rubbed his head. His hat was in the waiting room.

Tom hooked a thumb into the front pocket of his jeans and leaned against the wall. "What'd you find out?"

The sheriff told them.

Chapter Thirty-three

Cody knew something was up that morning the minute he stepped out of the car in Curtis Gaines' yard. Curtis' much younger and unusually well-dressed girlfriend came off the porch steps to meet him. "Howdy, Sherri Lynn."

The slender woman shifted from one foot to the other. Her simple Broadcloth white shirt with print flowers and casual brown culottes belted at the waist made her seem even younger. The south wind blew her straight brown hair in her face. "Sheriff."

He slammed the door on his sheriff's car. "I'm sorry about Curtis."

Her eyes flicked from Cody, to his badge, and then his car before twitching back to his face. "None of us expected it."

"Least of all him." Cody watched her twitch. "You're nervous."

"No I'm not."

"Yes you are." He'd learned long ago to be direct with people. "You want to tell me what's up?"

"Other than my boyfriend was hired by two city fellows driving a dark car to do something he wouldn't talk about, and then it killed him?"

"That's a start. They pay him enough for his trouble?"

Her gaze slipped away. He watched her look for an anchor in the pasture behind him, then skip across the wide yard before resting on the airplane hangar to his left.

"Sherri Lynn, what do you know about it?"

"Not much." She paused. "I drove by the hangar that morning and saw them over there. Curtis told me he had a job that day and didn't need me around, so I ran some errands and went back by an hour later and saw the men sitting on the hood of their car. The plane was gone. I came back past again on the way to his house after they left and his plane was there.

"When Curtis came in for supper, he showed me a stack of bills and said our ship had come in. He said we didn't need to worry about money anymore, and gave me some cash to go buy us a new color television set."

"How much did they give him?"

She shrugged, still holding the hair out of her face. "I don't remember."

Cody looked off in the distance at a line of trees. A martin house not far away was working alive with birds. "You know, money is an interesting thing. When I was a kid, I was at a family gathering when one of my uncles called Uncle Ned around behind a car. I went with him, because I was nosey.

"This uncle, who I won't name 'cause he's still alive, dug in his pocket and pulled out a wad of bills. He counted out a hundred and fifty dollars into Ned's hand, paying him back for what he'd borrowed years before."

Cody paused and waved a honeybee away from his face. "Here's the thing. I was just a kid, but I remember the amount. Money sticks in your head. So let me ask you again, how much money did those city people pay?"

She shifted from foot to foot, bleeding off energy. "He didn't tell me."

"'course he did, and you're already spending it and him barely in the grave."

Shocked, Sherri Lynn stepped back. "How'd you know?"

He crossed his arms and leaned against the hood. "Them shorts or whatever they are still have the tag on 'em."

She looked at the tag and deflated.

"So how much was it?"

"*One* pack was ten thousand dollars."

"What does that mean?"

"They ripped him off. There was a second pack, but it was a bunch of ones with hundred dollar bills on either side."

"They call that a flash roll in Vegas."

"Whatever you want to call it. It all came to ten thousand and four hundred dollars."

"To spray for one day."

"Said they'd send him more every year. They thought it was important, and so did he."

"That ain't it. They paid him an ass-load of money and he took it, not caring if it was dirty or not."

They stared at each other for an entire minute before Cody surrendered. "Anything else?"

"He was coughing the next day and didn't fly. He'd come down with a bug that wore him down until he finally started spitting up blood. That's when we come to the hospital."

Chapter Thirty-four

"And died." Judge Rains half-sat on the edge of the bed.

"That's right. Y'all know the rest."

"So this all leads back to those two men?"

"I don't know where it leads, Judge. I'm just telling you what I found out."

Tom Bell's eyes went flint hard. "What were they wearing?"

Cody crossed his arms and half sat on the bed. "She said dark suits and sunglasses."

"Driving a dark car."

"That's what she said."

"I bet it was a rent car. Those sound like government men." He shook his head. "The damned Cold War has come to Texas, and it's a cryin' shame."

O.C. turned his attention to Tom Bell. "You have an idea."

"Yessir. Sounds to me like they hired Curtis to do something for them that killed him."

Ned shook his head. "But what would city people want a crop duster to spray?"

Before Tom could offer an answer, a nun with a pursed mouth appeared in the doorway. "Gentlemen, this is not a meeting room. We'll have to clean it again now."

All four ducked their heads, not wanting to draw the wrath of the sour woman wearing a black habit. "Mr. Parker?"

Cody and Ned looked up.

Her expression softened. "Mr. Ned Parker. Someone's on the waiting room phone for you."

"Who is it?"

"I didn't ask. He called you by name, though."

Ned walked down to the waiting room and picked up the receiver that was lying on the table. "This' Ned."

"You don't know me, but I have some information you need."

He frowned at the unfamiliar voice. "About what?"

"Your grandson. Now listen carefully. I'm only going to say this once and I'll hang up. The kid is sick from a bacterial agent the CIA released in your community. They call it simulated warfare experiments. It was supposed to be benign, but that isn't the case. This isn't the first time they've done this in the U.S.

"They ran one in Canada and a few years ago the experiment they conducted in San Francisco wound up making people sick, too. More than one person died. That's all I can tell you."

"You know so much about this, you're in on it too. Why'd you call?"

The caller hesitated. "I can't do this to our people anymore. I just thought you deserved to know what happened. Goodbye."

"Wait!" There was no answer, only the dial tone that quickly turned into an annoying buzz. He hung up, but the phone rang again. He snatched it off the cradle. "Ned Parker here."

The voice was different, and very familiar. "Mr. Ned. This' John. Didn't expect you to answer. How's Top?"

"He ain't good right now."

"I'm sorry about that, and for not being there with y'all, but my baby boy Bass Reeves is in the hospital, sick and coughing, and I'm hoping it ain't the same thing Top has."

Ned's blood ran cold. "This hospital?"

John grunted. "Nossir. We're at the Negro hospital, South General."

Ned picked up his hat from the end table and weighed it

in his hand. "That baby has a cold in his chest all the time. It's probably nothing."

Tom Bell returned and Ned hung up when they finished, ignoring the looks from those who'd been listening. He crossed the floor and leaned in to the old Ranger. "Tom, I just got a call that said the CIA's behind Top's being in here, and Curtis Gaines' death. We've got to track this thing down."

"Cody'll do it."

"No. Not the law. You and me."

"Ned, you *are* the law."

Ned didn't tell him that the fear and anguish over using the Poisoned Gift was rapidly overtaken by a building red rage that pushed everything else to the side. "That, and a granddaddy who's mad as hell."

Chapter Thirty-five

Deputy Anna Sloan and Stan Ewing waited for Lucas DeWitt on Monday morning in the parking lot full of blowing dirt in front of the Round Rock sale barn. Covered cattle pens attached to the sale barn took up two-thirds of the structure and stretched a hundred yards behind the building. The only sound above the growling trucks was the bawling of uneasy cattle.

The constant south wind was setting her teeth on edge and she looked forward to the promised cool front the weathermen said was on the way. The air was full of dust and the smell of cow manure, diesel exhaust, and cedar. Most of the vehicles in the lot were pickups, and many were attached to cattle trailers. A two-lane highway rose and fell into the distance, following the rolling contours of the hill country.

Anna was in the passenger seat of Ewing's new 1968 Ford pickup. "Who is this guy?"

He rolled down the window and hung his arm out the door. "Stock salesman. I've met him a time or two in the past. He knows just about everybody in the business and can sell you some cows direct, or steer you towards a feller in your part of the country that'll do the same."

"It'll cut out the middle man, as far as sales are concerned. What do you think he'll charge me for the introduction?"

Stan's eyes changed for a moment. "Make sure it's money."

Her forehead wrinkled. "What do you mean by that?"

He held up a hand. "Nothing on you, but this is a man's world. Some of these old boys don't think the way I do, or you. Talk to him straight, and ask him what it'll take to buy his cows, cash on the barrelhead."

Anna studied the man she'd only known for a short time. You never knew what was going on behind another person's eyes, especially a near-stranger she'd met in a dance hall.

"Fine then. What do you think you'll get out of all this?"

"Maybe another date?"

"We haven't had one, yet."

"We danced."

"That's not the formal definition of a date."

"It's a start."

"It could be a finish too, buddy." She gave him a grin to soften the comment.

A truck slowed on the highway and pulled into the lot, stopping even with Stan's door. A thick, gray-haired man with a crewcut mirrored Stan's elbow out the window. "Howdy."

"Lucas."

"Who's that with you?"

"Anna Sloan. She's the one wants to buy some cows."

"She don't look like no stock buyer to me." Lucas chewed the soggy stub of his cigar. He grunted. "I don't usually deal with women. Go inside and buy all you want."

Anna leaned forward, already disliking the man. "I'm trying to save money. In the end, you'll be dealing with cash, not a woman."

"You got it on you?"

"Of course not. Am I buying from you?"

"I doubt it. I can give you a phone number or two for a price."

"Folks down here?"

"Could be. Where you from?"

"Northeast Texas."

"That covers a lot of territory."

"Give me numbers for people from Amarillo to Texarkana, then."

Lucas grunted, and Anna disliked him even more. She never cared for men who sounded like hogs when they were thinking.

"Come get in the truck with me."

Stan pitched his hat onto the dash. "Now hold on, Lucas."

The man held up a hand. "I just don't want to holler across you."

Anna yanked the door handle, glad she had a little snub-nosed thirty-eight tucked into her right boot. There was also a folding knife in the back pocket of her Levi's. "It's all right, Stan." She slammed the door and spoke to him through the open window. "Why don't you come pick me up tonight at the Belle Air motel about nine? You know where it is?"

"Sure do."

"I'll see you then." Holding her hair out of her face, she rounded the truck before Stan could argue and climbed into the cab with Lucas. Stan pulled away with a spurt of gravel, leaving them sitting apart from the other trucks and trailers.

"This'll cost you." Lucas adjusted the cigar with his tongue.

Anna pulled two twenties from her shirt pocket and laid them on the bench seat between them. Already irritated by the grit in her teeth, she packed down the anger swelling in her chest. "That's all you're gonna get."

He studied the bills for a moment. "That ain't enough."

She added a third. "I'm just looking to buy cows."

"No you ain't."

"What do you think I want, then?"

"I don't know what it is, but it ain't cows."

She opened the door and scooped up the twenties. "Fine then."

"Hey, wait a minute." Lucas reached across the seat and grabbed her wrist.

"You better turn a-loose if you want to keep that hand."

Seeing the look in her eyes, Lucas let go as if he'd grabbed a hot branding iron. "Okay. Okay. Just stop."

"What?"

"You really *are* in the market for cattle."

"I said I was."

"Why not get them in there, or at a sale barn somewhere close by your ranch?"

"I have my reasons."

"You want Mexican cattle?"

"No. I don't want anything with diseases."

"That's what it is." Lucas took the cigar from the corner of his mouth and used it like a pointer. "You're losing stock and you want to replace them without people around you knowing they're dying. You better be careful. What have they got? Hoof and mouth?"

She looked around as if to be sure no one was within hearing distance. "Brucellosis."

He drew a sharp breath.

"Don't worry. We bought some cows from Wyoming and they brought it into one pasture. We've cleaned 'em out, but Daddy don't want folks to know what happened, or we'll never sell another cow again."

"So that's it. A little sleight of hand?"

"That's all."

"One hundred and I can give you an old boy who's working cows up in Vernon right now. He knows folks on both sides of the river and they can set you up."

She only studied on it for a second. Vernon was less than two hundred miles west of Chisum, the perfect distance for rustlers in her part of the state to feel safe. "Deal."

Anna counted out the bills while Lucas wrote a phone number down on the inside of a pack of Gopher matches. He traded the matches for the money. She glanced down at the cover and read, "Steak Island, Austin's 'Most Exotic' restaurant. Now I know where to find you." She tucked the matchbook into her shirt pocket with the remaining cash.

Lucas followed her hand with his eyes, keeping them on her chest far too long. It took a moment for her comment to soak in and he snapped back to her face. "What for?"

"Just in case this whole thing turns sour." She slipped out of the cab and slammed the door.

"Hey, honey-child."

She stopped, squinting her eyes at the blowing dust. "Yeah?"

"I don't like you."

"I don't care, people prob'ly don't like you, neither."

Chapter Thirty-six

The blue norther finally arrived nine days after the Gold Dust fiasco and with it, plummeting temperatures. The old-time Texans always said that if you didn't like the weather, just wait a few minutes for it to change.

They were right. The rustlers swung their trailer full of stolen cattle into the dusty gravel lot of the Vernon stockyard, three hundred and fifty miles north of Austin. The cold north wind blew sand, small gravel, and trash across the truck.

Dale glared out the window. The redhead's eyes were listless, and he looked to be shrinking in on himself. "I hate this country."

The cattle that had been in the trailer for over twelve hours bawled for water and stomped the filthy floorboards.

Owen pulled around to get in line behind two other trailers waiting their turn to unload the stock at the sale barn. Owen tilted the stained Stetson back on his head and turned up the heater. His hair was even greasier than the day they murdered the Center Springs farmer.

"We got here just in time. I can't believe they're this busy on a Monday morning."

Dale pointed. "They're having a sale tomorrow. Things're different out here."

"I'll be damned."

"You sure this is safe?"

"Safe as can be."

"I don't want to get caught by no stock inspector."

Owen spoke with authority backed by nothing but arrogance. "Don't worry about that. I hear tell he don't show up here more'n once a month, and he was here two days ago. That's why we came out and I didn't figger on such a busy day. We're golden."

The trailer at the chute pulled away and the next truck swung around to back up against the pipe gate. Metal slammed as the hands unloaded a herd of complaining shorthorns. The rustlers waited their turn, and Owen backed in.

A freezing cowboy in broken-down boots and faded jeans motioned for him to roll the window down. Tightening the scarf around his neck, he tucked it into the barn coat that didn't look thick enough to turn the icy wind. He passed the clipboard through the open window. "Fill this out."

Keeping the window down despite the falling temperatures, Owen finished the paperwork while the cowboys unloaded the cattle. Nothing on the form was true. The owner of the sale barn would make the check out to their own bank in the name Owen was using. He'd drive directly to the bank and cash it, using the fake driver's license in his billfold.

The cowboy pulled his sweat-stained felt hat down tighter. He took the clipboard back. "No brands?"

"Naw, we got lazy. Our boss is 'bout done with ranchin' and is sellin' out."

"That's a dangerous business. There's folks who'll steal 'em if you ain't careful."

"I know it."

"You didn't put the name of the ranch down there."

Owen scribbled "Cobb Ranch" and handed it back.

Dale coughed, deep and wet. The cowboy looked concerned. "This weather's gonna make us all sick." He glanced down at Owen's handwriting. "Where's this? I don't recognize y'all."

"Montague County." Owen kept up the conversation to let Dale rest. "We were here last year. I remember *you*."

Embarrassed that he might have forgotten, the cowboy turned his back to the wind like a cow and chewed his lip. "How come y'all to bring 'em out this far?"

"The prices are better'n back home. It's been a good, wet year. Everybody and his duck's trying to sell off their stock, and they ain't getting what they ought to bring."

"Sure 'nough." Eyes tearing in the cold wind, the cowboy nodded with pride. "We do a fair business here."

"I know. That's why we came back."

The cowboy handed them a receipt and waved the next truck and trailer forward. "See y'all next time, and, buddy, you better get in out of this weather. That cough sounds like you're coming down with puh-monia."

Dale flicked a hand. "I believe you're right."

With a pocket full of cash three hours later, the rustlers pulled out of the bank parking lot and drove east, looking for their next mark as Dale's cough increased with every mile they traveled.

Chapter Thirty-seven

"Bass' gonna be fine."

Sitting in the hospital waiting room that Monday morning, Sheriff Cody Parker was relieved to hear John Washington's cheerful voice on the other end of the line. Despite what Miss Sweet, the local healer, told them about Bass being allergic to most everything he came into contact with, the stocky four-year-old boy woke up Tuesday morning with clearing lungs and an appetite.

A nun passed in silence, her habit scraping the polished floor. Cody wondered how she could almost float across the floor. "The folks here say he has the same thing Top's down with, but he's not near as bad off."

Cody swallowed a rising lump in his throat. Top was in bad shape and not getting any better. He was in an oxygen tent, wired to machines, and pumped full of antibiotics. He hadn't opened his eyes in days.

"That's what my doctor says, too. But little ol' Bass don't have weak lungs like Top. He's strong for his age, and he'll be all right even though he keeps a snotty nose most all the time. The doc looked in the rest of our kids' heads and says he don't see nothin' wrong with any of 'em."

"I bet Rachel's relieved."

"You ain't a-kiddin'. How's Top?"

"Not good. Doc Heinz says we'll know by tomorrow, but he thinks the medicine they're giving him is working." He swallowed again. Heinz remained optimistic, but Cody could tell by the look in his eyes that despite what he said, the doctor was losing hope.

"Would you tell Mr. Ned I'm sorry I can't come by…"

"Don't you worry about it. He knows you have to stay and take care of your family. I've got a question for you, though."

"Shoot."

"I got to tell you first that Curtis Gaines is dead from the same infection. He's had some problems and that pulled him down before this stuff got ahold of him. I hear he did some business with two men in dark suits and sunglasses before he got sick. You see any strangers in town by that description?"

The line crackled while John thought. "I don't reckon, but that don't mean much. There's folks coming and going these days to beat the band with this gold rush Miss Pepper's started."

"Well, check around when you get back to work and see what you can find."

"Are they tied up with all this in some way?"

"I believe they might be."

"I'll poke around."

"You do that. Oh, by the way, I got a call from the Dallas Sheriff's office to be on the lookout for grave robbers."

"Good lord, people digging up cemeteries?"

"Indian grave robbing. There's lots of stuff like skulls, bones, bowls, pipes showing up all of a sudden. They say a couple of leads point back here."

"They know for sure it's coming from Lamar County?"

"No, but he heard about Pepper's gold rush and thinks there might be some connection, like people are up here digging for treasure but finding graves and selling our people's bones. Ned says this whole part of the county is thick with graves we don't know about."

"I remember him saying there was a lot of tradin' here at one time."

"Yep, the river crossing was close, and all these springs were good for camping. I told Anna, and some of the others to keep an eye out. You do the same."

"Yessir."

Chapter Thirty-eight

The cattle rustlers were sitting in The Rig, a smoky honky-tonk restaurant southwest of Fort Worth, eating steak and washing it down with whiskey. Everyone who pushed into the warm interior shivered in relief to be inside the dim building lit by neon beer signs. Loud country music made it difficult to hear each other talk.

The bartender came to their table, wiping his hands on a stained apron tied around his waist. "Owen."

The greasy-haired rustler looked up and squinted his close-set eyes. "What do you need, Dennis?"

"Phone call for you."

Owen met his partner's lethargic gaze and cut another bite of T-bone. He didn't like Dale's gray color that matched the half-eaten, well-done steak on his plate. Dale stifled a phlegm-thickened cough. "I bet it's Ben."

"It would be, since he's the only one who knows we're here." Owen followed the bartender to the phone sitting beside the register. "Yeah?"

The man, who sometimes helped them move questionable cattle, got right to the point. "Somebody wants to buy some cows."

"Got a name?"

"Nope. It's a phone number. A feller I know in San Angelo knows a feller in Round Rock named Lucas DeWitt, who gave the number to a woman named Anna."

"A woman?"

"That's all I know. A woman who's looking for cattle."

"Why don't she go to a sale barn?"

"How the hell do I know? You want the number or not?"

"Sure." Owen motioned for Dennis who brought him a pencil and order pad. He licked the dull point. "Shoot." He wrote down the number and hung up. "Dennis, gonna call long distance."

"I'll put it on your bill."

He dialed the number and a female voice answered. "Hello?"

"I hear you want to buy some cows."

"Sure do." The voice brightened. "Who is this?"

"Oh, let's say Mr. Smith."

"All right, Mr. *Smith*. I'm looking for thirty or so head."

"What breed?"

"What do you have?"

"Whatever you want."

"I hear music. That's pretty confident from a guy doing business in a honky-tonk."

"I'm a broker, and I work out of this restaurant. If you'd do a little reading in the library, you'll find that cattlemen have been doing business in restaurants since the Civil War."

Owen might look like an addled high school dropout, but he'd graduated with honors. He was too lazy to make money by hard work. He intended to let others do the work and he'd get rich off *them*.

The woman on the other end hesitated, as if the dressing-down hurt her feelings. "I see your point. Look, I'd like to buy some Herefords if you have any stock. I hear you can deliver."

"Sure can, depending on this cold front. They say there may be some falling weather out of this norther. When and where would that delivery be?"

"How about my daddy's ranch in Roxton?" She read him the route address and gave him directions.

Dale was staring absently at his steak when Owen returned

to the table. It took a moment to realize Owen was back. "Was it Ben?"

Owen shook his head in disgust. "A woman wants to buy some cows."

"A woman?"

"That or a man with a really sexy voice. I'm lookin' forward to meetin' her. She sounds like a real man-eater, if you know what I mean."

Dale didn't catch his drift. "Where do we deliver them?"

"Roxton. That's not so far from where we've been watching that two-thousand-acre ranch in Bonham."

Dale nodded and wiped a sheen of sweat from his forehead. His eyes were red and liquid. "It's gonna be a cold bitch, loading them up, though."

"The timing's perfect. Everybody'll be inside by the fire at night. Hey, are you all right?"

Dale shivered as a customer pushed through the door, bringing a gust of cold air that washed over their table. He sipped from a glass of whiskey beside his plate. "Let's get some aspirin when we leave. I got a fever and my stomach don't feel all that great, neither."

"Drink some more whiskey. My old man always said that a toddy'd fix whatever ails you."

"Forget the toddy part, but he was right." Dale finished the bourbon and held it up for a refill. "I'll have another."

"I'll join you." Owen swallowed the last of his beer. "I believe I'll move to Scotch."

"You never ordered that before."

"I never had the money. We're gettin' rich, and I intend to enjoy what's coming to me."

"Us."

"Yeah. That's what I meant. Us."

Chapter Thirty-nine

Deputy John Washington steered into the Holiday Inn parking lot. Chisum had only two motels decent enough for tourists or travelers. The other was the Ramada Inn on the opposite corner of Highway 271. The norther had arrived in full force, and though the heater was on, cold radiated through the windshield.

Instead of going to the office to ask around about the visitors in dark suits, John parked under the distinctive sign where he could see all of the rooms in the two-story L-shaped motel. He kept the engine running to stay warm. Fifteen minutes later a door opened on the ground floor and a colored maid in a dingy white cotton uniform stepped outside with an armload of sheets.

She flinched at the chill and dropped the linens into the bin. John exited his car as she knocked on the next door. "Maid service!" She knocked again and when no one answered, used a passkey and cracked the door open. "Maid!"

John moved up behind her and took one arm, pushing the short, round woman into the room. "Hey!" She twisted in his grip and stopped. "John!" She threw herself into his great arms and he hugged her back with the same enthusiasm.

"Howdy, baby!"

She squealed and wrapped both arms around his neck. "It's so good to see you!"

"Same here."

"Shut that door. You're lettin' all the heat out."

He closed the red door and tilted his hat back, eyeing Junie, his youngest sibling.

She looked up at him and smiled. "How's Bass?"

"Right as rain. I done took him home and Rachel's tending the whole bunch."

"My stars, I don't know what that good woman sees in you."

"Can't say myself."

"What'choo doing here, and why'd you push me inside that-away?"

"You ain't got no coat on, and you'd catch double walkin' pu'mony if we was to talk out in that icebox. I need to ask you some questions."

"Well, as long as we're inside, I got work to do. First things first." She stepped into the bathroom and flushed the toilet. "I swear, lazy folks don't think they got to flush in a motel." She turned the television off as well.

"Ain't that the truth? It's a shame we take indoor plumbing for granted."

"We should all be ashamed. Got kinfolk who still use out-houses not twenty miles from here who'd dearly love a flush toilet."

John leaned against the chest of drawers and crossed his ankles. "President Nixon says we're gonna put men on the moon in the next few months, and here people still livin' like when we was kids."

Junie pulled one corner of the wrinkled bottom sheet free and stripped the bed. "What kinda questions you here to ask me?"

"I'm looking into something and wondered if you'd seen two suspicious men staying here in the past couple of weeks."

"Suspicious how?"

"City people. It was back before this norther came in, a week to ten days or so, if that'll help. They wore dark suits and had crewcuts. Wore shades a lot."

She rolled the sheets and pillowcases into a bundle and pitched it on the floor. "Drove a dark car."

John raised an eyebrow. "That's right."

"Yep. I seen 'em. They stayed here for a couple of days."

"Tell me about 'em."

She picked up a full ashtray and dumped it into the trash. "They's quiet. One coughed up a storm like smokers do. He looked at me like I was dogshit, and never spoke a word. They's goin' out one mornin' when I was cleaning the rooms. The other'n was nice enough. Held the door for me to come in and said they'd be gone and out of my way. The mean one call him Mr. Brown. Like that a real name. Shoulda said Mr. Smith. It'd be the same thang."

"You see anything? Papers. Notes?"

"You mean newspapers?"

"No, stuff businessmen carry."

"I wouldn't look at it if they did. I ain't about to get fired from this job, and I ain't no snoop. Mama'd blister my hide even today if I was go to diggin' through customers' business."

John held up a hand. "Didn't say you'd do that. I was just wondering if you saw anything out of the ordinary."

"Like two men who look a lot alike, same haircut and suits, but didn't smile much. Out of the ordinary like that?"

He laughed. "Yeah."

"No, but I did notice one thing. One of 'em took down a phone number on one of them pads we put out with the motel's name. I only noticed 'cause it wasn't like our numbers and he left a five-dollar bill beside it for a tip. I wish ever'body else'd tip me like that."

"How so?"

"How so what?"

"How was the number so different you'd notice?"

"Why, Miss Sweet's phone number is SU4-8135. But that'n was long as my finger. It had one of them new area codes on it, and at the end of that long line was an X and three more numbers. I never saw nothing like that befo'."

John saw a similar pad lying on the dresser. "I don't suppose you remember that area number do you?"

"Sho do, part of it anyway, cause it's one number away from Nanny's house number. That's why I can remember it."

He waited.

"It's two-forty, Nanny's house bein' two thirty-nine."

John hugged her again. "I'll let you get back to your rat-killin'."

"Think that'll help you?"

He picked up the phone book and opened to the front pages, quickly finding what he was looking for. A map of the United States that covered two pages was broken into dozens of jigsaw pieces showing what part of the country was assigned each code. Area code 240 was Washington D.C.

He closed the book and put it under the telephone. "It already has."

Chapter Forty

Dr. Heinz called Miss Becky and Ned into the hall outside of Top's room. "Y'all, we're losing your boy."

The hair stood up on the back of Ned's neck. His chest tightened and he choked down a sob.

"No." Miss Becky backed against the wall, one hand over her mouth.

"We're doing everything we can, but now he's barely able to breathe on his own. If he keeps failing, we're gonna have to put him on a ventilator."

"What's that?" Ned knew the answer, but he needed to hear Heinz say it.

"That's a machine that'll breathe for him."

"For how long?" Miss Becky's eyes were closed.

"Until he's rallied and can take over, or…"

Ned's sharp question cut the doctor off. "Or what, Heinz?"

Dr. Heinz looked into Ned's flashing blue eyes and took half a step back. "Ned, I'm just telling you what I know. If the boy—"

"Top. His name is Top, and you'll use it instead of calling my grandson 'the boy,' you understand?"

"Fine then. Top will stay on the ventilator until he can breathe on his own again. That could be for any length of time. If this infection does things we're not expecting, the results could be worse."

"Worse?" Tears ran down both of Miss Becky's wrinkled cheeks.

"We honestly don't know what's happening inside his body. The bacteria seem to attack the lungs, but that could change and damage other organs, and that could include the brain or his kidneys. We just don't know any more. The truth is we'd need to autopsy…"

Heinz stopped at the looks of anguish on their faces, realizing what he'd almost spoken aloud. "Look, I just needed to let y'all know what's happening. Hang on and I'll keep you updated. We're doing everything we can." He paused. "This is hard. I'm sorry." Heinz spun and left as quickly as possible.

Miss Becky buried her face in her hands as deep sobs racked her body. Not knowing what else to do, Ned gathered her into his arms. After five long minutes, her crying lessened and Miss Becky wiped her tears. She tilted her head up at her husband. "Ned."

"What, hon?"

"You don't want me sayin' this, but I'm gonna do it anyway. If they put Top on one of them machines, he might never come back. I've heard of people they've taken off and they didn't do nothin' but lay there for years afterward. If that happens, you know what you have to do."

"I'm not gonna do it."

"Ned." Her eyes flashed at him for the first time since they were newlyweds. "You'll help him go on. That's the reason you have your Gift, and you'll use it to ease that baby into Heaven, if need be."

Ned's eyes burned. He swallowed. "Will it be right?"

"You'll know that when you hold him."

"I hope that never comes."

"But if it does, you do what you have to do. Promise me."

"I ain't makin' no promises, but one."

"What's that?"

"I'm mad as a Jap, and somebody's gonna pay for this."

Chapter Forty-one

The Broken Spoke's dance floor was crowded for a Tuesday night when Deputy Anna Sloan and Stan Ewing gave up and returned to their table. The house bandmembers on the low stage were sweating under the lights in a blue cloud of cigarette smoke, playing current hits sprinkled with Hank Williams songs which always brought couples onto the floor. Harried waitresses moved through the crowd, doing their best to stay ahead of the empty bottles and cans.

Anna sipped from her warm beer on her last night in Austin. "I never did like to dance in that kind of crowd."

"The music's good, though. I'm glad we came."

"I wasn't going to leave town without saying goodbye."

The song ended and the band launched into another.

Stan laced his fingers on the checkered tablecloth. "Can I come up and see you in a week or so?"

Anna felt her stomach sink. She found herself becoming attached to the lanky cowboy, but their whole relationship was based on lies and false pretenses. "I'll give you a call."

"Why can't I call you?"

"Well…"

Her answer was interrupted when a drunk in a cheap hat stumbled into their table. Stan barely caught his beer bottle as it sloshed a foamy eruption into the air. The drunk leaned over, his face only inches from Stan's. His breath was pure alcohol. "Hey, buddy. I'm gonna whip your ass."

Surprised, Stan pulled his head back. "What for?"

"You've been hoarding the best-looking woman in the place." The drunk leaned toward Stan. "Me and the boys want a dance with her."

"Well, sorry. We're here with each other."

"You don't need to speak for me." Anna bristled at Stan's response. "Look, there's some cute gals over there. Why don't you go ask one of *them*?" She inclined her head toward a group of single women at a nearby table.

Cheap Hat shook his head. "Nope. You're my girl."

"I'm nobody's girl."

Stan started to stand, but Anna put one hand on his leg. The light pressure held him in place. She felt the situation spinning out of control.

Cheap Hat leaned forward with both hands on his thick thighs. "Get up, or you a coward?"

Keeping her hand on Stan's leg, Anna would have sworn she could feel the air suck out of the room. The music receded into the background and the voices around her became indistinct. "He's not a coward. It's me that don't want him to get up."

"Who you gonna listen to, sissy? A woman? Get up and let's go outside."

"He's not getting up."

Stan's expression hardened. "Anna, don't speak for me, neither."

She saw that she'd already lost the argument. "I'm trying to get this creep away from us."

Cheap Hat flicked out one hand, flipping Stan's Stetson onto the table and knocking over a bottle. Foam spilled onto the table. The lanky cowboy placed both hands on the tabletop and rose slowly. "Outside."

"Good." Cheap Hat spun and headed for the door, followed by four others.

Anna took Stan's arm. "He's gone. Let's go out the back."

"I'm not running."

"You're not proving a thing. This is nothing but a dick-measuring contest and I really don't care."

"I *live* here. I come to this dance hall pretty regular. I can't run."

"I'll make it look like I've pulled you away and it'll be my fault."

"That's just as bad." Stan jerked his arm away and snatched his hat from the table. "You stay in here. I'll be back."

"You won't win against five of them."

"I only have to whip one."

"Look, I have experience in this. They're gonna jump you as soon as you step out the door."

"Experience? You talk guys out of fights pretty regular?"

Anna weighed the options and decided her undercover work was over. "I'll tell you everything later, but right now you need to listen. I'm a sheriff's deputy and I've seen fights like this before."

Stan paused and looked down on her. "First you're a rancher's daughter, and now you're a deputy? Look, we can finish this conversation later and you can tell me the truth if you know it, but see all these people staring at us? Right now I have to deal with this guy."

Her heart sank when another man in western clothes joined them at the table. "Stan, you gonna stand here and make goo-goo eyes at this gal, or you gonna go out and whip that guy's ass for knocking your hat off?"

Caught up in a testosterone-driven male ritual stretching back centuries, Stan abandoned common sense and squared his shoulders. "I'm going outside."

Neon lights reflected off the bottles as Anna pushed away from the table to follow him outside. "Dammit!"

Chapter Forty-two

It was dark outside when I opened my eyes, wondering why I was in a clear plastic tent.

The room was lit by a dim bulb. Nothing was right. My bed was narrow, and the other window in my bedroom was missing. It took a few seconds to remember I wasn't at home, but in the hospital.

I turned my head to find Miss Becky asleep sitting up in a chair. Her hands were folded over the Bible in her lap. A tickle in my chest made me want to cough, but I held it down for a second and it passed.

Drowsy, I closed my eyes again and the little cough came anyway. Nothing big, just a little chuck that would have been a quiet little poot if it'd come from the other end.

The sound was enough to wake her up, though. She leaned forward to see inside the oxygen tent. I turned my head so she could see my eyes were open. "Howdy."

Her breath caught and the frown on her face disappeared to be replaced with wrinkled smiles. She pulled back a flap so we could talk. "Praise the Lord! You're back with us. Hallelujah! How you feeling, baby?"

"Pretty good."

"You breathin' all right?"

I drew a deep breath mixed with a wide yawn. It felt good

to pull air down deep without coughing it back out again. "I believe so. It's night."

"You've been asleep for a long time."

I closed my eyes for a second and remembered the Poisoned Gift's dream, the white operating room, and my spiral toward the light. "I was bad for a while, wasn't I?"

"We thought we'd lost you once." Her voice broke.

"There was a bright light."

"That was God. I guess He decided it wasn't time for you to go."

My mouth was dry. "I need a drink."

She helped me sip from a paper straw stuck in a glass. That cool drink of water made a lot of difference in the way I felt. I laid back and closed my eyes. "Where's everybody else?"

"They all went home to get some rest, all except for your grandpa. He just left to get some coffee down in the café." Miss Becky started for the door. The soft sound of her shoes on the floor told me she was going to get somebody. "Wait a minute."

"I need to tell the nurses you're awake, hon. Your Grandpa'll want to know you're past the crisis."

"In a minute. I have to tell you what I dreamed before I forget it."

I needed her to hear what the Poisoned Gift had put in my mind.

"All right."

"They were from the Poisoned Gift."

She went back to her chair and sat heavy, like her legs had give out. "What was it?"

I told her about the white room and the gray rat that stood and ran from the stream and into hills that rose in the distance. She listened, nodding, with her eyes closed until I finished. "Does that make any sense to you at all?"

She rubbed her hand over the Bible's leather cover. "None of them dreams make sense right off. We'll figure it out directly."

"That usually comes later, after everything's happened."

"That's how the Lord wants it to work."

"It don't make no sense, giving me these visions but in a way we can't make 'em out 'till it's all over and done with."

"We don't get to understand everything."

"Is my Poisoned Gift like Grandpa's?"

She was quiet for so long I thought she was holding her breath. "His helps people through the Gates. Yours ain't the same…it's different."

A picture flashed in my mind of Grandpa sitting on the side of the bed, holding my head in his lap and raining tears on my face. A cold chill went down my back. "Did he think he was going to have to help me pass like Mr. Jules? Was I that close, seeing the light?"

Miss Becky's voice hitched. "How do you know about that?"

"I heard y'all talking after you thought I was asleep. I was too sick to go under and heard everything you said. I think I saw it from up there in the corner of the ceiling, but it didn't last long. Then I felt a hard yank, like somebody pulling a rope tied around my head, and the next thing I knew I was dozing in and out while people talked. Was he about to help me?"

The wind rose until the moan became a shriek. The window leaked a little, and I felt a soft kiss of cold air on my arm.

"He thought he might have to, but nothing happened."

We both had a Gift we didn't like and all of a sudden I needed to know about his, so maybe I could understand mine. "Tell me how his started. Maybe I can see some other doctor about my Poisoned Gift if I needed to. Maybe somebody can teach me how to stop it. Is that what Grandpa did? You mentioned it a while back, but did he just quit using it?"

"Hon, you're too weak."

"You won't be able to tell me later when folks start coming in, once they hear I'm not dying. Please, Miss Becky. "

Her face went hard and it was the first time I'd ever seen her like that. Miss Becky's wrinkled forehead and cheeks were a roadmap to her life, but she always wore an expression that was mostly pleasant, though sometimes worried.

This one was as strange as if I'd talked ugly. It took a good long while for her to come back, and she shuddered like she was cold. She finally found one of those wrinkles at the corner of her mouth and I was relieved to see it turn up.

"All right, hon…" She trailed off for a minute and I watched her gather the words.

Chapter Forty-three

Folks in Center Springs dealt with the Great Depression better than some other places. Rain was scarce in 1934 and all of Texas withered in the heat, but there was barely enough moisture to sustain life. Prices were down and even if a crop made, the return was less than substantial.

The Parkers were having a hard time making ends meet like everybody else, but a young family with four little kids down in the bottoms was in worse trouble. Ned and Becky drove their Model T to town one Saturday and bought a sack of groceries to drop off at the Woods' so they'd have something to eat besides beans.

On the way home, they took the graded dirt turnoff in Powderly and wound through the hardwoods, enjoying the shade provided by a thick canopy of trees. Only half a mile from the gin, a wider gravel road intersected the one they traveled. A commotion caused Ned to slow, but he would have bled off what little speed they had anyway for the people who tended to drive their cars much faster on the gravel road. There'd been two or three near-misses between the new Model A cars and wagons. Sometimes a horse and buggy blocked the road, or slowed things down so much the fast drivers had to take to the ditch.

That's what happened. It was as bad a wreck as they'd ever seen, stopping a line of cotton wagons beside the gin. A Model

T and a Model A were all tore up, steaming and smoking. A wagon lay on one side, one wheel still spinning slow and lazy.

A horse thrashed and screamed in pain. A confusion of shouting farmers worked to cut it free of the harness while others yelled over the cacophony to shoot the animal and put it out of its misery.

"Somebody's probably dead in all that." Ned wasn't the constable yet, but he pulled around the wagons and drove as close as possible to see if he could help.

Hands over her ears to block out the horse's human-like screams, Becky closed her eyes. "Dear Lord, please spare those people in the wagon, and put that poor thing out of its misery."

The injured gelding lay on its side, kicking its life away in a tangle of harness. Ike Reader put his skinny knee on its neck and sawed at the leather harness with his folding knife. He cut the last strap and jumped back. The horse thrashed for a moment and struggled to its feet. Planting its back hooves, it spun toward Ned's car. A huge knot on its right front cannon told the farmers gathered at the scene that gelding's leg was broken.

Showing the whites of his eyes, and despite the leg, the injured horse charged Ned's Model T. Instead of escaping, the gelding reached the car and planted his rear hooves as if reined to a dead stop.

"Easy boy." Ned spoke low and easy, stunned that the horse was even standing.

Shivering and blowing, the gelding stumbled closer and lowered his head. Ned reached out and the horse stuck his head inside the car, resting it against the future constable's shoulder.

Becky's eyes filled with tears. Used to raising and slaughtering their own meat, she still felt for an animal's suffering and this one was hurting more than any she'd ever seen.

With his left hand, Ned curled his arm and rubbed the gelding's soft nose like he'd done thousands of times to other horses. At the same time, he reached with his right hand and felt for the revolver on the seat beside his leg. The right thing to do was to shoot it right then and there.

An electrical jolt numbed Ned's shoulder at the same time the horse's muscles twitched and hardened. "Damn it!" Ned grabbed his shoulder, his face twisted in shock.

The animal moaned, groaned and shivered like he was being electrocuted. A heartbeat later, his head snapped up and he stepped back like a young, healthy horse.

"What happened?" Becky leaned forward to see. "He bite you?"

"No. I don't know what happened!"

The injured horse whirled and charged back down the dirt road toward the wreck on a leg that flopped and slapped the ground.

"Listen, y'all look out!" Ike Reader warned the men trying to help the woman driver hanging limp halfway out of her Model A. "Here comes that damned horse again!" They scattered as the gelding ran to the woman and stuck his head against her.

She convulsed and woke up screaming at the same time the other car burst into flames. The gelding dropped as dead as if he'd been shot.

Ike hollered. "We were wrong! She ain't dead! Quick, get her out!"

Ned gave that old Model T the gas and they slid to a stop just feet away. Ike and Frank Flynn threw a chain around the front bumper. The other end was already attached to the revived woman's axle. Ned mashed down on the reverse pedal, pushed the throttle lever and they shot backward. The chain snapped taut and he jerked the Model A away from the burning wreckage. Ned pulled the car to safety and killed the Flivver's engine.

They jumped out and Ned ran to check on the woman who was still alive, despite the frightening wound in her head, and recognized her as a teller at their bank in Chisum. "Don't worry, Fannie. We'll get you out."

She blinked, revealing only the whites of her eyes. "Ned, I need you to come close." Shocked, he leaned in and she whispered, her voice sounding dead. "You have to do it for them."

"What's that?" He refused to look at those eyes, and instead found himself staring at the horrible open gash revealing the woman's brain. "Do what for who? You got somebody else in there?"

"Ned, I was there, and He said for you to listen."

"You were where?"

"Heaven. He said for you to listen."

"Who?"

"I was there, but your horse pulled me back for a minute to tell you this."

"I don't have a horse…"

"You have a job to do."

"What?"

Her eyes twitched, as though the very eyeballs were trying to escape their sockets. "Help them release. Sometimes folks need help and it's all right to open the door for 'em."

"Huh?"

"Open the Gate."

Her eyes closed to slits and she fell silent and limp.

Ned and Becky helped tidy the dead for Sheriff Poole and drove home. The sun was down and they ate supper by kerosene light in the old Apple homestead they rented, talking about what happened at the accident. They went to bed that night and the next morning the entire incident seemed like a dream.

A week later, a colored family showed up in their bare yard and a shirtless man in overalls and worn-out brogans knocked on the porch post. The mother in a faded flour sack dress looked twenty years older than her age. Her six children wore similarly faded hand-me-downs, but all were clean and patched.

Becky opened the door and stepped out on the porch to find a stout man holding a profoundly retarded child wrapped in a ragged quilt. She saw the child move a feeble arm. "Help y'all?"

"Miss Becky. I'm Marcus Roosevelt. Is Mr. Ned in, please, ma'am?"

"We ain't hirin', Marcus. It's hard times and we're doing our own harvest."

"Not lookin' for work, ma'am." Marcus and his wife exchanged looks. "We heard Mr. Ned can help us." He adjusted the quilt around the little girl. "Last night an angel with glowing wings come to us and said to bring our little girl to your house."

Ned came to the door behind her. His face was white as a sheet. "Y'all don't need to be here. I can't help you." He dug in his pocket and pulled out a wrinkled dollar bill. "Here. Hope this helps." He turned and went into the living room.

Stunned by his unusual action, Becky watched his retreating back. She couldn't bear for the family to stand scorching in the sun. She did something she'd never done before. Becky Parker invited a colored family into her house. The nervous couple filed in behind her, through the kitchen, followed by their children. They stood quiet in the living room, watching Ned in his rocking chair.

He refused to look at them. Marcus cleared his throat. "Mr. Ned. I for shore ain't used to this, but an angel come to us in the night and said you could help. See, this here baby in my arms is dyin' hard and we done been to the doctor and he said there ain't nothin' nobody can do for her. She's sufferin', suh, and that ain't right for a baby that ain't done nothin' to nobody."

Ned rocked and refused to meet Marcus' eyes.

Marcus moved the quilt and Ned's dull gaze followed his hands. The blind child who was nothing but a sack of bones with a swollen stomach looked to be about eight to ten years old. She was deformed worse than anyone he'd ever seen, her face misshapen, with jumbled teeth that protruded from her slack mouth. She convulsed in Marcus' arms.

"I can't help you." Ned's eyes fell to the rag rug under Albert's feet. He shook his head and rocked until a precocious five-year-old with dimples and short hair held in abeyance by strips of blue ribbon circled her daddy.

She stepped between Ned's legs and climbed into his lap, taking his face between her little hands, forcing his chin up to listen. "M'name's Pickles and a beautiful angel come to my house said it's okay for you to help my sister. Her name's Tom-Tom and she's a full ten years old today."

Ned choked out a reply that sounded as if his heart was breaking. "No."

"The Lord told my daddy. It's all right."

Marcus stepped forward without asking and placed Tom-Tom in Ned's lap. The ragged quilt fell off, revealing her wasted body in a rag diaper.

Ned held the invalid child like a baby. With her head under his chin, he rocked while tears leaked down his cheeks.

"You don't need me to tell you how." Pickles rubbed his knee and rested one hand on her big sister's bony leg.

Ned twitched, gasped, and tightened as if his whole body was cramping.

"See, you already know."

From the corners of his eyes, Ned saw electricity sparkle like fireflies in the air. One of the fireflies became a narrow bolt of lightning that shot upward, disappearing into swirling red storm clouds built near the ceiling. A high-pitched humming filled Ned's head and he was sure it was swelling like a balloon. He closed his eyes and held Tom-Tom who relaxed in his arms.

Ned went rigid and the silent clouds above opened at the same time a warm glow ran through his body. A feeling of love and peace replaced the taut vibration of electrical current and he felt Tom-Tom's thin little soul sweep past his face like a soft, warm baby's breath.

A cool, unseen set of tiny hands caressed his cheeks. The clouds broke at the same time a soft yellow ray of light pulled the phantom hands away. Tom-Tom took one last breath and let it out. Ned collapsed inward and closed his eyes.

The clouds were gone when Ned opened them, feeling completely worn out. The room was silent as Pickles put one knee on the rocker's seat and pulled herself over Tom-Tom's still body high enough to reach Ned's face. She kissed him on the lips. "Thank you, Mr. Ned."

Becky took her eyes off the animated little girl and realized her parents were weeping. It was then she saw Tom-Tom was gone. She'd died without even a sigh.

Marcus gently took Tom-Tom from Ned's arms. "Thank you, sir. That angel was right."

The mama handed Becky a bundle wrapped in a clean flour sack. By the feel, she knew it contained something precious to the family, a slab of bacon. "Hon, I cain't take this."

"We need to give y'all something for releasing our baby from this cruel ol' world."

"Feed this to your kids." Becky handed it back. "Come with me."

They went into the kitchen. Becky took a pound of butter wrapped in cheesecloth from their secondhand icebox. "I want you to take this with you, and I won't ask nothing but your name."

The woman accepted the gift. "Wilma."

"Well, you take care of these babies, Wilma."

In the living room, Pickles grabbed Ned around the neck and gave him another wet kiss. "You take that one to somebody else who's gonna need it when it happens again."

Ned cried for an hour after they left with Tom-Tom's little body wrapped again in her quilt, barely gathering himself before another wave washed over him. He knew what was going to happen the minute Marcus, Wilma, and their family showed up in the yard. He'd seen it all before in a flash when the gelding put his head against his chest and passed something to him that no one could explain.

Chapter Forty-four

I was afraid to say anything when Miss Becky stopped talking and took a deep, shuddering breath. She dabbed her eyes with a towel she'd thrown over her shoulder. "He asked me what would happen if somebody else needed help passing over, because he wasn't sure he could do it again, and I told him it'd happen when it happened and that's what he was supposed to do.

"We wondered for weeks about it and thought the Gift was gone, that maybe it was only supposed to happen that one time, but around Thanksgiving we went to visit some kinfolk who had their grandmother and she was just barely hanging on, praying for death, but Death wouldn't come.

"They'd heard about Tom-Tom and asked if Ned would hold her for a minute to see if he could ease her pain and release her. He didn't want to, but I convinced him to go in there and sit on the edge of the bed. He sat near the head, and put that old woman's head in his lap. She got easy, went limp, and went home to Jesus.

"That's when we knew for sure he had the Gift."

"So if it was for good, and y'all knew what was going to happen, why'd he quit?"

She swallowed. "Some people from town thought he was doing more than holding those poor people. There was a hotshot lawyer here in town at the time and he went after Ned, wanting to convict him of murder. There was a trial, and it was a mess. O.C. took Ned on as his lawyer, and after a long, long trial, he was...what's the word?...acquitted. But at the same time, some church folks accused him of thinking he was Jesus, and that hurt him worse'n anything.

"When the smoke finally cleared, he said he'd never help anyone cross again, and didn't do it until Old Jules needed to pass."

"I never heard anything about it."

"Most everybody that had anything to do with it is dead and gone, and them who're still alive put it aside and went on with their lives, just like us."

I started to ask another question, but she gave my leg a pat and stood. "Now, I don't want any more questions, and you just let it be."

She walked out as quick as you please, leaving me laying there with about a million questions. I dozed off a little later, trying to make sense of it all.

Chapter Forty-five

Anna was right. Cheap Hat and his friends were waiting for Stan the moment he stepped out the Broken Spoke's front door and into the dark parking lot. She shivered, more from nerves than a chill and found herself in the middle of the events that quickly spun out of control.

Stan stopped near the cars parked behind the cedar hitching posts and pointed at Cheap Hat. "Tell these other bastards that it's you and me."

"Naw it ain't!" A short, squatty guy with hair curling over his collar stepped forward and threw a right toward Stan's jaw.

His eyes were on Cheap Hat, but Stan saw the blow coming in his peripheral vision. He pulled back just enough for the jaw-breaker to miss. He caught the man's wrist and used his attacker's momentum to yank him off balance and into a drugstore-cowboy watching the action unfold.

Taking advantage of his surprise move, Stan spun and threw his shoulder into a left that exploded Cheap Hat's narrow nose. Blood spurted as he wailed and stumbled back.

The other four no-accounts closed in. Stan hit another, but the punch left him wide open. A fist hard as cement caught him in the temple and his head snapped sideways. Ears ringing and stunned, Stan juked to his left to gain some room.

Recovering from the pain and his surprise, Cheap Hat threw

himself at Stan as the group closed like wolves. The lanky cowboy went down fighting.

Her head buzzing with fury, Anna lunged forward and grabbed a collar and jerked the attacker backward. She hit him with a fist at the point where his jaw hinged. The crack was as distinct as a hammer blow and he staggered sideways.

Knowing she was outweighed and outmatched, she tugged a lead-weighted sap from inside the waistband under her shirt and cracked the nearest skull, knocking the man's hat spinning. "Back off! Sheriff's deputy!"

Anna's announcement went unnoticed, but her assault gave Stan enough room to regain his feet. He drove a fist into Cheap Hat's stomach. She drew her arm back for another blow and a guy with curly girl's hair grabbed her around the waist. He slung her into the side of a car. Her head dented the door and the world spun.

The point of a boot connected with her side, knocking the air from her lungs in a painful whoosh and Anna curled into a ball to defeat the next kick. The distinct meaty sounds of fists, grunts, and exclamations filled the night air as she struggled for breath.

She was only out of action for a few seconds, but it was long enough for Stan's attackers to put the boots to him. Groggy, Anna saw the combatants ringed by patrons of the honky-tonk who'd come outside to watch. Struggling to roll onto her hands and knees that refused to cooperate, she saw two pairs of polished boots push through the crowd.

Loud, authoritative voices rang overhead. "That's it, boys! This fight's over!"

Anna's vision cleared enough to see two Austin police officers shove the combatants back. "Deputy sheriff!" Sitting against the car and holding her badge aloft with one hand, she felt blood running from her nose.

● ● ● ● ●

Stan was unconscious when the ambulance unloaded him at the Emergency Room at Austin's Brackenridge Hospital. Half a dozen listless patients slumped in their chairs, waiting for the doctors to finish with the more urgent injuries involving a car wreck, one knifing, and another fistfight from a different club.

Sitting on an examination table, Anna identified herself to the doctors on duty as a sheriff's deputy from Chisum. The Austin police officers stood between her and the nurses' desk.

They wore khaki-colored shirts and midnight blue, almost black, caps. The oldest was in his sixties and the lines in his face mapped a hard life on the capital's streets. He nodded toward the icepack Anna was holding on her eye and cheek. "You're gonna have a nice shiner, and that nose don't look none too good."

"I'll live."

"Um, hum. M'name's Earl. So you're here doing undercover work."

His wasn't a question as such, but it required a response. Her ribs ached, but didn't feel broken. "Yessir. I used to work for Harris County, but then took a job not long ago with the Sheriff's Office in Chisum. We've had a lot of rustling in our part of the state and Sheriff Parker sent me down to see what I could find out."

"You should have told us first."

Anna had nothing to say about that, knowing she was clearly in the wrong.

"Your sheriff thinks they're unloading them here?"

She turned her attention to the younger officer. "Yep. Well, the truth is that we don't know where they're turning them. I'm following up on a lead, and that's all."

Earl thought for a minute. "Jim, have you heard anything about stolen cattle?"

"Nope." He tilted his cap back. "But we don't get around the stockyards much."

She didn't mention the contact she'd made. "That's all right.

I was finished. Stan asked me out tonight and I wanted to go dancing one more time before I go home tomorrow, but then before things got out of hand, I had to tell him." She glanced at the doors leading to the ER.

"Oh what a tangled web we weave." Earl stood with a basset hound look on his face and slid both hands into his pockets.

"It's not like I'm down here slutting around." Anna's face reddened at the quote. "It's called undercover work. You guys know that."

"What time you leaving tomorrow?"

"You trying to get me out of town, Earl?"

The older man nodded. "Yep. Go on back up where you came from. Chisum, wasn't it?"

Tim adjusted his cap again, as if it wasn't tilted enough to suit him. "Hey, where'd you say Chisum is?"

"I didn't. It's about a hundred miles northeast of Dallas."

For the first time since they arrived, Jim looked interested. "Earl, wasn't there some connection there with that dead man from the motel?"

Anna's eyes flicked to Earl. "Dead man?"

"Yep. A maid at a motel in Round Rock called it in a day or so ago. Found a guy dead in his bed and brought him here. They screwed up and should have sent him to the county morgue, but the driver was new. Had a receipt in his pocket from some place in Chisum."

She wondered if it was anyone she knew. Her neck prickled, a warning sense she'd come to rely on as a peace officer. "You have a name for him?"

"Nope. We weren't involved. Just heard about it. Say, is there some connection between the two of you?"

"Not that I know of." She rose and went to the nurses' station.

A young woman who looked to be barely out of her teens was writing on a pad. Her cap and uniform were snow white. She popped her gum. "That's gonna be a nice shiner. Help you?"

"I'm Deputy Sheriff Anna Sloan. Those officers over there told me a body came in that was D.O.A. a few days ago."

"So?"

"Were you working then?"

"Who'd you say you were?"

"Deputy Sloan."

The woman's eyes roamed Anna's features, taking in her boots, jeans, and western shirt. "Where's your badge, *Deputy?*"

Her right eye and cheek throbbing, Anna slapped the ice bag on the counter and dug in her pocket. She hammered the badge beside it. "It's right here, and in about two seconds I'm gonna make a phone call and slap you with a warrant to look through your purse, or even wherever it is that you live. You look to me like one of those dope-smoking potheads that spends their nights stoned on grass, or the pills you snitch during the day."

The nurse's eyes flicked toward the cops, then down to the counter. "Hey, chill out, man! I was only asking."

Anna felt the officers move up behind her. "Were you working last Friday morning a week ago when they brought that body in instead of taking it to the morgue?"

The nurse's eyes went loose in their sockets, trying to find somewhere to rest. "I wasn't, but Ethyl was."

"She here?"

"Yes."

"Go get her."

The nurse's gaze finally settled over Anna's shoulder. Apparently one of the officers nodded and she stood. "Okay, okay. Just be cool, man."

Chapter Forty-six

Mr. Brown adjusted his overcoat and watched the numbers above the St. Joseph Hospital's elevator door. The two passengers in the car with him were nuns who waited with their hands clasped, eyes on the floor. The door opened and one of the women held out a hand. "This is the intensive care, sir. Is that where you want to get off?"

He glanced out at a cluster of tables in a small, three-walled waiting room across hallway. "Yes, ma'am."

"All right, then. God bless, and son?"

"Yes ma'am, uh, Sister?"

She smiled. "You'd better get yourself a hat. You'll catch your death of pneumonia with that bare head uncovered in this weather."

"I'll be fine." He stepped out and the elevator closed behind him, rattling upward to the next floor.

A complete stranger to those in the waiting room, Mr. Brown chose a seat in the corner, away from the family that he hoped were the Parkers. Most of those in the waiting area smiled at the unusually dressed stranger. He felt the sheriff's eyes on him, evaluating his overcoat and the suit beneath. Glancing down at his glossy lace-up shoes, he realized that no one else wore anything even resembling his clothes.

Mr. Brown smiled a hello, picked up a magazine, and settled

into a vinyl-covered chair. Just another family member or friend waiting on a patient.

An elderly woman with a bun held in place on the back of her neck raised a worn Bible in one hand. "Praise the Lord, they're lettin' Top come home tomorrow."

The sheriff nodded and returned to the conversation, leaving Mr. Brown to soak up everything they knew about the bacteria and Gold Dust.

Chapter Forty-seven

Ethyl Grimes sat at a flimsy table across from Deputy Anna Sloan in the Brackenridge Hospital's break room and lit a cigarette. She took a sip of the sludge they'd found in the coffeepot. Her two-pack-a-day voice was pure gravel.

"I was there when he came in. Those dumbasses shoulda took him to the morgue instead of here. We keep people alive, not bring them back from the dead." She held out a crushed pack of Kools and shook one up.

Anna grinned at the crusty old nurse who'd seen thirty years of Austin's emergencies. She shook her head at the offer of a cigarette. "Don't smoke."

Ethyl shrugged and tapped the cigarette back into the pack with a forefinger. "I shouldn't. I know these things'll kill you, but it's harder'n hell to quit." She took a long drag and let it out through her nose. The smoke drifted over her white cap. "I really shouldn't be doing this. Dr. Fenning'll shoot me if he hears I'm talking out of school. You ought to talk to him."

"I'd rather talk to women." Anna cut her eyes toward the door. "Men usually turn the conversation around on me, if you know what I mean."

Ethyl squared her shoulders, pushing her chest out. "They talk to these, too."

They laughed and Anna nodded. "And I'm tired of talking to their foreheads."

"Fenning's forehead goes all the way back to here." She chopped the side of her hand against the back of her head. "So we're usually talking to a cueball."

They laughed again. Bonded.

Ethyl took another drag, leaving lipstick on the filter. "Look, honey, I don't know how much I can help you."

"That little girl at the desk says the dead guy came in a week ago today was from Chisum. How'd she know that?"

"Linda? She's barely one step up from a candy striper."

Anna repeated her question. "How'd she know where he's from?"

"There was a motel receipt in one of his pockets."

"He was dressed when he came in, then?"

"No. He was nekked as a jaybird, but somebody'd rolled his clothes up and stuffed 'em in a pillowcase. I was trying to find some ID and the receipt was in there."

"Any ID? A drivers license?"

"Nothing. He had a Zippo, a pocketknife, two packs of Camels, and a wad of cash."

"A wad?"

"Over a thousand dollars stuffed into the toe of his shoe."

"Why'd you check there? Most people would have stopped with the pockets."

"I had a sorry ex-husband that squirreled cash away in his shoes. He picked up the habit of doing that when he shacked up with them old whores he went home with, to keep 'em from rolling him."

Anna couldn't help herself. "You knew he was sleeping around and stayed with him?"

"Honey," Ethyl tapped the ash off her cigarette in a metal ashtray, "he was so good you'd have stayed with him too."

They shared a laugh before Anna held up a hand. "I'd have run him off the first time."

"Oh, I did, after about the *tenth* hussy." Ethyl patted her bun into place under her white cap. "After he came home with something that needed a butt-load of penicillin."

"Let's get back on track here. You checked the toe of the dead guy's shoe and found cash."

"Yep. Like I said, he reminded me of my old man and looked like the kind of guy who had something to hide. Gave the cash to the guys at the morgue, too, when they finally came to collect the body. I don't know what happened to it after that."

"Did you get a receipt for it?"

"Sure did."

Anything else you can tell me about him?"

"He had a couple of purty tattoos."

"Military?"

"One was a Navy tattoo. Another was different. It was the outline of Vietnam under a mushroom cloud. That man had hell before he died. Coughed his lungs out. Literally. There was tissue on his chest, mixed in with all the blood."

"Did you keep any records here of a diagnosis, or death certificate?"

"I can get you something."

"Fine. Anything else you can recall?"

"One thing."

"What's that?"

Ethyl leaned forward, waved Anna closer, and whispered in a conspiratory tone. "I wish I'd have known him when he was alive, if you know what I mean."

Chapter Forty-eight

Ned felt light as a feather after seeing Top sitting up in bed, eating soft foods, and breathing without the aid of an oxygen tent. After visiting with his grandson for a while and spreading the good word, Ned met John Washington the next day in Frenchie's rear booth.

He got to the café first and sat with his back to the rear to keep an eye on the front door. The smell of frying onions, old grease, and hamburgers made his stomach grumble, reminding him that he hadn't been eating well.

Not surprising, John came in through the rear entrance. His people ate in the back, and he often visited with friends and family where they didn't have to suffer the stares and glares of the café's white patrons. It didn't make any difference this time, the café was empty.

John touched Ned lightly on the shoulder as he passed and slid into the opposite seat. "Glad to hear Top's better."

"So are we." Ned's voice caught, surprising them both. John reached across and patted his friend's hand. Ned clasped his on top. "How's Bass?"

"Tolerable well." John stopped when Ned's eyes flicked over his shoulder.

Tom Bell and Judge O.C. Rains came in and joined them. Ned and John slid toward the wall to make room. O.C. laced his fingers on the scarred table beside Ned. "Boys."

Cody arrived and spoke to Frenchie. She nodded and locked the front door, then flipped the sign in the window to read "Closed." Cody took the pedestal seat at the end of the booth. "I miss anything?"

"We're just talking about that area code John got from his sister." O.C. wiped his palm across the table, collecting grains of salt. He shook them onto the dark floorboards. "It's for Washington D.C."

"That fits." The muscles in Ned's jaw flexed. "The feller that called me said the CIA's behind all this. That area code fer sure puts them right 'chere in Chisum, and with this Mr. Brown's name, we have a start."

Cody crossed his arms. "It doesn't give us everything we need. Now we know it was the government who sprayed that crap all over Center Springs. It's killed more than we thought. Anna called from Austin last night and told me about another guy down there who most likely died from the spray. Interesting thing is, she can't find anything about him. Just a wadded motel receipt that ties him to the Holiday Inn here in Chisum. I checked the registration, ran the name, and I believe it's bogus."

Ned dug a thumbnail into the soft finish of the table. "That bollixes things up. We don't know if it has anything to do with Pat's murder or this disease that's killin' folks, or cattle rustlin', 'ner nothin' else. What's to happen if I was to call them people and ask who was in charge of sprayin' that stuff down here, or if that feller that died was one of theirs?"

O.C. shrugged. "For one thing, I doubt the CIA is listed in the phone book, and even if you did manage to get a number, they'll deny it or have an alibi ready."

"*Alibi.*" Ned leaned back. "Here's what I think I'm gonna do. I'm going to Washington and find that place and *make* somebody talk to me."

O.C. rapped his knuckles on the table. "Nobody's gonna *talk* to you there. They'll just say they don't know nothing about it and show you the door. And who you have in mind in the first place? You don't have nothing but an area code."

John's deep voice cut in. "Maybe not.'

They waited while he pulled a thin pad from his shirt pocket. "My sister called me last night and said she might have something else for me. She takes these used pads out of the motel rooms when folks check out. She's supposed to throw 'em away, but she gives 'em to her kids to draw on. She remembered she'd put some in her purse and forgot 'em. When she went back to look, she believes this one came from them government men's room."

He held the black pad up. "They's nothing wrote on here, but if you turn it to the light, there's a phone number dug in the top page with that same area code and the X with three more numbers after that. I called it, and a lady answered Bureau of Public Roads.

"When I told her who I was, she said I had the wrong number and hung up. I don't believe them fellers from Washington had anything to do with our roads down in here."

"Well-well." Ned took the pad and angled it to the light. "Looks like we know who to talk to."

"You still can't go off half-cocked!"

"O.C. I'm not just gonna sit here and do *nothin'*. Somebody needs killin' for this."

"You ought to at least try to *arrest* 'em first, if you find who you're looking for." O.C. used his judge's voice. "Your jurisdiction don't exactly extend to the East Coast."

"Mine does. I'm not a U.S. Marshal, but I can guarantee you that if I showed up there, somebody'll take notice of this here *cinco peso* on my chest."

Cody shifted to make more room. "That don't mean anything. Just like Ned, you can't go walking in and demand to see whoever was in charge of spraying poison in our county."

"You know, I've seen Ned work. Even when he doesn't have all the pieces of a puzzle, he noodles around until other pieces shake loose, right?" Tom Bell ran a finger under his mustache to smooth the clipped ends. "Maybe that's what we need to do. Those people up there feel pretty safe, right? All us rubes are down here. What if a couple of Texas lawmen show up and start asking questions? Making themselves known. Somebody might get nervous enough for a piece of the puzzle to come loose."

"Y'all'll most likely get hurt and that's all."

"I've been hurt before." Tom Bell's statement floated in the air without response.

Ned drummed his fingers on the table. "So me and you drive up there, because I ain't flyin', and make ourselves known."

"You have a better idea?"

"No."

Cody drew a deep sigh. "I know there ain't no use in trying to talk you two hard-headed old coots out of it. Y'all go ahead on, but check in and let us know what you're finding out. I need to get all this wrapped up here."

"What's today, Wednesday?" Tom Bell counted on his fingers. "We can be there in three days of hard driving."

"It's a good long piece over there. We leave before daylight in the morning." Ned pulled at his ear, thinking. "Cody, you need to do something for me while we're gone. Bill Preston's bein' a real butthole. He was down with a bulldozer a ways from where they're working, getting fill dirt for the foundation. Merle Spahn saw them digging close to a spring and he got all riled up, hollering that half the springs in this county are drying up and here they are, maybe killing another'n. Y'all keep an eye out on what Preston's doin' before that blows up, too."

"That sounds like something we need to worry about later."

"You'll worry about it if they get crossways and start fightin' one another."

The pained look on Cody's face was enough for Ned to give him one more nudge. "You've got another case you need to close, too."

The Lamar County sheriff sighed. "What's that?"

"You're gonna have to stop whoever's digging holes all over my precinct in that gold rush Pepper's started." As soon as the words were out of his mouth, a whisper of a thought crossed Ned's mind. He grasped at it like a floating soap bubble, but it escaped, leaving a maddening sense that it was important.

Chapter Forty-nine

Mr. Gray fidgeted across the desk from *his* superior, wishing he could light his pipe. A veteran in covert operations, Gray spent his entire career doing what he was told, but making sure that he was covered in every way. He'd been in that office dozens of times, but this was the most uncomfortable debrief he'd ever experienced.

The spacious corner office and large mahogany desk bespoke of the well-dressed man's status in the organization. Thick carpet, paneled walls, and valuable art made the office seem more like the cushy lair of a CEO than a government employee.

Resembling a college campus built in the 1950s, the 1.4-million-foot building in the middle of nearly two-hundred-fifty wooded acres eight miles from D.C. housed dozens of departments that mostly worked independent of each.

The tiled hallway outside was full of art donated from a local elementary school, an attempt to humanize the building full of people dedicated to working in gray areas beyond the ken of the average citizen. Beyond that bit of humanization, the inhabitants worked in a world of compartmentalization that insulated them from the rest.

After Agent Gray finished his report, the Supervisor checked his Rolex. His soft blue tailor-made suit cost more than Mr. Gray's salary for a month. The man's mouth pinched in concentration. "You say this isn't your fault."

"We did our jobs." Agent Gray saw the man had missed a small triangle of whiskers on his chin when he shaved that morning and it made him feel a little better. He folded his arms across his chest and quickly reversed the move. His supervisor would notice the defensive body language and use it against him. Instead, he removed the cold pipe from his teeth and cupped it in his hand. "I believe it was mechanical failure. The sprayers malfunctioned."

"You think that's what killed your agent?"

"Yessir. The…Gold Dust…was on the bottle and sprayers. I think my man came in contact with the material."

"What about the other one? The civilian pilot?"

"Same thing. We're learning that pre-existing medical conditions allows the bacteria to cause damage to those with lowered immune systems. The information I'm receiving from the research team back in Chisum says that healthy people are unaffected by it."

The Supervisor examined the documents spread on the desk between them. "You're confident this *benign* bacteria is dangerous."

"My *research* team is." Gray replaced the pipe, thinking that his Supervisor was trying to trap him into taking responsibility for the conclusion that Gold Dust was deadly. The man wasn't dealing with an amateur. Deflect to the research team and let them take the fall, one way or another.

"Fine. Pull the rest of your team from the field." He closed the file allowing Gray to read the large Confidential stamp on the cover. "This experiment is terminated. It never happened."

"Yessir."

"You've dealt with your fatality?"

"Yes. The body was cremated as an unnamed entity, and the family compensated."

"The civilians?"

"Other than the deceased pilot, an elderly man is in the hospital along with a boy about fourteen years old. Neither is expected to live, and both illnesses trace back to Gold Dust. The boy's grandfather is a local constable, and his uncle is the sheriff."

Supervisor laced his fingers and rocked, giving Gray a good view of his buffed fingernails. "Okay. What of it?"

"I have reason to believe that the grandfather is investigating this beyond what you'd expect."

"Meaning?"

"We think he has a lead on my team."

"Get to the point."

"My man just called from Arkansas. He says the constable is coming here."

Supervisor shook out a cigarette. "That can't happen. You know what to do."

"Yes sir."

Chapter Fifty

On Tuesday, thirteen days after Curtis Gaines sprayed Gold Dust over Center Springs, Ned and Tom Bell drove through the heavy traffic flowing toward the nation's breathtaking capitol building. Stunned by the grandeur and spectacle of the columns on the Lincoln Memorial, Ned could only shake his head.

"Good lord, this place looks like what I imagine Heaven to be, without the gold streets…and the traffic."

Tom Bell twisted in his seat to see the bright marble Washington Monument beyond the reflecting pool. "Make no mistake, my friend. This ain't Heaven. It's closer to Hell, in my opinion. Look all the money they spent on marble. This is what the Roman Empire looked like not long before it fell."

Not knowing where they were going, Ned simply followed the flow of traffic. They soon found themselves driving past the Smithsonian Institution. Tom Bell pursed his lips. "This place has changed since the last time I was here." He pointed to the Capitol Building. "That hasn't, though."

"That the Capitol?"

"It is, and if you want to see something impressive, we can go in there."

"Nope. I don't have any intention of going in there. Tom, I'm so out of my territory they'll put me in jail the minute I step through those doors."

"Ned, did you see Lincoln sitting in that big memorial we passed back there?"

"Sure did."

"Well, he did what was right at a bad time in this country. I believe anyone worth their salt in that capitol would see what's in you."

"What do you mean?"

"I mean we're here for what's right, even though there's people who work for the government who's on the opposite side."

"I still don't get what you're saying." Ned turned left, away from the mall.

"What I'm saying is even though you and me are Davy fighting Goliath, all these great buildings have given me faith in what we're doing, despite the corruption going on behind some of those walls. It's gonna be all right."

Ned drove in silence for several minutes. Tom Bell opened a map and squinted through a pair of reading glasses. "Take this road out of town for a little bit so we can figure out what to do."

"I'm getting' hungry."

"I know just the place, if it's still there."

The Texans took the table farthest from the door in the nearly empty tavern called T.C.'s outside of Tyson's Corner, Virginia. As the name implied, the little community was nothing more than a crossroads west of Washington, anchored by T.C.'s on one corner, and a gas station on the other.

They were stiff and sore after the long, uneventful drive leading to the lonely crossroads in the country, thirteen miles west of Washington D.C. Eisenhower's interstate system helped on their journey East, but many of the roads they followed meandered through small towns reminding them of Center Springs. Neither man had slept well since they left. Most of the privately owned tourist cottages sported refrigerated air conditioning and color television, but the lumpy, sagging beds took their toll on men who started the trip with aching joints and questionable backs.

Ned squinted at the menus in the dim light. "I'god, Tom, the least these folks could do is put in some stronger light bulbs. I bet these ain't but twenty watt."

"I believe this place is called a roadhouse in this part of the country." Tom's eyes crinkled at the corners.

Ned's eyes began to make out the dark paneled walls, the plaid seat covers on the booths and chairs. Wooden shutters on the windows looked as if they hadn't been opened in years. "I don't like bars and we ought-not be in here. It's a nervous place, if you ask me."

"It's not Frenchies. I believe I'll order a beer."

"Sweet tea for me, and a hamburger sounds pretty good right about now." Ned scanned the room, glad they were the only customers in the early afternoon. The odor of spilled beer and frying onions filled the thick air.

"I doubt they'll have sweet tea, and you better ask for extra ice, too."

"Why's that?"

"They don't use much ice in their drinks out in this part of the country. Oh, and I 'magine you'll be charged for every glass. They don't have free refills, neither."

"Well, this ain't my kind of place. That's for sure." Ned shook his head and dropped the menu behind the condiments and napkin dispenser on their sticky pine table. He laced his fingers. "You were right, I may have bit off more'n I can chew."

"I been tellin' you this place was more than you expected."

"I figured we'd just walk in to that Bureau of Public Roads and ask who's in charge."

"The one we couldn't find."

Ned studied his hands. "I never saw such a place. All that marble and such, it's bigger'n Dallas. I figured we'd find that building right off, but I reckon it's gonna take some doin'."

Tom nodded slowly, letting Ned work it all out in his head.

The bartender/grillman with oiled hair came around, wiping his hands on a stained apron. "You guys decide?"

"Burger and sweet tea."

"We have regular tea."

"Is it sweet?"

"No." The owner pointed at the sugar dispenser on the table. "You'll have to add your own. You?"

Tom Bell hid a grin. "Burger for me, too, and a Hamm's."

The man turned on his heel. "Be right up."

Chapter Fifty-one

Mr. Brown steered into a Gulf station, one of only two buildings at the intersection of two two-lane highways. Directly opposite, a wooden roadhouse squatted amid bare hardwoods. He'd passed a fresh new mall only two miles away, proof that Tyson's Corner was poised on the edge of a boom.

An attendant popped out of the office at the sound of the bell. "Fill 'er up?"

"Sure."

"I'll get that windshield, too."

Brown shrugged. The bug-splattered glass of the rent car that wasn't supposed to leave Texas was the least of his worries. All the way from Chisum, he had time to watch the old men and think. He'd run operations all over the world, but this one was bothering him.

"Pay phone?"

"Around the side." The attendant used the Ethyl pump without asking if Brown preferred the more expensive gas blend. "Bathroom's unlocked."

Brown nodded his thanks and dug in his pocket for a dime. He could see the parking lot of the tavern across the street, and Parker's red Fury parked in front. Crows cawed and fluttered in the leafless trees.

Sticking his finger into the rotary dial, he spun it several times, following a series of numbers he'd long since memorized. It rang twice.

"Gray here."

"This is Brown."

"Where are you?"

"Tyson's Corner, at the Gulf station. Ned Parker is at the tavern called T.C.'s across the road."

"That the man who's coming to see me?"

"Yes, sir."

"Take him out, now that you're close enough for a cleanup team. I'll have them there in…"

"Sir, with all due respect, I don't do wet work. I never have."

There was a long silence on the other end, and Mr. Brown wondered if they'd been disconnected. Gray's clipped voice came back sharp in his ear. "Did you just refuse a direct order?"

"That sounds like a military term to me, and we're far from military. We all have specialties. I don't do wet work. I'm covert operations."

"You do as I say."

"Not in this sense, I don't. My lack of morals only goes so far, and it isn't gunning down innocent Americans." Brown felt the emptiness inside drain out like water down a bathtub drain, to be replaced by a dull anger and strong indignation. Surprising himself, he'd hit the end of the road and was finished. "In fact, sir, conducting tests on U.S. citizens is as wrong as it gets for me. I'm done."

"Hold on." Silence returned to the other end. Brown started to hang up, but Mr. Gray came back on the line. "Fine. You go in and engage until a team shows up."

Brown swallowed. The gray sky darkened, becoming even more threatening. The incessant cawing of the crows emphasized the dismal, chilly weather that added to the downward spiral of his mood. "No. I'll stay here and cover from the outside, then leave when the team gets here."

"Fine." Gray's answer came far too fast. "Call me when they're finished."

Brown hung up the phone and returned to his car as a soft shower fell on the pines lining the road. "I wasn't born yesterday."

He started the engine and pulled out, headed back to D.C., where he could hide in the never ending throng of people.

Chapter Fifty-two

CIA Agent Matteo was in his tiny, closet-sized office. His phone rang. Recognizing the line, he snatched it up before it could ring again. "Yes, sir."

"Get a wet team out to Tyson's Corner right now. You know where that is?"

"Yes, sir, Mr. Gray. It's out on highway…"

"You don't have to map it out for me. I know where it is. There's a Texan inside. Take him out."

"Done."

"Hold on."

"Sir?"

"We have an agent across the street at the Gulf station keeping watch."

"We won't break his cover."

"That's not what I want. He's your second target."

Agent Matteo felt the hair prickle on the back of his neck. He took a deep breath to gain a moment. "Sir, confirm. You want us to take out an asset, a *Company* man?"

The deep voice was all business. "Yes. He's turned. He's now a throwaway."

"Name?"

"Codename in this operation, Mr. Brown. Confirm his identity before taking action."

"Yes, sir."

Matteo hung up with a shaking hand and leaned back to gather himself. He'd just moved up in the Company. He grabbed his coat and went to find his best friend in the CIA, Sammy Fontaine. Matteo's move would bring Fontaine right along with him.

It was a great day for both of the young agents.

Chapter Fifty-three

Ned and Tom Bell had finished their meal when the red padded front door opened, admitting a shaft of bright light silhouetting a voluptuous woman in a tight skirt and blouse. She moved across the dim room without hesitation and slid onto a barstool with the fluid ease of a cougar.

Ned watched the woman spin on her stool and give them the once-over. He didn't make eye contact, afraid it would encourage her to come over. Neither he nor Tom Bell were interested in other women, especially those who frequented bars.

"She don't need to be in this place." Ned pursed his mouth.

"I doubt she's in here to eat." Tom jerked a thumb toward the wall, and Langley, Virginia. "Back to what we were talking about. We'll find what we're looking for, but no matter what we do, you go in these places without me at first. We need to see what you find out on your own."

"You're the ace in the hole, then."

"You can look at it that way."

The door opened again and the silhouettes of several loud young men filtered in. Laughing, they let it slam shut behind them and paused, allowing their eyes to adjust.

Already accustomed to the gloom, Ned gave them a quick glance, and met Tom's gaze. Neither liked what he saw of the rawboned men in casual clothes and fresh haircuts who moved together as smooth as sharks.

They took a table in the middle of the café with a loud screeching and thumping of chairs. The shortest of the group wearing a plaid shirt and jacket pointed at the two old men sitting against the wall. The others followed his finger.

The female barfly watched them with an appraising eye. She flicked a gofer alight and lit a cigarette. Shaking the paper match out, she pitched it into an orange glass ashtray and blew a lungful of smoke toward the ceiling.

One member of the group whispered something and they all laughed. A muscular blond in white jeans and gray jacket waved at the counter. "Hey, how about a round of beers here?"

The bartender/owner stopped wiping the bar. "What kind?"

"What difference does it make? We'll just piss it away in an hour. Just make sure it's cold, that's all."

They laughed again, apparently proud to have a comedian in their midst.

White Jeans threw a thumb at the bar. "And buy that cute lady there anything she wants."

The woman raised an eyebrow and flashed them a smile. "It's gin. Bombay and tonic."

"Whatever you want, sweetcheeks."

She tipped her glass in thanks and turned back to the bar.

The two old men turned back to their conversation. Tom spoke softly. "Anyway, I think we find out where all those CIA guys go after work and follow 'em to a bar or something. Maybe we can get someone who'll talk to us then."

"We have a name they used at the motel in Chisum."

"That's right, but if we ask for Mr. Brown, they'll look us straight in the eye and say they never heard of him. Ned, these people are something like you've never seen before. They lie for a living. They lie when the truth is easy, like what they had for breakfast. They make things up, and if they get called on them, they make up stories to cover what they made up."

Already tired from traveling, Ned felt deflated. "So what are our chances of finding who we're looking for?"

"Not a snowball's chance in hell, but then again, I have a good feeling about this for some reason."

"That don't make no sense."

"I know it." Tom Bell straightened when one of the loud young men slid his chair back with a loud squall of wooden legs on the polished plank floor. He headed for their table, followed by two others just as big.

Ned felt a cold knot form in his stomach at the sight of their faces drawn tight and smooth. The men were hard and solid. The one Ned thought of as Muscles wore a jean jacket over a blue broadcloth shirt and he wondered what kind of weapons might be hidden.

Muscles stopped and planted his feet at the head of their table. "What did you say about us?"

Instead of meeting the man's angry gaze, Ned kept his head low. He choked down a whimper of frustration at the rising situation that felt like an approaching thunderstorm. The brim of his hat hid his eyes. He didn't need to see the man's face. His hands held his attention. Both were doubled up in fists that had seen a lot of punishment.

"I don't know what you're talking about, feller. We're waitin' for our check, that's all."

"Well, Tex, I think you're talking about us, all quiet so we can't hear."

"I knew we shouldn't have come in this place, Tom. This ain't like back home."

Tom Bell was a mirror image of Ned, head low so his hat could cover his eyes. He sighed. "Look, friend..."

Muscles leaned in. "I ain't your *friend, buddy!*"

"Fine. My mistake."

"Yeah, well, my buddy over there reads lips pretty good and he said you're talking about us."

Ned felt his face flush, sensing a pressure wave of trouble on the way. The man was a freight train that wouldn't be stopped, and Ned knew his kind from the beer joints across the river back home.

Lacing his fingers, the Texas constable stared at his work-hardened hands, figuring the loudmouth might back away if he didn't respond.

"Hey, old man. I'm talking to you, too." Muscles rapped the table. "Didn't your mama teach you to take your hat off inside?"

If there was anything the world that made Ned mad, it was someone who presumed to tell him where wear to a hat. Instead of responding, he ground his dentures and waited for the man to leave.

The man in white jeans raised his voice. "Look at me when I'm talking to you!"

"Hey, you guys!" The owner leaned over the counter. "That's enough!"

White Jeans put an index finger to his lips. The owner quieted. The dark-haired woman rose and backed toward the swinging door leading to the grill behind the counter.

Ned met Tom Bell's eyes. They'd widened slightly, not from fear, but from something deep down inside that Ned once saw in a honky-tonk across the river. A roaring in his ears told him things were quickly building to a head.

Tom Bell shifted in his seat and hung an elbow across the back. He pushed his hat up with a thumb and met Muscle's gaze. His voice was quiet, conversational, exactly opposite the gathering storm. "Son, you and I need a talk. See, I've known men like you all my life."

"That so?"

"And every one was the same. Full of piss and vinegar, but not *near* enough sense to know what to do with it." He tilted his head toward Ned. "That feller right there's good, and decent, and calm in most weather, but when he gets mad, people get hurt."

Muscles started to laugh, but saw something in Tom Bell's eyes that slowed his roll.

"Now you're getting it." Tom Bell's voice was low and steady. "Look at him. He hasn't paid your struttin' any attention, and I bet you think he's afraid, right, but look at his hands, son. They ain't shaking, and his voice didn't quiver when he spoke. I bet you didn't notice that either, right?"

"I don't care."

"You should. He's just waiting like a big ol' rattler that wants to be left alone, but he ain't rattled yet. If I's you, I'd go back on over there and drink those beers you ordered before he gets up out of that chair and goes to work."

The short twenty-something man at the table snorted, but his attempt at bravado died in the thick, silent air.

Muscles swallowed. "Goes to work, how?"

Tom Bell finally raised his head to look the man in the eyes. "You need to learn to pay attention, son. See, how he's sittin'? You think he can't do anything, but he's an old he-coon that's still pretty spry for his age and if you keep going the way you are, I doubt you'll get so ripe."

Muscles raised a lip. "This fat old man ain't never hurt a fly. Who are you, anyway?"

"I don't matter, but that fat old man carries a badge, for one thing, son, and for another, I have a sneaking suspicion there's a feller or two would say different, if they could still talk."

The tough young men wavered and the leader went soft and indecisive. Suddenly confused, he looked to his friend near the bar. "A badge?"

"Now y'all are getting it."

White Jeans gave his partner a head shake and took over. "No damn badge scares me. He ain't from around here, so he ain't got any juris, jury…"

"Jurisdiction." The short man rooted at the table seemed to have a little more on the ball than the other three.

"Shut up, Dewayne. Yeah, jurisdiction."

"I'm tired of talking to you." Tom Bell pushed his chair back. The sudden move caused Muscles to move back a step.

Ned finally swung one leg from under the table so he could see the bar. "Hey, bartender."

"What?"

"Call the hospital and tell them to send out a couple of ambulances."

Muscles tried to maintain his cool. "For what?"

"Because somebody's fixin' to need one." A lead-weighted sap appeared in Ned's hand and snapped outward, catching Muscles in the knee with the crack of an axe biting into pine.

"Shit!" He howled and dropped to the floorboards. The woman gasped.

At the same time, White Jeans threw a low punch at Tom Bell's jaw. Tom pulled his head back just enough for the swing to whiff past and grabbed the man's thick wrist. White Jeans' center of gravity was off and Tom slammed him face-first into the table.

White Jeans snapped upright from the pain, holding his broken nose. Tom again used the man's reverse momentum to push his head back and deliver a solid blow under his chin that knocked him unconscious. The tough young man hit the floor like a felled tree.

Suddenly uncertain, the third troublemaker backed away from the two old fighters as the shorter man rose from their table, knocking his chair over with a clatter. The lawmen were on their feet in a flash, backing the others down with nothing more than their readiness to continue the fight.

The door opened, allowing a beam of light to spill across the tables. The two surprised troublemakers beside the table turned toward the silhouette of a man that paused inside the door, taking in the scenario.

The newcomer in a suit and fedora crossed the silent tavern. "You gentlemen stay right where you are. I'm Police Chief McDaniel." He held a revolver in his right hand, pointed at the floor. "Arnold, what the hell's going on in here? Why are these men on the floor with you standing there with that phone in your hand?"

The bartender glanced at the receiver as if he didn't know where it came from. "Hey, Aloysius. These four young men came in and started bothering those two there. That's when that one in the silver hat told me to call an ambulance."

Ned tilted his head like a dog looking at a new pan.

Chief McDaniel stepped between the men squared off between the tables, noting the sap still in Ned's hand. "Why?"

Muscles rolled over, holding his knee. Tears streamed down his face. "We came in to have a drink and these two threatened me and Clayton here and broke my knee."

Lying on his back, Clayton was unable to respond.

Chief McDaniel paused to think. "Well, then I guess I'll have to take these two old-timers in for disturbing the peace, and the four of you, too, for disorderly conduct."

He stepped forward and the third of the hard-looking young men beside Ned's table moved to cut him off. "We're not going anywhere…"

Chief McDaniel's arm flashed and the revolver cracked against the man's head. He went down like a rock.

The snick of a released blade followed a second later and the short guy still standing beside his table chose to join in by flashing a switchblade.

"I wouldn't." Ned's .38 pointed at the little man's chest.

At the same time, Muscles had gathered himself enough on the floor to reach under his shirt. He stopped when Tom Bell's Colt .45 appeared from nowhere. "You boys are outgunned."

"Nobody move!" Chief McDaniel stepped back and leveled his snub-nosed pistol. "Drop your weapons or I'll shoot every one of you!" The switchblade clattered to the floor.

"Chief McDaniel." Tom Bell's soft voice was loud in the silent building. He slowly raised his left hand to pull the lapel back on his coat, revealing the *cinco-peso* Ranger badge on his shirt. "This one doesn't give me any jurisdiction here, but it sure tells who I am."

"There's a badge under my coat, too." Ned also spoke softly and lowered his revolver. "Now, we're gonna put these pistols back in our holsters, but watch 'em while we do it."

Chapter Fifty-four

Sheriff Cody Armstrong, Deputy Anna Sloan, and Deputy John Washington huddled in Cody's office, listening to the north wind shove against the windows and moan under the courthouse eaves. Snow flurries dusted the streets with dry powder that swirled on the pavement and collected on the shrubs, trees, and dying grass around the building.

"Nice shiner." Cody adjusted his chair and propped his boot heels on the desk, relieved that Anna was back, but distressed over her swollen nose and black eye. He was sure the mayor was going to call him into the office as soon as he heard about her face. "Glad you're back all safe and sound. How was your vacation?"

Anna snorted. "Some vacation, hanging around honky-tonks and looking for rustlers."

"Miss Anna, you know he's just givin' you the bidness." John chuckled and leaned against the wall.

"I know it, but I didn't come back with a prisoner, that's for sure."

"Didn't expect you to. Just information." Cody tried not to stare at her nose. It looked worse than her eye and cheek. "What have you got?"

"A meeting with a supplier later today, and I've already told you what I learned about that guy who died in a Round Rock motel."

John worried at the brim of the hat in his hands. "There wudn't nothin' else but the motel receipt from the Holiday Inn."

Cody tilted his head, thinking. "Was there a date on the receipt?"

Anna opened the small notebook she carried in her back pocket and read the date. "Why?"

"Because that's when my sister says two citified strangers were staying here."

Cody studied his black boots, puzzling it out. "The ones who were here at the same time Curtis Gaines sprayed Center Springs."

"Yep." John took out his own notebook.

Anna wrinkled her forehead. "What's up? I've been gone, remember?"

Cody explained the connection between the motel room, the strangers, and the telephone number on the notepad. "Ned and Tom Bell are gone to Washington. Those two strangers are tied to death and sickness here, and now one of 'em's turned up dead hisself."

John rolled his big shoulders and straightened up. "So what does all of this mean?"

"I don't know. We're getting close to something, but it's not fitting yet. I'll have to let you know about them when he calls in."

"It doesn't tie in with the rustling, though, does it?" Anna adjusted her position to see the men on either side of her chair.

"No." Cody dug a toothpick out of his shirt pocket and stuck it in the corner of his mouth. "We still don't have any concrete leads on the rustlers and who killed poor old Pat Walker."

"Have you thought maybe the two aren't connected?"

Surprised, Cody stopped chewing and gave Anna his attention. "I hadn't thought of that."

"Maybe the cattle were rustled by one guy, but Pat was shot by a completely different person. Could it have been these two city guys? Maybe he ran into them and saw something he shouldn't have."

The office was silent as they pondered the possibility.

"I'll be dog." John growled deep in his throat. "This one's a tangle, ain't it?"

Cody bit down on the toothpick. "It'd be as clear as the nose on your face if somebody explained it. Look, we're pro'bly making this harder than it is. Let's not tie the two together right now. Anna, when are you supposed to meet these *cattlemen*?"

"This evening in Roxton."

"On the side of the road, or what?"

"I know a retired U.S. Marshal out there who's letting me use his farm. I worked with him down in Houston and when I called and told him what I needed, he was all for it." She gave him the retiree's name and address.

"Good. John, go with her. Wear some overalls and act like a hand. That'll let you get close to keep an eye on Anna. I'd feel better with John behind you with that scatter gun of his."

She met his gaze and he wondered if she saw through his decision. "Works for me."

"Good. Y'all get gone and let me know what happens."

Anna stood. "Call you on the radio?"

"As far as I know. I'm gonna be in Center Springs, trying to put a stop to this gold rush of Pepper's. Somebody went into Ike Reader's pasture and left the gate open. Half of his cows got out and he's fit to be tied."

Chapter Fifty-five

Ned, Tom Bell, and Police Chief McDaniel were sitting in the back corner of the still-empty bar in Tyson's Corner, Virginia. The four young men were on the way to the local lockup with the promise of medical help if they really needed it.

The female barfly was still there, calming her nerves with still another gin and tonic. Chief McDaniel had already taken her statement and that of Arnold, who Ned learned was the bar's owner, chief cook, and bottlewasher.

"They won't be in jail very long." The Chief shook out a Lucky and fired it up. "They aren't who you think they are."

"What does *that* mean?" Ned was getting frustrated with all the cloak-and-dagger stuff. "I don't understand all I know about this."

"Constable Parker, if I had to bet your farm on it, I'd say they were hired by the Company to do a job. The question is, why is it you two who got the nod?"

"The Company?"

McDaniel took a long drag. "The CIA. So why were they here to take you guys out?"

"Take me out?" Understanding raised Ned's eyebrows. "That was all planned from the start?"

"Mr. Parker, those guys were here to, at the very least, beat the hell out of you and send you back home, or to kill you. From the looks of them, I'd say you were about to disappear."

"How do you know that?"

"I got a hangup call that said some guys were coming in here with trouble on their minds. I don't get those very often, and it sounded legit. Then when one of my boys came to pick them up, they popped their trunk full of shovels and lye. They had nothing on them but a little cash. No licenses, cards…hell, they don't even have billfolds. I'm sure they gave us fake names, but we're running background checks on them anyway.

"In fact, I have a good idea those guys in my jail will have some mysterious visitors come by with official government papers signed by people you've never heard of ordering me to release them, and I will. So the question is, why were they here to make *you* disappear?"

Ned sipped at the weak tea cooled by only a few chips of ice and told Chief McDaniel the story, from the farmer murdered by cattle rustlers, to the crop duster, to Top. He spoke softly so the woman at the bar couldn't hear, but went into more detail than he'd planned and by the time he was finished, he'd lost the spirit to do anything other than sit there and drink iced tea.

The Chief listened without speaking until Ned finished. He stubbed out the cigarette in a nearly full ashtray and spun the pack on the tabletop. The woman ordered another gin and tonic in a voice amplified by liquor.

"Sounds like a story, don't it?" Tom Bell absently ran his fingertips along a gouge in the yellow wood. "I'd think it was all made up, if I heard it like that the first time."

"It would sound fishy if I lived anywhere else. But I know this area and, God help me, it makes more sense than I'd like to admit."

Tom watched the woman slide her empty glass across the bar. "How so?"

"I was in the Army, and I watched those Spooks work. That's why I recognized those guys for what they were. The only problem is, you two are in over your heads. If you stay on this track, you'll disappear in less than a week, despite what's happened here today." The Chief gave a half chuckle, half grunt. "Or because of it."

"So you think we should just tuck our tails and *run*?" Ned's frustration landed on the last word harder than he intended.

"No. I didn't say that, Mr. Parker."

Ned cleared his throat. "If this was going on all the time in my county, I'd be worried."

"They call it clandestine operations, and these people are thick as roaches this close to Washington. I've turned my head from time to time, so this one won't sting near as bad. A certain amount of corruption this close to the capital is to be expected."

Tom Bell held McDaniel's gaze for a long moment. "Why are you taking all this as the truth so fast?"

McDaniel cupped his hands around a gofer match and lit another cigarette. He watched the woman slip off her stool, steady herself for a moment with the bar, and concentrate on her walking skills as she left.

"I know Texas Rangers don't lie, and they do what's right, and because my granddaddy wouldn't have left something like this alone, either, if it had happened to me when I was a kid."

Chapter Fifty-six

Pastures and thick woods alternated as Owen and Dale hauled a stolen trailer-load of cattle down a narrow, two-lane county road. Owen drove slowly, looking for the white pipe gate described on the scribbled note in his hand. Newer metal fenceposts alternating with wooden posts told of slow but inevitable changes coming to the area.

The roller coaster weather continued. The day was chilly and the tail of another cold front headed for Texas was forecast to drop temperatures even more as it dragged across the southern tier of states. The brunt of the storm was predicted to strike Washington D.C. head-on.

Owen grimaced when Dale coughed into a blue bandanna that was spotted with blood. "You sound like hell."

"Feel like hell."

"Well, hang on. We'll sell these cows and get gone. Then I'll carry you to Dallas and you can see the doctor there."

The heavy trailer full of Herefords rocked behind the pickup. They came to a dirt drive leading up to a two-story farmhouse. A faded wooden barn rose from the pasture a hundred yards behind a bobwire fence.

"This is it."

The dirt track made a wide loop around the open yard and ended at a pipe gate leading into the pasture. Owen pulled up to the gate as ordered and killed the engine. He stepped out and met a man and woman walking from the house.

The older unshaven man in overalls and light jacket waved. "Howdy."

Owen returned the wave, paying more attention to the woman than the man. She looked as if someone had given her a good beating and wondered if it was the hard-looking farmer beside her. "Are you the young lady called me to bring out some cows?"

"Sure am."

They shook and the older man slipped both hands into the warm pockets of his jacket. "I don't believe I've ever bought cattle sight unseen."

Owen handed him a handwritten bill, noticing a herd of slick, good-looking Herefords staring in his direction. "You've never bought cattle of this quality for this price, either. You got a name, sir?"

"Edward White."

"And you?"

"Anna."

"Y'all married?"

"No." Anna's answer was clipped.

"Well, it's good to meet y'all." Despite her black eye and swollen nose, he was even more interested, now that he knew they weren't a couple. "These are from a ranch out west of Vernon. An old boy I know's getting a divorce and he told me, he said, 'Jimmy Don, she ain't getting nothing. Sell these cows quick and give me the cash.'"

Anna frowned. "That doesn't seem fair to her."

Owen shrugged and tried not to lick his lips. Anna was the kind of woman that made him all loose and jittery inside. Even the bruises made her more interesting. "It's not my dance. How do you want to do this? You want me to pull through here and let 'em out?"

Dale coughed and Anna shifted to see over Owen's shoulder. "Somebody sounds sick."

"That's my buddy. He's got a bad old cold. He'll be fine. In fact, I bet he goes to sleep early tonight. You have any supper plans?" He licked his lips. His tongue protruded far too long.

"Ed and I are eating with my folks. That's why we need to get done."

"Oh." Owen's possum eyes lingered on her breasts half-hidden by a light barn coat. He was disappointed, but had her number in his pocket and figured he'd call in a few days, in case she was really interested but wouldn't say anything in front of Ed. He jerked a thumb toward the fence. "That gate?"

"That'll be fine."

"Good. You have the cash first." He drug his eyes up to a busted blood vessel in the corner of her left eye. "It ain't that I don't trust a pretty little lady like you, but…you know…"

"I understand." She turned toward a red smokehouse not far away. "John, would you come out here and help us unload these cattle?"

A huge black man in overalls and a well-worn canvas coat came around the corner and waved. "Sho' will." He stopped beside the overgrown corner fencepost by the truck's right front fender.

Owen watched him unlock the gate. The healthy cattle on the other side of the fence weighed on his mind. He tore himself away and back to the conversation at hand. "The cash?"

"In a minute. We're waiting for the stock inspector to get here. He'll check the brands and then we can finish the deal."

"Stock inspector? You didn't say anything about a stock inspector." All those warm feelings about Anna rushed to the bottom of his pot belly.

Alarm bells went off in his head. The big black man wasn't acting right, either, still fooling with the gate and the wire. Owen glanced at the overgrown vines. Nothing is straight in nature, and the lines of a shotgun leaning against the corner post stood out in the tangle. Owen realized they'd been set up and dug into run.

"Dale! He's going for a gun! Shoot that sonofabitch at the gate!"

Dale lost a moment opening the door and leaning out to pull the trigger on the German Luger as fast as he could. Ducking, John missed his grab at the shotgun. He dove for cover against the truck's grill and out of sight from the cab.

Owen yanked a .38 revolver from his belt and fired at both Anna and Edward at the same time. The first round snapped close to Edward. The retired marshal produced a revolver from his coat pocket. Off balance and trying to get out of the line of fire, he shot and missed.

Anna dropped and scrambled behind Edward's truck, pulling the trigger on her double-action revolver three times as she scurried to shelter. Caught in the open, Owen grunted at the impact and stutter-stepped between the truck and trailer. Edward sprinted to cover, shooting single-action all the way. One of the rounds plowed up a gout of sand from the yard. Another punched through the side of the rustlers' truck.

The outlaws were in trouble. There was no way to back up a trailer-load of cattle in the middle of a gunfight. The only option was to drive straight through the gate, but that move would get them deeper into the pasture with no clear escape route.

"Deputy sheriff! Give it up!" Anna fired as Owen jumped over the trailer's tongue, putting the load of cattle between him and the guns spitting lead in his direction. Dale piled out of the cab and followed, firing over his shoulder to keep John down.

With the truck and trailer between them and the law, the rustlers sprinted across the yard and into a thin line of trees lining the drive. Pistol rounds whined overhead and ricocheted off the trunks.

Owen glanced over his shoulder and saw the black man snatch the pump twelve from the tangle of vines. "Shotgun!"

Deep booms punctuated the sharper slaps from the handguns. Dale grunted and lurched against Owen at the same time a pickup turned off the gravel road, heading in their direction. He grabbed his off-balance partner's collar and dragged him behind a ragged row of thick cedars.

"Down!" On his stomach and bleeding from his own wound, Owen peeked between the trucks to see the unsuspecting driver leaning over toward the floorboard. The windows were up on the truck moving at a walking pace down the dirt drive.

Owen stepped into the open and aimed his pistol. "Stop!"

Shocked upright, the man slammed his brakes. Dale rounded the front of the vehicle and Owen yanked the door open. A round snapped past, causing him to duck. He raised up just in time to see the driver's badge as the lawman twisted in his seat, bringing a Colt to bear.

Owen stuck the snub-nose into the man's side and pulled the trigger twice. Ignoring his grunts of pain, Owen grabbed a handful of jacket and dragged the already limp body out of the way. "Get in!"

Dale fired back toward the house and stumbled through the passenger door. Owen slammed the truck into reverse and spun backwards. He hit the country road, jammed the shift lever into gear, and spun out, throwing gravel in a wide spray.

The last thing he saw as they sped away was the huge black man in overalls charging in their direction. He slid to a stop beside the dying lawman, raised the shotgun, and shot three times as fast as he could pump the twelve-gauge.

Chapter Fifty-seven

A cold rain met Ned and Tom Bell outside the bar in Tyson's Corner. The drunk woman was sitting behind the wheel of her brand new Mustang Mach 1. The engine growled in Park, but she was staring straight ahead, the car radio blaring a rock 'n' roll song by a woman who kept saying, "Don't you want somebody to love?"

The Chief's car was parked at the opposite end of the building, but McDaniel stayed inside.

Ned opened the door on his Plymouth and, despite the light rain, stopped with one foot in the floorboard, studying the Mach 1 and its occupant. Crows circled the trees behind the roadhouse and Gulf station across the street. "Tom, that poor woman's too drunk to drive."

"It ain't our business."

"I know it, but she's gonna cause a wreck on these slick streets, or kill somebody."

"Give me a minute. I'll go in and tell the Chief."

"Hang on. He's already had enough from us today. I'll just get her keys and we can lay them on his hood over there. McDaniel'll know what to do when he comes out."

"What if she won't give them to us? This ain't Texas. We can't haul her in."

"I'll get her keys out of the ignition. She's so drunk she

won't notice, and I bet she'll go to sleep right where she's sittin'. McDaniel'll be out directly."

"I believe you're spinning your wheels there, Ned."

"I've spun 'em before." Leaving his door open, Ned rounded her car. "Hey, missy."

It took several seconds for her to turn her head and give him a crooked grin of recognition. "You were inside."

Cold rain dripped from the brim of his hat and he was glad for the sport coat. "Sure was. You feeling all right?"

"I'm just a little dizzy and sleepy. I was fine until I came outside."

"Yep. You can sit and drink for hours at a bar, but the minute you get up, all that alcohol sneaks up on you."

Her forehead furrowed. "I'm not drunk!"

"Didn't say you were." He reached over her. "This is awful loud and I can barely hear you over that noise." He turned the volume knob and killed the engine. The radio faded away as the tubes died. "That's better."

He straightened and rested one hand on the roof of her wet car, leaving the keys there.

"Why don't you sit right 'chere and rest for a while?"

"I'm not drunk."

"Still ain't said you are, but you're slurring your words a right smart."

Ned sighed and met Tom Bell's gaze over the top of the low car. Tom frowned and shook his head. "I done told you what was about to happen."

"Lady, can we call somebody to come and carry you home?" The quizzical look in her face made Ned grin. "Can somebody come get you?"

"I don't have anybody here. My folks are all back in Dallas."

"I ain't leavin' no Texas girl to get home by herself in this condition." Ned dug in his pocket and pitched the Fury's keys to Tom Bell. "You follow us and I'll drive her home."

The old Ranger caught them with one hand, shaking his head. "We ain't got *time* for this."

"It won't take but a few minutes. This gal needs help and Miss Becky would say this is the right thing to do, so I'm a-doin' it. Lady, slide over and I'll drive."

Ned averted his eyes as she straddled the console, her dress riding high enough to show her stockings and garters. "Lord help me." Unused to bucket seats and shifters in the floorboard, he felt as if he were going all the way to the ground before he settled behind the wheel. "Good goddlemighty. Where do you live?"

"In Alexandria."

"How far is that?"

Her eyes went loose in her head. "About twenty miles."

"That ain't much farther than Center Springs to Chisum. We can be over there and back in forty-five minutes." He was talking more to himself than her.

"Where's Center Springs?"

"A long way from here, that's for sure."

Chapter Fifty-eight

Driving with one hand, Owen kept his beady eyes on the broken white line as the stripes vanished under the hood. "Hang on, buddy." His other hand clutched his bloody chest.

Dale slumped against the door and coughed into the blue bandanna that was fast turning red. "This is bad."

"It don't look good." Owen saw a Motorola radio mounted to the floorboard. He turned up the volume to hear a deep voice.

"All units. Be on the lookout for two men who murdered Stock Inspector George Nobles. They stole his truck and fled the scene. This is Deputy John Washington. I need for somebody to call in with a description of George's truck. I barely got a look at it. It's a late model Ford and that's all I know."

Dale leaned his head back, breathing through his mouth. "Where you taking me? I need a hospital."

Owen moved his hand that came away wet and sticky. "I believe I do too." He put pressure against his wound again. "Where you hit?"

"My back. I took a load from that damned shotgun." Dale coughed, deep, wet, and thick. "Hey, where does this road come out?"

Owen's eyes flicked to his partner and back to the road. "Hang on."

"I think I need some sleep."

The truck's engine roared as Owen leaned on the foot-feed. "You can sleep at my brother's house. That's where we're headed. He'll fix us up." Still amped up by an adrenaline dump, Owen slapped the steering wheel. "We're gonna be all right."

When he didn't get a response, Owen reached across the cab and shoved Dale's shoulder with a bloody hand. "Dammit, boy! You so scared you can't talk?"

Dale's eyes were slits staring at nothing.

"Dale? Oh shit."

Chapter Fifty-nine

The barfly named Kathleen dozed in and out in the passenger seat as Ned threaded his way through the wet, leaf-strewn streets of Alexandria, Virginia. Federalist townhouses, streets canopied by stately old maples, and brick sidewalks reminded him of feed store calendars featuring autumn in New England.

He stopped at an intersection and shook her shoulder for the umpteenth time. "Hey, where to now?"

She raised her head and focused through the rain-spotted windshield. "Turn left."

They followed the tree-lined residential street lined with parked cars. "That's it." She pointed a weak hand at a row house that looked like all the others.

"There ain't no parking places out front."

She could barely raise her head and squinted as if her eyes wouldn't focus. "There's one up there on the next block."

The hair prickled on the back of Ned's neck, but he couldn't figure out why. He saw the space and pulled in. He opened the passenger door and took her arm. "Come on. Let's get you inside." Kathleen stepped out, giving him still another view of her underclothes. He took her arm and pulled her upright.

A space in front of her row house had opened up after they passed, giving Tom Bell space to park Ned's red Fury. He killed the engine and hurried down the wet sidewalk to meet Ned and Kathleen. "I got a bad feeling about this."

"Don't make no difference. We're here now."

Their breath fogged as snowflakes mixed with the light rain. With Kathleen's arms over their shoulders, the lawmen guided her down the wet sidewalk and up the steps.

Ned handed Tom her key ring. "I 'magine her house key is on there."

"It's not locked." Kathleen leaned heavily on Ned and clutched his right arm as they reached the door. "I don't have enough to steal."

Tom stuck the keys in his pants pocket and turned the knob and stepped aside "Get her on in here."

The drunk woman's voice steadied. "I feel *sick*."

Tom Bell's head snapped around at the tone of her voice.

Supporting her weight, Ned half pushed her through the door, noticing a staircase inside the door to their left. He hoped there was a bathroom on the first floor. "We need to hurry, then."

"I feel really *sick*!" Her voice rose again, no longer slurring.

A hallway beyond the staircase split the house in two, with an office on the right, and a living room on the left. A man holding a huge pistol appeared at the end of the hallway. Tom Bell fanned his coat back, recognizing Muscles. "Watch out, Ned!" He drew his 1911, shoved Kathleen forward, and pulled the trigger.

The report filled the well-appointed house.

Chapter Sixty

Owen pulled the stolen truck into the Piggly Wiggly parking lot in Bonham. Weak from shock, he leaned back and rested for a minute. The radio had been busy with the description of the stock inspector's truck, and the two involved in the shootout.

His familiarity with many of the county and farm roads allowed Owen to stay off the main highways and make his way into the small northeast Texas town. He needed to keep moving, to get to his brother's house where he could heal up. He plucked the Luger from Dale's dead hand. "Many thanks."

Leaving his empty revolver on the floorboard, Owen slid out of the bench seat and pulled his coat together to hide his bloody shirt. He groaned at the jolt of pain that shot through his chest like a bolt of lightning.

Rows of cars and farm trucks fanned out from all sides. He checked the door on a Dodge truck beside him, and when it proved locked, he went to the next one, confident that he'd find one that was open. The odds were on his side. Rural folks tended to leave their keys in the ignition.

Chapter Sixty-one

The heavy .45 slug from Tom Bell's Colt 1911 caught Muscles in the chest with the sound of a wet slap. At the far end of the house, the big man staggered back against the kitchen's doorframe, pulling the trigger on a new Colt Python .357 magnum revolver. It spat a streak of fire down the dim hallway with a deafening roar. The round struck Kathleen in the shoulder with devastating results.

Sober as a judge, she shrieked and spun, pushing away from the lawmen as more guns from different angles in the hallway opened up. Tom Bell fixed on a second gunman two doors down on the right, throwing two rounds at him in a roll of thunder. Both drove home and the wounded man disappeared into a room and out of sight.

A bullet plucked the padded shoulder of Ned's wet sport coat with a spray of fine droplets and a puff of damp fill. To that point he'd almost been shocked into immobility. The whipcrack of the round snapped him back into the budding firefight. Ned whipped the Colt .38 revolver from the holster on his belt. He thumbed the hammer back and fired at White Jeans, who stepped out of the kitchen with a leveled shotgun.

Knees buckling from the wound, Kathleen stumbled against a narrow table against the wall, knocking over a vase and turning with a Walther in her hand. Tom Bell saw her raise a small automatic in his peripheral vision. He crooked his left arm, stuck the .45 around his side, and pulled the trigger.

Her light blouse sparked from Tom's shot. The material caught and a small flame rose from the dead woman's blouse.

The .38 barked as Ned pulled the trigger on the double-action revolver. White Jeans disappeared. Tom Bell's 1911 roared in measured beats as if he were on a gun range. The rounds found their mark half a second later, knocking the short man back. He fell half in and half out of the second doorway. Stunned by the Texans' viciously accurate response, the surviving CIA agents pulled back.

The long entry hallway running the length of the house was a shooting gallery. Ned ducked into the empty living room on his left, glancing up the empty staircase as he passed.

"These are the sonsabitches from the bar!" Ned snapped a shot at a figure ducking behind a door on their right.

"I know it!"

"It's a setup!"

"I know it, I said."

The two lawmen separated. Ned yanked the pin on his revolver, dropping the cylinder. He slapped out the empty cartridges and reloaded. Tom Bell ducked into a formal living room on his immediate right. His pistol roared twice more.

The empty magazine from Tom Bell's Colt thumped on the hardwood floor. He slammed a full one into the handle and fired three times in rapid succession, followed by a thump further inside the house. "That's the sawed-off little runt with the knife, Ned! Think that last feller's upstairs?"

"I ain't looked up there yet." Holding the pistol in his familiar Old West stance, Ned peeked around the door and into the entry hall. "You got anybody down in white jeans?"

"Nope."

The woman was obviously dead. A large patch on her blouse had already burned off, charring her skin in places, but dying out.

Tom Bell flickered past the open door and disappeared deeper into the row house.

Ned crept through the line of rooms on his side of the house, following the muzzle of his pistol, looking for White Jeans. Except for the ticking of a clock somewhere out of sight, the only sound was his own breathing and light footsteps. Heart thumping like a jackhammer, he swallowed his fear and tried to warn anyone else in the back of the house to clear out while they still could.

"Feller, if there's a back door to this place, you better take it!"

Passing an open door, Ned glanced across the hallway to see half a man's body sprawled on the floor, a victim of Tom Bell's .45. The old Ranger waved his arm around the doorframe at the same time his voice floated soft through the still air in the silent house. "It's me. Don't shoot."

"I see you. I'm right here."

Temples pounding and half deaf from the gunshots, Ned paused to glance at the plaster ceiling, hoping the floor joists above would creak and give away anyone upstairs. Taking a deep breath, he passed through a dining room and into the kitchen, trembling from tension.

Tom Bell appeared at the same time. Muscles' body lay in a spreading pool of blood. Tom leaned in so close to Ned's ear he felt his warm breath. "There's a staircase back here. The guy in white jeans is prob'ly above us. I have an idea."

They made their cautious way back through the narrow house. Ned expected to hear sirens at any minute. Heart pounding, he kept an eye on the doorway opening to the entry at the far end. They reached the living room and paused only a few feet from Kathleen's still body.

Tom Bell covered the stairs with the 1911. He held up a hand to keep Ned still. "Let's get out of here!"

He backed to the front door, opened it for three seconds and slammed it. Stepping lightly to join Ned in the living room, he held the constable still with a palm out gesture to wait. They could see the front door from their position, but were out of sight from the staircase, at least until anyone coming down would be exposed in the doorway.

The clock measured seconds off their lives, then a full minute. A car started on the street and another hissed on the wet pavement.

Chapter Sixty-two

Owen lay on a filthy cotton mattress in the extra bedroom of his brother's sixty-year-old farmhouse. There were no sheets, and the blue-and-white ticking was stained in several places. "What do you think?"

"I had an old dog that got shot in the stomach like that once. He laid under the porch for two weeks and then crawled out one day and ate some old baloney I had in the icebox."

"So he made it?"

Ellis grunted and sat back in his cane-bottom chair. "Naw, the baloney was bad and it killed him."

Owen grimaced. "Oh damn. Don't make me laugh. It hurts too bad. Tell me the truth. What do you think?"

"Well, you'd quit bleeding by the time you got here. While you was passed out, I checked that bullet hole. I think it broke a rib and glanced up. It cut through some muscle and missed everything else. Come out through the meat under your arm. It ain't infected, at least not that I can tell."

"You ain't no doctor, you know."

"I know it, Possum, but I doctored plenty of calves and dogs." He glanced through the dirty farmhouse windows at the sprawling cotton fields of Prosper, Texas. "I believe you'll be all right."

Though he hated the nickname, Owen had always bowed to his brother. He swallowed. "I hope you're right."

"Well, you can stay here for a good long while, if you'll stay out of sight."

"What'd you do with that car I came in?"

"It's in the barn. It'll stay there till you're healed, but then you get gone in it."

"I'll go quick as I can. Anybody see you put it there?"

"Probably. It sat out there in the yard for a couple of hours, too. I guarantee Dodd Dobbs saw it and he'll likely tell everybody he knows. He's worse than an old grammaw." Ellis studied the peeling wallpaper.

"It's hottern'n a six-shooter."

"I figured as much. Guess I ought not ask, but who was it that shot you?"

"I don't know for sure. One of three people."

"Damn. You tangled with three at one time?"

"One of 'em was a nigger deputy sheriff. I heard him on a police radio in a truck I stole. That's how I got away. If I was to bet, I'd say the others were the law too."

"Didn't they have no uniforms on?"

"No. I was pulling a cattle deal and they was acting like buyers."

"But they weren't." Ellis barked out a laugh. "That's why I got out of the business. It goes to show you can't trust nobody these days, not even the laws."

"I said don't make me laugh." Owen grimaced and held his side. "It hurts too bad. Go on and get out of here and let me sleep."

Ellis shook a brown bottle of thick liquid. "I'm gonna give you a shot of this, just in case."

"What is it?"

"Livestock penicillin. It works on a cow, it oughta work on you."

"That stuff might kill me if it ain't made for people. Besides, I remember from when I caught the clap that different medicines work on different things. How you know that's the right one?"

"Well, it's all I got, unless you think blackleg medicine'll work better." He drew a glass syringe full of white liquid that looked like Elmer's glue. "Roll over. This goes in your hip."

Owen rolled to his side, gasping as the wound pulled. "Oh God, that hurts. I hope you sterilized that thing."

"Boiled it." Ellis leaned over and jammed the dull needle into muscle.

Owen tightened up and groaned. "Damn that hurts."

"Wait'll I push this plunger."

"Oh *hell!*"

Ellis rocked back on his knees. "That'll do it. I'll give you another shot, day after tomorrow."

"You didn't use alcohol." Owen lay back, gasping from the pain in his chest. "You're supposed to wipe the skin with alcohol first."

"I never do it with the cows, so I forgot. I'll do it next time."

Chapter Sixty-three

Sirens rose in the distance. Apparently, White Jeans upstairs heard them at the same time and came thumping down the stairs. Instead of rushing out the door, he stopped on the last few steps, maybe listening, maybe wondering if the slamming door was a ruse.

Ned held his cocked pistol aimed at the open doorway. The muzzle wavered, but Tom Bell's .45 held as steady as if he were using a rest.

The guy on the stairs was in a bad position. If he was right-handed, either the pistol, a shoulder, or his head would be the first thing to appear. Ned estimated his height and steadied his aim where he expected a body part to materialize.

Tom Bell wasn't waiting, though, as the first distant siren was joined by a second, then a third. The moment he saw the muzzle of a shotgun emerge past the doorframe, he opened up with the big .45, punching holes through the plaster and lath.

White Jean's body fell into view, tumbling onto the hardwood floor and losing the pump shotgun in the process. He groaned and reached for a pistol in his belt, but Ned sprang forward and snatched it away.

Tom Bell quickly holstered his pistol. "Grab his other arm." They yanked the wounded man to his feet and he shrieked as the bones in his shattered, bloody shoulder ground together. "Shut up, buddy. You started this." Tom Bell yanked the front door open with one hand. "Let's get him in the car and get out of here."

Ned took in the wet street, surprised there were no onlookers watching. "Don't you think we should stay and explain what happened to the laws?"

"These guys *are* the laws, in some way. What I'm gonna do is find out what we need to know. That's what you wanted, right?"

The sirens grew closer and they rushed the wounded man across the sidewalk and into the backseat of Ned's Fury. Tom handed Ned the keys and followed their hostage into the car. "I told you I had a bad feeling about bringing that gal here."

"I'll listen to you if there's a next time." Ned pulled onto the street as the cold rain turned to wet snow.

Chapter Sixty-four

Ty Cobb and Jimmy Foxx Wilson paused at a barbed-wire fence hanging loose on bodark posts. Behind them, thick hardwoods stretched down to the Red River. On the opposite side, an overgrown pasture was quickly going back to nature everywhere except for a long, fresh trench dug along a line of mature oaks.

Ty Cobb rested one wader-covered foot on the bottom wire that stretched through loose staples with a creak. "I swear, I hate to see this."

"Old Gary Tidwell wouldn't've let this happened when he was alive." Jimmy Foxx scratched at the longish hair sticking out from under his cap.

"Well, he's gone and now Bill Preston has it."

"I reckon he won't care if we shoot a few squirrels over there on the creek." Jimmy Foxx threw a grin at his brother that said more than the words.

Ty Cobb scratched at a three-day stubble. "You know, this place used to be working alive with quail."

"They'll still be here. I 'magine Bill won't care if we bust up a covey or two, neither."

His brother laughed. "Hold my shotgun." He handed the humpback Browning to Jimmy Foxx who put one foot on the bottom strand and raised the next wire. Ty Cobb bent at the waist and stepped through the gap. They traded shotguns and repeated the process.

"Listen!" Jimmy Foxx pointed his nose into the wind like a retriever. "Them are quail talkin'."

"Sure 'nough. Let's go bust 'em up."

They hadn't taken two steps before a covey of birds exploded one hundred yards down the fencerow. The brothers paused, looking in that direction, and saw two men and a woman walking their way.

"Who's that?" Neither cared that they were on Bill Preston's land. They'd grown up hunting the river bottoms of Lamar County and knew every landowner who owned pastures, fields, woods, and meadows. "It ain't Bill."

"Naw, he's usually over there working on that new house they're building, or diggin' in that gully not far from his house." Jimmy Foxx squinted at the trio. "They're not huntin'. I do believe they're carryin' shovels."

"Gold diggers!"

Seeing the brothers, the trio froze.

Ty Cobb waved. "Y'all come on over here!" Cradling his shotgun in the crook of one arm, he watched them hesitate, bend their heads in discussion, and walk in their direction. Jimmy Foxx rested the barrel of his shotgun over his right shoulder.

The two men and a woman in casual city clothes took their own sweet time making their way through the knee-high weeds. All three wore coats that looked brand new. Recognizing them from Neal Box's store, the woman's face broke into a wide grin. "I know you two. You're the Wilson boys."

The brothers nodded as one. Jimmy Foxx tilted the time cap up on his forehead. "We know you, too. What're you doing out here, Scottie?"

The men waited, silent, holding their shovels as if they were war axes. Squaring her shoulders to make her breasts stand out, Scottie took the lead. "Mack Vick told me that big old oak tree standing out there all by itself is most likely where that Palmer Lake gold might be."

Jimmy Foxx grunted. "Mack knows cattle, but he don't know nothin' about trees. That there red oak come up when I was filling my diaper. They grow fast and big."

The men behind her looked disappointed. "Is this your land?"

Ty Cobb studied the young man in a flat top. "Good-looking haircut. I don't know you."

"Billy Taylor. I'm Scottie's boyfriend."

Back to her friends, Scottie raised an eyebrow. Neither brother knew whether it was a question or reaction to the man's statement. Ty Cobb couldn't help himself. "I didn't know for sure you had a boyfriend. You and Mack Vick looked kinda chummy up at the store the other day."

"Boyfriends come in all sizes and styles." Disinterested, Scottie cut her eyes toward the distant tree line and trench obviously dug by a bulldozer. "So do you know where we need to look?"

"Sure do."

They leaned forward, anticipating Jimmy Foxx's statement.

"Jewelry store. There ain't no gold out here, and you two fellers ain't got no business digging on this man's land, 'cause I bet Scottie didn't tell him y'all were coming out. I'd get myself gone if I was y'all."

"He's doing enough digging himself, he won't notice we were here." Scottie's smile disappeared in a flash. "Well, you're no friend at all. Come on, boys. Let's go back up to the store and see if anyone's had any luck. Maybe we'll find someone more accommodating to help us."

She spun on her heel and stalked away through the grass. Her boyfriend Billy paused. "Say she was running with another guy?"

Jimmy Foxx shrugged. "Said I saw her talking to Mack Vick."

Billy frowned at the ground, looking defeated. "How big an ol' boy is he?"

Ty Cobb's hand measured six inches above his head.

The boyfriend shrank even more. He met his silent buddy's eyes and they followed Scottie down the fence row.

Ty Cobb watched them climb the fence where they were first sighted. "They ain't got no sense at all, riding an old fence like that."

"Naw, and can you believe it, city folks just come out and start diggin' on private land like they got good sense."

"Aint' that the truth? Well, let's get after them quail before they all die of old age."

• • ● • •

Sheriff Cody Parker leaned against his car in the parking lot of Neal Box's store, his arms were crossed and he studied the half dozen cars parked around the domino hall. The news of the shootout between Anna, John, and the rustlers followed by hours of investigation had taken a toll.

Mayor Stratton had called him into his office, questioning Cody about Anna's bruised face and the incident with the rustlers. Halfway through the mayor's tirade, Cody figured out Stratton's concern. It wasn't budgetary issues that had him all twisted up. He had the hots for Anna and didn't want her to be placed in danger.

He needed to get out of Chisum and think, back home to the little community that was as comfortable as an old shoe.

He'd also driven out to keep an eye on the people coming into Center Springs. More and more complaints were being filed over trespassers looking for gold, though neither Neal Box or Oak Peterson cared. They were having a banner year, selling food, shovels, and buckets to the out-of-towners caught up in the gold rush. Oak had even hired some of the local boys to build screened trays that hopefuls bought to sift the dirt, in the hopes they could get permission to dig.

The only problem was that most of the landowners didn't want strangers driving through their pastures, leaving gates open, and digging exploratory holes. All except Neal Box, who gladly let anyone pay for the privilege of investigating the five hundred acres a mile from Palmer Lake that he leased from the owners who lived in Dallas.

The Wilson Boys pulled up and shut off their truck's engine.

The brothers joined Cody. Ty Cobb spat a long stream of tobacco juice onto the bottle caps that served as cheap paving and kicked one rubber shoe against the other to dislodge a clod of dried mud. "I had to run some of these treasure hunters off Bill Preston's land a little while ago."

The back of Cody's neck tingled. "They close to the big house on the overlook?"

"Down at the far end." Jimmy Foxx sat on the trunk of Cody's car and fished out a pocketknife to clean his fingernails.

Ty Cobb scratched under his hat. "Bill's new house is purty as a picture. Took him a while to get it built, though. The grade dropped off more than he expected and it took considerable fill dirt to level it off. They set the foundation and then changed their minds and doubled the size. It's gonna be a showplace when they're finished."

"How come 'em to make it bigger?"

"Had plenty of money to spend on his house, I reckon. He owns a big car dealership in Dallas. I heard he got some kind of deal and made a killing in the last few months."

"Where'd they dig it?"

"Dig what?"

"The fill dirt to level the foundation."

"On the northwest side of his place. Down on a draw that drains off toward the river. We shot some quail down there where he dug it out. Looky here what I found in some of that dirt he turned up." He held out an arrowhead. "First one I've seen in a couple of years."

Cody grunted a response. "That's what Ned was talking about when he told me some folks around here are mad 'cause he's digging too close to some of these springs. So you run some folks off for him?"

"Sure 'nough. That big-titted gal brung 'em out, but when we asked if she had permission to be diggin', she hauled it on out of there."

"Scottie?"

"You know her?"

"Know of her, like ever'body else." Cody grinned. "They were out prospecting?"

"Yep." Jimmy Foxx carved on a ragged thumbnail.

"What were y'all doing out there?"

"Huntin', a 'course."

"With or without permission?"

Ty Cobb scratched under his cap. "Don't know which. Didn't ask."

They watched a beat-up fifty-nine Plymouth roll to a stop in front of the store. Ike Reader emerged, looking embarrassed to be driving a car instead of his truck. Miss Mable stepped out of the backseat and waved.

Cody couldn't resist. "Miss Mable. Whatcha got in your overnight bag today?"

She set a battered blue train case beside Jimmy Foxx and flipped the metal latches. It was filled with baby chicks that popped their heads up and looked around, peeping at the sudden light.

The men chuckled. Cody reached out and lowered the lid before they could jump out in the cold. "You taking 'em in to sell?"

"Why, gracious no. I'm keepin' 'em in there so my cat don't get 'em while I'm gone."

"Shoulda thought of that."

Miss Mable locked the case, waved goodbye, and walked around behind the store.

Ike Reader couldn't stand not being part of the conversation. "Boys. Listen listen. Y'all know this is the wife's car, but my brakes went out on the truck and I had to carry it over to Tim's for him to fix 'em. Good thing too, 'cause I picked Miss Mable up out by Arthur City and she was so tired I doubt she coulda climbed up in the truck, even with the running boards."

"I wasn't gonna say anything, Ike." Cody grinned and crossed his arms. "But your old lady's gonna be mad when she sees how much mud you got packed in those wheel wells."

"Well, I been huntin' and almost got stuck."

Jimmy Foxx's interest perked up. "Get your deer?"

"Sure 'nough. It's in the trunk."

Ty Cobb winced. "It's gonna be full of blood."

"I put some 'toesacks under it."

Jimmy Foxx pushed off the car. "Let's see it." They followed Ike to the back and he raised the trunk. A huge ten-point buck was curled up like a dog and appeared to be sleeping instead of dead.

Jimmy Foxx leaned in close. "Good lord. That's the purdiest rack I've seen on a deer in ages."

Ty Cobb pushed in beside him. "Ike, how come you to curl him up like that?"

"I didn't. I just heaved him in and closed the lid. I shoulda gone ahead and gutted him, though. I nearly herniated myself trying to get that big bastard in there."

Standing beside the back bender, Cody glanced in from the side. "If I didn't know any better, I'd think it was just sleeping."

All four men stiffened when the deer slowly raised its head and blinked.

"It's *alive*," Jimmy Foxx whispered.

"It can't be." Ike crossed his arms and stepped back to argue. "I hit that thing so hard with the car it was knocked forty feet. You can see the dent in the fender. It was dead when I threw it in."

"I thought you said you *shot* a deer." Ty Cobb turned to face Ike.

The little farmer planted his feet. "I said I *got* a deer. You asked me if I got a deer, and I said yes. I didn't lie. I ain't like that."

He was interrupted when the deer regained its senses and

proceeded to kick the living dog-water out of the trunk and the backs of the taillights. For some unknown reason Ike Reader rushed to the car, reached in and grabbed the buck's antlers like he was going to hold it still. The deer braced its back feet against what was left of the passenger seat, planted his forelegs on the edge and leaped out. The buck's head hit Ike squarely in the nose so hard that water squirted from seven orifices.

They all agreed later the sound of their heads smacking together was like a raw egg dropped into a mixing bowl.

While Ike held his bleeding nose, the deer ran off down the highway toward Lake Chisum with the Wilson boys trailing behind, howling and loading their rifles. Cody watched them go.

It was the first time he'd laughed in days.

Chapter Sixty-five

Pepper and Mark were in her living room by the fireplace, enjoying the winter smell of woodsmoke. The big windows leaked cold air. They were listening to Tommy James and the Shondells on Pepper's radio and watching the last of the leaves drop off the red oaks in the Ordway House's front yard.

Miss Mable came around Neal's store and passed on the oil road. Pepper nudged Mark and pointed. "Looky there. She's flat-out crazy, walking in this cold, and without a coat."

A sadness fell over Mark in a dispirited wave. He'd seen people living not far from his aunt's house in Oklahoma who barely had a decent shirt to wear outside, let alone a good coat.

"Don't your mama have one we could give her?"

"I'll go ask."

The song "Mony, Mony" ended at the same time a car pulled up in front of the white two-story. Mark ran his fingers though his long hair to get it out of his eyes. "Do you know whose car that is?"

"No." Pepper turned down her radio, curious to see who would get out.

Three men waited inside while the shifty looking driver wearing a turtleneck and a coat buckled at the waist knocked on the door. Mark felt the hair rise on his arms at the way the man's eyes darted everywhere. Life had taught him to respect his instincts. Pepper started to answer, but he held her back. "Wait."

She frowned. "What's wrong with you?"

"Something ain't right."

"It's a car. What's not right with a car?"

"I don't like cars full of nothing but men. Not that many men."

Ida Belle came from the kitchen. "I'll get it. You kids wait right here." She opened the wooden door, but left the screen latched. "Hello?"

The man stuffed both hands into his coat pockets. His three-day stubble covered a dimple in his chin like Kirk Douglas', and Mark didn't like that, either. "Howdy. We're from Dallas and looking for a girl named Scottie. We heard tell she knows more about this buried treasure than she's lettin' on. We'd like to talk to her."

Pepper and Mark looked through the windows. "Shit! Look at that stupid coat. It has more pockets than all my clothes put together."

"You better lower your voice. He might hear you."

"So what?"

Ida Belle shook her head. "That's just a story started by my daughter. There's not any gold."

"We heard about it in Dallas, then a few minutes ago over at that little grocery."

"That's none of my business. We can't help you."

Pepper turned to Mark, fear in her eyes. "It went all the way to Dallas? Shit, I just wanted to get that big-titted gal's goat. I didn't mean for it to turn out like this."

"Shhh." Mark took her arm.

"Y'all better leave…" Ida Belle quit talking when the doors slammed and the car's occupants kicked through the leaves on their way to the house.

Mark spun and disappeared into the rear of the house. He cut through Pepper's bedroom and into her parents' room. Uncle James kept a twelve-gauge leaning in the corner. He grabbed the heavy humpback Browning and stepped into the entry hall just in time to see the men who'd been waiting in the car spread across the yard. One pitched an empty beer can into a drift of leaves.

"I need to talk to Scottie a minute. We hear you have somebody living here with you. Is it her? Is it Scottie?"

"I've said too much." Ida Belle latched the screen door. Her voice trembled. "Y'all need to go on now. You've been drinking."

One of the three dressed in square-toed work boots, jeans, and a dirty jean jacket scuffed a cigarette out under one foot and lit another. His face hardened. "Lady, we just want some information."

"Aunt Ida Belle said for you to go."

Mark stopped beside the staircase with the twelve-gauge in his hands. Carrying it port arms, he angled his body and waited. In any other fourteen-year-old's hands, the twelve-gauge would have looked too big, but he'd filled out in the last couple of months and the heavy shotgun didn't look odd at all. He was surprised that the barrel wasn't waving around, because despite his outward appearance, his nerves were jangling like a telephone.

Pockets raised both hands. "Hey, kid. Careful with that thing."

At the sight of the shotgun in Mark's hands, Ida Belle shifted to the side, giving Mark a clear view of the stranger on their porch. "My father-in-law is the constable. You better leave before he gets here."

"Is that an Indian?" Pockets squinted through the screen and lowered his hands to the wooden doorframe. "You got an *Indian* in the house with your white daughter?"

"I saw her in the window when we walked up." The chain-smoker who'd spoken unscrewed the cap on a nearly empty pint of whiskey and spoke around the cigarette in his lips. "But a long-haired *Indian*. That's as bad as having a nigger in the house."

Mark leveled the muzzle. "She said to get gone."

Chain-smoker glanced sideways toward something none of those inside could see. He stiffened and held up both hands. "All right, all right. We're going, but if I ever catch you out without that shotgun, it'll be me and you, *boy*."

Pockets also caught something in his peripheral vision. His eyes widened and he sidestepped down the plank steps. Their attention kept switching from Mark behind the screen to something else just out of sight on the road.

They took their time returning to the car. Pockets glanced over his shoulder and tried to build a little bravado that blew away in the wind. "These hicks don't know nothing. Let's go."

Pepper couldn't leave well enough alone. She joined her mother at the screen, frustrating Mark and getting between him and the two strangers. "Hey, dumb ass, I have your license number."

"Big deal." Pockets and Chain-smoker returned to the car after one more look at the oil road and slammed their doors. The car crunched slowly over the gravel drive and turned toward the store.

Ida Belle placed one hand over her heart, as if to steady it. "They're gone, but I bet they won't be the last. I wonder who the next fool will be."

Pepper watched them drive away and angled her head against the screen to see what they'd been looking at. "Mama, come looky here."

Curious, Ida Belle unlatched the screen and stepped out on the porch to see Miss Mable standing at the corner of the house, tucking a revolver back into her train case full of chicks. "My God. Miss Mable, get in this house where it's warm."

"They didn't look like nice men and I told them so when they tried to pick me up in Arthur City." Carrying the case in the crook of her arm, she allowed Ida Belle to hustle her inside. "The good Lord told me it'd be warm in here."

Ida Belle shook her head. "Arthur City! You walked that far in this cold? I swear. You don't carry that gun around everywhere you go, do you?"

"Why, I don't know." Miss Mable looked surprised. "Do I?"

Knees shaking in relief, Mark leaned the shotgun in the corner. "Aunt Ida Belle?"

She took a long, shuddering breath. "What hon?"

"You have any idea where Uncle James keeps the shells for that shotgun? That thing's as empty as Pepper's head."

Miss Mable placed her case on the telephone table. "I'd like a teacake, please." She pushed past them toward the kitchen.

Hearing the faint cheeping inside the case, Pepper rolled her eyes. "This place and these people are gonna drive me crazy."

Chapter Sixty-six

Ned drove through the increasing snowfall for ten minutes before the man in the backseat moaned and held up a weak hand, as if the gesture would make his shoulder stop hurting. "I'm bleeding to death."

Tom Bell's .45 slug had entered the tip of the CIA assassin's right shoulder, shattering it and tearing into his chest. His breathing was labored and he struggled to sit upright.

Ned squinted through the slapping windshield wipers with no particular destination in mind. They'd driven past the biggest graveyard he'd ever seen and finally saw a sign that said Arlington National Cemetery. Wet snow covered the ground.

His eyes flicked to the rearview mirror. The man's pale face told him he didn't have long. "We have a problem. I don't know where we're headed."

"Anywhere the road goes." Tom Bell's expressionless gray eyes stayed on the wounded man. "We need to do this fast. You're fading, buddy. I'm gonna ask you some questions and you better answer right quick."

Following the traffic, Ned passed a massive statue also covered in snow and lit by high-intensity lights. He recognized the iconic posture of marines planting the American flag, and the famous memorial only made him feel worse.

"I'll tell you anything you want. Get me to a hospital."

"In time." Tom Bell's voice was cold as the falling snow. "After we get some answers."

"Fine."

"What's your name?"

"Larry."

"Larry, who are you with?"

The wounded man groaned. He rested his head on the back of the seat. "What difference does it make?"

"A lot to us. You're with the Company, right?"

Larry swallowed and nodded.

"Why'd you try to kill us?"

"They'll kill *me* if I tell."

"Don't matter. You're dying as it is."

Ned shivered at the Ranger's emotionless voice. They passed over a bridge and the Jefferson Memorial. Few tourists braved the weather so the steps to the round classical revival structure were untracked. The marble and columns modeled on the Parthenon should have been inspiring, but the open-air structure at that moment was nothing more than a pole barn to him.

"Look buddy, I'm the one who shot you and I'm about to do it again if you don't tell me what I want to know. Who told you to start something with us in that bar and why?"

Larry's weak voice was wet. Blood dripped from his lips. "You know too much."

"What were you supposed to do with our bodies?"

"Agent Matteo ordered us to bury them. He set up the operation."

"Then what?"

"Louise was supposed to report that you were dead."

"Who was Louise?"

"The woman at the bar. She's...she was...an agent too."

Ned's eyes roamed from the mirror to the world beyond the wipers. His stomach rolled at what was going on in the backseat, but it was why they'd driven halfway across the country—to get answers.

The road drifted around a small lake. A sign pointed to the left. Tidal Basin. Ned glanced at the Washington Monument barely visible through the snow. The wipers packed slushy ice and snow to the bottom of the windshield.

"I'm getting weak, man. Get me to the hospital."

"He's taking us there. Now, who told you to kill us?"

"Mr. Gray. A guy that goes by the name of Mr. Gray."

"Mr. Brown, and now Mr. Gray?"

Larry coughed and grinned past the blood in his teeth. "We… they…all use alternate names."

"Then that won't do us any good. How do we find Gray?"

"You can't."

"We will."

Larry's shallow breathing became more labored, his voice thick and wet. "Hospital. Hurry."

"I'm not seeing one." Ned shifted his mind into neutral. For the second time that day he steered past the Roman architecture of the Lincoln Memorial. The earlier awe he'd felt about the monuments and buildings that housed the precious documents that were the foundation of a fragile framework of government was gone, because he knew the majesty of that two hundred years of trust and honor was on the brink of winking out. He glanced through the columns to see the sad, chiseled face of Abraham Lincoln defined by bright lights that were yellow in the falling weather.

Ned felt exactly the same.

Larry faded and Tom Bell nudged him awake. "Hey. You're in bad shape. You need to tell us where your boss is headquartered."

"It won't do you any good."

"We'll decide that. Where is it?"

"Route 123 in Langley."

"How'll we know when we get there?"

"Cross into Virginia. It'll be on your right. There's a sign that says Bureau of Public Roads. That's the Company."

Ned nodded. They already suspected it, but hearing it from the agent was progress. They completed the circle around the Lincoln Memorial and headed back past the Tidal Basin.

"Fine, then." Tom Bell shifted with his back against the door. "What's Gray's real name?"

"It won't do you any good. Get me to the hospital."

"Tell me now, then we'll get there. You don't have much longer."

Larry coughed blood. "I don't think I'm gonna make it."

The light went out of his eyes and Ned saw they were back at the Jefferson Memorial at the same time Larry died.

"Dammit." Tom Bell leaned back in his seat. "You were right, Larry, you were worse off than I thought."

Chapter Sixty-seven

Sheriff Cody Parker's office in the Lamar County Courthouse was much smaller than O.C. Rains' digs. A wooden desk and four oak filing cabinets set side-by-side took up one wall. A bank of windows usually brought in plenty of light, but the day was so cloudy Deputy Anna Sloan needed the desk lamp to finish her report on the shootout. She screwed the cap back onto her fountain pen when the phone rang. "Sheriff's office."

"I'm looking for Sheriff Cody Parker."

"He isn't in and I'm afraid he'll be out of the office for most of the day. I'm Deputy Anna Sloan. Can I help you?"

"I didn't expect *you* to answer."

Recognizing Stan Ewing's voice, her fingertips unconsciously touched her black eye and cheek. The swelling had gone down, but it would take weeks for the bruise to fade. She took a moment to answer. "Well, hello, cowboy."

"Bet you're surprised to hear me."

"Flabbergasted is the word."

He chuckled. "I feel the same way myself, but I'd say thunderstruck. I never expected to hear your voice again."

She swallowed and searched the ceiling for the right words. "Look, I didn't either. I expected that we'd run our course…"

"Hold on. Let's save that for the next date. I really was calling the sheriff. Can you take a message?"

Anna took a deep breath to calm her suddenly jangling nerves. "Shoot."

"I know who it is that he's probably looking for after that shootout with a couple of cattle rustlers. I was gonna leave this anonymously, if there's any way."

"That's hard to do at this point. How do you know about that incident way down there?"

"It's easy when the guy called and said I better be careful because some folks think I set the whole thing up, but I didn't. You know what happened that day at the sale barn."

"You're talking about Lucas DeWitt, the guy who gave me the contact information to set up my buy."

"Your buy? It was you that was there?"

"It was me, all right, and two other deputies."

"I'll be damned. You really are a deputy. I never figured you for the law."

Her mouth was suddenly dry. Now he knew almost everything about her and here she was, feeling like a high school girl with a crush. She pulled a strand of hair behind her ear, as if he could see through the receiver. "Let's get this taken care of first. You know the name of the guy who got away?"

"Sure do. His name is Owen Lee Bass, and he sent word back that he's gonna kill me when he gets the chance, but you know I didn't do anything, Anna. I just set up a meeting to get you some cattle."

"Don't worry about that. You know anything else?"

"No, but I bet he has a record and it'll probably include rustling somewhere."

"I can pull it up. What happened?"

"Like I said, Lucas caught up with me at the sale barn yesterday and told me that Owen called him to find out who'd given him his name. Lucas said it was me who introduced you to him. That's all I know, except I'm carrying a pistol now."

"Don't worry. We'll pull up his sheet and track him down." She paused. They were finished with that part of the conversation.

Stan stepped in to help. "Look, you have my number. Why don't you gimme a shout when you get the chance? I promise I won't call the sheriff's office every day, asking to talk to you."

Relief washed over her. She was back in control, or so she thought. "Good. Stay out of the honky-tonks and away from the sale barn for a while until we can pick this guy up. I'll give you a call when the smoke clears. How's that?"

"Fine. Hey…thanks."

"You're welcome."

"I hope that 'smoke clears' comment wasn't prophetic."

She thought about what she'd just said and smiled at the ten-dollar word used by a cowboy. "Me, too. I'll call you soon."

They hung up and she wondered why she'd said it would be soon. It didn't matter. She went to work tracking down Owen's rap sheet. The phone rang again and she snatched it off the cradle.

"You forget to blow me a kiss goodbye?"

Mayor Stratton's voice sounded surprised. "Why, no. Who do you think this is?"

Shocked, Anna put her hand over the mouthpiece and stifled a scream. "Uh, no, Mayor Stratton. It…was my mom. I was just talking to her. How can I help you?"

"Well, I wanted to see how you were feeling and if you're all right, ask you to supper one night soon."

Her breath caught. "I don't know. What night would be good for you and your wife?"

Chapter Sixty-eight

Agent Joe Hill sat behind his desk on the third floor of the nearly ten-year-old building in Langley, Virginia, bearing the sign Bureau of Public Roads. The walls were filled with memorabilia gathered from across the country, but there were no photos of him with a family, only government officials, friends, or alone on a spring creek in Missouri where he liked to fish.

Two other agents were in cushioned chairs on the opposite side of Hill's desk. Deep in thought, he opened a tobacco pouch and filled his pipe with cherry blend. In his office, there were no aliases. "Did they get the house cleaned up in time, Matt?"

The dark-skinned agent named Matteo adjusted the knot in his tie. "No, sir. The police got there first."

"I'm assuming protocol was followed in renting it."

"Yes. Louise did everything right, except for what happened once they were inside."

"You're right about that. I never expected the others to fail."

Matteo fidgeted as if their failure was his fault. "They underestimated their man."

"Do we know it was that old man? Maybe it was another agency."

"It was him, and another guy that's even older."

Irritated at the news, Hill finished packing the pipe and put the pouch in a desk drawer. He moved a snub-nosed revolver to the side and plucked out a Zippo. He lit it, puffed twice, and leaned back in thought. "So, two old country rubes took out five of our best agents."

"They're good." The second speaker had hair as reddish orange as a clown. "I'm not sure they don't have any training."

"Or your pros got overconfident."

Matt jerked a thumb. "Sammy here says they're working with another team. It makes sense. Two old men can't do that kind of damage, so try this idea. Maybe they were decoys like we were using Louise. Let's say they took Louise to the house and were followed by their secondary team. They opened the door, got out of the way, and let the pros do their job. They were in and out in minutes, leaving everyone dead but Larry Brimley. He's missing."

Men who moved through the world as invisible as ghosts were having trouble understanding how others with apparently less skill could outmaneuver them at every turn. Hill clicked the stem against an incisor. "You think this rogue team, or the two old men if that's who it was, took him for questioning, Agent Fontaine?"

"It's the only thing that makes sense." Sammy sat up straight, the same way he did to answer questions in school. "We checked the hospitals, but there's no sign of him. I called our usual doctors, thinking he might have gotten away, but none of them have seen him."

"Safe houses?"

"No. He vanished."

"He didn't vanish. They're probably working on him right now."

The two agents exchanged glances, but remained silent.

"Find them."

Agent Matteo laced his fingers. "How?"

Hill flipped the lid open on a small box, revealing several trout flies he'd inherited from his father. Gently touching the vintage flies, he worked on his next move in the game of chess called subterfuge and planned to go fishing as soon as the operation was cleaned up. "Figure it out. We're the CIA."

Chapter Sixty-nine

Cody, Anna, and John Washington were in Judge O.C. Rains' office. The judge was busy signing a warrant for Owen Lee Bass. "Where's Prosper, Texas?"

Elbows resting on his knees, Cody fiddled with his hat brim. Half sitting with one foot on the ground, Big John Washington took up most of a corner, leaning against a file cabinet with his arms crossed.

Anna perched herself on a stack of books taking up most of the other chair in the office. "It's a little farm community north of Dallas."

"Collin County?"

"Yep."

"Run it down for me, Anna, how you got this name." Cody hid a grin at how fast Anna's leg was swinging. He wondered if it was a sign of nervousness over serving the arrest warrant, or over a tall Austin cowboy that she'd been defensive about.

She described the phone call and her tenuous relationship with Stan while John and Cody tried to maintain their composure. She'd already growled at them over their grins and nudges, and they didn't want to set her off again in the judge's office.

"After that, it took me a while, but I pulled up his history through the new National Crime Information Center. It's only a year or so old, but NCIC had everything I needed. He was arrested here once for a DUI, so that gave me a start. Then I went from there, AKAs, family, known associates. A lot of people know him and Dale Thompson, who got killed in the shootout the other day."

"Sorry to hear George Nobles died." O.C. signed another paper. They were all silent at the mention of the stock inspector's name. "He was a good man."

"When I started running family names, Owen's brother popped up." Anna frowned at the smirks on Cody and John's faces." He'd been in jail for grand theft auto, armed robbery, assault, sexual assault, and…are you ready for this?…cattle rustling. Found him living in Prosper and called the local constable down there. His eyebrows were already up over folks around there talking about strange goings on at his place."

"How so?"

"He hadn't been working his fields much, and his kids had been talking about a sick relative that was staying there. The constable hung out up at the co-op gin for a while, just fishing around and learned that one of the local farmers had seen an unfamiliar car in Ellis' barn when the door was open. You know how folks talk. There ain't no secrets in a small town."

O.C. finished the paperwork and handed it over to Cody. "You hook up with the Collin County sheriff and y'all go in with them to make the arrest. I don't want you just knocking on the door by yourselves."

Cody slid the folded documents into the inside pocket of his uniform jacket. "We won't."

"That means all three of you. And you two quit grinnin' at her like you know something."

Eyes toward the floor, they nodded like recalcitrant children.

"Good. Now, y'all go get that sonofabitch."

Chapter Seventy

Doc Heinz said he'd let me go home pretty soon, and boy, was I glad. I'd always thought I'd enjoy being in the hospital, lazing around bed with nothing to do but sleep and read. I'd imagined days of being propped up with pillows, waited on hand and foot by pretty nurses, and digging through a stack of library books.

Instead, those nuns were in and out every fifteen minutes, poking and prodding at me, jamming needles into my butt, and generally fussing around. Most of 'em were sour old maids with lines around their mouths from keeping their lips pursed all the time, like they lived on green persimmons.

But there was one young nun who always had a grin and a mischievous look in her eye. It was her job to give me my shots when I needed 'em, and it was kinda embarrassing, because every time she stuck me, it was in the hip.

She saw my drawers more than Miss Becky did on washday, and the funny thing about it was that I heard her in the hall one morning, saying that she wanted to be the one to give me shots.

Doc Heinz came in one day when Miss Becky was gone. He sat at the end of the bed and watched me over the tops of his glasses. "How you feeling today?"

"I'm doing good. I still have that cough, but it's not as deep."

"Your asthma bothering you?"

"Not so's you'd notice."

"Stick out your arm."

I did, and he took a syringe out of his pocket.

"I'm gonna use you as my guinea pig." He laid a syringe flat on the inside of my forearm and barely slid the end of the needle under the skin. "I talked to your grandmother, and she agreed to let me try something to get your asthma under control. This is gamma globulin. You're gonna get one of these every six weeks for a good long while. Now, this is gonna sting a little."

"What is that stuff?" It looked like dirty water in the little window on the syringe's side.

"It's a serum made out of human blood that's supposed to boost your immune system."

He pushed the plunger and a bubble formed under the skin, like a blister. He wasn't kidding, it felt like a bee sting, but I held still.

"Good boy." He kept my arm in his soft hand, watching the blister. "So tell me about that dream you had, the one with rats in my operating room."

I told him, but without getting into the Poisoned Gift. When I finished, he chewed a lip. "You have a lot of dreams like that?"

"About rats?"

He chuckled. "No, about the future."

"How'd you know?"

"I've known your Grandpa since before the war."

He didn't need to say anything else about that. "Sometimes."

"Do they ever come during the day?"

I felt uneasy about where he was going, but had been taught not to lie to adults. "Sometimes."

"Umm, humm." He rubbed his thumb over the blister that I saw it was getting smaller. "Have you ever talked to anyone about it?"

"Miss Becky and Grandpa."

"No, I mean like a doctor."

"What would a doctor know about dreams?"

"Some doctors know a lot. That's not my line, but I know a couple of people you could talk to."

I saw something in his eyes I didn't like. I wanted to yank my arm away, but he was still rubbing that blister away. "I don't need to talk to anyone."

"Umm, humm. If you felt like you wanted to make those dreams stop, would you tell me?"

"Sure, but you can't stop dreams."

"Talking might help."

I looked out the window. "That won't help at all."

He waited a couple more beats. "Fine, then." He slapped my leg and stood. "I'm sending you home tomorrow, but you take it easy. No running, jumping, or playing for a while 'till those lungs clear up. I don't want to see you back in here again." He paused by the door and gave me a smile. "Now you enjoy the rest of the day and then get out of here before you ruin one of my nuns."

Dr. Heinz left and I lay there, wondering what he meant until the pretty nun came in with a steel tray. "Last shot. I'm gonna miss you. Now, roll over and show me that hip."

Chapter Seventy-one

Ned Parker steered the Fury into a motel parking lot. A snowplow was at work clearing over two feet of snow. Traffic on the streets moved at a snail's pace while more continued to fall.

Tom Bell shook his head. "I can't believe you."

"What does that mean?"

"You just drove back to that house where we killed all those people and unloaded a dead man into that woman's Mustang like we were delivering mail."

"They were all gone."

"I know it, but I never would have thought of that."

"The man deserved that much respect."

They'd spent the previous night in a motel while Larry Brimley rested in the Fury's trunk, perfectly preserved during the long cold night and following day.

The police were gone when they returned to the row house at dusk, but the woman's snow-covered car was still where they parked it on the next block up. Tom unlocked it with her keys and they quickly transferred Larry's body behind the wheel. The heavy snow kept folks inside, and no one saw them set him up behind the wheel.

Tom Bell chuckled at the memory. "The police are gonna be surprised when all this melts and they find him."

"It won't be long."

"So now what?"

Ned studied the neon-lit underside of the Holiday Inn's porte cochere. Outside, the bright star atop the familiar sign flickered and brightened every few seconds as the neon starburst spread outward, artificial fireworks in a snowstorm. "I'm gonna get a room in here under my name."

"Then what?"

"Either some of these people are gonna come see me, or I'm gonna use that number we have to call this Mr. Gray and talk to him myself. If that don't work, we're driving over there."

"Good lord."

Chapter Seventy-two

"I want to go in before daylight."

Cody didn't like the look in Sheriff Hawkins' eye. The Collin County lawman was a little too eager. "There's kids in there."

Anna sat between Cody and John in Hawkins' utilitarian office. "I don't like having murderers and rustlers in my county. Let's go get it done."

"We don't know how Ellis is going to react. It's a school day. Let's just wait until the kids are gone, or for him to feed his cows, or go to the field, if that's what he does. We can take him away from the house.

"His wife works at the Sav-U grocery store. She'll be gone then, too. That should just leave Owen in there by himself and nobody but him'll get hurt if he acts the fool."

Sheriff Hawkins paced his small office, alternately looking at photos of himself and local dignitaries, or studying a small bronze replica of the Texas state capitol on his desk. "Should we notify the local paper? They may want to cover it."

Understanding dawned on Cody. The man had ambition, but not the sense or bottom to make it work. "We'll call them as soon as we have Owen in custody. This may be nothing more than knocking on the door and he gives up. That wouldn't make a very good story, would it, getting them excited about something and then just have the guy hold out his wrists."

The attention-hungry Sheriff Hawkins thought for a moment as he straightened a photo on the wall. "I guess not. Maybe we can take a picture afterwards."

Anna rolled her eyes.

Chapter Seventy-three

Tom Bell was in the shower when Ned turned down the sound on the color television and picked up the phone. He hated showers and was aggravated because the room didn't have a tub. "Long distance to Center Springs, Texas. I'm calling Miss Becky Parker. This here's Ned Parker."

He studied the oily sheen on two pump shotguns lying on the bed as the call went through. He thought the operator had cut him off, but the phone in Center Springs finally rang through a storm of static. The receiver clacked and a voice spoke through a low buzz. "Hello?"

The operator came through loud and clear. "I have a person-to-person call to Miss Becky Parker."

"This is Pepper."

"Is Miss Becky Parker there?"

"Yeah, but who's calling?"

"Ned Parker."

"Well put him on."

"Are you Miss Becky Parker?"

There was a brief silence. "Sure."

"You said you were Pepper."

"That's my nickname. If you'd asked for Pepper you'd have known right off."

"Pepper!" Ned had no idea she couldn't hear him. "Operator. Pepper'll be all right."

"Fine, then. Here's your party. I'm connecting you now."

The line clicked. "Pepper. Can you hear me?"

"Grandpa! Where are you?"

"A long way off, honey. Who's there with you?"

"Miss Becky. We just got home from the hospital. Uncle James and Aunt Ida Belle are staying with Top tonight."

Ned started to ask her about his grandson, but was afraid of what he'd hear. He needed to get either the good news or the bad from an adult. "Good. Put your grandmother on the line."

"I just went through all that so I can talk to you. She won't tell you, but Tucker's out there in his car asleep again."

"Why does that bother you?"

"Cause he oughta have sense enough to come inside. It's colder than a well-digger's butt out there and he's asleep with the motor running to stay warm. If he's trying to earn extra money, why's he wasting it on gas? He's liable to kill himself breathing that exhaust."

"I'll talk to him when I get back. Now let me talk to your grandma."

"But I wanted to talk to you. Mark has an idea that Tucker's up to something else."

Ned rubbed his bald head in frustration. "Now why would he say that?"

"I don't know."

"Put Mark on."

"He's over at Uncle Cody's, stacking wood on the porch. He wanted to make a little spending money."

"All right. Have him tell Cody what he's thinking."

"I don't know when Uncle Cody'll be back. He's gone to Collin County."

"Good goddlemighty, girl, where's Miss Becky?"

"She's in the kitchen. But Grandpa, I want to talk to you about something else. There was a guy who come up to the house yesterday and wanted me to sell him that gold piece of

Daddy's. He had that big-titted gal from the store with him and I got nervous."

"You should have been, and I'm thinking about blistering your butt when I get home over it. Tell that to Cody, too. Now, put your grandmama on the line."

"Fine then." He heard the receiver click against the wooden telephone table, then Pepper's faint voice. "It's Grandpa. He wants to talk to you, not me. You can tell him about the stole still, too. He wouldn't let *me*."

Miss Becky rattled the phone some more and Ned closed his eyes when she spoke. "Ned?"

"Hi, honey." The tight muscles in his neck eased and he settled down at the round table beside the window, nearly bumping his head on the swag lamp suspended directly over the ashtray positioned in the exact center. "What about the stolen still?"

"More whiskey is already showing up and they're thinking it's from that one."

"I told them not to set it up on the square. Now somebody's already fired it up again."

"That don't matter much right now. Where are you?"

"We're in the Holiday Inn just outside of Washington. Maryland, I believe. We're still trying to find the man who started all this. How's Top?" He held his breath.

"He's better. The doctor says he's out of danger and his lungs are clearing up every day."

"So they got a good handle on it? He's gonna be fine?"

"I didn't say that. Dr. Heinz says he's getting stronger. If the medicine keeps working and he don't backslide tonight, they'll send him home tomorrow. I'm worried about you, too. When are you coming home?"

"As soon as I find that man."

"Ned, you don't have to do this. Top's gonna be all right. Come home."

"You'd want me to keep on after him if somebody *shot* Top. It's the same thing."

"We need you here."

"You have Cody and John and James. I need to find this feller before he hurts somebody else."

"We need you."

"It won't be much longer."

"Ned, let the Lord handle this. Vengeance is…"

"…Mine. It's *mine*. You've told me that before. I believe the Lord is using me to find the man responsible. You know, others died besides Top getting' sick. That's how He works, in mysterious ways."

She was silent with nothing but static on the long distance line. "Y'all had any trouble?"

"Not so's you'd notice."

She was silent on the other end of the line. "What are you gonna do when you finally root him out?"

"I don't know yet." He absently watched a commercial featuring a knight on a white horse, aiming a lance at people and whitening their clothes. "You tell Cody to keep an eye out. I believe these people know who I am, and I wouldn't put it past them to try something."

"What do you mean?"

He heard the shower shut off. "I mean keep an eye out." He glanced out the window at the snow-covered parking lot. A car with smoke pouring from the tailpipe and bad shocks on the rear made him think of Tucker asleep in the cold yard and he grinned. "Hey, tell Cody to pick Tucker up next time he sees him."

"Well, my stars, Ned. How come?"

"He's running whiskey in the back of that car. That's why it's sittin' low in the rear."

"How do you know that?"

"I don't for sure, but I have a good idea. He'll know who took the still and it'll lead back to Doak who I 'magine has it fired up already."

"I never had no idea."

"That's because Tucker's kinfolk."

"What if you're wrong?"

"Tell him I'm sorry, and to go get a real job so I won't be suspicioning him, but I'm not."

"All right. I'll let you go. Ned, you be careful."

"It seems like we have this conversation a little too often."

"I was thinkin' the same thing. I'll keep prayin' for you."

Ned thought about the men and one woman they'd left dead. "We're gonna need it."

Chapter Seventy-four

Tom Bell flicked a speck off his black hat in the Holiday Inn and rested it upside down on top of the metal television cabinet. "You think this is a good idea?"

Ned stuck his index finger in the dial and spun it. "I do."

"They can trace the call if you stay on long enough."

"That's what I'm hopin' for."

Tom glanced out the window at the nearly empty, snow-covered lot. Only one car was parked in front of the coffee shop less than fifty yards away. "Go ahead on, then." He settled in the chair, lacing his fingers across his flat belly.

"I intend to." He dialed the phone. "Yes, hello? This is Constable Ned Parker. I need to speak to a Mr. Gray who had a...whatta ya call it?...assignment in Center Springs Texas."

He listened for a moment. "I know you don't know who that is, or where Center Springs is, either. I intend to talk to your Mr. Gray right now, or I'm gonna drive over there and go through you to do it."

Ned waited and nodded at Tom. He put one hand over the mouthpiece. "She's seeing if anybody knows anything...hello?" He listened. "She's transferring me."

Ned tilted the phone and Tom Bell leaned in to listen. "To who?"

"Didn't say."

A male voice came through the earpiece. "Hello?"

"This is Constable Ned Parker."

"That's what my secretary said. How can I help you Mr. Parker?"

"So she already knew who I was calling, huh? Is your name Mr. Gray?"

"How can I help you, Constable?"

"That's good enough for me. You were in Chisum and Center Springs a couple of weeks ago."

"No, I wasn't."

"Yes you were, and some of your friends too. That crap you had Curtis Gaines spray from his airplane killed some folks, and made a bunch of others sick, some of my people."

"Mr. Parker. I'm sure you don't know much about the CIA or clandestine operations, but even if an operative went to Texas and did the things you say, they wouldn't be talking with you on an open line. You never know who's listening."

"*I'm* listening. I want to know who you work for and what *operative* ordered you to do what you did."

The man on the other end of the line laughed and Ned knew for a fact that the guy had been toying with him from the minute he picked up the receiver. "I don't know what world you live in, but no one here is named Mr. Gray, and no one here will talk to you about your accusations or about who they work for, or with. Are you getting my message Mr. Parker?"

"I'm gettin' pretty tired of your guff. I believe you're responsible for those deaths or that little gal a minute ago wouldn't have put you on the line. I intend to take you in. I'm coming to your office before the end of the day and putting you under arrest."

"You can't arrest me!" The voice laughed again. "This is ridiculous. You won't even get through the *gate*. I don't know why I'm even talking to you. I'm going to hang up now."

"One of your men died in Austin."

The line was silent. Ned met Tom Bell's eyes.

"Four more were killed in a house yesterday. One was a woman."

"I heard about four murders on the news. They say another was taken hostage. Do you know anything about that, Mr. Parker?"

Ned turned it back on him. "I heard something about it."

"Did you do it?"

"I want to talk to you face-to-face."

"That's not going to happen."

"Then I'm coming through your front door, like I said."

"You do that, and you'll be arrested, badge or no badge."

Ned figured they'd had enough time to trace the call. "I'll be there in an hour."

"Wait a minute."

Ned paused.

"It's snowing hard out there and the roads will be clogged. I don't know how you got this number, because it isn't published. You say you know where I am? Drive on in and give your name to the guard at the gate. I'll make sure he lets you in. You've obviously gathered a lot of information, all of it incorrect. Let's clear all this up. I have a previous appointment. Be here in three hours."

"Fine. I'll see you there."

The call disconnected and the two lawmen studied each other across the motel room.

Tom Bell's eyes were battle-bright. "They'll be here before you know it."

"I'm countin' on it."

Chapter Seventy-five

Joe Hill punched another line. "Did you get it?"

The voice on the other end was clipped, all business. "Just a minute. We're working on it."

Hill waited, knocking the dollop from his pipe into a glass ashtray and scraping the inside with a metal pick.

"Got it. Room Twelve at the Holiday Inn just across the line in Maryland."

"Good." He hung up and addressed the agent across the desk. "I want a team there in thirty minutes."

The Italian-looking agent nodded. "Orders?"

"He killed our agents and kidnapped another. Neutralize him and anyone else. Do it personally."

"Just exactly how do we recognize this guy?"

Hill's desk phone rang. "Sixties, pot belly, cowboy hat. He'll stand out. Leave the bodies there."

"Yes sir. Then locate and eliminate Agent Carl Hanson. He's going by the code name Mr. Brown. You know him by sight?"

Matt simply nodded.

"He's become a threat and we can no longer trust him."

"You're talking about wet work. You know I've never personally done that kind of thing."

"We all have to start somewhere, and I've been watching you. You'll do fine."

Chapter Seventy-six

Mr. Brown tracked through the snow in the Holiday Inn parking lot and pushed through the door into the coffee shop. He took a seat at a booth overlooking the two-story motel and Ned Parker's red Plymouth Fury. He was confident that his time with the Company was over.

Guilty over what he'd done in Center Springs, he felt even worse after setting up the old men. Mr. Brown had hoped Mr. Gray would come out to the roadhouse with his team to settle with the Texans. He drove down the road and parked on a turnout, watching the agents when they arrived. Disappointed that Mr. Gray wasn't with them, Mr. Brown drove back to the Gulf station and called the sheriff's department to tell them that trouble was about to break out.

What followed was a shock. A man in a fedora arrived in an unmarked car and went inside. Twenty minutes later the parking lot was crawling with local police who hauled the four agents away in handcuffs.

He was surprised to see Parker and the other Texan emerge not long after, speak with a drunk woman in the parking lot, and take her home. Confused, Mr. Brown followed them to a row house in Alexandria and after what sounded like an intensive firefight, emerged with a wounded man.

He followed at a distance as they drove aimlessly through the streets before pulling into the Holiday Inn and renting a room. He almost laughed aloud when they dragged the apparently dead hostage from the backseat and put him in the trunk like luggage. Mr. Brown spent the night in the chilly car, running the engine only when the cold became unbearable.

He trailed them back to the row house the next morning, this time chuckling when they propped the body behind the wheel. Those two old men kept him in stitches. Torn between simply walking away to disappear forever or watching to see what came next, he waited to see this final act of the drama that had been playing out for days.

Ordering coffee in the warm café, he lit a cigarette and watched the snow fall, thinking about where he'd come from and the jobs he'd been assigned since joining the Company. He didn't mind the overseas work, but the truth was that he wanted to see this thing done, so he could walk away and divest himself of the guilt he carried after performing experimental warfare on American soil that took the lives of his fellow citizens.

He liked the idea of vanishing forever, thinking of the skimmed money he'd squirreled away in his offshore bank account, and the twenty thousand dollars in cash stowed in the trunk that would support him and his family on a warm Mexican beach for the rest of his life.

Chapter Seventy-seven

Agent Matt Matteo killed the engine of the 1965 Galaxie 500 after backing into a snowy parking slot at the edge of the two-story, L-shaped Holiday Inn. There were only a dozen snow-covered cars scattered in front of the rooms. Tire tracks crisscrossed the buried blacktop.

It was Matteo's first "wet" assignment and he intended to do things right. He'd learned from the first team that got shot up in Alexandria not to take the two old men for granted.

Heavy snow fell as he studied the motel. Drapes darkened more than half of the rooms, while the occupants of several others had theirs opened to spill bright yellow light onto the exterior walkways on both the ground and second floors.

Agent Sammy Fontaine cracked the window, lit a cigarette, and studied the snow-covered cars. He was the only redhead in the department and often sported a sunburn in the summer months. Freckles spotted his nose, prompting the nickname Opie that he hated. "There's Room Twelve."

Matteo squinted. "Yep." Room Twelve was on the little end of the L-shaped motel.

They studied the motel with rooms opening onto the parking lot. The metal balcony rails were thick with fallen snow. The heated swimming pool steamed in the cold air, but still looked slushy. The interior of the coffee shop on the corner glowed with warm, yellow light.

"Glad they're on the first floor."

A nonsmoker, Matteo cracked his window to create a cross breeze. "Why?"

"Things could get tight on the second. Limited access from two directions. I like the first floor better."

"Well, Opie, you get your wish."

"Don't call me that." Sammy stopped when another car matching theirs swung past and pulled in at short end of the motel. "There's the rest of the guys."

"I see them."

"What do we do now?"

"Knock on the door."

"That's pretty smart."

Matteo shrugged at the sarcasm. "The drapes are closed."

"Doesn't matter."

Agent Matteo coughed softly and cracked his own window for more ventilation. "Good point." He rested suddenly nervous fingers on the butt of the Colt Python hanging under his left arm. "Let's wait a minute."

Chapter Seventy-eight

"They're here." Ned stood and shrugged on his barn coat that was much warmer than the sport jacket he usually wore. He picked up a shotgun and patted the heavy shells sagging his outside pocket. He didn't need to check the .38 in his holster. It was always loaded and there were more than enough rounds bulging the other pocket.

Tom Bell came out of the bathroom to the sound of the flushing toilet. "Folks need to learn how to flush after they pee. Whoever had this room didn't believe in pushing that little lever."

He hefted the other pump shotgun, checked the loads, and peeked around the heavy drapes in Room One. "I can barely see through all this falling weather. There's one government car backed in over across the lot. Another drove down to the far end by our room. How do you want to play this?"

Ned's stomach that had been rolling steadied. It was finally time. "I just want one man to get us through those gates."

"I'm not sure how this one's gonna work. Hang on. I have an idea." Tom Bell put the Remington pump back on the bed and removed his hat. "Follow me close so they don't see that barn coat and we're gonna just walk up while they're trying to get through that door.

"What're you doing?"

"We're gonna let them look down the muzzles of these shot-guns and persuade one of 'em to go along with us."

"If that don't work?"

"Why, they'll try to shoot us, but bunched up as they are, I believe these scatter guns'll level 'em all."

"We need one alive."

"I hope it works out that way."

Chapter Seventy-nine

Agent Matteo glanced up at the Holiday Inn sign as if its familiarity would settle his nerves. Opie's cigarette butt went out the
cracked window, and it was time. Nerves vibrating like guitar
strings, Matteo yanked the door handle and stepped out of the
car and pointed at Room Twelve. "Let's go."

Four agents piled out of the other car and drew their weapons.
They split up on both sides of the door and Agent Matteo rapped
his knuckles on the blue door of Room Twelve. "Federal agents."

Nothing moved behind the drapes.

"Federal agents. Open up!"

When there was still no response, redheaded Agent Fontaine
backed up and gave the door a kick. The steel frame refused to
yield, and he kicked it again while the other agents kept their
eyes directed at the knob.

Matteo glanced around to see what kind of crowd they might
be drawing. Through the heavy snow, he saw an old white-haired
man with a cane and an overcoat make his slow, creaky way out
of Room One beside the motel's office.

Seeing no threat, he followed the others.

Chapter Eighty

Ned Parker followed Tom's lead and kept the old Ranger between him and the shotgun that he carried. They'd barely stepped off the walkway and onto the drive when they heard a shout.

"Mr. Ned."

Tom tensed and almost raised his own shotgun held low against his leg. "It's you, Ned." Tom never took his eyes off the cluster of agents with their backs to him. He paused, not frightened, but curious.

Ned spun on his heel. The stranger's attention flicked back and forth between the twelve-gauge pointed at his stomach and the agents who finally breached the door and poured inside.

"Don't shoot me, gentlemen. I'm with you and we have to move *now*. Mr. Ned, you need to come with me."

"I saw you in the waiting room back at St. Joseph Hospital."

"My name's Mr. Brown. We only have a few seconds before those guys come pouring back out. They're here to kill you. Y'all have to come with me *right now* before they realize what happened."

Ned shot a look toward the opposite end of the parking lot. The only thing to see was snow, blue doors behind a veil of falling snow, and one dark opening where they'd kicked their way into Room Twelve. It was the familiar reference of 'Mr. Ned,' an age-old title of Southern respect that made his decision.

"Let's go, but don't run. Just follow me." Mr. Brown led them to a Mercury Cougar parked on the street around the corner of the coffee shop. "Get in."

Ned raised his eyebrows at Tom Bell, who returned the expression. "Constable, the situation has become fluid. You ride in the front."

Mr. Brown steered onto the street while the confused agents stood in the parking lot, scratching their heads, eyes searching the motel's doors and windows.

Ned twisted so his back was against the fender. "I don't believe I know you."

Mr. Brown glanced toward his passenger and then back to the rutted, icy road. "I'm one of the guys you're looking for."

The old constable's face hardened and he reached for the .38 on his belt. Tom Bell's voice came soft over the seat. "Ned. I've got this .45 pointed at his back. Let's hear what he has to say, then you can kill him if you want to."

Mr. Brown swallowed. "Let me explain."

Ned threw a look out the back window to see if they were being followed. "You better drive real careful."

"That's my intention. Look, I'm going to get some distance between us and those guys back there, then we can talk."

"You with them?"

"Yes and no."

"You're gettin' closer to Hell every second."

"Yes, I'm CIA, and they are too, but they're here to either kill you or take you into custody. I'm not with them. Not anymore. I'm trying to help you."

"Murderers don't kill people one week and then help them the next."

"You're right about that." Mr. Brown took a left and merged onto the icy highway. Only one lane was passable and he fell in line with other drivers leaving Washington. His eyes flicked to the rearview mirror and back through the windshield. "People weren't supposed to die. I went to your town as part of my job, but I was lied to."

"That's what you say."

"Look, I know you're going to find it hard to believe me, but I'm telling you the truth. I'm trying to do what's right here."

Ned angled his head to see Tom's .45 pointed at the driver just as he'd said. He forced himself to relax and settle back. "Go to talkin', but first tell me where you're from."

"Texas, sir. Gilmer."

"How could an East Texas boy turn out like you?"

It was evident the question stung. Mr. Brown stared past the rhythmic wipers and followed the single-file line of cars creeping through the storm. He told them everything that had happened from the time they arrived at Curtis Gaines' airplane hangar, to his final change of heart outside of the roadhouse. He explained Gold Dust, what it was supposed to do, and how it had mutated.

They listened without interrupting as Mr. Brown talked, though Ned's face stayed beet-red in anger. His explanation ended when an exit appeared. "We're getting off here."

Ned squinted into the storm. "Where we going?"

"To a safe house."

"What's that?"

"A place in the country that I've rented for a few years."

Ned rubbed the back of his neck in frustration. He wasn't in charge and it aggravated him to depend on someone else. "Where is it?"

"No. I'll tell you more when we get there."

Tom Bell slipped the Colt back into its holster. "I'm putting this up. That don't mean I believe you."

"I wouldn't either," Mr. Brown said and turned again, leaving the city behind.

Chapter Eighty-one

"How'd that happen?" Agent Joe Hill felt his blood pressure rise. The familiar burn of stomach acid rose in his throat.

Agent Matteo stood on the opposite side of the polished desk, hands folded in front of him. His gaze kept slipping off Hill's flashing eyes and toward the snow-covered trees outside. It had stopped for the moment and a flock of small birds swept through the sky like a school of fish in the ocean. He felt like a fish separated from the school, easy prey.

The operation at the motel was his, and his failure was unforgiveable. The only thing he could think to do was shift the blame and hope Hill saw a glimmer of truth in his story.

"I think someone tipped them off."

"I'm listening."

"This whole thing smelled from the outset, sir. It looks like those two old guys aren't who they say they are. They're too good, and they stay one step ahead every time we get close. Opie, I mean Agent Fontaine, agrees. We feel they may be working for another organization."

Agent Hill leaned back the chair and picked up the cold briar pipe on his desk. He bit down on the stem. "So you think the Russians are behind this?"

"Not at all. I've talked to a couple of the other guys. We think it's another agency here in the Company."

"Another department in this *building*?"

"We considered that possibility, but it didn't make sense. At first we thought it was an overlapping department, not realizing they were in our territory, but that's not it. I…we…think it's a different black team that's gone rogue."

Hill swiveled in his chair and clicked the pipe stem against his teeth, studying a photo beside his desk lamp of him with a glistening McCloud trout. Written in ink across the image was, *Crane Creek, Mo., 1967*. "You're saying it's an overlap."

"That's the only thing that makes sense. Our theory is they'd been monitoring the Gold Dust mission, and when it went south they saw an opportunity to take us down. You know as well as I do that our financial allocations have taken a hit the past couple of years, with most everything focused on the war in Vietnam.

"Somewhere along the way, word got out about what we were doing, and when the bacteria got out of hand, they pounced. They're taking out our guys, or turning them. I don't trust half the people in the other suits."

"You realize Parker is nothing but a small-town cop."

"He was. But we found out that a significant amount of the Gold Dust operating funds are missing. Some were paid out, but when the accountant got involved, he noticed that the payouts from Mr. Brown were much higher than other operations. Maybe cash turned him and Parker. Money does that.

"In my opinion, Mr. Brown paid this Parker guy to look the other way, but when his grandkid nearly died, he decided to take matters in his own hands. No amount of money can replace a child."

"That part I *do* know. Parker called *me*."

Surprised, Agent Matteo paused. "How'd he get your name and number?"

"Not just the number, my extension too. That gives credit to your idea of a rogue team. He's saying one thing, that he's looking for whoever coordinated the mission, but at the same time, he runs into some of our best men who were assigned to take him out…"

"See, this guy's a ghost! He knows more than he should."

"There's holes all through this thing, and a dozen amateur slipups."

"That's my point." Matteo's eyes returned to the window and the flock of birds swooping in unison. "The other old guy must be a pro, but we think he's not alone. Most likely an operative who came out of retirement, and he's good, too. We still have one agent missing from the team that was supposed to take them out in Tyson's Corner, and then failed again in the row house. The whole thing's suspicious. It looks like Agent Larry Brimley's working for them. In my opinion, that's how they managed to kill the entire team."

Hill lit the pipe with a paper match. "Back to the motel."

"Yes, sir. I called the mission a go, and we moved on the motel room. It was snowing hard. Those steel doorframes are a bitch, but we finally got in and the room was empty. We canvassed the entire motel, but found out they'd disappeared only minutes before we arrived. See, they know our schedule right down to the minute.

"We spoke to everyone, from the manager on down. The manager said he saw two old men leave with a younger man while we were in the target room. We think it was Brimley or Mr. Brown."

"I don't see the connection. It doesn't make sense for either one of those guys to wait until then, and Agent Brimley's possibly wounded."

"It does to us. Again, money. Brown's gone rogue, pulled Brimley in, and they tipped the old men off we were closing in. We think they're after you, and then they saw you weren't with my team, they disappeared to wait for another opportunity to take you out."

Hill realized his pipe had gone out and lit it again. He swiveled in his chair to study a second large photo on the wall of him kneeling and holding a fat trout in the same Missouri creek. An unfamiliar feeling of unease coiled in his stomach, knowing someone higher in the Company was looking for an opportunity to take him down for the Gold Dust fiasco. He'd never been personally targeted, but had seen it happen more than once. "Let's say you're right. Now what?"

Agent Matteo shrugged, uncertain. "That's the part we haven't figured out. If it was me, I'd be trying to learn more names. Real ones. "

"Mine?"

"Yes."

"Thank you. Let me know the minute any new information comes to light."

"Yes, sir." Relieved that he might have saved his job with a partially manufactured story and conjecture, Agent Matteo spun on his heel and left.

Agent Hill puffed his pipe. The whole failed mission was spinning out of control. He was too close to retirement for such an issue. For the first time in his career, he was going to kick this one upstairs.

The pipe stem clamped in his teeth, he rolled a sheet of blank paper into his IBM Selectric typewriter and wrote his resignation. Finished, he yanked it out and signed it with his Christian name.

With that done, he leaned back and reflected on how long it had been since he'd been fishing in his favorite Missouri creek, the Crane.

Chapter Eighty-two

The storm slacked off and the picturesque Virginia countryside was directly opposite the bustle of Washington. Leafless branches loaded with snow reached for the cloudy sky, making Ned homesick. Travel was slow on the buried two-lane road that wound like a snake through the rolling countryside.

Low rock walls stacked by the hands of slaves matched the length of the highway, defining the property lines of eighteenth- and nineteenth-century houses set well back from the road. The CIA agent ignored their glowing windows and concentrated on keeping the car between the ditches on the treacherous, icy road. Other cars and drivers hadn't been as lucky. More than a few abandoned cars were sideways in the ditches. One had plowed through one of rock walls.

It was dusk when Agent Brown turned onto a trackless driveway and killed the engine beside a dark farmhouse. Ned and Tom Bell stepped out, keeping their weapons close at hand as Mr. Brown unlocked the door. They entered the house that smelled musty from disuse.

Ned unsnapped his holstered pistol, just in case. "What'd you call this place?"

"A safe house I maintain. Not even the Company knows about it. We have to be gone in the morning, though. We can't take any chances by sitting still."

Once inside with an alarm set, Mr. Brown moved around the kitchen, closing the blinds. "How'd you pull that off back there at the motel?"

Ned's attention never wavered from the agent. He didn't trust the man any farther than he could throw him. "Wasn't anything to it. Tom here saw a couple that rented the room for only a couple of hours."

Mr. Brown frowned. "I don't get it."

Tom Bell grinned. "They went in without any luggage. I waited about fifteen minutes and knocked on the door. They were…how do you say it?…*in flagrante delicto*. That's Latin for—"

"I know. A misdeed."

"Indeed. Folks caught with their pants down, or off, tend to do what an officer of the law says. I suggested they leave right then and go back to their own spouses, and we kept the room."

Shaking his head, Mr. Brown adjusted the thermostat and the farmhouse rattled as the furnace in the basement bellowed glorious heat smelling of burned dust. "I saw what you were doing. So your plan was to ambush those guys and kill them all?"

"Not all of 'em." Ned hung one arm over the back of the chair and crossed his legs as if they were having a family discussion back in Miss Becky's kitchen. "We were gonna take one of 'em with us, whether they all surrendered, or there was only one left breathin'."

"But lawmen can't do that, Constable." Mr. Brown lit a cigarette, shook the match out, and dropped into an ashtray from the Washington Diplomat Motel.

"You're not one to be talking about rules and what the law can and can't do."

Mr. Brown took a long drag as if would help him think. "You're right about that, but I knew right from wrong growing up." He made eye contact with Tom Bell. "You a Constable too?"

Tom moved his coat's lapel. Mr. Brown's eyebrows rose. "You're a Texas *Ranger*? You don't have any jurisdiction here."

Ned snorted. "Don't you Washington people know anything?"

"What do you mean by that?"

"Our jurisdiction comes from what's right."

"What did you intend to do once you *kidnapped* an agent?"

Ned didn't like the word, but had to swallow his pride. It was rough going down. "You're putting a lot of polish on that word *agent*. That guy and his buddies was aiming to kill us. Your people had already tried it before. Our idea was to take one of 'em somewhere we could persuade him to give us the information we're looking for."

Tom Bell broke in. "It's Ned's idea of working his way up the ladder, and the truth is, there's a certain amount of logic to his method, though we might have encountered some problems along the way, right?"

"Breaking the law doesn't suit you two."

"How do you know what suits us, son?"

Mr. Brown let his gaze slip from the Ranger's cold eyes. "I grew up with men like you. Taking someone against their will is one thing, but now it sounds like you're talking about torture, and I don't think it's in either one of you. Specifically what information are you looking for?"

"We want to find this Mr. Gray."

"That's a code name, just like Mr. Brown for me. You guys know you're out of your league here, don't you? Even if you find the name Mr. Gray goes by, it won't be real either. He'll have a whole dossier on that one as well, but it'll be fake. Guys like him operate under so many layers of cover that you'll never find out who they really are."

"You tell us."

"I don't *know* his real name. He wasn't like my partner. He lives well above my paygrade and I've only known him by whatever moniker he uses for each mission. I know how you feel, Mr. Parker. I don't have your trust right now, but I want to help you guys and put an end to these experiments on the American people. I don't have any stomach for that kind of thing."

Tom Bell remained silent, watching Ned. Rubbing his bald head, Ned tried to make sense of it all. "Let's get back to it. What do *you* want out of all this?"

"For one thing, I'm done with the Agency. I plan to disappear with my wife and kids. They don't have any idea what I do for a living, other than I work for the government. We can make a clean break and when we're somewhere safe, I'll tell them the whole story."

Ned nodded. "You know they're gonna come looking for you."

"They will, but every now and then an agent will disappear. They'll investigate for a year or so, but with no proof that I'm alive or dead, they'll stop and I'll be gone."

Tom Bell inclined his head. "For a CIA agent, you're pretty naive."

Mr. Brown frowned. "I don't follow."

Tom Bell tilted his head again as he watched. "You know the truth, don't you, son?"

"The truth?"

"You know as well as we do that there's only one way to deal with this man. You'd talked yourself into believing that you can disappear, but you'll be looking over your shoulder every day for the rest of your life when you're not worried sick that something's going to happen to whatever family you have.

"These people will keep them under surveillance until you finally think it's safe to contact someone, or feel that you've covered your tracks enough that you can go home at some time. But they'll be waiting, and when you do, you'll find yourself in a shallow grave somewhere." Tom Bell paused. "Your idea to get away clean is for us to kill Gray for you."

The house was silent except for the wind moaning under the eaves.

Tom Bell stood and drifted toward the window. "Now, you listen to me, son. This whole thing is out of control, right? You aren't the law. In fact, you're a long way from it. So far, I see you as the only option to solving this problem, so here's what you're fixin' to do.

"Before we leave this house, you're going to give us everything we need to help me and Ned here track him down. Give me what we asked for and I'll turn my head long enough for you to disappear. If your information proves correct, you can stay gone and we'll deal with Mr. Gray, right? It appears to me that if he's gone, you're most likely off the hook. We'll take care of our part. But if you lie to us, and you need to know I despise a liar, I'll track you down and kill you for the skunk you are."

Mr. Brown swallowed. "You're a Texas Ranger. You and Parker have to follow the law."

"That's where you keep getting it wrong, son. We shed those shackles when you almost killed his grandson with that junk you sprayed over our little community that only wants to be left alone."

Tom Bell startled both Ned and Mr. Brown when he drew the .45 on his belt. The 1911 was already cocked and locked, and Tom Bell pointed it at the CIA agent with his finger on the trigger, guaranteeing he meant business. "You told us yourself that nobody knows we're here. You see, our plan came together. We have an agent who knows everything we need. It's time to start talking. I sold my soul to the ol' Devil a long time ago, son, so you don't have any idea what I've had to do to preserve the safety of Texans. But now the stakes are larger and your people involved me."

Ned saw Tom's finger tighten. "Tom, if you kill him, we'll have to start over."

The Ranger lowered the muzzle toward Mr. Brown's knee. "I'll break him down then, until he talks."

Mr. Brown's face turned white. He'd been around enough to know the old man wasn't kidding. At the same time, years of deception kicked in and he worked the angles. If he gave Mr. Gray up, they'd kill him, satisfying their need for retribution, and leave. If they failed and were killed, he'd manufacture a convincing story that he'd saved the agents back at the motel and fed the old men the information that led to their deaths.

He almost smiled. It was a win-win. "Fine. I'll do it. You'll let me walk out of here and disappear."

"I already told you I would. I don't lie, son."

"All right. As long as you leave my name out of it if you get caught."

Ned leaned forward on the table. "We're listenin'."

"I know where you can get your hands on Mr. Gray. But he's not going to like it."

Tom Bell smiled. "What he won't like is tangling with Old Country sittin' here."

Chapter Eighty-three

Over twelve hundred miles from Washington D.C., and only five miles from Center Springs, Cody's Motorola crackled. "Cody?"

"Mornin', Miss Martha."

"Right back atcha, but you're not gonna be as happy in a minute. Got a call from Oak Peterson out in Center Springs. There's some people fixin' to fight up at his store."

He was barely at the Powderly water tower on Highway 271 and spun the wheel, screeching into a U-turn. "I'll be there in five minutes."

"It might be over by then."

"Good, then I'll just collect them that's able to walk and bring 'em in."

"I'll stand by with an ambulance."

"You do that."

John Washington's deep voice filled the speaker. "I'll be there by the time you show up."

"Save some for me."

John's car was already on the shoulder in front of the little frame country store. The lot was buzzing with unfamiliar cars instead of the usual pickups and dusty sedans. Big John had a local farmer backed against the fender of a Chevrolet, and was pointing a finger at two seething strangers.

Leaving the motor running and the door open, Cody slipped from behind the wheel, almost knocking his hat off and aggravating him to no end. Loud voices across the lot full of onlookers told him a fistfight was only seconds away. "What's going on here!?"

The sun-browned farmer named Herman Wales pushed away from the car fender. "Cody, you need to do something 'fore the rest of us do it for you."

"One of 'em was fixin' to swing on Herman here when I pulled up." John interrupted. He spoke directly to the sheriff, his voice unusually friendly. "I told them two to back off and that feller in the hat called me a nigger. Don't matter that I wear a badge, he don't know me well enough to call me that."

Cody's irritation faded at the comment. John's voice was of normal tone, not low and dangerous, as when he was mad. He was having fun with the strangers wearing jeans and jackets. The one with a hawk nose had his receding jaw set, his face red with anger. His eyes were glassy and he looked like he'd torque off at any second. He wore a battered fedora that had been recreased into a rough semblance of a cowboy hat.

Cody aimed a forefinger at him. "We'll talk about what you called my deputy in a minute. What's your name?

"Clint. This's my runnin' buddy, Marshal."

"Where are you two from?"

"Over in Stumptown."

Cody shook his head. Stumptown, a small town from "behind the pine curtain" in East Texas, was nearly two hundred fifty miles from Chisum. The gold rush was gaining momentum if it had reached that hotbed of racism. Only Grove Town down on the Gulf Coast was worse. "That clears up a lot."

As if dismissing the two, he turned back toward Herman. "What got y'all tangled up?"

"Cody, I've done had it with this gold business. I run these two off from my place once this morning. They'd parked in front of my gate and were heading across the pasture when I got there. After that I come in here to get a loaf of bread for the missus and they pulled up and got to saying things about us folks that live here."

"Did they threaten you?"

"Naw, but I'm tired of this, and it wouldn't surprise me none to find 'em sneakin' back onto my place the first time I turn my head. If I do, they're gonna get a load of birdshot in their asses."

"You won't shoot nobody." Clint smirked. "All I said is that these scratch farmers up here ought to be more friendly to their betters."

John's eyebrows raised. "Betters?"

"You ought to know about that, mor'n most."

"Sheriff Cody." John's voice had an edge this time. "Can I visit with this feller around back of the store for a minute?"

Marshal seemed to have more sense than his friend. He took half a step back. Clint on the other hand, didn't seem capable of controlling his mouth. He pointed at Herman. "We wasn't hurtin' anything. All we wanted to do was poke around a little, and this sonofabitch got to raising his voice…"

"Be careful." Cody's words floated out, calm and cool.

The younger man didn't get to finish his statement. Digging his right heel into the gravel-and-bottle cap parking lot, Herman threw a right, powered by more than a lot of shoulder. It landed flush on Clint's jaw and his feet left the ground. He landed on his shoulders and didn't move, knocked clean out.

John grunted. "Never mind."

"Told you." Cody caught Marshal's eye. "So, what do you have to say?"

"You gonna let him beat up on my friend."

"Wasn't gonna *let* him do anything. He kinda surprised me, too. Herman, you're under arrest."

The farmer shrugged and examined his knuckles. "Okay."

"Now buddy, I suggest you drag your friend's carcass there

into the car and leave. There ain't no gold treasure in Center Springs. I'd advise you to tell everyone who brings this nonsense up that it's not a good idea to come around." He chuckled. "Or to insult a former lightweight boxer."

Marshal stooped to pick up his friend. John stopped him. "Hey."

"Uh, yeah?"

"What was that you two from Stumptown called me?"

"He said it."

"Remind me."

"Sir, he called you…"

"You can stop there. The 'sir' done got *you* off the hook for the time bein'. Now, y'all get on out of here."

They watched him drag Clint's dead weight into the backseat of their Dodge Monaco. Marshal slipped behind the wheel and started the car. Cody stepped forward and put one hand on the man's open window. "Y'all don't come back here no more."

"Yessir."

He left and steered toward the Lake Lamar Dam. John watched the car pass the cotton gin. "You know where Miss Pepper is right now?"

Cody grunted. "No, but I want to find her first."

Chapter Eighty-four

Three days after leaving Mr. Brown and the safe house, and exactly three weeks after Gold Dust entered the Lamar County atmosphere, Ned and Tom Bell sat in pale-yellow shell-back lawn chairs outside the Candlelight Motel, not far from Crane Creek in Missouri. It was unusually warm at forty-nine degrees, but the cloudy skies promised to keep the temperature from falling much farther. Ned sipped on a bottle of Coke.

Tom Bell had a water glass full of ice and whiskey. He tilted it, swallowed, and sighed in satisfaction. "You sure don't look like yourself."

Ned looked down at the pea coat over his new blue cotton shirt and khakis. "I don't know how folks wear these kind of britches. They don't fit right."

Tom plucked at the collar of his flannel shirt with two fingers. "These wool pants don't fit like jeans, neither, but they'll do the job. This ugly coat's warm, though."

"I'll be glad to get back into my own clothes."

"It won't be long. These are working, though. We blended in just fine. The manager behind the desk didn't raise an eyebrow."

"Texans sound enough like Missourians that he don't know, or care."

Ned bit his lip, staring at the Missouri plates on his Fury. They were off a rusting car sitting on two flat tires on a rundown road in a town south of their location. He chuckled. "That was a good trick back there in Washington, giving that feller twenty dollars to go get our car out of that motel parking lot."

Tom's teeth gleamed in the fading light. "He didn't know what to think when I told him I couldn't go back and get it because I'd got caught with another man's wife and had to leave. That couple I run off gave me the idea."

They'd met a down-on-his-luck drifter in a coffee shop a mile away and told him Tom needed to get his car back, but was afraid the fictional woman's husband would be waiting. Twenty dollars was a fortune for the drifter and he took the job after Tom convinced him that the husband was looking for a white-haired man with a matching mustache, and not a youngster in bell-bottom jeans and sneakers.

"He walked right up there before daylight and drove that car away like nobody's business."

A dark car containing two men followed it out onto the street, but Mr. Brown pulled out in front of them, blocking the sedan at the entrance long enough for the drifter and the Fury to disappear around the corner. His headlights blinded the agents, who were so frustrated they simply waved Mr. Brown out of the way.

Not realizing the missing agent they were also looking for was sitting in front of them, they spun out of the lot. By then the CIA agent lost the advantage and couldn't pick out one set of car tracks from any other in the slushy streets. Mr. Brown pulled through the lot and out the other entrance, where he disappeared forever.

Ned suddenly felt homesick, watching waves of complaining southbound geese fly over the Missouri motel. "I want to get those tags off there as soon as we can."

"Tomorrow."

Ned watched a tall man emerge from his room and unlock his car. He withdrew a long tube from the backseat and slammed the door. The motel was an historic stop for fly-fishermen headed to the Crane Creek that wound down a wooded and bluff-lined canyon less than ten miles away.

"Say this place is full of fishermen?"

"Yep. We're just two more anglers in a bunch of other fishermen."

"Anglers."

"Don't worry, you won't have to say that."

Ned sighed. "Tomorrow I want to go home."

Chapter Eighty-five

An early morning mist drifted across the smooth surface of spring-fed Crane Creek, a twenty-three-mile tributary of the James River south of Springfield, Missouri. Hungry McCloud rainbow trout finned in the current, sipping the last of the late season bugs behind the protection of rocks and the occasional downed log. The creek wound through its rocky bed, trimmed by box elder and sycamores wearing colorful autumn leaves.

Standing calf-deep in the frigid water, recently retired CIA agent Joe Hill gripped the pipe stem in his teeth and made a false cast with a bamboo fly rod he'd purchased at an ungodly price from a high-end fishing store in Alexandria. It was worth the price to fish the Crane with class. The spring creek was home to one of only three populations of McCloud Rainbows in the country. Hill waded two steps farther upstream, feeling the current melt the gravel under his wading shoes.

The yellow humpy fly fell exactly where he wanted, at the edge of an eddy beside a rock protruding from the far bank. He mended the drift and watched the water. Even then he was surprised when the surface boiled and he missed the strike. "Dammit."

He yanked and the leader tangled in the small branches that grabbed the line and refused to let go. Mumbling under his breath, he unwound the thin monofilament and noticed a wind knot that he hadn't seen.

"Dammit again." He perched a pair of reading glasses on his nose and squinted at the tiny knot. The Missouri fishing trip was exactly what he needed to separate himself from the Gold Dust fiasco that would take weeks to unravel. A realist, Hill knew the organization and saw the writing on the wall. His superior knew the operation's failure spelled the end of Hill's career and accepted his resignation on the day he submitted the letter.

If Hill called the Company when he got back to the motel and asked for himself, no one there would ever admit he'd existed.

He plucked a stainless steel pick from one of the many pockets in his fishing vest. Angling his head, he turned toward the bank to get better light. The end of his pick, as sharp as a needle, caught the knot. He worked it into the tight loop.

I got out just in time. I'm slowing down and things are starting to slip, like my eyes.

The knot loosened and he put the pick away.

Gold Dust is going to be what people remember me for at the Company. Not all the good I've done all these years all over the world, but for a mission that wasn't my idea in the first place, headed by a bunch of eggheads who assured me the bacteria was safe.

He didn't like the looks of the leader. The knot had weakened it to the point that it might break with a big fish. He clipped the fly off with a hemostat.

At least I put most of the onus on Brown and Brimley.

He grinned around the pipe, remembering the body of Agent Larry Brimley was found in a car parked in the northeast side of D.C., the roughest section of the nation's capital. It was a perfect setup. His death provided the backstory they needed to hang the failed Gold Dust operation on his shoulders. The in-house report listed his misdeeds, plans, and associates, who would also fall. It wasn't the first time Joe Hill had manufactured an alibi.

Mr. Brown on the other hand disappeared like smoke in the wind, along with his family. The Company was patient, though. Sooner or later Mr. Brown or his wife would contact relatives and those watching would backtrack to whatever dirt-water country they were hiding in and the Company machine would send in a team to extract their vengeance.

The hemostat cut through his fly line and he clipped the device back onto a flap covering the uppermost pocket of his vest. One thing he'd miss, though, were the Company's missions that impacted the advancement of worldwide democracy, such as that little LSD project in Iran. Who cared what happened to a bunch of sand spooks if the experiments would show how effective the new synthetic drug was at expanding a person's mind? Maybe those guys over in Psych Ops could find a way to use their special subjects to read Russian minds.

Mr. Hill shook his head at the advancements in psychological warfare. Someday a guy in an office somewhere could just close his eyes, take a dose of acid, and open them in a Soviet agent's mind. Mind control! What a wonderful thing! Maybe they could get in deep enough to control an agent and turn him around to actually kill Leonid Brezhnev!

Well, it didn't matter here on such a clear, wonderful trout stream. He was free of worry and stress.

With renewed enthusiasm, he finished tying a new bloodknot and was reaching for his fly box when he noticed two fishermen splashing in his direction, driving the fish down. Hill frowned. "Dammit!"

He felt his blood pressure increase when he saw spinning gear in their hands.

How does anyone not know that you don't wade a creek coming from upstream?

Chapter Eighty-six

Collin County Deputy Jimmy Bright took a surprised criminal-turned-farmer named Ellis Bass into custody at the local post office as he picked up his mail. For the moment there were no plans to arrest his wife for harboring a fugitive. She was presumably checking folks out at the Save-U, and the kids were in school.

At the same time, Cody and his people were headed for Ellis' farmhouse. Anna rode in the front passenger seat. Big John and his shotgun took up most of the back. Sheriff Hawkins was waiting over the hill on the oil road that ran in front of Ellis' house about half a mile away.

Cody parked around a bend blocked by a thick stand of hackberry trees. Nerves on edge, he leaned one arm over the back of the bench seat. "I don't know how the sheriff is going to handle this. When we get the go, I'll pull up and, John, you go around back. I doubt Owen can move very fast if he's shot up, but you be ready with that twelve-gauge just in case."

"He got away from me once before." The big man wrinkled his forehead. "Ain't gonna happen again."

Cody registered a Collin County deputy sheriff's car that pulled up behind him. "Anna, this guy's gonna shoot if he gets the chance."

She nodded. "I expect it to happen."

He took in her yellowing bruises. "I just don't want any of us to get hurt…."

His radio squawked with Sheriff Hawkins' voice. "Move in!"

"Here we go." Cody rounded the bend. The overanxious, big-eared deputy following their cruiser gunned his engine, as if riding Cody's back bumper would spark him into racing up to the house. The sheriff's car was still a hundred yards away when Cody slowed to turn in the dirt drive. When the distance suddenly closed, the deputy showered down on the brakes and nearly rear-ended them.

"What's with these bozos?" Anna glanced into the side mirror, seeing the deputy throw up his hands in frustration.

"I believe that jugheaded little feller back there's excited. Must be kinda peaceful around here most of the time." John grinned from ear to ear. "They wouldn't know what to do in our part of the country."

Cody's eyes flicked from the rearview mirror back through to the house coming up on the right. Lights flashing, Sheriff Hawkins swung into the gravel drive and punched it enough to shoot around Cody. He cut across the yard and slammed the brakes, almost sliding into the front porch.

"Good Lord." Cody's comment was under his breath, a quiet statement on a suddenly escalating situation. "I'm surprised that fool didn't hit his siren."

A screeching *yip yip* from the deputy sheriff's car behind them cut off his words as the driver hit the switch a couple of times.

The cat was out of the bag.

"Hang on!" Cody punched the accelerator, steered behind the house, and hit the brakes. "Change in plans."

"I figgered." Before the car stopped, John piled out of the back with the shotgun to his shoulder in a move that looked practiced.

Cody was out in a flash with Anna at his side, pistol in her fist. Cody didn't remember drawing his 1911 and was surprised to see it in his hand.

Two hard reports, as sharp as a plank slapping concrete, came from inside.

"Door, John!"

Big John vaulted up on the small covered porch and planted his size seventeen shoe beside the flimsy lock. The entire frame splintered and he ducked to the side to get out of the line of potential fire.

A wall ran the length of the rectangular house, dividing it in half. Cody followed his .45 into a dingy but clean kitchen. Seeing no resistance, John pushed past the sheriff and into the living room on the right side. Cody glanced to his left to find a door leading into a bathroom off the kitchen. Another shot came from somewhere in the house.

Anna brought up the rear. From the opposite side of the dividing wall, three shots in rapid succession filled the air, hammering their ears. She dropped to one knee and with her shoulder pressed against a cabinet door, aimed into the bathroom beside them. A string of shots sounding like firecrackers told them the action was somewhere deeper in the house.

Chapter Eighty-seven

Rod and reel in his left hand, Ned Parker's footsteps crunched on the gravel streambank. The narrow creek meandered down a corridor of hardwoods and grasses, reminding him of what the smaller spring-fed creeks in northeast Texas looked like when he was a kid. Shimmering, gurgling water flowed under bare limbs overhanging the surface.

"I swear, the only clear water these days is the Blue River up in Oklahoma. I'd give anything to swap ten of them muddy creeks of ours for just one like this."

"This river's a sight, all right." Tom Bell carried a new Zebco thirty-three spinning rod. Both men wore chest-waders under their jackets. "I do love live water, though I don't see how fly-fishermen keep from tangling up in all these limbs."

A flock of starlings wheeled overhead, wind whistling over their feathers. They turned as one like a school of fish and settled into a bare oak overlooking the streambed.

Ned also carried a new fishing rod. He shivered and pulled the collar of his new jacket up around his neck. "I'druther use a cane pole in here."

"Let's get us a couple of poles and go fishing when we get back home. Catch us a mess of crappie." Tom rested the rod on his shoulder and pointed downstream. "Look. If your friend Mr. Brown was telling the truth, there stands who we're looking for."

The fisherman standing knee-deep in the narrow stream was as red as a beet. He shouted at them long before they were within comfortable talking distance. "Don't you two know anything about *fishing!!!??*"

Ned and Tom Bell waded closer. Sticking his fishing rod under his arm, Ned mimicked Tom Bell and tucked both hands inside the loose bib of his waders. It was a move modeled by farmers for decades as they rested in conversation. "I've been fishing all my life. What do you mean?"

"Those are *spinning* rods. This is fly water! Catch-and-*release* fly water. You've driven all the fish down. They won't rise again for hours."

Ned glanced down to examine the rod under his arm as if it had suddenly appeared there out of thin air. "Well then."

He dropped it into the river.

The fisherman's eyes widened. "Are you crazy?"

"Well, you just said that wasn't the right rig."

The stranger held his bamboo rod at port arms like a rifle. "Have you lost your damn *mind?*"

"That'll give you time to visit with us, then. That's why we're here, to talk to you if you're Mr. Gray."

The man's eyes narrowed, calculating. "Who?"

"We're the law and you match the description of the man we're looking for. You're under arrest, Mr. Gray, for murder."

"How…for *what?* Show me a badge."

Tom Bell opened his fishing jacket to reveal the badge pinned high on his shirt. "This work?"

The fisherman squinted and ripped his glasses off. "What's that?"

"A Ranger badge. Texas Ranger. I'm here to arrest you for crimes against the people of Lamar County, Texas."

The fisherman's face paled. "I don't know what you're talking about."

"Yes you do." Ned splashed a step forward. Water gurgled around his legs, adding volume to the chuckling stream. The starlings chirped, a back chorus to the events below. "I'm a constable in Lamar County. It was my friends you killed with that… that Gold Dust you had sprayed. My grandboy almost died." His voice broke. His jaw muscles worked as he gathered himself and cleared his throat. "I'm taking you back to Texas to stand trial."

The fisherman held out his hand. "Show me a duly signed warrant for my arrest."

Ned fell silent.

"You don't have a warrant, do you, buddy boy? No judge in the world would issue an out-of-state warrant to anyone other than a U.S. Marshall."

Tom Bell gave a semi shrug. "You know a lot about the law, sir."

"A lot more than you know. Identify yourselves."

"I'm Tom Bell, Texas Ranger. This is Constable Ned Parker, from Texas."

The fisherman visibly flinched. "Parker."

"That's what he said. I believe we've talked on the phone in the past."

"Well, if you two really are who you say, you're completely mistaken about my identity."

"Could be. So who do you say you are?"

"Joe Hill."

"You have ID?"

"Sure. Right here." He reached into the inside pocket of his vest with a nervous hand and removed a thin wallet. He paused, staring down the bore of Ned's revolver. "Easy with that thing."

"You better hand me that billfold real slow, and the name in it better be…what did you say?"

"Hill."

"Give it here."

The fisherman extended his arm and took a step closer to the constable. The starlings took wing with the soft sound of padded applause as if anticipating what was about to happen.

Ned squinted, looking for the truth in the fisherman's eyes. "You're pretty nervous for an innocent man."

"I'm scared of course. You're threatening to shoot me, but I'm not your Mr. *Gray*."

Hill's pronunciation of the word "Gray" sent Ned's mind reeling with Miss Becky's description of Top's vision.

A gray rat in an all-white operating room.

A gray rat escaping up a *hill*, white marble columns…like the ones on the monuments in Washington.

Mr. Gray really *is* Joe Hill!

Ned's eyes widened and that's all it took for Joe Hill to recognize that he'd made a mistake. Ned saw the muzzle of a double-barreled derringer concealed in the wallet. Hill curled his finger through a hole in the leather and fired. The .22 magnum round cracked past Ned's cheek.

Feeling the shock wave of the passing bullet, Ned stumbled to the side, fighting the pull of the current. Gravel shifted under his feet. Splashing down on one knee, he pulled the trigger on his cocked revolver. The .38 round punched Joe Hill AKA Mr. Gray on the left side of his chest-waders.

Hill grunted as the slug plowed through his lung. He fired the Hi-Standard derringer's second barrel. The hollow-point slug ricocheted off the water and whined away.

Ned shot again, steadier this time, and missed, clean as a whistle.

Two heavier reports from Tom Bell's 1911 echoed down the creek valley. The first round struck Hill's waders within an inch of Ned's first shot, and the second caught the falling man under the chin.

The CIA agent toppled backward, already in Hell before he splashed into the gin-clear water.

"I hope you can still hear me." Trembling with rage, Ned struggled back to his feet and spoke to the partially submerged body. "You hurt my grandkids, you sonofabitch."

Tom Bell swiveled to check their surroundings. "Serves him right." He slid the Colt back under his waders. "Ned."

The old constable watched the current push at the body. Tendrils of blood stained the water. "What?"

"He drew on us. He would have killed one of us if you hadn't shot."

Ned shivered as if a possum had run over his grave. "He was so close, it's a wonder he missed with both of them shots." He swallowed. "You don't have to make me feel better about this. I'd-a shot him anyway, once I was sure who he was."

Tom Bell absently smoothed his mustache, pondering the statement. "I know it. I was gonna do it even if you didn't."

"He's the one we've been looking for."

"He is, that. But you know, this won't change much. This man's dead, but you've only broken off a fang, not taken the snake's head."

"I know that, too. I did what I intended. I've settled with the sonofabitch who hurt my family."

"And the rest of them back in Virginia?"

"I can't do any more than what we've done. It's just too big."

The current pushed at the limp body, but the gravel bottom held him in place. Tom Bell dipped his hand in the water and pulled up Hill's wallet and empty derringer. He slipped it into his shirt pocket before turning his serious gaze back to Ned. "I need to know, to satisfy the Devil. How were you sure he's the right one? I still didn't know until he tried to shoot you."

"Top had a vision about a gray rat running up a hill. He told Miss Becky. She told me when I called the house last night. I put it together and saw it in his eyes at the same time he shot. It's him, all right." Ned cleared his throat and opened the long blade on his pocketknife. He swallowed and knelt beside the Gray's body. "I've done my do. Let's finish this and go home."

"I'd like that just fine."

Chapter Eighty-eight

The phone rang on Sheriff Steve Brigman's desk. Reading a newspaper article on still another firefight in Vietnam, he lifted the receiver. "Sheriff's office."

"This the sheriff?"

"Said it was." The sheriff of Stone County straightened as if proud of the title.

"I'd like to report a dead body in Crane Creek."

Brigman put down the paper and gave the caller his full attention. "Who is this? Where?"

"The best I can tell you is that he's a-layin' 'bout a mile and a half south of the Old Wire Road near that big turnout where people pull in and park to fish. You know where that is?"

"I do. Who is he and how…?"

"He's been shot dead."

"Who's been shot by who?"

"By me, and he ain't got no identification. Good luck figuring out his name, but I wouldn't worry. He's a murderer that I settled with. And by the way, I'd just as well tell you, there ain't no bullets in 'im. I done dug 'em out, what didn't go plumb through. Now, I'm calling from a pay phone, and I've done told you all I'm gonna say."

The caller hung up and Brigman ran a hand though his short blond hair thinking this one was going to be difficult in more ways than one.

Chapter Eighty-nine

Propped on feather pillows facing the window, Owen rested with Ellis' freshly sawed-off semi-automatic Remington 1100 shotgun lying alongside his leg. The head of the bed was against the long wall that divided the rectangular house lengthwise. A door on his left led to the bathroom that also accessed the kitchen. One on the right opened into Ellis' bedroom at the front of the house just off the living room.

The short yelp of a siren broke the silence. Out in the country, sirens mostly announced volunteer fire trucks and ambulances. The two yips told Owen everything he needed to know.

Even with the windows locked tight against the cold, the car tires popping on the gravel drive were crisp and distinct. The roar of an engine rose as a car flashed past the window, headed for the rear. A Collin County deputy peeked into the window fifteen seconds later.

"This is it!" Owen raised the three-foot shotgun and fired, grunting as his wound tore from the recoil. The deputy disappeared as the glass-and-wire screen shattered.

The front door slammed open. Voices shouted in the living room. Trembling with pain, Owen couldn't take the shotgun's punishment again so soon. He waited until a big-eared Collin County deputy appeared in the doorframe to his right with a revolver pointed at the rustler.

"Don't move! Don't move! Get both hands in the air!" The over eager deputy who only minutes earlier sounded his siren in excitement stepped into the room. He motioned with the cocked pistol. "Hands *up!*"

Owen held up his empty left hand in a magician's move to gain the deputy's attention. "I can't." At the same time he raised the Luger hidden in the folds of the chenille bedspread and fired. The 9mm round shattered the deputy's pelvis. He shrieked and returned fire before falling out of view.

The deputy's lucky shot shattered Owen's right femur. The rustler howled from the impact. Two pools of warm blood flowed onto the sheets as an adrenaline dump shorted-circuited the sensors in his pain center.

Still in the kitchen, Cody flinched at the firefight erupting on the other side of the wall. Anna knelt, taking stock of the situation. Cody caught a glimpse of Sheriff Hawkins dragging his fatally wounded deputy onto the front porch at the far end of the long house.

Finding himself afraid that Anna was going to get hurt again, and still feeling responsible for the fading bruises on her face, Cody pushed down on her shoulder to keep her in place. "Stay here. Going through the bathroom!"

Big John rushed past Anna and into the cluttered living room to find a closed door leading into what he suspected was a bedroom where Owen was holed up. He kicked at the paint-splattered metal doorknob. It gave enough for him to see the back of a large piece of furniture in the way.

The heavy chifforobe blocking the door behind Owen's right shoulder jolted as someone kicked it from the other side. He twisted and emptied the Lugar's magazine through the wall.

• • ● • •

Temples pounding at the gunfire, Cody saw what he suspected to be a door leading from the bathroom and into Owen's room. Following the front sight of his 1911, he took a deep breath and stepped into the bedroom, hoping Owen's attention was focused on where John was kicking through the door.

• • ● • •

Frustrated by Cody's overprotective attitude, Anna ignored the sheriff's warning and rushed past John as rounds punched through the wall. He recoiled from the slugs snapping through the faded wallpaper only a few inches away. "I think there's a damned chifforobe in the way!"

Holding her revolver in the classic battle stance she'd learned as a recruit in Houston, Anna sidestepped toward the deputy's blood smear leading to the front door. "He's right through *there*." She peeked into the empty front bedroom at a perfectly made bed.

• • ● • •

Owen dropped the empty pistol and caught a glimpse of someone in the bathroom doorway. He instinctively twisted to see who was coming through and groaned at the electric bolts of pain shooting through his body. With a grunt, he once more raised the sawed-off shotgun from his lap at the same time the Lamar County Sheriff appeared in the doorway.

• • ● • •

"Don't do it." Cody's voice came soft and low. Conversational.

The shotgun's muzzle wavered, rising. Surprised at how calm he felt, Cody fired three times in quick succession. Deflected by bone and the steel barrel, one .45 round angled up into Owen's chest. Another blew the rustler's thumb off the shotgun's grip, but his index finger tightened in reaction. The hard crump of the sawed-off was deafening in the small room. The buckshot missed, leaving nine .38-caliber holes in the wall only two feet to Cody's left.

Owen fell back. Cody lowered his pistol in relief.

Like a bad dream, Owen rallied and raised the shotgun again. The twelve-gauge bore looked big as a culvert. Shocked that the odd-looking man was still drawing air, Cody brought the pistol back to level, but knew it was going to be close.

Three hammer-blow reports from Cody's .45 told Anna the sheriff had found his man. Then came the heavy blast of a shotgun.

She peeked around the doorframe at the same time a bloody and dying man attempted to bring a nasty-looking little shotgun to bear on Cody. Anna blew three holes into the rustler's chest as if she were on a firing range and would have kept shooting had she not felt Big John's hand on her shoulder, telling her it was over.

As Owen's nerveless hands dropped onto the bloody sheets for the last time, Cody sagged against the doorframe, knowing the gal he was worried about had saved his life.

Chapter Ninety

Cody met Anna in Bill Preston's yard the next time Bill came in from Dallas. The extravagant modern house overlooking the Red River far below was completely out of place in that part of Northeast Texas. They waited beside their marked cars until Bill came outside at the sound of Cody's car horn.

Bill was the definition of an oily used car salesman, which is what he was before he started working for a dealership only ten years earlier. Cody's suspected the snake with legs had earned enough money to acquire a dealership through illegal means.

The arrogant car salesman wiped his palm on his gray slacks before extending it toward Cody. "Sheriff. Can I help you?"

They shook. Cody tilted his head toward Anna. "Howdy Bill. This is Deputy Anna Sloan."

Preston didn't offer his hand to Anna at all. "You're the deputy the mayor was telling me about."

Anna face turned white. "What's he said to you?"

Bill smirked. "Oh, that you were doing a good job." He'd made his point. "What can I do for you, Sheriff?"

Cody waved a hand at the two-story house, then toward the western slope. "I see y'all had to bring in a lot of fill, but this is the place I'd pick, too."

"That's the truth." Bill was proud of his house. "Took ten thousand dollars just to build that retaining wall, but it was worth it. No matter the cost."

"The cost to people, history, and the law, huh?" Insulted at being snubbed, Anna's voice was stiff with anger.

Bill's expression went cold. "What does *that* mean?"

Cody decided to be direct. "She means that I bet if we was to be invited into your house, I'd find some pretty interesting things on the walls and shelves."

Caught between their discussion, Bill seemed indecisive. "Uh, what?"

Anna pressed forward. "Will you invite us inside to look at any Indian artifacts you might have?"

"What makes you think that? And no, we can talk out here, unless you have a warrant."

Cody tilted his hat back. "Bill, why don't you tell me what I want to know before I have to come back with that warrant you mentioned?"

Bill rubbed his bulbous nose. "Indian stuff. Yeah, bought a few things for the walls. I can provide canceled checks for those."

"Did you keep records of the artifacts you dug up with the fill dirt? If I'm right, based on how much that house cost, I'd estimate you earned enough from the sale of those items to interest the IRS."

Bill deflated. "All right. Yeah, we found some old Indian stuff, bones, and a few trinkets."

"Like breastplates, bowls, weapons, and how many gold coins?" Anna crossed her arms, waiting for an answer.

"What? *Gold?*"

"I'm tired of playing around, Bill." Cody took his arm. "We know you sold that and a bunch of Spanish gold coins. Probably what those old Indians found at some point out by Palmer Lake. My ancestors didn't have much use for gold coins except for decoration, so I imagine they buried them with their people."

"There wasn't that much. It was just some old bones."

Cody was surprised when his voice cracked. To him digging into Indian burial grounds was the equivalent of robbing graves at the Forest Chapel Cemetery.

"Maybe not much there, but what about the other places you've been digging with that bulldozer. Sounds to me like you've found more than one grave. You've gotten pretty good at it, after finding the first one. You made enough off the sale of my ancestors to build a much nicer house, huh?"

"Most of the money came from my business."

"We'll let the lawyers figure that out." Anna opened the back door of the sheriff's car. "Get in."

A horse snorted and Cody watched Mack Vick ride up. The cowboy's eye was black and both lips had been split, but healing. He tilted his hat back to reveal an ear decorated with several stitches. He crossed one leg over the saddle horn and took the makin's out of his shirt pocket. "Chickens finally come home to roost, huh?"

Bill glared. "You want to keep your job, you'll get back to work."

"Smoke break." Mack built a cigarette and grinned. "I told them what they were doing was illegal. There's a dozen 55-gallon barrels out there behind the house, every one of 'em's full of bones and stuff."

Cody studied the cowboy. "Looks like you tied into a buzz saw, from the looks of that face."

"Just some city fellers who were a little upset when their cupcake Scottie took up with me for a little bit."

"How little?"

Mack shrugged. "'till the idea of gettin' rich soured. Ol' Bill there was nice enough to let Scottie stay here in the big house while his wife's in Dallas. I believe he liked looking at her. Anyway, Scottie took us both, Bill. She stole my heart, and the rest of your Spanish coins. She left this mornin' and good riddance."

Bill blanched and it wasn't because Scotty was gone. "You're fired."

"Naw. I quit."

Anna took out a pad and clicked her pen. "I'll get something out on the radio about her."

Cody sighed. "Bill, you're under arrest."

"What for?"

"Grave robbing. It's called looting…"

"Well, hell, Sheriff."

"The charges are looting of Indian artifacts, theft of private property, and trespassing."

Bill's face fell. "What do you mean?"

"That little draw where you're got your fill dirt belongs to Harp Johnson. Your line is on *this* side of that big oak tree. I went over to his pasture and took a look around." Cody pointed at a line of bare trees in the distance. Already devoid of leaves, the crooked limbs looked like arms and fingers pointing toward the sky. He shivered at the image of Top's vision that Miss Becky'd told him about only days before. "See there? That line of trees that've already lost their leaves?"

"All these leaves are falling. It's that time of the year."

"It is, but those started falling first. You cut the roots, the trees died, and those are a couple of hundred years old. A couple are marker trees the Old People bent to point toward water and springs. You killed a spring over there, too. That's where you dozed first, to find the graves this past summer. Add malicious destruction of private property and natural resources to the charges."

"They're just old Indian bones. What of it?"

Cody felt his face redden as his anger built. "Those *old bones* were people. Miss Becky's people. It was their graveyard, and you dug 'em up with a damned *bulldozer*."

Bill sulled up. "You wouldn't have found out about it if it wasn't for this damn gold rush everybody's all worked up about."

Cody took his arm. "Yeah, the one my granddaughter started when you traded a coin you dug out of a grave for building supplies. Come go get in the car."

Bill went with him to Anna's car. "It was the first one I found. I didn't think it would be worth much with that hole drilled in the top."

"That's so it could be a necklace." Cody slammed the car door and turned to Anna with a grin. "The mayor, huh?"

"I'm going to nip that in the bud as soon as we get back to town."

"You do that. Book him for me, because I have one more thing to do."

"What?"

"Pepper started this. Now she's gonna finish it."

Cody drove back to Center Springs to end the gold rush. The parking lots of both general stores were filled with strange cars and trucks. Knots of men loafed in small groups that formed then dissolved. Others spread maps over the trunks or hoods of their vehicles, looking for possible places to explore.

He crept past, making sure they all got a good look at his sheriff's car. He accelerated on the oil road past Neal Box's store and turned into the long drive in front of the Ordway Place. He tapped the horn and pulled to a stop under the spreading oak trees.

James came out on the porch. "What's going on?"

Leaving the motor running, Cody stood and leaned on his car door. "Pepper here?"

"Yep."

"Get her and y'all come go with me."

"Where to?"

"To put an end to this gold rush foolishness."

James stepped back inside and reemerged thirty seconds later with Pepper and Mark. Pulling on their coats, the stone-faced kids got in the back and James took the front passenger seat. Cody spun the wheel and headed back to the stores, glancing in the rearview mirror.

"Pepper, I'm gonna pull up there beside the domino hall and block the road with this car. Then you're gonna climb up on the roof here and when I get everyone gathered around, you're gonna explain that this whole gold rush idea came out of your empty head, and then you're gonna apologize."

Her jaw fell open and Mark had to cover his mouth with one hand so she couldn't see his grin. "But Uncle Cody, I didn't *mean* for all this to happen."

"We don't mean for a lot of things to happen, but when they turn out wrong, we have to pay the piper."

He pulled the car across the oil road at the intersection between the domino hall and Oak Peterson's store. He killed the engine, turned on his lights, and gave the siren a quick punch. The shrill yelp caught the attention of everyone in the area and they drifted in his direction. He stepped out and waved for them to gather around.

"Y'all come on over here!" Cody ducked his head back inside the car. "I know you didn't mean for this to get all out of control, but people have been hurt and arrested after you got crossways with that gal on Neal's porch and told her a big windy. Now, get on up there and do what I told you."

Eyes full of tears, Pepper stepped out of the car. She hesitated until Cody held out his hand to steady her as she used the back bumper for a step. Her tennis shoes left distinct prints on the dusty trunk lid. She had to use a knee on the back glass to crawl onto the roof. By that time, a mix of strangers and Center Springs residents gathered around the car.

Cody faced the crowd. "Folks, my niece Pepper here has something to say to y'all, and I want you to listen. Go ahead on, gal. Tell 'em who you are and what you did."

Face flushed red with embarrassment, she pulled her hair behind one ear and adjusted the feather. Her first words quavered, but gathered strength as she went on. "For y'all that don't know me, I'm Pepper Parker, and my grandaddy's the constable here, Ned Parker. This is my Uncle Cody Parker, and I guess y'all can tell he's the sheriff." She took a deep breath, staring down at the faces looking up, mostly strangers. "I got aggravated at that big-tittied…"

"Pepper!" Her daddy's sharp voice caused her to jump.

"*Jeeze*. Don't have a *cow*. All right. I got mad at a girl over there at Neal Box's and made up a story about finding a gold coin at Palmer Lake. There *ain't* no lost gold that I know of, and all you greedy people just took a little fib and blew it all up."

Cody didn't call her on the observation, because it was true. Instead, he watched the faces of those around him. "What else?"

"Oh. I'm sorry. I'm sorry for the trouble I've caused. I didn't mean to do it. " She scrambled down and took off walking down the road toward home, her bell-bottoms flapping around her ankles.

Mark started to follow, but James held out a hand. "Stay right here for a little while, son. It's time you start learning about women. She needs to be alone and think about what she's done. If you go with her, she'll cry and let you shoulder some of what she needs to deal with."

"You all heard what she said." Cody raised his voice so everyone could hear. "The buried treasure is an old wives' tale and nobody's found anything, so I want all y'all to go on back home and pass the word. You've been snookered by a little ol' teenage gal who's fessed up. This is over, and anybody I catch trespassing from here on out will be charged with a helluva lot more'n that. Judge O.C. Rains has cleared his calendar for the next three days and says he'll levy the maximum fines the law will allow, and by the way, once we have somebody in custody, I'm gonna run background checks and that'll take several days. So y'all need to get gone."

A few grumbled, and more than one person in the crowd voiced an opinion that Pepper's behind should be worn out. One that Cody agreed with. Five minutes later, the parking lots were nearly empty and Cody's car was still sitting across the oil road.

Neal Box stepped outside and crossed his lot. "Well, I guess it's over."

"It is, that." Cody reached in and clicked off his lights.

"It was good while it lasted."

"What do you mean?"

"I made a buttload of money these past few days. Now it's back to carryin' most of these folks on credit till the end of the month."

Cody laughed and drove home to spend some long hours with his redhead for the first time in weeks.

Chapter Ninety-one

I still had a dry cough that came and went a full two weeks after Uncle Cody's gunfight with the cattle rustler. We were between cold fronts, and I was finally back at school. The day was warm and sunny. I thought it was gonna be a good day until I saw Harlan Ketchum twist a quarter from the hand of another kid.

His toady Frankie laughed when he saw me and pointed. The look in Harlan's eye told me nothing had changed while I was in the hospital.

I was sitting with my back against a tree, an open math book in my lap, trying to figure out some problems the rest of the class had already learned. Kids of all sizes screamed and played chase, or swung, or did what Pepper and Mark were doing, wandering around the trees at the edge of the playground like lost cows, talking and not paying any attention to anything going on around them.

Harlan stuck the quarter in his pocket and moseyed in my direction. He steered shy of me for a while, but I wasn't dumb enough to think it was because he was afraid. He just didn't want to tangle with Mark, who'd already seen a lot of life and was tough to boot. Harlan was afraid of Pepper, too. We all knew she wouldn't think twice about punching him in his big ol' nose.

He kicked the sole of my tenny shoe. "Hey, Mouse."

I marked my place in the textbook and looked up. "Don't call me that." Mouse is what Cale called me when he wanted to get my goat and Harlan remembered. I never let on it bothered me, but I'd about decided that I was tired of people calling me names.

"I'll call you anything I want."

My heart started pounding when I realized Harlan had that look in his eye. It was the same glassy expression he got when he tried to stick my head in the commode. "I'm just trying to study here."

"How much money you got on you?"

"Look, all I have in my pocket is a buckeye, a pocket knife, and two dimes."

Frankie giggled down at me. "Turn 'em out, like he said."

For the first time in my life, I hit the wall. I'd almost died and come back, and now here was some stupid kid who spent most of his time terrorizing people littler than him. I'd had it. "Nope. Go bother somebody else."

He kicked the side of my shoe with his steel-toed work boot and it hurt like the dickens. "Give it here."

"Ain't got nothing to give. Go on and leave me alone, bone-head."

The look in Harlan's eyes was frightening. "Get up, Mouse. I think you got that coin Pepper's been talking about. Thom Batch told it to me for the truth."

I didn't like the fact that he was standing over me, and was getting tired of looking up at him, so I stood. He was a head taller, but the tree had pushed the ground up around the base of the trunk and that gave me enough height that we were close to eye level.

"That'll be after the fight."

It must have startled him. He stepped back and angled his body so one shoulder was pointed in my direction. He doubled both fists and raised them like one of them old-time boxers. It was all scary at first, but then he thumbed his nose at me.

I'd read that old school boxers thumbed their noses to be sure their hands were high enough to protect their faces in a fight. At the same time it was a sign of disrespect. It was the first time I'd ever seen anyone do that, and I got tickled.

"What are you grinning about, Mouse? Come on!"

He thumbed it again with his right hand, and I busted out laughing. "What are you doing?"

He thumbed again. "I'm waiting."

"I'm not fighting *both* of you."

Harlan jerked his head toward Frankie. "He can have what's left when I'm finished."

Frankie set his feet to get ready. That familiar sinking feeling dropped the bottom out of my stomach. I remembered Uncle Cody telling me one time that if you know you're gonna get in a fight, throw the first punch and make it a good one. I dug in with my right foot and jabbed straight out with my left fist. We were both surprised when Harlan's nose exploded in a gout of blood.

Instinct kicked in and I hit him with a right in the same place. Harlan rocked back. Frankie stepped up to hit me and that's when a mane of black hair flashed by. The meaty sound of a punch was followed by a wail and I knew then that it was just me and Harlan.

"*Take him, Top!*"

Mark's voice made my chest swell and I threw a left jab that missed, but I followed it with a hard right in the eye and Harlan's legs went all loose and rubbery. The next thing I knew, I'd thrown myself at him and we were on the ground. Harlan covered his bloody face and tried to twist away, but I was finally mad. I hit him half a dozen times, but couldn't tell you where they landed if my life depended on it.

He finally rolled away and got up running. I was almost out of gas and knew better than to chase after him. A coughing spell caught up with me and I doubled over until it passed. When I straightened up, Mark was straddling Frankie, who was rolled up in a ball, crying and holding the side of his head. It was a shock to see we were in the middle of a ring of kids who were laughing and clapping like they'd just seen a magician pull a rabbit out of his hat.

Mark kicked Frankie in the side. "Get up and get on outta here."

Frankie rolled over and got up. He ran toward the gym without looking back and passed Miss Russell who was steaming in our direction. That little redheaded teacher pushed through the ring of kids and planted both fists on her hips.

"Y'all get to class now." The ring scattered and she turned to Mark. "Mr. Lightfoot, do you want to tell me what's going on out here?"

I didn't want him to get into trouble, so I spoke up. "It was me, Miss Russell."

Her pale eyebrow rose. "Fine then, Mr. Parker. What would your granddaddy say about you fighting at school?"

"He wouldn't say nothing if I didn't start it."

The eyebrow rose higher. "You trying to be smart, mister?"

"No, ma'am. Just telling you truth."

She knew good and well that it wasn't my fault. I felt like I was on stage and everything was scripted. It made me feel good, though, because I'd never been on the winning end of a fight.

"Harlan started it, and I finished it. Mark didn't do nothing but keep Frankie off of me."

"Didn't do anything," she corrected, but I saw the corners of her mouth lift. "So I take it you were just sitting here studying and he was the instigator?"

"Yessum. I was minding my own business. He wanted something I didn't have...and, well...he's been taking the little kids' lunch money and I got tired of it."

Miss Russell crossed her arms like she did when we were reading our oral reports. "Go on. You're suddenly Lancelot, protecting Camelot?"

I must have grown another inch. "Well, I didn't intend for it to be like that, but I guess that's how it turned out."

"Umm, humm." Miss Russell's attention shifted. "And you, Miss Beatrice Parker. What's your role here?"

Pepper's face reddened. She hated her real name and for anyone to use it. "I didn't do nothin'. I just came over here to watch." She couldn't keep her mouth closed, though. "But I'da knocked the snot out of both of 'em if I'd got here in time."

Miss Russell wet her lips and whistled loud and long, louder than any man I've ever known. "All right, students. Everyone inside and right now." She nodded as if it were all settled. "I'll have to call your granddaddy, but it won't be too bad. I'll make sure he understands, but you have to serve penance, Mr. Lancelot."

"Yes, ma'am. What's that?"

She gave me a wink that only I saw. "I want a twenty-page report on whatever library book you're reading, and I expect it in two days."

I was grinning ear from ear, especially when Pepper spoke up just loud enough that Miss Russell couldn't hear. "Well, shit. You'd do that anyhow if you wanted to."

Mark held out his closed fist. "Open your hand."

I did, and he dropped a quarter in my hand. He grinned. "Spoils of war. I guess it fell out of Harlan's pocket."

I collected my math book, and went looking for the little kid to return his quarter.

Chapter Ninety-two

Dinner at Ned and Miss Becky's house was over and the sun chased most of the cold away. It was one of those Texas winter days that started in the low forties and warmed into the seventies by the afternoon.

Fresh air flowed through the open windows and the adults gathered in the living room. Us kids were sitting on the floor, listening to their conversation about the past few weeks.

Tom Bell chuckled at Cody's description of Ike Reader's escaped deer. "And that happened in the middle of a gold rush and all those other troubles."

"Just goes to show that the good Lord's got a sense of humor." Miss Becky laughed.

I wanted to keep the discussion going. I always loved to hear their stories. "Nobody ever found anything, either."

"Yeah, they did." Uncle Cody patted Norma Faye's leg. "That's how the Prestons wound up with that big old house overlooking the river."

She picked up his hand and put it back in his own lap. "I thought they inherited some money while the house was going up."

"They got some money, all right." Grandpa rocked back and forth. "While they were digging for fill dirt on that draw not far from the house, they dug into a bunch of Indian burial mounds.

It's against federal law to rob graves, but he didn't care. Cody found out the rest."

Tom Bell cleared his throat and stood. "Well, kids, this so-called gold rush ain't quite over." He picked up his hat.

Pepper perked up. "What's that?"

"Come go with me to find out. You boys get a couple of shovels out of the smokehouse."

Grandpa stopped rocking. "What fer?"

"I know where there's some gold buried."

Pepper couldn't understand it. "Where? We going to Palmer Lake?"

Mr. Tom smoothed his mustache. "You know where you kids burned scraps in Cody's yard, back when I was working on the house?"

"The one we pass every time anybody comes down the drive and the grass is thick and green?"

"Yep. Remember what I told y'all about hunting for gold?"

"You said to look for landmarks, places that people could remember after a few years."

"Yep."

I got caught up in the conversation. "What's there?"

"About twenty thousand in gold double-eagles."

Norma Faye put a hand over her mouth. "In our *yard?*"

"It was the best place I could think of at the time where it wouldn't be found."

Grandpa started rocking again. "It would have been lost, then, if you'd stayed dead down in Mexico."

Tom Bell's smile twitched his mustache. "Not really. I wrote to you about it in one of those envelopes I told you not to open."

"I'll be dog."

Tom Bell put on his hat. "It was for y'all, for later, but now I think you're gonna need it at some point soon for these kids' college, Ned. Now let's all go over there and dig up some gold, but Pepper, you say a word about it...."

"I know. I know. You'll blister my butt."

His eyes flashed with that light that made me shiver. "And you know I would."

"And I'd hold you while he did it," Grandpa said as we left to dig up a treasure. "Even though I wouldn't take for her."

To see more Poisoned Pen Press titles:

Visit our website:
poisonedpenpress.com
Request a digital catalog:
info@poisonedpenpress.com